iThe Teleport Company

DANIEL J. FORMOSO

DEDICATION

For the family, J.E.N.I.

CONTENTS

ACKNOWLEDGMENTS

I must thank my family for letting me start this during the COVID lockdown and then through five years of writing, editing, and rewriting.

Finally, to my readers: Thank you for taking a chance on a new voice. I hope this story brings you as much joy in reading as it brought me in writing it.

1 ROTTERDAM TRANSFER

The call came at 05:00, three hours before the demonstration that would change global commerce forever.

"Dr. Franco, someone's been in the power systems." Lars's voice crackled through the encrypted connection. "Professional work. If I hadn't run early diagnostics—"

Ren was already moving, yanking on her jacket in the predawn darkness of her Rotterdam hotel room. "How bad?"

"They knew exactly where to hit. Cascade failure set to trigger during peak MTU load. This wasn't industrial espionage, Ren. This was industrial sabotage."

Her mind calculated probabilities, suspects, countermeasures. Only someone with deep knowledge of their power requirements could have been this precise. "Can you fix it?"

"Already started, but—" A pause. "Whoever did this had inside information."

The words hung between them like a death sentence. Ren grabbed her secure tablet, pulling up facility schematics. "Lock down everything. No one goes near the MTU without my direct authorization. And Lars?" Her voice dropped. "Start background checks. Priority on anyone hired in the last six months."

She ended the call and immediately dialed Koji in Nagasaki. Through her window, Rotterdam's port sprawled in the darkness, its lights like a constellation of commerce about to be reorganized.

Today would be very different, transporting twenty containers of zero emission, electric motorcycles from the Port of Nagasaki to the Port of Rotterdam. A container ship would take over one month to make the trip at a cost of almost $7,000 per container and a total cost of $140,000.

Two weeks earlier, Koji Ozakashi gazed over the bustling Nagasaki port from his temporary office window, absorbing the vibrant chaos below. His imposing 188 cm frame and long gray-streaked black hair made him stand out among the workers scurrying below.

"Takahashi-san, what's the status of the MTU installation?", he called over to his chief engineer.

Meeka Takahashi looked up from her holographic display. "Final calibrations are underway. The quantum entanglement rates are stable at 99.8%, well exceeding our minimum threshold." Her fingers danced through the projection, adjusting parameters on the control panels. "The cooling system gave us some trouble yesterday, but we've reinforced the cryogenic seals."

Koji nodded, his gaze drifting away from the window, a pensive look crossing his face. "And the test objects?"

"Three successful transfers of increasing mass. The apple arrived intact, then the bicycle, and finally the refrigerator. All molecular structures preserved within acceptable parameters."

A young technician burst through the door, breathless. "Ozakashi-san! The first motorcycles have arrived at the staging area."

Koji checked his watch. "Right on schedule. Let's begin the documentation process." He picked up his secure tablet. "And someone find Yamada from customs. We need those forms processed immediately."

Outside, a convoy of electric trucks had pulled up to the designated area. Workers began unloading sleek, metallic motorcycles – the GreenRider X9, the world's first fully carbon-neutral electric motorcycle with a range of 800 kilometers on a single charge.

"Careful with those!" barked Sosuke Matsuda, the manufacturer's quality control supervisor. "Each unit is worth more than you make in a year."

Koji approached him with a slight bow. "Matsuda-san, welcome. I trust the journey from the factory was smooth?"

Matsuda's perpetual frown deepened. "Smooth enough. But I still don't understand why we're shipping through your company instead of our usual logistics partner." He lowered his voice. "The CEO is taking an enormous risk on this contraption of yours."

"A risk that will cut your shipping costs in half and eliminate your carbon footprint entirely," Koji replied smoothly. "Please, let me show you our facility while the motorcycles are being loaded into the containers."

He led Matsuda to an enormous warehouse where the yellow MTU stood, humming with latent energy. Technicians in white lab coats moved purposefully around the machine, checking readings and making adjustments.

"This doesn't look like any shipping equipment I've ever seen," Matsuda muttered.

Koji smiled enigmatically. "That's because it isn't."

As they approached the MTU, Matsuda's eyes widened. The machine dominated the warehouse floor—a massive yellow structure with complex arrays of what appeared to be sensors and emitters covering its surface. The MTU looked exactly like an enlarged shipping container that was a meter and a half wider, taller, and longer.

"What exactly am I looking at, Ozakashi-san?" Matsuda asked, his skepticism giving way to curiosity.

"The future of global shipping," Koji replied, gesturing toward a control station where several engineers worked. "Meeka, would you explain the basics to Matsuda-san? Technical details only, of course."

Meeka approached, tablet in hand. "The Mass Teleportation Unit utilizes quantum entanglement principles to disassemble matter at the subatomic level, transmit the exact pattern instantaneously to a paired receiver unit, and reassemble it perfectly." She spoke matter-of-factly, as if describing something as mundane as a forklift.

Matsuda laughed nervously. "You're joking. This sounds like science fiction."

"Ten years ago, it was," Koji acknowledged. "But Dr. Franco's breakthrough in stable quantum field generation changed everything."

"Dr. Franco? You mean Ren Franco? The physicist?" Matsuda's eyebrows shot up. "The one who disappeared from academia after publishing those controversial papers on matter transmission?"

"The very same," Koji confirmed. "She didn't disappear—she went private to develop this technology without interference."

A technician approached with a clipboard. "Ozakashi-san, the first container is ready for inspection before loading. Customs officer Yamada is waiting."

"Excellent. Matsuda-san, would you like to verify the motorcycles yourself before we proceed?"

Matsuda nodded firmly. "Absolutely. My company's reputation rides on those bikes—quite literally."

They walked to a staging area where workers were carefully positioning the motorcycles inside a standard shipping container. Each bike was secured in a specialized rack, protected by minimal packaging—a testament to the manufacturer's environmental commitment.

"Our normal procedure uses significantly more protective materials," Matsuda noted, running his hand along one sleek frame. "You're certain they'll arrive undamaged?"

"More than certain," Koji assured him. "The quantum transmission process doesn't involve physical movement as you understand it. There's no turbulence, no vibration, no impact. Each atom arrives exactly as it departed."

Yamada, the customs official, approached with an electronic tablet. "All documentation is in order, Ozakashi-san. I'll need your final verification before sealing the container."

Koji signed the digital form. "Thank you, Yamada-san. We appreciate your department's cooperation."

"It's... unusual," Yamada admitted, glancing toward the MTU. "But my superiors are quite interested in the potential applications. Especially regarding contraband interdiction."

Koji nodded. "A valid consideration. The scanning process is thorough enough to create a complete molecular inventory. Nothing can be hidden."

As the container was sealed and moved toward the MTU loading bay, Matsuda watched with visible apprehension. "How many times have you done this successfully? With cargo this valuable?"

"This specific cargo? Never," Koji admitted. "But we've conducted over three hundred tests with progressively larger and more complex objects. The physics doesn't change based on monetary value, Matsuda-san."

"My company is taking an enormous risk," Matsuda said, his voice low. "If this fails..."

"It won't," Koji assured him, placing a hand briefly on the man's shoulder. "But I understand your concern. That's why Ren—Dr. Franco—offered a significant discount on shipping costs. Your company's willingness to be first makes you pioneers."

Matsuda squared his shoulders. "The GreenRider X9 is already revolutionary. Perhaps it deserves a revolutionary shipping method as well."

"Exactly." Koji smiled. "Now, shall we begin?"

In Rotterdam, preparations were equally intense. Ren stood in the center of the enormous tension membrane structure that had been erected at the port, directing the final placement of equipment.

"The power coupling needs to be secured with the vibration dampeners," she instructed a team of engineers. "Even a two-millimeter shift during operation could disrupt field integrity."

Lars Van Der Westhuizen, the Dutch engineer heading the local team, wiped sweat from his brow despite the cool air. "We've triple-checked the foundation. It's solid to bedrock, and the power grid is isolated as you requested."

Ren nodded, her eyes never leaving the massive yellow MTU. "Good. Now show me the security perimeter."

As they walked the edge of the structure, a port official approached with a clipboard. "Ms. Chen, I need additional signatures for these temporary operation permits. The harbormaster is concerned about potential electromagnetic interference with ship navigation systems."

"There won't be any," Ren said flatly. "Our technology doesn't operate on those frequencies."

The official looked skeptical. "Nevertheless, we need these waivers signed before tomorrow's demonstration."

Ren took the clipboard with a sigh. "Fine. But I want it noted that your concerns are unfounded."

After he left, Lars leaned closer. "You can't blame them for being cautious. What we're attempting has never been done before."

"That's precisely why we've spent three years in development and testing," Ren replied, her voice softening slightly. "This isn't some reckless kitchen experiment, Lars. The mathematics is sound. The physics is sound."

"I know," he said. "That's why I joined your team. But you have to understand—for most people, this will seem like magic."

Ren's lips curved in a rare smile. "Any sufficiently advanced technology is indistinguishable from magic. Arthur C. Clarke."

"Let's just hope our audience tomorrow appreciates a good magic show," Lars replied.

As they walked back toward the MTU, Ren's phone buzzed. A message from Koji in Nagasaki: "First batch of motorcycles containerized. All systems nominal. Ready when you are."

She typed back: "Rotterdam MTU at 98% readiness. Proceeding as scheduled."

Ren pocketed her phone and surveyed the facility. The tension membrane structure, stark white against Rotterdam's gray skies, housed not just the MTU but a complex array of support systems. Superconducting power conduits snaked across the floor, connecting to cooling units that hummed quietly in the background.

"Dr. Franco," called a voice from the control station. "We've detected a minor fluctuation in the quantum field stabilizers."

Ren moved quickly to the bank of monitors where Sarah Jensdotter, their quantum engineer, was frowning at a display. "Show me," Ren demanded, leaning over the console.

Sarah pointed to a waveform that pulsed irregularly. "The entanglement synchronization is dropping to 98.2% every 73 seconds, then returning to optimal levels."

Ren studied the pattern, her mind racing through calculations. "It's a harmonic resonance with the port's power grid. Increase the isolation factor on the primary shield by 0.3%."

"But that will require recalibrating the entire—"

"Do it," Ren interrupted. "We can't risk even a 1.8% variance during actual transport. The molecular reconstruction could show anomalies."

Lars joined them, concern etched on his face. "How long will the recalibration take?"

"Three hours," Sarah estimated.

"We have four until the scheduled demonstration," Ren noted. "Begin immediately."

As Sarah gathered her team, a security guard approached. "Dr. Franco, there's a representative from the European Energy Commission requesting access. Says they needed to conduct a safety assessment."

Ren's expression hardened. "Denied. We have all of the required permits. This is proprietary technology."

"They're quite insistent," the guard said uncomfortably. "They have some kind of regulatory override."

Lars touched Ren's arm lightly. "Perhaps we should allow it. Showing transparency might help with future approvals."

Ren considered this, then nodded curtly. "Fine. One representative, thirty minutes maximum. No recording devices, no samples, no direct access to the MTU core."

As the guard departed to relay these terms, Lars studied Ren's tense posture. "You've been preparing for this moment for years. Are you really not nervous at all?"

Ren's dark eyes met his. "Nervousness implies uncertainty. I'm not uncertain about the technology." She paused. "I'm uncertain about how the world will respond to it."

Before Lars could reply, Ren's secure tablet chimed. She glanced at it, then straightened her shoulders. "Koji's team has completed the final container loading. One hundred GreenRider X9 motorcycles, packaged and ready for transport."

"And on our end?" Lars asked.

"We'll be ready," Ren stated with absolute conviction. "We have to be. The observers arrive at 07:30 tomorrow. First transport begins at 08:00 sharp."

She walked to the center of the facility, where the yellow MTU stood silent and waiting, its potential still hidden from a world that had no idea how dramatically things were about to change.

"Run a full diagnostic on the quantum receiver array," she instructed a nearby technician. "I want every atom in this machine operating at peak efficiency."

As teams of technicians swarmed around the MTU, following Ren's precise instructions, Lars found himself marveling at her composure. Tomorrow, they would either make history or become a cautionary tale in the annals of failed technological moonshots.

Either way, the world would never be the same.

Five kilometers away, aboard the freighter Kumo no Ito, Bora watched the port through night-vision scopes. The emergency vehicles converging on the TTC facility looked like fireflies in the green-tinged darkness.

"The sabotage failed," Klaus Bernheimer wheezed beside him, clutching his fourth whiskey despite the early hour. "They found it too quickly."

"Of course they did." Bora lowered the scope. "It was meant to be found."

Háo from Xìngyún Trade Transport stepped forward. "You wanted to fail?"

"I wanted to test their response protocols." Bora turned to the three shipping executives he'd summoned. "You don't kill what you don't understand. The power grid was reconnaissance."

Victoria Henryson's British accent cut through the bridge's darkness. "Expensive reconnaissance. If they trace it—"

"They'll find breadcrumbs leading to eco-terrorists who vanished last week." Bora activated his wall of monitors, each showing different angles of the port facility. "The real asset was confirming they have someone inside willing to be turned."

"You compromised their staff?" Bernheimer's eyes widened.

"Gambling debts are wonderfully motivating." Bora pulled up thermal imaging of the facility, watching Ren's team swarm the power systems. "Sarah Jensdotter. Quantum engineer. She's probably being discovered right about now."

Through the monitors, they watched Lars's team work with military precision. Bora made notes on a tablet—response time, personnel deployment, security protocols.

"She's good," he admitted quietly. "But everyone has a breaking point."

Friday, 09 June 2056. The digital watch on Ren's wrist read 08:00 in Rotterdam. The morning's sabotage attempt had cost them ninety minutes and one trusted team member. Ren watched the observers gather, her tablet showing seventeen different security protocols now running simultaneously. Every power coupling triple-checked. Every data line verified.

Lars appeared at her shoulder. "Jensdotter confessed. She was supposed to trigger a quantum field collapse during the third container."

"The third?" Ren's mind raced through implications. "After we'd proven initial success but before establishing reliability. Maximum credibility damage."

"Should we delay?"

"No." Ren's voice carried steel. "They wanted us rattled. We proceed exactly as planned."

Mr. Tanaka approached, sweat beading despite the cool morning. "Dr. Franco, I've heard concerning rumors about security incidents—"

"Handled." She met his nervous gaze. "Someone preferred the status quo. They've been disappointed."

Ms. Davies materialized beside them with practiced stealth. "This 'someone' wouldn't happen to own container ships, would they?"

Ren kept her expression neutral. "I couldn't speculate about motivation. Only guarantee safety."

Davies smiled thinly. "I'm sure. Though industrial sabotage does suggest someone takes your technology very seriously."

Before Ren could respond, her secure phone buzzed. Koji's message was brief: "Nagasaki secure. Ready on your mark."

She was waiting, fidgeting almost imperceptibly – a tiny trembling tremor in her otherwise still hands – with a few others, at the designated berth waiting for the shipment.

They were protected from the persistent Atlantic drizzle by a tension membrane structure, a temporary shelter erected specifically for this clandestine demonstration. The structure, vast and stark white, covered the operational area, shielding the core technology from curious eyes and satellite surveillance.

Inside the structure was what resembled a bulkier-than-usual gamma-ray radiography system that looked like two TEUs could fit inside. It was boxy, industrial, and humming with a low, resonant energy that vibrated through the concrete berth.

Painted a utilitarian yellow with "TTC" stenciled starkly on its sides, the machine looked simultaneously mundane and utterly alien against the backdrop of traditional cranes, cargo mountains, and the grey, choppy waters of the harbor. This was the Mass Teleportation Unit (MTU), the culmination of decades of theoretical physics, relentless engineering, and a truly absurd amount of personal wealth and risk.

The designated berth in Rotterdam wasn't just occupied by the official observers. A small crowd had gathered at the perimeter—dock workers on break, curious security personnel, and a handful of journalists who'd caught wind that something unusual was happening.

Among them stood Elise Vos, Rotterdam Port Authority's Environmental Compliance Officer, her critical gaze fixed on the yellow MTU. "Another tech 'solution' that'll probably cause more problems than it solves," she muttered to her colleague.

Officer Pieter, a burly harbor police veteran, shrugged. "If it works, it could mean fewer ships to patrol. I wouldn't mind that."

"And fewer jobs," added Sven, a longshoreman whose family had worked these docks for generations. He spat onto the concrete. "My grandfather loaded ships, my father loaded ships, I loaded ships. What happens to us if this thing works?" His voice was flat, laced with fear for the future of his trade. A heavy silence settled over the dockworkers nearby.

"Progress always comes at a cost," said Elise, her tone softening slightly. "But remember when automated cranes were introduced? Everyone said the same thing, but we adapted. Found new roles."

"This is different," Sven insisted, gesturing toward the MTU. "That thing doesn't just change how we work—it eliminates the need for the work entirely. No ships, no cargo handling, no stevedores. Just magic boxes appearing from nowhere."

Another dockworker, younger than Sven, leaned forward. "My cousin works in retraining at the labor union. Says we should start learning quantum mechanics now." His attempt at humor fell flat among the worried faces.

Near the official group, Dr. Jela Reeves from the European Union's Technology Assessment Board took meticulous notes. She'd been tracking Ren's patent applications for years, piecing together the puzzle of what The Teleport Company might actually be developing. Now, watching the nervous Mr. Tanaka fidget with his tie, she felt a surge of professional excitement. If this demonstration succeeded, her report would shake Brussels to its core.

"Care to share your preliminary thoughts, Dr. Reeves?" whispered her assistant, a recent physics graduate named Marco.

"If it works as theorized," Jela replied quietly, "we'll bear witness to the most significant transportation breakthrough since the Wright brothers. Perhaps more significant." She adjusted her glasses, studying the MTU's exterior. "The energy implications alone are staggering."

"And the economic disruption?" Marco pressed.

Jela's expression grew somber. "Incalculable. Shipping represents about 90% of world trade. This technology wouldn't just change shipping—it would fundamentally alter global economics, labor markets, energy consumption patterns..." She trailed off, watching Ren check her equipment. "And it appears to be in the hands of a single private company."

"Three minutes to initiation," announced a technician manning the control terminal, his voice carrying across the tension-filled space.

Ms. Davies, the government observer, casually positioned herself closer to Ren, her seemingly relaxed posture belying her heightened alertness. She glanced at the grey, choppy water. "The wind's picking up," she observed, her tone mild, but her eyes assessing Ren's reaction. Her agency had flagged TTC as a potentially disruptive technology years ago, but even their most speculative analysts hadn't predicted anything of this magnitude.

"Nervous?" she asked Ren quietly.

"No," Ren replied simply, checking her watch. It wasn't bravado; it was mathematical confidence. The equations were balanced. The technology would work. Her voice was low, precise, reflecting absolute certainty in the data.

"You understand our concern," Ms. Davies continued, keeping her voice low enough that only Ren could hear. "Technology with this potential... It changes everything. Security implications, economic stability, geopolitical balance."

Ren's gaze remained fixed on the MTU. "Change is inevitable. Better it comes from transparent commercial application than military development."

Ms. Davies raised an eyebrow. "Is that why you turned down three different defense contracts?"

"You've done your homework," Ren noted without surprise. "Yes. This technology doesn't belong exclusively to any government or military."

"Noble," Ms. Davies murmured, "but potentially naive. If this works today, you realize you won't be able to control who develops similar systems."

"Perhaps," Ren conceded. "But we'll have a significant head start. And the patents are... comprehensive."

There was a representative from the motorcycle manufacturer, a nervous, tie-loosened logistics manager named Mr. Tanaka, whose career likely depended on this working. There were two grim-faced port authority officials, skeptics radiating polite disbelief, clipboard in hand, ready to document everything – or nothing. Then there was the single, quiet individual introduced only as 'Ms. Davies' from a discreet government agency Ren suspected was tasked with observing potentially disruptive technologies. They watched the yellow MTU with a mixture of apprehension and morbid curiosity.

Mr. Tanaka approached Ren, checking his watch for the fifth time in as many minutes. "Dr. Franco, perhaps we should consider a delay if there are any... uncertainties. My company could arrange conventional shipping as a backup plan."

"That won't be necessary," Ren assured him, her calm confidence in stark contrast to his anxiety. "The system is functioning perfectly."

"But the financial exposure if something goes wrong—"

"Is covered by our insurance," Ren completed his sentence. "As outlined in clause seventeen of our agreement. Your company's investment is protected, Mr. Tanaka."

One of the port officials cleared his throat. "Speaking of

protection, we've received additional inquiries from the Maritime Safety Board regarding potential electromagnetic interference."

Lars stepped forward. "Our system generates a self-contained quantum field. There is no electromagnetic radiation that could affect navigation or communication systems."

The official appeared unconvinced but nodded stiffly. "We'll be monitoring nonetheless."

Ren raised the hardened satellite phone to her ear, the connection crisp despite the distance. She called Nagasaki. It was 15:00 in Japan. "Koji-san! Hello and good afternoon. How are you? And, more importantly, how is the shipment?"

"Kon'nichiwa, Ren-san. An excellent day here," replied Koji Ozakashi. Koji was more than a colleague; he was a longtime friend from graduate school, one of the few people Ren trusted implicitly with both her ideas and her vulnerabilities.

They had navigated the complex theoretical landscapes of quantum mechanics and computational physics together years ago. Koji had readily agreed to oversee the Nagasaki end of this monumental first test. "Next time you're here, I'll take you to this great ramen stand." Koji's voice was steady, injecting a note of familiar, grounding normalcy into the tense situation.

"While I admire the thought, you don't have the best taste buds, Koji. I'll pass," Ren retorted, the mild teasing of a release valve for the pressure building within her. "Are we ready?"

"All set here," Koji confirmed. "Customs documents complete. Coordinating key codes and sending the first container in sixty seconds."

"Remember our first experiments with entanglement at MIT?" Koji added, his voice tinged with nostalgia. "Professor Zhao said we were wasting university resources on science fiction."

"And now he's requesting a demonstration for his department," Ren replied, allowing herself a small smile. "Funny how success changes perspectives."

"Indeed. The first container is positioned and scanned. Quantum signature locked and synchronized with your receiver." Koji's voice shifted to pure professionalism. "Initiating transmission on your mark."

Ren glanced at the observers gathered around her, their

expressions ranging from skepticism to barely contained excitement. "Proceed, Koji. Standard protocol."

On the Nagasaki end, Koji turned to his team after ending the call. "It's time. Meeka, begin the quantum field initialization sequence."

Meeka nodded, her fingers flying over the control panel. "Initializing primary field. Superconductors at optimal temperature. Quantum entanglement is stable at 99.9%."

"Yamada-san," Koji called to the customs official, "final verification of container contents, please."

The customs officer held up his tablet. "Container JPNA-4482937 verified and cleared for transport. Contents: twenty-five GreenRider X9 motorcycles, serial numbers matching manifest."

Matsuda from the motorcycle company paced nervously behind them. "This is insanity. Absolute insanity. If those bikes arrive damaged—"

"They won't," Koji assured him. "Quantum transport maintains molecular integrity. They'll arrive exactly as they are now."

The massive yellow MTU began to hum more intensely, its internal chamber glowing with a blue-white light as the first container was moved into position by an automated loader.

"Quantum field established," called out a technician. "Container in position."

"Begin molecular scanning," ordered Meeka.

A series of laser-like beams swept over the container from multiple angles, mapping every atom of its structure.

"Scan complete. Molecular pattern stored. Establishing entanglement with Rotterdam MTU."

Koji watched the progress bar on his monitor fill rapidly. "Rotterdam link confirmed. They're ready to receive."

"Initiating transport in ten seconds," announced Meeka, her voice tight with concentration.

The team fell silent, watching the container sitting innocuously in the MTU chamber. Matsuda had stopped pacing, his eyes wide with disbelief and a hint of fear.

"Five... four... three... two... one... Initiate."

The blue-white glow intensified to blinding brightness for a split second. When it faded, the container was gone.

Koji exhaled slowly. "Transport complete. Awaiting Rotterdam confirmation."

The control room erupted in hushed murmurs. A junior technician crossed himself reflexively.

"Did it... did it work?" Matsuda asked, his voice barely audible.

Meeka's eyes remained fixed on her monitor. "Quantum dissolution complete. Pattern integrity maintained throughout transmission." She looked up at Koji. "It worked on our end. Now we wait."

Koji stared at the empty chamber where the container had been moments before. Despite years of theory and smaller tests, the reality of what they'd just accomplished struck him anew. They had just disassembled a multi-ton object at the subatomic level and sent its perfect pattern across thousands of miles.

"Prepare the next container," he instructed, his voice steady despite the momentous occasion. "We continue as planned."

The line went quiet for a few seconds as Koji relayed instructions on his end. Ren held her breath, watching the yellow MTU in front of her.

As Koji stated, precisely one minute later, the large yellow MTU machine in Nagasaki, seven thousand miles away, lit up. A deep, resonant hum filled the Rotterdam structure, building in intensity. The stenciled "MTU" seemed to pulse with contained energy.

Simultaneously, the MTU in Rotterdam began to respond, its internal space shimmering with an almost imperceptible distortion, like heat haze but colder, more focused. "Loading the first container," Koji announced.

To the growing amazement, then outright astonishment, of the others waiting with Ren in Rotterdam, a solid object began to materialize within the distortion field of the MTU. It started as a faint outline, a spectral suggestion of form, then rapidly resolved into the undeniable, physical reality of a steel shipping container. The familiar corrugated sides, the locking bars, the worn paint – a standard TEU, coalescing into existence from nothingness.

Aboard the Kumo no Ito, Bora stood perfectly still as the first container materialized on his monitors. Behind him, Bernheimer dropped his whiskey glass. It shattered on the deck, the sound sharp in the sudden silence.

"Mein Gott," Bernheimer whispered. "It's actually real."

"Yes." Bora's voice held something almost like admiration. "Despite our interference, despite the pressure, she delivered."

He touched his earpiece. "Are you seeing this?"

A cultured voice with a slight Eastern European accent responded. "Every frame. The energy readings are... extraordinary."

"And the vulnerability assessment?"

"Processing. But Bora—" A pause. "This changes everything. Every assumption about commerce, borders, control—"

"I know." Bora watched Ren directing her team with calm precision. "Which is why we move to Phase Two immediately."

He turned to the assembled executives. "Gentlemen, lady—you're about to witness your industry's extinction event. The question is whether you'll help me control the aftermath or be buried in it."

On the monitors, the second container began materializing.

Lars, standing at the control panel, called out readings in a voice fighting to remain professional. "Quantum coherence at 100%. Molecular reconstruction proceeding at optimal parameters. Mass verification in progress."

One of the technicians, a young woman named Sarah, stared at the monitor in front of her, her face illuminated by the scrolling data. "It's... it's perfect," she whispered. "Every atom, exactly as transmitted."

The sight reminded Ren of a conversation years ago, when she had first explained her vision to a potential investor. The woman had been skeptical but intrigued.

"So you're saying this machine will know everything about whatever it's moving?" the investor had asked.

That investor had signed the check the next day.

Now, years later, Ren watched as theory became reality before her eyes. The container solidified completely, settling onto the platform with a soft metallic thud that echoed through the suddenly silent structure.

"My God," breathed one of the port authority officials, dropping his clipboard with a clatter. "It's actually appearing from nothing."

Mr. Tanaka fumbled for his reading glasses, comparing the stenciled number on the container to his manifest. "The... the TEU number... it matches!" His voice was shaky with disbelief and dawning realization.

Dr. Reeves scribbled furiously in her notebook, a small, triumphant smile on her face. This was more than she had dared hope for.

"Koji, it's here." Ren's voice was her normal, unexcited tone, a lifetime of disciplined emotional control holding back the tsunami of relief, triumph, and sheer awe flooding her senses. "Coordinates locked. Quantum field stabilized." She allowed herself only the slightest exhale, a tiny release of the tension coiled tight in her chest for years.

"Congratulations, Ren-san!" Koji's voice crackled with genuine excitement, a rare breach of their usual scientific reserve. "You are now a pioneer of history. As agreed, one TEU every five minutes."

One of the longshoremen in the perimeter crowd shook his head slowly, his earlier fear turning to a deep unease. "They weren't kidding," he muttered. "Just... gone from there, here now. What does that even mean?"

His colleague, an older man with weathered hands, leaned against a stack of conventional containers. "Means we better start learning new skills, Jakob. The world just changed."

"Changed? For who?" another dockworker interjected, his voice tight with anger. "It just looks like another case of the rich getting richer while we lose our livelihoods. My father lost his job to automation, now my children will have nothing because of this... this witchcraft."

"Keep it down," hissed a supervisor. "This is happening whether we like it or not. Better to figure out how to adapt than fight the inevitable."

The dockworkers fell silent, but their expressions spoke volumes—a mixture of awe, fear, and the dawning realization that their world had just been fundamentally altered.

Mr. Tanaka approached the container cautiously, as if it might disappear again. "Can we... can we open it?" he asked Ren. "I need to verify the motorcycles are intact."

Ren nodded to Lars, who pressed a sequence on his control panel. The container doors unlocked with a mechanical click.

"Be my guest," Ren said.

With trembling hands, Mr. Tanaka pulled open the heavy metal doors. Inside, perfectly arranged in specialized racks, stood twenty-five gleaming GreenRider X9 motorcycles, their metallic blue finish catching the light. Not a scratch, not a dent, not a single molecule out of place.

"Impossible," whispered one of the port officials, peering over Mr. Tanaka's shoulder.

Mr. Tanaka moved into the container, examining the motorcycles with meticulous care. He checked serial numbers against his manifest, ran his fingers along the pristine surfaces, and even started one of the bikes, its electric motor instantly humming to life.

"They're perfect," he announced, his voice filled with an equal mix of wonder and suspicion. "Exactly as they were in Nagasaki. Not even a fingerprint out of place." He turned to Ren. "Dr. Franco, this is nothing short of revolutionary."

Ms. Davies moved closer to Ren. "How soon until the next one arrives?" she asked quietly.

"Four minutes," Ren replied, checking her watch. "We'll complete all one hundred containers before noon."

"And the energy requirements?"

Ren allowed herself a small smile. "Less than what a container ship burns crossing the Pacific. And zero emissions."

"The implications for national security—" Ms. Davies began.

"Are substantial," Ren finished for her. "But not my primary concern. This technology exists to solve logistical and environmental problems, not create military advantages."

Ms. Davies studied her carefully. "Noble intentions, but as smart as you are, you must surely realize that governments worldwide will be extremely interested in what you've done here."

"I'm counting on it," Ren replied. "But on my terms."

The freighter Kumo no Ito—Spider's Thread—sat motionless in Rotterdam's harbor, a rusted black presence that blended in perfectly in the industrial sprawl of Europe's largest port. From its top deck, the massive cranes and container mountains looked like toys, a child's construction set about to be swept away.

Inside the ship's bridge, multiple screens displayed various angles of the yellow MTU at the port, frozen frames of the container materializing, data streams of energy readings that shouldn't exist according to conventional physics.

Bora stood perfectly still, hands clasped behind his back, watching the replay of the demonstration for the third time. His tailored suit showed no wrinkles despite the late hour. His expression revealed nothing—not surprise, not anger, not fear. Only careful, meticulous observation.

"It's impossible," Klaus Bernheimer wheezed from a worn chair, his third whiskey trembling in his hand. The German shipping magnate's face was florid with panic and alcohol. "The physics alone—"

"The physics are irrelevant," Bora interrupted softly, not turning from the screens. "What matters is that it happened. Denial is a luxury we cannot afford."

"But the implications—"Háo from Xìngyún Trade Transport began, his voice tight with barely controlled hysteria. "If they can move containers instantly—"

"They can move anything instantly," Bora finished. "Ships become museums. Ports become graveyards. Your empires become memories." He finally turned, his dark eyes sweeping across the three executives he'd summoned. "Unless we act with precision and purpose."

Bernheimer stood abruptly, swaying slightly. "We should expose them! The energy requirements must be massive—environmental concerns, safety violations—"

"Sit down, Klaus." Bora's voice carried a quiet authority that made the larger man immediately comply. "Crude attacks will fail. Dr. Franco has been preparing for this moment for years, perhaps decades. Look at the execution—flawless. The timing—perfect.

The security—impenetrable. This is not some startup we can simply overwhelm with lawyers and lobbyists."

He touched a control panel, and new images filled the screens—satellite photos of installations in remote locations, financial records showing vast capital movements, patent filings dating back years.

"TTC isn't just a company," Bora continued. "It's a revolution disguised as a corporation. They've been building in the shadows while we've been fighting over scraps of the old world."

"You've been watching them," Háo said, a statement rather than a question.

"I watch everything that threatens the natural order," Bora replied. "And this"—he gestured to the frozen image of the materialized container—"is the greatest threat we've ever faced."

The third executive, Victoria Henryson from Oceanic Maritime Alliance, had remained silent until now. "What do you propose?" she asked, her British accent clipped with tension.

Bora smiled then, an expression that didn't reach his eyes. "First, we must understand our enemy. Dr. Franco—brilliant, driven, but fundamentally naive about how power truly works. She believes technology alone can reshape the world." He pulled up an image of Ren from the demonstration, her face showing that moment of quiet triumph. "She doesn't understand that every system, no matter how advanced, has vulnerabilities. Every network has its ghosts."

"Ghosts?" Bernheimer asked, confused.

"Unintended consequences. Hidden flaws. Exploitable weaknesses." Bora moved to the window, gazing out at the port where the demonstration had taken place. "Their technology appears perfect, but perfection is an illusion. They're moving quantum information through conventional infrastructure at some point. They're interfacing with existing systems. They have human operators with human weaknesses."

"You're talking about sabotage," Victoria said carefully.

"I'm talking about survival," Bora corrected. "The natural order—where distance creates value, where control of movement means control of commerce, where we decide what moves and when—is under assault. We either adapt and absorb this threat, or we're extinct within five years."

He returned to the screens, pulling up a complex organizational chart. "I've already begun reaching out to... alternative partners. Organizations that understand the value of controlling flow—of goods, of people, of everything. They have networks Franco can't imagine, capabilities she'd consider beneath her ethical standards."

"Criminal networks," Matsuda said flatly.

"Practical networks," Bora countered. "While Dr. Franco dreams of saving the world, they understand the world as it actually is—brutal, hierarchical, driven by power and profit. They'll be eager to either control this technology or destroy it."

"And if we're caught collaborating with—"

"We won't be." Bora's tone brooked no argument. "I've spent years building walls between my public face and my true operations. Shell companies, intermediaries, encrypted communications that make Franco's quantum security look like a child's lock. Officially, we'll be concerned business leaders seeking dialogue and regulation. Unofficially..." He let the implication hang.

Bernheimer drained his whiskey. "What do you need from us?"

"Resources. Intelligence. Political pressure through your existing channels." Bora pulled up a new display showing TTC's known facilities. "But most importantly, time. We need to slow their expansion while I find their weakness."

"You seem very confident you'll find one," Victoria observed.

Bora's smile returned, colder than before. "Every system I've ever encountered has had one fundamental flaw—it was designed by humans. And humans, no matter how brilliant, always make mistakes. Franco's mistake was believing she could change the world without the world fighting back."

He moved to a secured cabinet, withdrawing a slim tablet. "I have assets within the technology sector who understand quantum systems. People who've worked on similar theoretical projects. Some may even have connections to Dr. Franco's past academic work. We'll understand her technology, then we'll find its ghosts."

"And then?" Háo asked.

"Then we offer her a choice," Bora said.

The ship shifted slightly with the harbor's tide, a subtle reminder that even the most stable platforms were subject to forces beyond their control.

"I must warn you," Bora added, his tone shifting to something darker. "Once we begin this path, there's no return. Dr. Franco has already shown she can make the impossible real. We must be prepared to be equally... creative in our response. Some of what needs to be done will be unpleasant. Necessary, but unpleasant."

The executives exchanged uneasy glances, but none objected. They understood the stakes.

"My father commanded a container vessel for thirty years," Bora said suddenly, his voice taking on an unexpected personal note. "He used to say that controlling the sea meant controlling the world. Franco has made the sea irrelevant." His expression hardened. "I won't let his life's work become meaningless. I won't let our entire civilization be reshaped by one woman's hubris."

He turned back to the screens showing the Rotterdam port, where cleanup crews were already dismantling the temporary structure that had housed the demonstration.

The spider was beginning to spin its web.

The technician at the control panel called out, "MTU recharging. Ready for the next transport in three minutes, forty seconds."

Lars approached, his face flushed with excitement. "All systems nominal. The quantum field is actually more stable than in our test runs. We could potentially reduce the interval between transports."

"We stick to the plan," Ren instructed firmly. "Five minutes between containers. Safety protocols remain in place."

As the officials and observers gathered around the first container, examining it with a mixture of disbelief and wonder, Ren stepped back, taking in the moment. This was just the beginning. Soon, they would be moving more than motorcycles. Food, medicine, building materials—anything that could fit in a container could be transported to the furthest reaches of the globe.

"Dr. Franco," Dr. Reeves approached, her professional demeanor barely containing her excitement. "Would you be willing to discuss the broader implications of your technology? The EU Technology Assessment Board would be extremely interested in collaborating on regulatory frameworks."

"In due time," Ren replied. "Today is about demonstrating viability. Tomorrow we can discuss the future."

From the control station, Sarah called out, "Second container transmission initiating from Nagasaki!"

All eyes turned back to the MTU as the process began again. The quantum field shimmered into existence, atoms assembling into molecules, molecules into structure, invisible forces weaving together the fabric of matter across impossible distances.

As the first container settled fully onto the berth with a final metallic groan, solid and real, its impossible journey complete, Ren felt a profound sense of vindication. But looking at the faces around her – the awe, the fear, the skepticism turning to disbelief – she knew this was just the beginning. The world was about to change, whether it was ready or not.

As the fourth container materialized, Ren's secure phone vibrated. Unknown number, but it had bypassed three layers of encryption.

The message was simple: "Impressive demonstration. We should talk about your future. Or lack thereof. - B"

She deleted it immediately, but Lars had seen her expression change.

"Problem?" he asked quietly.

"No," she lied, watching the fifth container begin its impossible journey across seven thousand miles. "Just the beginning."

In her peripheral vision, she caught Ms. Davies speaking rapidly into her own secure phone, her gaze never leaving Ren. The government observer had seen the message too, or at least Ren's reaction to it.

The war for the future of global commerce had begun. The first shot had been fired this morning. The response had just arrived.

And somewhere in Rotterdam's harbor, Bora smiled.

2 REN'S GENESIS

The quantum field collapsed at 03:47 AM.

Ren jolted awake in her quarters at TTC headquarters, the emergency klaxon cutting through the Newfoundland night. Her secure tablet was already lighting up with cascading system failures.

"Dr. Franco, we have a breach in Satellite Array Three." Terri's voice crackled through the intercom, professional despite the hour. "Someone's attempting to access the core transmission protocols."

Ren moved before Terri finished speaking, pulling on clothes while her mind calculated attack vectors. Only someone with intimate knowledge of their quantum architecture could have gotten this far.

"How deep are they?" She grabbed her badge and tablet, already pulling up the satellite's diagnostic interface.

"They've bypassed the first two encryption layers. If they reach the entanglement matrix—"

"They'll have our entire network blueprint." Ren was running now, her footsteps echoing in the empty corridors. "Lock down all ground stations. Initiate Protocol Seven."

"That'll take the entire network offline for twelve hours."

"Do it."

The command center was bathed in red emergency lighting when Ren arrived. Wall-mounted screens showed the attack's progression—elegant code sliding through their defenses like water through a sieve.

"This is sophisticated," Terri said, fingers flying across her holographic interface. "They're using a modified version of our own error-correction algorithms against us."

Ren studied the attack pattern, something familiar nagging at her. The code structure, the approach to quantum decoherence...

"Dr. Franco." Lynn appeared at her shoulder, somehow perfectly dressed despite the hour. "I've been monitoring communications chatter. There's unusual activity in several shipping conglomerate channels. Encrypted, but the timing—"

"It's coordinated." Ren's voice was flat. "Someone leaked our architecture."

"That's impossible," Bruce interjected, arriving breathless. "Our NDA's are airtight. The financial penalties alone—"

"Unless someone doesn't care about money." Ren pulled up the attack code on her personal screen, dissecting its DNA. "This uses theoretical frameworks from my doctoral thesis. Unpublished sections."

The room fell silent except for the hum of servers and the soft chime of system alerts.

"You're saying this is personal?" Katya asked from her position by the financial monitors.

"I'm saying whoever wrote this studied my work extensively." Ren's fingers moved across her tablet, building a counter-algorithm in real-time. "There. Look at this approach to maintaining quantum coherence during the attack. It's based on a paper I presented at MIT fifteen years ago."

She paused, her hands suddenly still.

"Singh," she whispered.

"Your old professor?" Terri looked up sharply. "But he dismissed your work. Called it fantasy."

"Publicly." Ren's mind raced back to that office, those conversations, the way Singh had studied her calculations with an intensity that went beyond academic skepticism. "But he kept my papers. All of them."

Ren remembered one conversation vividly, the smooth laminate of the kitchen table cool under her forearms. She was twelve, maybe thirteen, her quantum mechanics book open between the dinner plates her mother hadn't cleared yet.

"So, things can be in two places at once, Dad?" Ren asked, pointing to a fuzzy illustration. Her voice, even then, held a quiet intensity, a desperate need to be understood.

Her father smiled, ruffling her hair. "That's just theory, Ren. Interesting stuff, sure, but—"

"It's not just theory," Ren interrupted, something fierce flashing in her eyes. "Scientists have done it with photons, with atoms. They've teleported quantum states across rooms, across cities."

"In laboratories with million-dollar equipment," her mother cut in, not looking up from her tablet where market reports scrolled endlessly. "Not exactly practical applications, honey."

"But if we could scale it!"

"Ren." Her father's voice took on that patient tone she'd grown to hate. "You're talking about science fiction. I work with real materials, real structures. They follow rules. Predictable, reliable rules."

"Quantum mechanics has rules too! Just different ones. If we could harness entanglement for actual transport—"

Her mother laughed, sharp and dismissive. "Transport? Honey, the energy requirements alone would bankrupt a small country. I analyze markets for a living. Trust me, if teleportation was viable, someone would be monetizing it."

"Maybe they just haven't figured out how yet," Ren said quietly, her knuckles white as she gripped the book. "Maybe everyone's been thinking about it wrong."

Her parents exchanged that look, the one that said their daughter was brilliant but impractical, gifted but naive.

"Focus on real problems," her father said gently. "Problems with solutions. That's how you make a difference in the world."

"What if I told you I could solve this?" Ren asked, her voice barely above a whisper. "Would you believe me then?"

"When you do, we'll be your first investors," her mother said with false brightness, already turning back to her screen. "Until then, how about focusing on your actual homework?"

Ren closed the quantum text carefully, feeling something harden inside her chest. They'd see. Eventually, everyone would see.

Ren shook off the memory, focusing on the present threat. Her parents never had believed in the impossible. But someone else had—someone who'd pretended not to.

"Terri, can you trace the origin of the attack?"

"Already on it. The signal's bouncing through multiple proxies, but—" Terri frowned. "That's odd. One of the relay points is registered to a company called Cerberus Holdings."

Lynn's tablet chimed. "Cerberus Holdings. Shell company registered in Cyprus. But look at this—" She pulled up a complex ownership chart. "If you follow the paper trail far enough, it connects to Infinite Crossings Logistics."

"Bora," Bruce said quietly. "Has to be."

"We don't know that," Lynn cautioned, but her expression suggested otherwise.

"We know enough." Ren's counter-algorithm was complete. "Terri, implement this. It'll create a quantum feedback loop in their infiltration pathway."

"That could damage their hardware."

"Good."

As Terri uploaded the countermeasure, Ren's tablet buzzed. Another unknown number, another impossible breach of her security.

"Impressive response time. Your old professor speaks highly of your theoretical work. Perhaps we should discuss practical applications. - B"

This time, Ren didn't delete it. She forwarded it to Lynn. "Add it to the file."

"The legal file or the other one?" Lynn asked quietly.

"Both."

The screens shifted from red to amber as Terri's countermeasure took effect. The attack retreated like a tide, leaving behind corrupted data packets that would take days to analyze.

"They're out," Terri reported. "But they got deeper than they should have. They have partial schematics for the MTU's quantum entanglement matrix."

"How partial?" Katya asked.

"Enough to be dangerous in the wrong hands," Ren admitted. "Not enough to replicate, but enough to potentially disrupt if they understand what they're looking at."

Bruce was pacing, his runner's energy needing outlet. "We should accelerate the public announcement. Get ahead of whatever they're planning."

"No." Ren moved to the window, looking out at the North Atlantic. Dawn was still hours away. "They want us to panic, to move before we're ready. We stick to the timeline."

"Even if they have Singh?" Terri asked.

Ren turned back to her team. "Especially if they have Singh."

It began with a relic in her grandparents' basement, an ancient computer that became her first love. While other children played games, Ren learned BASIC, wrote code, dissected programs. She spent months building adapters and cables to bridge decades of technology, transferring games from modern drives to ancient floppies.

Then came the challenge: bridging the gap. She wanted more, newer old games. She spent months, maybe a year, piecing together a solution. Adapters, homemade cables, drivers she wrote herself, painstakingly deciphering protocols no one used anymore. The day she successfully transferred a game from a modern USB drive to that ancient floppy disk, loaded it into the beige machine, and watched it boot up, it felt like a victory over time itself. She wasn't just playing with history; she was connecting it, understanding the fundamental principles that spanned decades.

This wasn't just a hobby; it was where she learned the language of systems, the joy of elegant code, the power of bending technology to her will.

Those early years teaching herself to bridge incompatible systems had prepared her for this moment—defending the impossible network she'd built from someone who understood it almost as well as she did.

"You're thinking about the Rotterdam demonstration," Terri said, studying Ren's expression. It wasn't a question.

"I'm thinking about patterns," Ren replied. "The sabotage attempt, now this. Someone's testing our responses, learning our protocols."

"Building a profile," Lynn added. "It's what I'd do if I were preparing a legal assault. Test the defenses, find the weak points."

"Except this isn't legal," Bruce pointed out.

"No," Ren agreed. "It's worse. It's personal."

Her tablet chimed again. This time it was Koji calling from Nagasaki.

"Ren, we've had an incident. Someone tried to breach our facility. Physical attempt, not digital. Security stopped them, but—"

"Let me guess," Ren interrupted. "They had inside knowledge of our security rotations."

"How did you—"

"Because we're under coordinated attack." She looked at her team. "How quickly can we implement Protocol Nine?"

Terri's eyes widened. "Full lockdown? That's never been tested on the complete network."

"Then we test it now." Ren's voice carried the same certainty she'd had as that twelve-year-old arguing about quantum mechanics. "Katya, what's our financial exposure if we go dark for seventy-two hours?"

"Significant but manageable. Our contracts have force majeure clauses for security events."

"Lynn?"

"Legally defensible. I'll file the necessary notifications."

"Bruce?"

"I'll handle client communications. Spin it as a planned security upgrade."

Ren nodded. "Do it. And Terri—" Their eyes met across the room. "I need you to run a deep audit on everyone who's had access to my academic work. Every student, every peer reviewer, everyone."

"That's hundreds of people."

"Then we'd better get started."

The lecture hall buzzed with chatter of excited students as Ren slipped into a seat near the front. The quantum mechanics course was notoriously challenging, but Ren thrived on intellectual stimulation. Professor Singh, a renowned physicist with wild grey hair and thick glasses, strode into the room, his presence commanding immediate silence.

As the lecture began, Ren found herself engrossed in the complex equations and mind-bending concepts. The idea that particles could exist in multiple states simultaneously, that the very act of observation could alter reality—it was both thrilling and terrifying.

Ren's hand shot up, almost of its own accord. "Professor, could you explain how quantum entanglement relates to the idea of teleportation? If two particles are linked, could information be transmitted instantaneously between them, regardless of distance?"

Professor Singh paused, a slow smile spreading across his face. "Ah, the dreams of teleportation. It's a fascinating question, Miss Franco. In theory, yes, entanglement could allow for information transfer that appears to defy the speed of light. But the practical challenges are immense. Maintaining coherence, compensating for noise and interference... we're a long way from beaming anyone up, Scotty."

The class chuckled, but Ren's mind was racing. Her hand shot up again before Professor Singh could continue.

"But you're treating entanglement like it's just a curiosity," Ren pressed, her quiet voice carrying surprising force. "What if we're thinking about the energy requirements wrong? What if the problem isn't power but precision in the quantum state mapping?"

Professor Singh's smile tightened. "Miss Franco, I appreciate your enthusiasm, but there's a difference between theoretical mathematics and physical reality. The decoherence alone—"

"Is a solvable problem if we use a distributed network approach with redundant error correction across multiple entangled pairs," Ren interrupted, her words tumbling out faster now. "I've run the simulations. The math works."

A few students shifted uncomfortably. Professor Singh removed his glasses, cleaning them slowly, a gesture Ren would later recognize as his way of controlling irritation.

"Simulations," he said, replacing his glasses with deliberate care, "are not experiments, Miss Franco. And undergraduate assumptions are not breakthrough physics. Perhaps we should continue with the actual curriculum?"

The dismissal stung more than Ren expected. She sank back in her seat, face burning, but her mind churned with defiant calculations. She felt certain she could make breakthroughs that would change the world.

Three days later, Ren sat across from Professor Singh in his cramped office, quantum mechanics texts towering around them like fortress walls. She'd spread her calculations across his desk—pages of dense mathematics, circuit diagrams, probability matrices.

"This is... ambitious," Singh said carefully, studying her work. "But you're making assumptions about maintaining coherence that simply aren't supported by—"

"By current technology," Ren finished. "But if we build a new architecture—"

"Miss Franco." His voice carried a warning edge. "I've been in this field for thirty years. Every few years, a brilliant student comes in convinced they've solved teleportation, or time travel, or perpetual motion. Do you know what they all have in common?"

Ren remained silent, jaw clenched.

"They confuse mathematical possibility with engineering reality. They ignore the brutal constraints of thermodynamics, of noise, of the simple fact that the universe doesn't bend to elegant equations." He pushed her papers back across the desk. "Your math is impressive. But this? This is fantasy."

"Heisenberg's uncertainty principle was fantasy once," Ren said quietly, her voice steady despite the tremor in her hands as she gathered her papers. "So was quantum tunneling. Every breakthrough looks like fantasy to the generation that couldn't achieve it."

Singh's expression hardened. "Arrogance isn't insight, Miss Franco. I suggest you focus on your coursework instead of trying to revolutionize physics before you've even graduated."

"I'll do both," Ren said, standing. "Thank you for your time,

Professor."

As she reached the door, Singh called out, "Ren." His voice had softened slightly. "You're brilliant. Don't let that brilliance become blindness. The world is full of brilliant failures who couldn't accept limitations."

"And full of mediocre successes who never tried to exceed them," Ren replied without turning around.

The next morning, Ren faced a different kind of skepticism in her Advanced Computational Physics seminar. Professor Wetherby, a woman who wore her Nobel Prize nomination like armor, paced before the holographic board.

"Miss Franco," Wetherby said without preamble, "would you care to explain to the class why your proposed quantum computing architecture violates basic thermodynamic principles?"

Ren stood slowly. She'd submitted her preliminary MTU designs as part of her coursework, knowing they pushed boundaries.

"It doesn't violate them, Professor. It redistributes the heat signature across multiple dimensional—"

"Dimensional?" Wetherby's laugh was like breaking glass. "Are we doing science or writing poetry? Energy is conserved, Miss Franco. You can't simply shuffle it into theoretical dimensions."

"The math supports—"

"Your math assumes conditions that don't exist outside of theoretical frameworks." Wetherby pulled up Ren's equations on the display, red marks slashing through them like wounds. "This here? You're assuming perfect quantum coherence across fifty-four separate processors. That's not ambitious; it's delusional."

The other students were silent, some sympathetic, others smirking. Ren felt her face burn but kept her voice level.

"Delusional, like assuming we could put a man on the moon? Or that we could split the atom?"

"Those had physics on their side," Wetherby snapped. "This is wishful thinking disguised as mathematics. If you want to write science fiction, Miss Franco, I suggest you transfer to the English department."

The jab was unexpected, personal. Ren's hands trembled slightly as she sat down.

"I'll prove it works," she said quietly, but loud enough for everyone to hear.

"Proof requires more than conviction," Wetherby replied, already moving on. "It requires accepting reality, not trying to rewrite it."

As the memory faded, Ren found herself back in the present, Singh's dismissive words echoing with new meaning. He hadn't been skeptical—he'd been studying her.

"Ren." Terri approached quietly while the others worked. "That paper Singh kept, the unpublished sections—what was in them?"

Ren hesitated. "Theoretical frameworks for bridging quantum states across dimensional barriers."

"That's what we use for—"

"For the Life MTU. Yes." Ren's voice was barely audible. "If they understand what they stole tonight, they'll know we're working on human transport."

Terri's face paled. "That's still years away from being safe."

"We know that. But would Bora care? Would anyone trying to stop us care?"

Before Terri could respond, Lynn called out. "Ren, you need to see this."

On the main screen was a news broadcast from Rotterdam. "Breaking news: Questions arise about the safety of yesterday's teleportation demonstration as anonymous sources claim massive energy discharge detected by nearby monitoring stations..."

"It begins," Katya said quietly.

Ren watched the manufactured crisis unfold on screen. "Bruce, wake up our media team. Lynn, prepare cease and desist orders. Terri, how long until we can bring the network back online with enhanced security?"

"Seventy-one hours, minimum."

"Make it forty-eight."

She saw Alexis manipulating holographic equations one afternoon during her graduate studies, slender fingers dancing through the projection. Ren, usually hesitant to initiate contact, felt a pull.

"That's an elegant solution," Ren said, surprising herself. Her voice was quiet, analytical, finding common ground in the beauty of math.

Alexis turned, dark eyes widening slightly. "Thanks. I'm using a modified Shor's algorithm to—"

"—reduce the decoherence problem. I see it now." Ren moved closer, drawn in by the intellectual puzzle, by the mind that could navigate these abstract spaces with such grace. "Brilliant."

Something fluttered in Ren's chest. Not the familiar anxiety, but a warmth, an unfamiliar insistence. Their shoulders nearly touched as they both stared at the hovering numbers. It wasn't physical beauty that captivated Ren, but the sheer, undeniable brilliance of a mind at work.

"Want to grab coffee and discuss it further?" Alexis asked.

Ren hesitated only briefly. "I'd like that."

Later, in late-night lab sessions at TTC, wrestling with energy transfer equations and network architectures, Ren found herself working alongside Terri. There was a shared language between them, not just of code and physics but of long hours, mutual respect, and a deep, unspoken understanding of the maddening complexities they were tackling. It was in these moments, these shared intellectual battles, that the warmth returned, deeper, more complex than just admiration for a brilliant mind. A connection formed, subtle but undeniable, a shared look across a terminal screen that spoke volumes.

The command center had shifted into crisis mode, but Ren couldn't shake the feeling that this attack was more than industrial sabotage. It was personal on a level she was only beginning to understand.

"The attack code," Terri said suddenly, still at her station. "There's something else." She pulled up a specific section. "This subroutine here—it's designed to create a resonance pattern in the quantum field."

Ren studied it, her blood running cold. "That would cause—"

"Molecular disruption during transport. Not enough to notice in initial tests, but over time, with repeated use..." Terri's voice trailed off.

"They weren't trying to steal our technology," Ren realized.

"They were trying to sabotage it. Make it fail catastrophically during a public demonstration."

"The motorcycles in Rotterdam—"

"Were fine. This code wasn't fully implemented. But if they perfect it, if they find another way into our system..."

Ren straightened, decision made. "Add a new parameter to Protocol Nine. We're not just upgrading security—we're rebuilding the entire quantum architecture from scratch. New encryption, new pathways, new everything."

"That'll take months," Bruce protested, overhearing.

"Then we'd better get started." Ren looked at each of her team members. "They want a war? They just got one."

The years blurred into focused intensity. Degrees earned, legal residency obtained. Ren didn't launch her ultimate project yet. She needed more. More capital, yes, but also practical experience in manufacturing, in building complex physical systems, and a network of people she could trust implicitly.

Her private computer science company wasn't a mere cover; it was a crucible. Leading a small, brilliant team, she pushed the theoretical limits of chip design. The Multi-Dimensional Processor was the result. Sales soared. Advanced AI, climate modeling, complex simulations—the MDP was indispensable. The profits flooded into her secret accounts, managed behind layers of holding companies and trusts.

With immense capital amassed, the groundwork began for the truly radical. Specialty companies sprouted, each a carefully crafted piece of misdirection: advanced materials science, high-energy physics research, proprietary data encryption, orbital mechanics consulting, automated manufacturing.

The satellite launches began in the early 2050s. Twelve launches over two years, contracted through various companies. Publicly, they were failures. Silent payloads reaching orbit, then nothing. The satellites hadn't failed. They were in stealth mode, minimal power, listening. They had been moved into position in pieces, assembled in orbit by automated bots. The launches were a magnificent misdirection. The real deployment method was the technology itself. No one noticed when, after two years of silence, the satellite clusters began subtle orbital maneuvers, coordinating with uncanny precision. No one noticed when they consolidated into three very large, incredibly powerful satellites—each the size of a small space station.

The question that had driven Ren since she first read about theoretical teleportation as a teenager—Why couldn't people move from one point to another instantaneously?—was closer than ever to being answered. To bring this to the world, she needed structure. A single entity. She named it, with characteristic simplicity, The Teleport Company. TTC.

Three years after that successful test, TTC operated from a fortress of innovation built into Newfoundland's rugged coast, south of St. John's—chosen for isolation, secured by layers of automated defenses, powered by fusion. The staff consisted primarily of STEM personnel and their families—the brilliant minds Ren had recruited from around the world, drawn by the vision, challenges, and promise of changing life as they knew it. They formed a tight-knit, self-sufficient community bound by the knowledge that they were part of something truly revolutionary.

Within the secure conference room overlooking the tempestuous North Atlantic coast, bathed in the cool, blue light of holographic displays, Ren convened her core executive team. Not friends like Koji, but a carefully assembled collection of highly competent professionals, each a master in their domain, balancing Ren's intense focus, technical genius, and social awkwardness with essential expertise.

There was Katya with a quiet, unflappable gravitas that had navigated the labyrinthine world of international banking. Former President of the World Bank, tall, reserved, her words sparse but carrying immense weight and insight, often framed in financial metaphors. "The fiscal outlay is considerable," she might say, "but the return on disruption... incalculable."

Bruce, the Head of Sales, seemed to vibrate with barely contained energy. The youngest executive, an ultra-marathoner whose relentless physical drive translated directly into his professional approach. Two PhDs which provided grounding for his boundless enthusiasm. The public face Ren rarely wanted to be, charming clients, negotiating contracts, evangelizing TTC's power with evangelical fervor. "The market penetration is exponential," he'd declare, "we're onboarding entire sectors!"

Terri, the Technologist, with her understated beauty and a sharp mind. The bridge between Ren's theoretical breakthroughs and the physical reality of the network. Overseeing maintenance, upgrades, development. There was the subtle, knowing look she sometimes directed at Ren, a shared understanding forged over years of late nights, wrestling with quantum entanglement, energy transfer, system architecture. A connection that went deeper than professional respect, lingering on the edge of something unstated, powerful.

Finally, Lynn, Head of Legal. The iron fist in a velvet glove. Navigating the treacherous legal landscape, vicious when required, defending against lawsuits, challenging protectionist legislation with calm precision. Her friendly demeanor disarmed opponents just before her legal arguments eviscerated them. "Naturally," she might say with a pleasant smile, "we anticipated the legal challenges. Our injunctions are already filed."

This team—Ren, Katya, Bruce, Terri, and Lynn—was the core executive council of TTC.

"Our purpose remains clear," Ren stated, gesturing toward a display showing projected emissions reductions. Her voice was calm, precise, devoid of unnecessary inflection, focused entirely on data and mission. "Eliminate pollution, increase efficiency, connect the world."

Bruce leaned forward, his energy palpable. "The Rotterdam demonstration generated over three hundred serious inquiries. Shipping companies are terrified, which means they're ready to talk."

"They should be terrified," Lynn said, her friendly smile cold. "We've filed injunctions against the first wave of regulatory challenges. The EU is trying to classify us under outdated transportation laws."

Katya cleared her throat. "The financial implications are... significant. We're looking at disrupting approximately eighteen percent of the global economy in the first phase alone."

"Which means eighteen percent of the global power structure

will be coming for us," Terri added, her eyes meeting Ren's briefly. "The satellite network is secure, but we should expect sophisticated cyberattacks to increase by an estimated four hundred percent in the next quarter." As she spoke, she subtly adjusted a holographic projection, her movements efficient. "Quantum entanglement protocols are holding stable on current operational transfers."

"Good. That's... good work," Ren replied, her voice steady, but with a barely perceptible pause, a moment of hesitation unusual for her, her gaze holding Terri's for a fraction too long before returning to the larger strategic picture.

"Planned for technically, yes," Lynn countered smoothly. "But politically? The lobbying and legal cases against us will be unprecedented."

"Politics follows technology, not the other way around," Ren stated with quiet certainty. "They'll adapt or become irrelevant."

Terri smiled slightly at Ren's characteristic directness. Then her voice dropped slightly, holding a note of awe and apprehension. "The Life MTU Division has made progress." She looked directly at Ren. "We've successfully teleported complex cellular structures with ninety-nine point six percent fidelity. Getting to one hundred percent will take some additional time."

The room fell silent. The quiet hum of the fusion reactor beneath them felt suddenly louder. The vastness of the North Atlantic outside felt smaller than the implications contained within this room. The unstated connection between Ren and Terri tightened, a shared knowledge, a shared burden, the impossible becoming real, the line between theory and reality blurring in ways that would change everything.

3 THE FOUNDATION SHIFTS

Sarah Millerston, a graphic designer working mostly remotely but needing occasional in-office days, desperately wanted a new home for her family of four. Their current reality was living in a two-bedroom apartment in a rapidly gentrifying neighborhood on the outskirts of Chicago. Rent consumed over fifty percent of their combined income. The two kids, Lily and Tom, shared a cramped bedroom, their toys perpetually spilling into the tiny living area.

They spent their weekends in a demoralizing routine. Attending crowded open houses for dilapidated bungalows listed at impossible prices. Touring new developments where postage stamp-sized lots held cookie-cutter houses that felt sterile and overpriced, enduring bidding wars they inevitably lost to buyers with deeper pockets or fewer contingencies.

David, slumped on their worn sofa after a particularly disheartening Sunday, would flip through online listings, a ritual of self-inflicted pain. "Look at this, Sarah. A three-bedroom, decent size, built in the 50s... listed for that? And it needs work!"

Sarah would massage his shoulders. "I know, honey. It feels impossible."

"Remember that little blue house we saw near Evanston?" David sighed, closing his tablet with a frustrated click. "Needs a new roof, foundation work, probably rewire the whole thing... and it was still half a million over what we could even dream of borrowing."

Sarah slumped down beside him. "And the agent looked at us like we were wasting his time. Just because we weren't putting down cash." She looked around their cramped living room, strewn with Lily's coloring books and Tom's dinosaur figures. "I just... I want them to have space. A backyard where they can run without me worrying about traffic. A room of their own." Her voice caught slightly. "Is that too much to ask?"

David pulled her closer. "It shouldn't be. Not for people who work hard, like we do." He kissed the top of her head. "We'll figure something out. There has to be another way."

Sarah rested her head on his shoulder. "I hope so, David. I really, really hope so."

It was a few weeks later, buried in another late-night search, that David stumbled upon a niche forum discussing "structural teleportation" applied to real estate. It seemed like science fiction, a fringe theory. But the more he dug, the more he found references to TTC, their Rotterdam success, and whispers of a pilot housing program.

"Sarah," he said, voice hushed with a mixture of disbelief and frantic excitement, "you won't believe what I just found."

She came over, rubbing her eyes. "What? Another 'fixer-upper' for the price of a palace?"

"No, listen. There's this company... TTC. They're doing it. Teleporting buildings. Houses."

Sarah blinked slowly. "Teleporting... houses? Like, 'beam it up, Scotty'?"

"Kind of! They scan it, atom by atom, dematerialize it, and then rematerialize it somewhere else. They're starting a program where people can buy houses in cheaper areas and move them to land they can afford."

Sarah stared at him, then let out a shaky laugh. "David, that sounds completely insane."

"I know! But what if it's real? What if this is the 'other way'?" His eyes were wide with a hope she hadn't seen in them for years. "They have a waiting list, a qualification process. It's focused on affordability. I think we might qualify."

They talked late into the night, researching, skeptical but undeniably drawn in by the impossible hope it offered. Applying felt like buying a lottery ticket – the odds were probably astronomical, but the potential payoff was life-changing. When the email came through months later, confirming their acceptance into the pilot program, they read it aloud to each other in stunned silence, Lily and Tom asleep in the next room, oblivious to the seismic shift happening in their parents' lives.

When they discovered TTC's housing service, it seemed too good to be true. They could purchase an affordable home in upstate New York and have it teleported to a small, much less expensive lot they could actually afford in a Denver suburb with good schools.

Elena Rodriguez had been with TTC for eighteen months, but this was her first residential move as lead project manager. She arrived at the upstate New York property an hour early, double-checking her tablet's systems while sitting in her rental car. The Millerston file was extensive—financial qualifications, psychological profiles, community impact assessments. But the notes that caught her attention were Terri's handwritten additions: "First-time homeowners. Daughter drew a picture of a 'rainbow house .' Handle with extra care."

When the Millerston's aging minivan pulled up, Elena watched them emerge—Sarah helping the kids while David stretched his back, all of them staring at the house with expressions of wonder and disbelief.

"Mr. and Mrs. Millerston?" Elena approached with a warm smile. "I'm Elena Rodriguez, your project manager. How are you feeling?"

"Honestly?" David laughed nervously. "Like we're about to do something impossible."

"The impossible is our specialty," Elena said, then caught herself. "Sorry, that's the company line. The truth is, I get it. This is your home. Your first home, right?"

Sarah nodded, unconsciously reaching for David's hand. "We still can't believe we own it. And now we're going to... dissolve it?"

"Transport it," Elena corrected gently. "Every atom, every memory, every imperfection that makes it yours. Would you like to walk through the process?"

As they toured the house, Elena's scanner team began arriving. Marcus, the lead technician, was a tall, soft-spoken man who'd been with TTC since the early days.

"Marcus," Elena called him over. "This is the Millerston family. Could you explain the scanning process? They have some concerns about personal items."

Behind them, the House MTU dominated the cleared area—a massive yellow frame, twelve meters wide and ten meters tall, mounted on heavy-duty rails. Unlike the container units, this MTU could accommodate an entire single-family home. The rails would allow it to roll forward once the house materialized, making room for it to be moved to its foundation.

"That's going to eat our house?" Tom asked, eyes wide.

"Not eat," Marcus corrected gently, walking over. "Think of it like... a doorway. A really high-tech doorway that connects New York to Denver."

Marcus set down his equipment case and knelt to be at eye level with Lily and Tom. "You guys want to see something cool?" He pulled out a small demonstration scanner, no bigger than a smartphone. "This little guy can see things our eyes can't. Watch." He scanned a seemingly blank wall, and his tablet lit up with hidden pencil marks, old nail holes, even the ghost of a removed picture frame.

"Whoa!" Tom exclaimed. "It's like detective vision!"

"Exactly," Marcus smiled. "And the big scanners? They're even better detectives. They'll find every secret your house has and make sure it all comes with you."

While Marcus entertained the children, Elena noticed Sarah staring at that refrigerator drawing. She walked over quietly.

"Your daughter's?" Elena asked.

"She drew it the day we signed the papers," Sarah's voice was thick with emotion. "Said it was our rainbow house because it would make us happy like rainbows do."

Elena pulled up her tablet, creating a new priority flag in the system. "Marcus," she called. "I want a Level Five preservation protocol on this kitchen area, especially the refrigerator and its contents."

Marcus looked up, surprised. "Level Five? That's museum-grade. We usually reserve that for artifacts."

"I'm authorizing it," Elena said firmly. "Sometimes a child's drawing is as valuable as any masterpiece."

David had been listening. "This might sound stupid, but there's a stain on the garage floor. Oil or something. I noticed it during the inspection and thought I'd clean it, but now... it's part of the story, you know? The first thing I noticed would be mine to fix or not fix."

"Not stupid at all," Elena assured him. "The imperfections are what make it real. Marcus, make sure we capture that garage stain in full detail."

"You're going to think we're crazy," Sarah added, "but there's also this squeaky step, the third one? The inspector said it was nothing structural, just old wood. But it's become our alarm system—we always know when the kids are trying to sneak downstairs."

Elena was taking notes now, genuinely engaged. "We'll preserve the exact acoustic properties of that squeak. When you're in Denver, it'll sound identical."

As the scanning began, Elena noticed David watching the robots with increasing anxiety. She approached him.

"You're a teacher, right? High school physics?"

"Yeah," David nodded. "Which makes this even more surreal. I teach about quantum mechanics, but this..." he gestured at the scanning equipment, "this is beyond anything in our textbooks."

"Want to know a secret?" Elena lowered her voice conspiratorially. "Half our tech team were teachers once. Dr. Chen, who designed these scanners? Taught middle school science for ten years. Said the kids' questions made him think differently about quantum states."

"Really?" David's tension eased slightly.

"Really. In fact..." Elena pulled up her tablet. "If you're interested, we have an educational partnership program. Teachers who've been through the moving process can help develop a curriculum about quantum transportation. Paid consultation, of course."

David's eyes lit up. "That would be... I mean, my students would lose their minds. In a good way."

Elena's tablet suddenly blazed with warnings. "Marcus, kill the power! Now!"

The lead technician didn't hesitate, hitting the emergency shutoff. The scanning arrays went dark.

"What happened?" David asked, alarmed.

Elena studied her screen, her face pale. "Someone inserted corruption code into our scanning protocol. If we'd continued..." She looked up at the house. "Random molecular bonds wouldn't have reformed correctly. Your walls might have appeared intact but crumbled within days. Or worse—immediately."

"Someone's trying to sabotage our move?" Sarah's voice was barely a whisper.

"Not just yours." Elena's phone was already out. "This is targeted at our entire housing program." She stepped away, speaking rapidly. "Terri? We have a situation. The Cambridge breach—they got deeper than we thought."

When she returned, the Millerstons were huddled together, Tom clinging to his mother's leg.

"Should we... should we call this off?" David asked.

Elena's jaw set. "Absolutely not. Marcus, implement Protocol Seven. Manual verification of every quantum state. It'll take longer, but—"

"But it'll be safe," Marcus finished. "On it."

Elena knelt before the children. "Hey, know what? The bad guys just made our transport even more special. We're going to give your house extra protection, like a superhero shield."

"Bad guys want to break our house?" Lily's eyes were wide.

"No, sweetheart. We won't let them."

In a Montreal office tower, Bora watched the live feed from multiple compromised security cameras near the Millerston property.

"The corruption code failed," his technician reported. "They caught it."

"Of course they did." Bora turned to his property acquisition team. "Status on Operation Mirror?"

"Seventeen homes purchased this week under variations of TTC's name. The families are... upset. Social media is erupting with accusations against The Teleport Company."

"Good. What about the Millerston family specifically?"

"We've traced them. First-time homeowners, perfect demographic for TTC's program. If their transfer fails publicly—"

"It won't fail through technical sabotage," Bora interrupted. "Franco's too careful. But public perception?" He smiled. "That's more fragile. Ensure our 'TTC Holdings' acquisition in their old neighborhood makes the local news. Tonight."

Later, as the scan progressed, Elena found Sarah alone in what would be Lily's room, running her hand along the doorframe.

"Measuring her height?" Elena guessed.

Sarah nodded. "Every birthday since we signed the papers three weeks ago. Just one mark so far, but..."

"But it's the first of many," Elena finished. "Sarah, can I share something? This job, moving houses—it's not just about the technology for me. My family moved constantly when I was young. Military. We never had a door frame to mark heights on, never had that kind of permanence. What you're doing, giving your kids both stability and opportunity? It matters."

"You don't think we're crazy? Teleporting our house across the country?"

"I think you're brave," Elena said simply. "And I think, twenty years from now, Lily and Tom won't remember that you moved their house through quantum space. They'll remember that you kept their home intact, that you preserved that squeaky step and that rainbow drawing and their height marks. That's what matters."

Marcus approached with his tablet. "Elena, we're hitting some interference in the attic. Old aluminum insulation is creating electromagnetic noise."

"Can we compensate?" Elena asked, switching back to professional mode.

"We'll need to run a secondary scan with different frequency parameters. It'll add about six hours."

Elena turned to the Millerstons. "We need extra time to ensure perfect accuracy. I can put you up in a hotel, or—"

"We'll stay," David said firmly. "If you don't mind. We want to be here for all of it."

"Of course," Elena smiled. "Marcus, set up the secondary scan. And order dinner for everyone—my treat. What do you guys like?"

"Pizza!" Tom shouted.

"But not just any pizza," Lily added seriously. "Good pizza."

Elena laughed. "Marcus, you heard the lady. Good pizza. And Sarah, David? While we wait, want to hear about the family in Japan whose 400-year-old tea house we moved last month? Talk about preserving imperfections—they insisted we capture the exact pattern of wear on the wooden step where generations of tea masters had knelt..."

As the sun set over upstate New York, the scanning continued, and Elena shared stories of other moves, other families, other preserved imperfections. The Millerstons began to relax, to see themselves as part of something larger—not just customers of a service, but pioneers in a new way of thinking about home, place, and belonging.

When Elena's phone buzzed with a message from Terri— "How's the Millerston move going?"—she typed back: "Perfectly imperfect. They're going to be amazing advocates for the program."

She looked up to find David helping Marcus adjust a scanner while Sarah and the kids were drawing pictures of their "rainbow house" to document this day.

"Hey Elena," Tom called out. "Will our house be the exact same in Denver? Like, exactly?"

"Every atom," Elena promised. "Every memory. Every squeak."

"Cool," Tom grinned. "We're like time travelers, except for houses!"

Elena smiled. Sometimes, the seven-year-olds understood it best of all.

In the quantum lab at 2 AM, Ren and Terri worked side by side, analyzing the corruption code from the attempted sabotage.

"This is sophisticated," Terri said, her fingers dancing through holographic displays. "They understood our error-correction algorithms. Someone with deep knowledge wrote this."

"Or someone with access to our research papers," Ren replied, not looking up from her calculations.

Terri glanced at her. "You think it's Singh?"

"The mathematical approach is... familiar." Ren's voice carried an edge of something Terri rarely heard—hurt. "He kept saying my work was fantasy, but he understood it. He always understood it."

"Ren..." Terri's hand moved toward her colleague's shoulder, then stopped. "We'll stop them. The Protocol Seven defenses—"

"Won't be enough." Ren finally looked up, and their eyes met. "They're learning our patterns. Each attack teaches them more."

"Then we change the patterns." Terri's voice was soft but determined. "Together. Like we always do."

The moment stretched between them, years of late nights and shared challenges condensing into something unspoken but understood.

"The Millerston family," Ren said suddenly, deflecting. "They handled the sabotage well."

"They're fighters," Terri agreed, accepting the redirect. "Lynn wants them as ambassadors."

"Good. We need human faces, human stories. I can explain the physics, but they can explain what it means."

"You explain more than you think," Terri said quietly. "You just do it differently."

Before Ren could respond, her secure phone buzzed. Another message from 'B': "Nice save today. Next time, your Protocol Seven won't be enough."

Terri saw Ren's expression harden. "He's escalating."

"Let him," Ren said, deleting the message. "Every attack reveals his methods. He thinks he's hunting us, but we're mapping him."

"Just... be careful," Terri said. "This isn't just about the technology anymore."

"It never was," Ren replied, turning back to her calculations. "It was always about control."

Three days later, Elena stood at the Denver site with her receiving team. The morning air was crisp, and she could see the mountains in the distance. Her earpiece crackled to life.

"Elena, this is Marcus at the New York site. The Millerstons are here. They're... emotional."

"Expected," Elena replied. "Put them on."

There was a rustling, then David's voice: "Elena? Is this really happening?"

"It's really happening, David. In about fifteen minutes, your house will be standing right where I am now. The foundation is ready, utilities are standing by. How's everyone doing?"

"Lily won't let go of my leg," David admitted. "And Sarah's taking about a thousand photos."

"Good. Document everything. This is history, your history." Elena switched channels. "St. John's control, this is the Denver site. We're ready to receive."

Ren's voice came through, unexpectedly. "Elena, Ren here. I'm personally monitoring this transfer. The quantum coherence readings are optimal. Tell the Millerstons we've got their home safe in our hands."

Elena smiled—Ren rarely involved herself in individual moves anymore. "The founder is personally overseeing your transfer," she told David. "You're in the best possible hands."

"That's... wow. Okay. We're ready."

Elena watched as the receiving MTU powered up, its frame beginning to glow with that characteristic blue shimmer. She'd seen dozens of transfers now, but it still gave her chills.

"Initiating quantum capture," Marcus announced over the comm.

Elena could hear Lily's voice in the background: "Daddy, is our house going to disappear?"

"It's going on an adventure," David replied, his voice thick with emotion.

"Transfer in progress," Ren's calm voice announced. "Maintaining coherence across all scanning points. Sarah Millerston's kitchen drawing is intact at the quantum level. The garage oil stain, preserved. The third step acoustic signature, captured perfectly."

Elena felt tears prick her eyes. Ren had been reviewing the personal details, ensuring they were preserved. It was so unlike the stereotypical "cold" Dr. Franco the media portrayed.

"Dematerialization complete," Marcus reported. "The house is... gone."

"Not gone," Elena corrected, watching the shimmer intensify in the Denver frame. "In transit. David, Sarah, your house is currently existing as pure information, traveling through quantum space. In about ten seconds, it'll be home again."

The shimmer reached a crescendo, and then, like a photograph developing in reverse, the house materialized. First as a ghost, then gaining substance, until finally, with a soft thrum, it stood complete.

"Transfer complete," Ren announced. "All quantum signatures verified. Welcome to Denver, Millerston family."

Elena's tablet chimed with an encrypted message from Lynn: "The Millerston family testimony was powerful. Would they consider being program ambassadors?"

Elena looked at the family exploring their perfectly transported home. "Sarah, David? Corporate has a question for you."

Later, as Sarah stood in her relocated kitchen, looking at Lily's rainbow drawing still perfectly attached to the refrigerator, she made a decision that would put her family at the center of a larger conflict.

"We'll do it," she told Elena. "If our story helps other families access this technology, we'll speak publicly."

Elena nodded, knowing she was asking them to become targets in a war they didn't fully understand. "There will be opposition. The same people who tried to corrupt your transfer—"

"Will try to discredit us," David finished. "We know. But hiding won't stop them, will it?"

"No," Elena admitted. "It won't."

From her tablet, she pulled up a news alert: "TTC Holdings Accused of Predatory Property Acquisition." The article featured a photo of a crying elderly couple.

"That's not us," Elena said quickly. "Someone's impersonating—"

"We know," Sarah said firmly. "We did our research. The real TTC was transparent from day one. These vultures?" She gestured at the tablet. "They're exactly why we need to speak up."

Elena approached the house with her tablet, running final checks. The oil stain in the garage—perfect. She climbed the stairs, and the third one squeaked exactly as promised. In the kitchen, Lily's rainbow drawing clung to the refrigerator, down to the slightly curled corner of tape.

Her phone buzzed with a text from Sarah: "Is it really there? Is everything okay?"

Elena stepped outside, held up her phone, and started a video call. "Sarah, David—look."

She walked through their house, showing them every preserved detail. When she reached the kitchen and focused on the rainbow drawing, she heard Sarah burst into tears.

"It's perfect," Sarah sobbed. "It's absolutely perfect."

"When can we come?" David asked, his own voice unsteady.

"There's a flight this afternoon. I've already sent you the tickets," Elena said. "TTC covers your travel for the first visit. And I'll be here when you arrive, to hand you your keys in person."

"Elena," Sarah said, "I don't know how to thank you."

"You don't need to. Just... be happy here. Make new memories to go with the preserved ones. And when people ask about teleported houses, tell them the truth—that it's not just about moving buildings. It's about preserving homes."

After ending the call, Elena stood in the empty house, imagining it filled with the Millerstons' furniture, their laughter, their life. Her phone rang—Terri.

"Ren told me the transfer went perfectly," Terri said. "She also mentioned you authorized Level Five preservation for a child's drawing?"

"Was that overstepping?" Elena asked, suddenly worried.

"No," Terri laughed softly. "It was perfect. It's exactly why we hired you. The technology is Ren's genius, but people like you—you make it human. The Millerstons are lucky to have you as their guide."

"We're all guides," Elena reflected, looking out the window at the Denver mountains. "Helping people find their way home, even when home itself is taking a quantum journey."

That afternoon, when the Millerstons arrived, Elena was waiting with the keys and a small gift—a framed photo she'd taken of their house materializing, caught at the exact moment between quantum possibility and physical reality.

"For your new living room," she said. "To remember the day your house took a leap of faith, and landed exactly where it belonged."

Tom tugged on her sleeve. "Ms. Elena? Will you visit us? You're kind of part of our house story now."

Elena knelt down. "You know what? I'd love that. And maybe you can show me how much you've grown on that doorframe by then."

As she drove away, leaving the Millerstons to rediscover their perfectly imperfect home, Elena felt the deep satisfaction of work that mattered. Tomorrow, there would be another family, another move, another set of precious imperfections to preserve.

But tonight, the Millerstons were home.

At TTC headquarters, Terri watched the Millerston family's success story with mixed emotions. The data from the transfer was perfect—every atom in its place, quantum coherence maintained throughout. It was a technical triumph. But something else nagged at her.

"The Millerston's house vanished from a neighborhood in New York," she said quietly to Ren as they reviewed the day's operations. "What happens to that community? What happens when more houses start disappearing?"

Ren looked up from her data analysis, surprised by the question. "The land remains. It can be redeveloped, perhaps more efficiently. The property taxes were paid. The transaction was legal and beneficial to all parties directly involved."

"But communities aren't just transactions, Ren," Terri pressed, her voice gentle but insistent. "They're relationships, shared histories, interdependencies. When we move a house, we're also removing a family from a social ecosystem."

A junior technician named Raj, overhearing as he calibrated nearby equipment, nodded in agreement. "My parents' neighborhood in Mumbai—everyone knows everyone. The same families for generations. If houses started vanishing..." He trailed off, shaking his head.

Ren considered this, her brow furrowing slightly. It wasn't that she was indifferent to these concerns; they simply occupied a different priority level in her hierarchical view of progress. "The technology creates opportunities that didn't exist before. It doesn't force anyone to move. It just removes artificial barriers."

"Perhaps," Terri conceded, "but we should at least be studying the social impact. Maybe develop guidelines, best practices for communities experiencing significant housing flux."

Ren nodded slowly. "That's... a point. I suppose we could have the data science team run some sociological models. No commitments to anything, but tell me what they come up with and we can evaluate if we want to do anything."

Terri smiled, relieved that Ren was listening, even if it wasn't a commitment. This was why their partnership worked—Ren's brilliant vision balanced by Terri's awareness of the human element.

While moving individual, often unique, dwellings captured the public imagination and provided powerful, high-profile examples of the technology's capability, the real volume, the scalable engine of the Homes and Buildings division, lay in modular housing. This was where TTC could make a tangible difference in addressing the scale of the global housing shortage, particularly in developing nations and disaster zones.

At a sprawling modular housing factory on the outskirts of Shenzhen, China, automated machinery cuts, shapes, and assembles wall panels, floor sections, and roof trusses from sustainable materials. Instead of trucking finished components to a congested port on the coast for weeks-long sea voyages, they are moved directly to a large, dedicated MTU facility adjacent to the factory complex. Within hours, hundreds of containers filled with components for a thousand homes destined for a new development in a rapidly growing city in Kenya would be scanned, loaded into MTUs, and teleported directly to a prepared site outside Nairobi.

In the Kenyan heat, a large, flat area cleared of all vegetation, rudimentary infrastructure like roads and utility connections being laid by local crews, many trained and employed by a local partner organization working with TTC. Suddenly, with the familiar hum and shimmer of the MTU field, containers begin appearing. Not one by one over weeks from a distant port via unreliable roads, but dozens within minutes, perfectly sorted according to the assembly schedule. Local workers, many trained by TTC or partner organizations in rapid modular construction techniques, immediately begin unpacking and assembling the components. Structures go up with astonishing speed.

Mary Ochieng and her family, beneficiaries of this rapid deployment, stood in front of a newly assembled modular home, its walls clean and sturdy, a stark contrast to the cramped, unstable shack they lived in before. "It feels like a miracle," she said to a visiting aid worker. "One day, nothing. The next, walls. A roof. Safe. Clean. My children have a proper place to sleep, to study."

Bruce returned from a field visit to the Nairobi project, practically bouncing with excitement as he briefed the executive team. "The impact is immediate and visible," he reported, showing videos of entire small neighborhoods, schools, and clinics springing up in days. "We're working with NGOs and local governments, sometimes directly with community leaders, delivering emergency shelters after floods or earthquakes, building schools and clinics in remote areas that previously couldn't get materials, and providing affordable, durable housing in urban centers struggling with rapid population growth."

Katya frowned while looking at her tablet. "The paperwork for these international projects is becoming unwieldy. Each country has different import regulations, building codes, and labor laws. We need to streamline our compliance processes or we'll drown in documentation."

"Worth it," Ren said simply, studying the images of families moving into new homes. For a moment, her usual analytical detachment gave way to something softer. "This is what matters. Solving real problems for real people."

Terri watched Ren with a small smile. These were the moments she treasured—when Ren's brilliant mind connected with the human impact of their work. "We should focus on building local capacity too," she suggested. "Train more local engineers, create jobs maintaining the MTUs, and ensure communities have ownership of the process."

"Agreed," Ren said. "This isn't charity. It's infrastructure development. Sustainable communities need more than just houses—they need agency and opportunity."

This seamless, efficient delivery of housing and construction materials had profound, disorienting effects on the existing economic landscape. The construction sector, already under pressure from the housing shortage and labor costs, faced an existential challenge to its business model. How could local builders compete with homes that materialized fully formed, or with components arriving instantaneously from low-cost manufacturing centers anywhere in the world?

The ripple effect hit local and state governments hard. Their primary revenue source – property tax – was based on the assessed value of homes and land. If dwelling value was now tied to a global market and could literally disappear from their jurisdiction, how would they fund schools, roads, police, and local services?

Across different levels of government, from municipal councils to federal treasuries, frantic discussions were underway about how to adapt. One concept gaining traction, though fiercely debated, was the idea of a "teleportation tax" or "transit fee." This proposed tax would be levied by the sending jurisdiction on the value of any structure teleported out, and potentially a separate fee or tax by the receiving jurisdiction on the value of structures teleported in. Proponents argued this was necessary to compensate communities for the loss or gain of taxable assets and the associated demands or reductions in local services. Opponents, including TTC, argued it would stifle the very mobility and affordability benefits the technology offered, creating artificial barriers and double taxation scenarios. The legal and administrative complexity of such a tax across borders and jurisdictions was immense.

The Vancouver Community Center's main hall overflowed with angry residents. Lynn stood at the podium while Ren's face loomed on a large screen behind her, participating via quantum-encrypted video link from St. John's.

"Four families on my street were forced out!" A man stood, shaking a handful of papers. "All bought by companies with names like 'Teleport Housing LLC' and 'TTC Estates.' You're destroying our neighborhood!"

Lynn leaned into the microphone. "Those companies have no affiliation with The Teleport Company. We're investigating—"

"Investigating?" A woman laughed bitterly. "While you investigate, my elderly neighbors are being pressured to sell.

Constant calls, offers they can't refuse, threats about property values crashing when houses start disappearing."

From the screen, Ren's voice cut through clearly. "We have evidence of deliberate impersonation. Someone is using our technology announcement to manipulate property markets."

"How convenient," the first man shot back. "You destabilize everything, then claim it's not your fault."

"Sir," Lynn responded firmly, "we're offering to help track these false companies. We've already filed cease and desist orders against twelve entities falsely using our name."

"And what about the real damage?" Another resident stood. "My daughter's school is losing funding because three families teleported their houses out. The tax base is evaporating!"

Ren spoke again, her tone analytical but missing the emotional undercurrent. "The tax structure needs reform. Land value should be the basis, not improvements—"

"We don't need economics lectures!" someone shouted. "We need our community back!"

Lynn saw the disconnect—Ren solving equations while people faced emotional devastation. "What Dr. Franco means is, we're working with municipal governments on transition funding. We're proposing a stabilization fund—"

"Funded by what? The houses that disappeared?"

A younger woman stood up, different from the others—tired rather than angry. "My name is Sarah Millerston. Last week, TTC helped my family move our house from New York to Denver."

The room turned to her, surprised.

"We couldn't afford anything near good schools. Our kids shared one tiny bedroom. Now..." Her voice caught. "Now they have space. A yard. A future. Yes, we left a community, and that hurts. But we were being pushed out anyway by rising costs."

"So you're defending them?" the first man asked incredulously.

"I'm saying it's complicated. TTC didn't create the housing crisis. They're offering one solution. Maybe instead of fighting them, we should be asking why our communities became so expensive that families like mine had to leave anyway."

Lynn seized the moment. "Mrs. Millerston raises an important point. We're not the cause of displacement—we're revealing displacement that was already happening economically. But we want to be part of the solution."

Ren added, "We're proposing community benefit agreements. For every house teleported out, TTC will contribute to local infrastructure funds."

"Blood money," someone muttered.

"Transition support," Lynn corrected. "Change is difficult, but—"

The lights suddenly cut out. Emergency lighting kicked in, casting eerie shadows. Lynn's security detail moved closer.

A new voice called out in the darkness: "Looks like your technology isn't so reliable after all."

Lynn recognized the planted disruption immediately—Bora's signature move. "The building's power has nothing to do with our technology," she said calmly. "Though it's interesting, someone would stage this interruption just as we were making progress."

The lights flickered back on. Several people in the crowd were filming, ready to spread whatever narrative served their purpose.

Sarah Millerston stood again. "For what it's worth, when someone tried to sabotage our house transfer, TTC caught it. They protected us. Maybe ask yourself who benefits from making you afraid of this technology."

She sat down to mixed murmurs, having planted the seed Lynn needed.

The room remained tense, voices raised in frustrated questions and worried exclamations. The council members offered platitudes, but the underlying fear was palpable. Their town, their homes, their way of life, was suddenly vulnerable, subject to forces they couldn't control, let alone comprehend.

Lynn attended these hearings, or had her team provide testimony and detailed reports. They argued that TTC was enabling economic mobility, allowing owners to realize the value of their properties regardless of local market conditions, preserving historical properties that might otherwise be lost, and providing needed housing elsewhere. They pointed out that the original land remained and could be redeveloped, potentially increasing its long-term value over time if used more efficiently.

Back at headquarters, the executive team watched recordings of these hearings with varying reactions.

"They're afraid," Terri observed, her voice soft with empathy. "Their communities are changing in ways they can't control."

Bruce waved a dismissive hand. "Every disruptive technology faces resistance. Remember the backlash against ridesharing? Against online shopping? People adapt."

"This is different," Terri insisted. "We're not just changing how people shop or travel. We're changing the fundamental stability of neighborhoods, of communities. That matters to people in ways we ourselves might not fully appreciate."

Katya, ever practical, focused on the financial implications. "The tax issue is legitimate. If we want sustainable operations, we need to help develop new tax models that work with our technology, not against it."

Ren had been listening silently, her expression thoughtful. "All valid points," she finally said. "We need to address these concerns directly. Not just with PR, but with real solutions." She turned to Lynn. "Work with our policy team on model legislation for land value taxation that includes transition periods and protections for vulnerable homeowners. And Terri—" she met her colleague's concerned gaze, "—I want a comprehensive social impact study. Real data on how our technology affects communities, both positively and negatively."

Terri nodded, pleased that Ren was taking the human element seriously. "I'll put together a research team. We should include sociologists, urban planners, maybe even anthropologists."

"Good," Ren said decisively. "We're not just moving houses. We're reshaping how humans relate to space and place. We need to understand all the implications."

As the meeting concluded, Terri lingered behind with Ren. "Thank you for listening," she said quietly.

Ren looked up, slightly surprised. "Your concerns are valid. The technical challenges are only part of what we're solving here."

"That's... not something you would have said a few years ago," Terri observed with a small smile.

Ren considered this. "Perhaps not. But the technology itself isn't the end goal. It's what the technology enables that matters."

"Helping people," Terri said simply.

"Yes," Ren agreed, a rare warmth in her voice. "Helping people find their place in the world. Literally and figuratively."

As they walked toward the research wing, the vast windows of the headquarters revealed the wild Newfoundland coastline, waves crashing against ancient rocks. Nature's reminder that even the most revolutionary technology existed within a larger context—a world of complex systems, interdependencies, and human needs that extended far beyond the elegant equations of quantum teleportation.

4 THE NEW ARTERIES

The morning sun cast long shadows across the nearly empty parking lot of the Route 80 Travel Plaza. Inside the office, Mary Hendricks studied her monthly fuel report while her business partner, Tom, poured himself another cup of coffee.

"Diesel sales are down forty-two percent," Mary said, her voice flat. "That's worse than last month."

Tom set down his cup hard enough to slosh coffee onto the counter. "How the hell are we supposed to stay open? We've already cut staff to the bone."

"The long-haul routes are dying, Tom. I talked to Eddie yesterday—you know, drives for Haulage? He said they're down to local deliveries only. Everything else goes through those yellow boxes now."

"Those damn teleporters." Tom stared out at the empty fuel islands. "Thirty years we've been here. My father built this place when the interstate opened."

Mary closed the report. "The repair shop's keeping us afloat, barely. Local trucks still need maintenance."

"For how long? I heard one of the biggest box stores wants to build their own teleport hub fifty miles from here. Once that's operational..." Tom trailed off.

"Maybe we pivot. Convert some fuel islands to electric charging?"

Tom laughed bitterly. "With what money? The bank won't extend our credit. They know we're finished." He gestured at the empty restaurant section. "Remember when truckers would wait in line for Donna's pie?"

"Donna retired six months ago. Couldn't afford to keep her."

A single truck pulled in, heading for the furthest diesel pump. They both watched it like a rare bird sighting.

"One customer," Tom said quietly. "Used to be one every minute."

Mary stood up, gathering her papers. "We need to decide, Tom. Sell now while the property's worth something, or ride it into the ground."

"Give it another month," Tom said, though his voice carried no hope. "Maybe things will turn around."

They both knew they wouldn't.

The bell above the door chimed as a man in an expensive suit entered the travel plaza. Mary looked up from her inventory sheets, immediately sensing something wrong. No one who could afford that suit stopped here anymore.

"Mrs. Hendricks?" The man's smile didn't reach his eyes. "I represent a group of investors interested in highway-adjacent properties."

Tom emerged from the back room, wiping oil from his hands. "We're not selling."

"You haven't heard our offer." The man placed a leather folder on the counter. "Given your current revenue trajectory, I think you'll find it generous."

Mary opened the folder. The number was insulting—barely enough to cover their debts.

"This is half what the property's worth," she said flatly.

"It's twice what it'll be worth in six months." The man's pleasant mask slipped slightly. "The Secure Ports Act is going to pass. When it does, TTC will be forced to route everything through federal facilities. The small operators, the truck stops, the independent logistics—you'll all become relevant again. If you're still in business."

"You're betting against TTC?" Tom laughed bitterly. "Good luck with that."

The man leaned forward. "We don't need luck. We have Senator Morrison's ear. We have the Teamsters. We have public sentiment about lost jobs." He tapped the folder. "This offer expires at midnight. After that, we'll simply wait for the bank to foreclose and buy from them."

"Get out," Mary said quietly.

"Think about it, Mrs. Hendricks. You can exit with dignity and enough money to start over. Or you can be another casualty of progress." He straightened his tie. "Oh, and that new electric charging station permit you applied for? It's been denied. Safety concerns, apparently."

After he left, Tom slammed his fist on the counter. "Son of a bitch. They're not just letting us die—they're making sure of it."

Mary picked up her phone. "Maybe it's time we talked to TTC directly."

"What?"

"Think about it, Tom. If the old guard is this scared, maybe we should be talking to the new one. Elena Rodriguez—the woman who saved Paris? She started as a logistics coordinator at a truck stop in Texas. Maybe she'd understand."

Tom stared at his wife. "You want to work for the people who killed our business?"

"I want to survive," Mary said simply. "And maybe help others like us do the same."

Premier Janet Chanhall connected to the emergency video conference from her office in Victoria. On screen, Alberta's Premier David Morisone looked grim, while Quebec's Premier Marie Duschamp was already speaking.

"—forty percent drop in fuel tax revenue this quarter alone," Duschamp was saying. "We cannot maintain our roads with these numbers."

"It's worse here," Morisone interjected. "Alberta's entire budget model assumes fuel tax growth. We're looking at a five-billion-dollar shortfall. Highway maintenance, bridge repairs, snow removal— everything's on the chopping block."

Chanhall unmuted herself. "British Columbia is considering a distance-based road tax for all vehicles, not just commercial. But the public backlash..."

"The public wants perfect roads and zero taxes," Morisone said bitterly. "Meanwhile, TTC pays nothing for using our infrastructure to move their containers to and from their facilities."

"They use electric trucks for local delivery," Duschamp pointed out. "No fuel tax contribution at all."

"We could implement special fees for teleport facilities," Chanhall suggested. "Call it an 'infrastructure impact assessment.'"

Morisone shook his head. "TTC's lawyers would tear that apart. They'd claim we're discriminating against new technology. Plus, they're building on Indigenous lands now—completely outside our jurisdiction."

"So what do we do?" Duschamp asked. "My transport minister is recommending toll roads, but rural communities will revolt."

Morisone slammed his fist on the table. "While we're sitting here talking, TTC is building on Indigenous land! They're using sovereignty laws against us!"

"Then change the laws," Chanhall shot back.

"You think we haven't tried? Every bill dies in committee. TTC's lobbyists—"

"TTC doesn't have lobbyists," Duschamp interrupted. "They have believers. Every family that's moved their house, every business that's saved millions on shipping—they're all advocates now."

Elena Rodriguez gripped the emergency shutdown lever as alarms screamed through the Paris MTU facility. The newly installed unit, positioned in a converted warehouse near Charles de Gaulle Airport, was vibrating violently.

"Everyone out! Now!" she shouted in French, then English, pushing technicians toward the exits.

The MTU's yellow frame glowed wrong—not the clean blue-white of normal operation, but a sickly amber that pulsed like a dying heartbeat. Through her tablet, she could see the quantum field readings spiraling toward critical.

"Elena, talk to me!" Terri's voice crackled through her earpiece from St. John's. "Your field coherence is dropping fast!"

"Someone's introduced a virus into the initialization sequence,"

Elena said, her fingers flying across her tablet as she backed toward the exit. "If this field collapses with full power—"

"It'll take out more than just your building," Terri finished. "Can you stabilize?"

Elena watched the readings spike. The MTU frame began to buckle, metal groaning under impossible stresses. Through the windows, she could see Parisian emergency vehicles already responding, but they had no idea what they were dealing with.

"Negative. We need to dump the charge." Elena made a split-second decision. "I'm redirecting the quantum field into the ground grid."

"That'll fry every electronic within—"

"Better than vaporizing the neighborhood!"

Elena initiated the emergency protocol she'd never thought she'd use. The building's lights exploded in showers of sparks. Her tablet died instantly. Car alarms outside went silent as their systems failed. But the MTU's terrible glow began to fade.

The frame gave one final shudder, exploded, and went dark.

Elena collapsed against the wall, breathing hard. Through the window, she could see the lights of Paris flickering as the power grid struggled to compensate. But the city stood. The facility stood.

Her backup phone rang—an old analog model she kept for emergencies.

"Elena?" Ren's voice, tighter than usual. "Status?"

"Facility secure. MTU destroyed. Several injuries from the MTU explosion. Someone with inside knowledge did this, Ren. They knew exactly how to induce a catastrophic virus."

"Are you hurt?"

"No. But if we hadn't caught it..." Elena looked at what remained of the MTU frame, metal twisted in ways that shouldn't be possible. "This wasn't corporate sabotage. Someone wanted mass casualties. They wanted Paris to fear us."

"They wanted us to be monsters," Ren said quietly. "Stay there. Lynn's already coordinating with French authorities. We're moving in a new MTU tonight from Germany."

"Ren," Elena said, "whoever did this—they're escalating. This isn't about competition anymore."

"I know," Ren replied. "That's why we're accelerating tribal partnerships. We need sites they can't reach."

Ren, presiding over the global network from the control room in St. John's, watched the holographic map of Earth fill in with new nodes. Each blinking light represented an active MTU site, connected directly to the silent constellation of satellites in orbit. The map was a testament to meticulous planning, years spent analyzing global trade routes, identifying logistical bottlenecks, navigating complex international relations, and assessing the readiness of local infrastructure and political will.

"Phase Two rollout is exceeding projections," Bruce announced, his voice crackling with his usual high-octane energy, even over the secure comms link from his office. He was back from a week of intense negotiations in Southeast Asia, having secured agreements for two new major hubs.

He added, "Demand is spiking as clients see the tangible benefits – not just speed and cost for cargo, but entirely new capabilities like instant access to global housing markets and rapid deployment of modular construction. We're getting requests for hubs in locations we didn't anticipate needing them for another three to five years. Businesses that were hesitant during the initial rollout are now seeing their competitors gain significant advantages."

The location strategy for these major teleport hubs was pragmatic, designed for maximum impact with minimal initial disruption, while also building redundancy and resilience. They weren't building entirely new, standalone cities of transport; they were inserting themselves into existing infrastructure, leveraging what was already there but fundamentally changing how goods moved through it.

In coastal countries, the most logical points of entry were the existing ports. Think Rotterdam, where it all began, but also Shanghai, Singapore, Los Angeles, Hamburg, Dubai, and newcomers like Tangier Med or the expanded Port of Walvis Bay. These colossal hubs, previously defined by the endless arrival and departure of container ships, the cacophony of cranes, and the sprawl of warehouses, were subtly transforming. TTC didn't need deep-water berths or massive cranes in the same way. They needed space – secure, accessible space within the port perimeter to install their large MTU arrays, capable of handling multiple container transfers simultaneously.

At the Port of Singapore in 2062, the air was thick with humidity and the smell of the sea, but the soundscape had changed. The activity was now concentrated in a vast, new, hangar-like structure on the port's eastern edge, a building that hummed with a low, constant energy. Inside, multiple MTU arrays, each capable of receiving or sending several containers at once, were the port's new heart.

Integrating this 21st-century marvel with the port's 20th-century legacy systems had been a nightmare. A TTC technical team, led by a no-nonsense lead engineer named Marcus, had been on-site for weeks.

This was the reality of TTC's integration—bridging the instantaneous future with the tangled, slow-moving past, one line of code at a time.

Lynn, watching the flawless execution of a transfer that required navigating a legal and technical minefield, allowed herself a small, satisfied smile. "Integration has been... a learning curve," she commented during a review later that day. "Port authorities are grappling with concepts like 'zero loiter time' and 'instant customs clearance.' Their entire operational paradigm is built around delays, storage fees, and physical handling. We're not just installing equipment; we're forcing them to redefine what a port actually is— from a node for physical transfer to a node for instantaneous data-to-matter conversion."

For landlocked countries, the impact was even more transformative, a sudden liberation from geographical constraint. Historically, their access to global trade was throttled by their reliance on distant seaports and the often-unreliable infrastructure linking them – thousands of kilometers of roads or rail lines susceptible to delays, damage, political instability, and cost. Now, TTC hubs situated at existing transit centers – major rail yards in Switzerland, logistics parks near capital cities in Central Asia, industrial zones in landlocked African nations like Ethiopia or Rwanda – became their direct, instantaneous connection to the world market.

This wasn't just about convenience; it was about unlocking economic potential previously constrained by geography, giving landlocked businesses parity with their coastal competitors, allowing them to participate fully in the global just-in-time economy. It stimulated local production, made exports more competitive, and attracted foreign investment.

Perhaps the most strategically interesting, and later, politically significant, aspect of the network rollout involved partnerships with Indigenous communities. Ren and Lynn had identified that in many countries, recognized tribal lands held a unique legal status, granting a degree of sovereignty from federal regulations.

TTC approached tribal governments whose lands were strategically located to fill gaps in the network. The criterion was simple: if a tribe had suitable land more than 100 km from any other TTC site, a partnership was proposed. The pitch was straightforward: TTC would lease land, providing a substantial revenue stream. They would build and operate an MTU facility, creating skilled local jobs with comprehensive training. The tribe would gain instant access to the global trade network, and the facility would operate under tribal law, often independent of the very federal regulations that were being designed to stifle TTC.

Lynn, often accompanied by Bruce (who learned to channel his high-octane energy into patient listening and clear, respectful communication, a surprising but welcome development for the team), spent considerable time meeting with tribal councils, listening to their needs, and explaining the potential benefits of the partnership. They didn't arrive with pre-packaged deals, but with proposals for collaboration.

The pitch was straightforward, focused on empowerment and mutual benefit: TTC would lease land from the tribe, providing a substantial, long-term revenue stream – vital, unrestricted funds for tribal governments to invest in education, healthcare, and infrastructure. They would build and operate a state-of-the-art MTU facility on the leased land, creating skilled local jobs for tribal members, with comprehensive training provided by TTC. The tribe would gain direct, instant access to the global trade network, enabling tribal businesses – from agriculture to manufacturing to tourism – to import materials or export products without relying on external infrastructure or navigating complex bureaucratic hurdles off-reservation. And crucially, for both TTC and the tribe, the facility would operate under tribal law, often independent of federal or state regulations that might be influenced by TTC's legacy logistics competitors, a foresight that would prove critical when facing legislation like the Secure Ports Act.

This unique status proved invaluable. In late 2062, a major humanitarian organization attempted to ship a large batch of advanced, temperature-sensitive vaccines from a lab in Switzerland to a series of rural clinics in remote parts of New Mexico and Arizona. The shipment, routed through the Port of Houston, hit a wall of federal bureaucracy. A newly implemented, vaguely worded "Bio-Security Inspection Protocol," pushed by lobbyists with ties to the legacy pharmaceutical transport industry, held the shipment for "additional verification." Days turned into a week, the vaccines' narrow temperature window closing fast. The clinics waited in vain.

Simultaneously, Lynn, anticipating just such a bottleneck, had arranged for a second, parallel shipment to be sent directly from the Swiss lab to the newly operational MTU hub on the lands of the Cherokee Nation in Oklahoma. The container, flagged with the highest priority, materialized in the Oklahoma facility, was immediately loaded onto a waiting electric truck and driven directly to the clinics, arriving a full five days before the Houston shipment was finally released, some of its contents compromised by the delay. The incident was a quiet but powerful demonstration of the tribal hub's strategic importance, a sovereign artery bypassing the hardening sclerosis of federal regulation.

The impact on the Cherokee Nation itself was palpable. The MTU facility, a sleek, modern structure powered by vast local solar arrays, was a source of immense community pride. It brought not only jobs but a new type of one—high-tech, skilled, and future-oriented.

A young Cherokee woman named Alayna, who had left the Nation for a dead-end data entry job in Tulsa, was one of the first technicians hired and trained. Now, she sat at a state-of-the-art console, managing the complex data streams for incoming and outgoing shipments. Today, she was coordinating with a high-end art gallery in Paris, arranging the secure teleportation of a collection of contemporary Cherokee pottery.

Her voice was confident as she spoke French with the gallery manager, confirming the quantum signature lock on a delicate, hand-painted vase. "Oui, monsieur. The custom-molded foam cradle has been scanned. We are initiating the transfer. You should see it materialize in your receiving field within thirty seconds."

She felt a surge of pride as she initiated the transfer, watching the data stream across her screen. Two years ago, she felt she had to leave her home, her culture, to find a future. Now, she was at the heart of it, using cutting-edge technology to send her people's art, their stories, out into the world instantly. After her shift, she would use part of her paycheck—a salary that allowed her to help support her elderly parents—to buy supplies for the community center's language immersion class. The MTU hub wasn't just a building; it was a connection, a lifeline, a promise that their future could be built right here, on their own land.

On the lands of the Cherokee Nation, vast and beautiful, but historically facing economic challenges and 'brain drain' as young people moved away for opportunities. A TTC facility rises near a tribal community center – a secure, modern structure powered by local solar arrays and integrated with the tribal broadband network. Inside, Cherokee technicians, many previously working in various trades and retrained by TTC engineers, manage incoming and outgoing shipments – perhaps locally produced arts and crafts being sent directly to international markets, or essential supplies like building materials for new tribal housing projects arriving instantly, bypassing long truck journeys from distant cities.

Ren, making a rare site visit, looked intently at the integration of technology and community and tribal leader, Principal Chief Vance. Principal Chief Vance gestured out to the facility, where tribal members were working. "Our young people… they used to have to leave the Nation to find skilled work. Work that paid well, that was modern. Now? They work here. Operating machines, managing complex data streams. They are building a future for us, on our land. Using technology to strengthen our traditions, not erase them."

Ren, quiet as ever, nodded, observing the pride in the Chief's voice and the faces of the workers. "The economic self-determination and opportunity for your people was a key objective of this partnership. And your sovereignty provides a level of operational independence that benefits us both, allowing us to serve communities without external interference."

Lynn added, "Should certain proposed federal restrictions pass, this facility, operating under tribal law, would be exempt. It ensures continued access for the region, both for TTC and for the Nation's economic activities, regardless of external political pressure."

The tribal partnerships weren't merely strategic workarounds; they represented a deliberate choice by TTC to align with historically marginalized groups, creating alliances built on mutual benefit, respect for sovereignty, and a shared interest in operating outside the control of established, often oppressive, systems. These sites, seemingly small nodes on the global map, would later prove to be vital havens for TTC's operations when regulatory pressure intensified, embodying a different model of how technology could interact with traditional cultures and legal frameworks.

The emergency call came at 11 AM. Alayna was already at the Cherokee Nation MTU facility, having stayed late to coordinate a shipment of medical supplies to a clinic in Guatemala.

"Alayna, we have a problem." Security Chief Robert Stonecrow's voice was tense. "Perimeter breach, sector seven. Three vehicles approaching fast."

She pulled up the security feeds on her console. Three black SUVs, no plates, racing down the access road.

"Wake the Chief," she said, her training kicking in. "And call County Sheriff—"

"They won't make it in time," Robert interrupted. "These guys are thirty seconds out."

Alayna's mind raced. The medical supplies in the MTU—insulin, vaccines, antibiotics—were meant for a dozen clinics. If these intruders damaged the shipment...

"Lock down the MTU," she ordered. "I'm initiating emergency transport."

"The receiving site isn't ready—"

"They have ten minutes to get ready." Her fingers flew across the console, bypassing safety protocols. "I'm not letting them destroy medicine meant for children."

The SUVs screeched to a halt outside. Through the windows, she could see men in tactical gear deploying. Not government—too sloppy. Corporate mercenaries.

"Federal agents!" someone shouted through a megaphone. "This facility is under emergency inspection!"

"Like hell," Alayna muttered. She opened a channel to Guatemala. "Dr. Morales, emergency incoming. Clear your pad now!"

The front doors burst open. Men flooded in, weapons drawn—not guns, but industrial-grade electromagnetic disruptors designed to destroy electronics.

"Step away from the console!" one shouted.

Alayna looked him in the eye and slammed the transport initiation. The MTU flared to life, its quantum field building rapidly.

"Shut it down!" The lead mercenary raised his disruptor.

"You fire that, you'll cause a cascade failure," Alayna said calmly, not moving from her position. "The energy release will level this building with you in it."

The man hesitated. Behind him, his team looked nervous.

"You're bluffing."

"Am I?" Alayna's hand hovered over the emergency shutdown—the one that would contain the field but destroy the shipment. "Your employer didn't brief you on quantum field dynamics, did they? Twenty terajoules of energy, released instantly. They'll find your atoms scattered across three counties."

The MTU's hum reached a crescendo. The medical supplies vanished in a flash of blue-white light.

"Shipment completed," she announced. "Now, unless you want to explain to the real federal authorities why you're impersonating agents on sovereign tribal land, I suggest you leave."

The lead mercenary's earpiece crackled. Whatever he heard made him curse.

"Pull out," he ordered his team.

As quickly as they'd come, they were gone. Alayna's hands shook as she saved the security footage and began documenting everything.

Chief Vance arrived minutes later with tribal police.

"They wanted to destroy the shipment," Alayna reported. "Make it look like our operation failed."

"Or worse," the Chief said grimly. "Make it look like we were transporting something illegal. Discredit us and TTC together." He put a hand on her shoulder. "You did well, daughter. You protected our sovereignty and saved lives."

"They'll try again," Alayna said.

"Yes," the Chief agreed. "But now we know they're coming. And we'll be ready."

The core of the TTC network was, of course, the orbital infrastructure. The three massive satellites, silently holding their geostationary positions, were the heart of the system, the primary relay points for long-distance transfers. From the ground control center in St. John's, Terri's team monitored their status, managed the immense energy flows required for teleportation, and routed the complex quantum data streams.

"We're seeing a fundamental shift in inventory management for large corporations," Bruce explained to Ren during a market analysis briefing. "They don't need massive warehouses full of buffer stock near ports anymore. They can keep inventory at manufacturing sites and teleport it Just-In-Time to regional distribution centers as needed. This drastically reduces storage costs, eliminates spoilage for perishable goods, and frees up billions in capital previously tied up in inventory sitting on ships or in warehouses. It's a massive financial incentive driving adoption, especially for retailers and manufacturers with complex global supply chains."

This Just-In-Time teleportation model also reduced waste and increased responsiveness to market demand, allowing companies to quickly shift production or inventory based on real-time sales data, rather than forecasts made months in advance based on shipping lead times.

But while containers represented commercial volume, the absolute priority was always on essential goods: fresh fruit, food, and medicine. These shipments were flagged in the system, given immediate priority over all other cargo, often routed through dedicated MTU units or specialized transfer protocols with enhanced monitoring.

At a receiving center in a major city – not a port, but a clean, secure logistics hub located centrally for rapid distribution to supermarkets, pharmacies, and hospitals – pallets of perfectly ripe strawberries, picked in California the day before, appear instantly from an MTU, their freshness preserved by the speed of transit. Crates of vaccines, kept at a precise temperature during their instant journey from a lab in Europe, are immediately moved into cold storage units already positioned next to the MTU field. Boxes of specialized medicines, tracked by individual serial number, are cross-referenced against manifests and dispatched to waiting electric delivery vans heading for hospitals and pharmacies.

"Our 'Food and Medicine' division is having a quiet but profound impact," Katya said, highlighting data on reduced spoilage rates, improved access to critical pharmaceuticals in remote or underserved areas, and the ability to respond rapidly to localized health crises by instantly moving medical supplies. "The cost savings are significant, allowing aid organizations and healthcare providers to stretch their budgets further. More importantly, the speed eliminates bottlenecks that could mean the difference between life and death for patients awaiting critical treatment or medication." They were particularly vigilant with these shipments, using enhanced quantum signature analysis and monitoring protocols to detect any tampering or inconsistency.

The network was more than just a collection of physical sites and orbital assets; it was a complex, interconnected system of data, energy, and matter flow, orchestrated from the central control room in St. John's. Every shipment, every transfer, was monitored, verified, and secured using the layers of quantum encryption protocols developed internally by Ren's teams. Ren had insisted on this level of control, transparency (within the system), and security from the outset, foreseeing that such a powerful system would inevitably be a target for criminals, competitors, and state actors.

The control center had quieted for the night shift. Most of the day staff had gone, leaving only the essential overnight team monitoring transfers. Ren stood before the global map, the glowing lines of active transfers creating a web of light across continents and oceans.

Terri approached with two steaming mugs, offering one to Ren. "You missed dinner. Again."

"Did I?" Ren accepted the mug absently, her eyes still fixed on the map.

"You always do when the network adds new nodes." Terri stood beside her, close enough that their shoulders nearly touched. "Ten new sites this week. Five port integrations, three landlocked hubs, and two tribal partnerships."

Ren nodded, taking a sip from her mug and grimacing slightly. "What is this?"

"Actual tea. Not that synthetic caffeine you usually drink."

A small smile touched Ren's lips. "You sound like my mother."

"Someone has to look out for you." Terri's voice softened. "You're pushing yourself too hard."

"There's too much at stake not to." Ren gestured toward the map. "Look at the trans-Pacific routes. Volume up twenty percent just this quarter."

"I know. I've already adjusted the system to handle it." Terri studied Ren's profile, noting the shadows under her eyes. "Remember when we spent three days debugging that housing algorithm? You wouldn't sleep until we fixed it."

"And Koji kept bringing us that terrible ramen," Ren recalled, a genuine smile warming her features.

"God, it was awful. I can still taste it." Terri laughed. "He really has no taste buds." Ren's smile faded as she turned back to the map. For a moment, her shoulders slumped slightly, the weight of her vision visible in her posture.

Terri hesitated, then placed her hand gently on Ren's arm. "You're changing the world, Ren. But you don't have to carry it all alone."

Terri's phone buzzed—a reminder about old cloud storage expiring. She clicked to review what to keep, scrolling quickly through old files while monitoring the satellite feeds.

"Ren, the Mianyang site is requesting..." she started, then froze. Her thumb had accidentally selected and sent a folder labeled

"Montreal_2059."

Her blood turned to ice as she saw what had transferred to their shared work channel: professional photos from an artistic photoshoot she'd done years ago for a photographer friend. Tasteful but intimate, showing far more of her than she'd ever intended Ren to see.

"Oh God, no, no, no..." she frantically tried to delete them, but the quantum-encrypted channel had already synced.

Ren's workstation chimed. She glanced over, opened the message, and stopped completely still.

"Terri, I think you've—" Ren's voice was unusually strained.

"I'm so sorry! It was an accident, old storage, I didn't mean—" Terri's face burned crimson.

Ren closed the images quickly but not before Terri saw her screenshot one. "It's... fine. We should focus on—yes. The emergency."

"Ren, I—"

"Later," Ren said softly, not meeting her eyes. "We'll... discuss it later."

"We should check the polar route projections," she said, retreating to the safety of work. "Phase Three needs to be operational within six months."

Terri let her hand fall away, but the connection lingered. "It will be. I promise."

The private dining room in Hong Kong overlooked a harbor with noticeably fewer ships than just a year ago. Behind soundproofed doors, Bora watched the assembled executives with calculating eyes. Unlike the aging shipping magnates he had replaced, Bora moved with the coiled precision of someone who had fought for everything he possessed.

"The public goodwill from their humanitarian stunts is a temporary problem," Bora stated, his voice soft but commanding. "Emotion fades. Economic reality persists."

A frustrated aerospace executive slammed his fist on the polished table. "They're gutting us! Air cargo revenue is down forty percent!"

Bora raised a hand, silencing the outburst. "Anger clouds judgment. We need strategy." He activated a projection showing TTC's growing network. "Their vulnerabilities are public trust and political regulation."

He displayed footage of a tearful truck driver lamenting his lost livelihood. "We control the narrative. Make them the villain destroying livelihoods, not the hero saving the planet."

Switching to a legislative document, he continued, "In every major market, we push for regulation under the guise of security. The 'Secure Ports Act' will force all teleportation through existing, federally-controlled ports."

A woman in an expensive suit spoke up. "You seem to have a personal vendetta, Bora. Is this business, or is this going beyond that?"

Bora's expression remained neutral, but something flashed in his eyes. "I grew up in a shipping family. Three generations of ships' captains. My father commanded a container vessel for thirty years." He looked out at the half-empty harbor. "When TTC appeared, his company downsized overnight. He lost everything. At sixty-two, he was too proud to take charity, too specialized to find new work."

He turned back to the group. "My father ended his life six months ago. Left a note saying he couldn't bear to be useless." Bora's voice remained controlled, but ice-cold. "So yes, this is business. But it's also personal. TTC didn't just disrupt an industry. They destroyed lives and legacies without a second thought."

He straightened his perfectly tailored jacket. "We will not just slow them down. We will make the world fear them. Tie them in legal knots until they are begging to be acquired." A thin smile appeared. "And then we'll own the future they created."

The executives nodded, now seeing Bora not just as a strategic leader but as someone with an unshakable motivation driving his every move. His personal loss had become their rallying point, transforming corporate competition into a crusade.

TTC conversations weren't limited to system diagnostics. They also discussed the impact they were seeing reported from the new sites.

"Bruce sent footage from the Tashkent hub opening," Terri mentioned one afternoon, pulling up a short video clip of local workers and the Uzbek factory manager celebrating a successful transfer. "Seeing their faces... the potential this opens up for them. It's powerful."

Ren watched the clip, a faint smile touching her lips. "That's the point. Unlocking potential. Connecting people. It's not just about efficiency for major corporations. It's about creating opportunities where geography used to be a barrier." She turned to Terri. "Are our training programs for the local staff at the new hubs sufficient? Especially the tribal partnerships? They need to be fully autonomous, fully capable of managing their sites."

"Lynn's team is overseeing that," Terri confirmed. "Working with tribal leadership to ensure cultural sensitivity and long-term job development. Not just training operators, but technicians, maintenance crews. Building local expertise."

The network was functional, expanding, and undeniably powerful. It was changing the world with every transfer. But its very success was creating the conditions for a backlash that would test its resilience. The flow of goods was smooth and instantaneous, but the flow of power and resistance was becoming turbulent, seeking to disrupt the new arteries of the world.

This was precisely why the tribal partnerships were so critical. Back on the lands of the Cherokee Nation, Lynn was having a follow-up meeting with Principal Chief Vance, not as a lawyer negotiating a deal, but as a partner reviewing a thriving joint venture.

"We've seen the reports," Chief Vance said, his voice calm and measured as he looked out at the bustling MTU facility from his office window. "The proposed legislation in Washington, the 'Secure Ports Act.' It is designed to trap you, to tie your technology to the old systems."

"It is," Lynn confirmed. "But it has no jurisdiction here. Your sovereignty provides a sanctuary, not just for us, but for continued commerce in this entire region if it passes. It makes the Cherokee Nation a vital hub, economically and strategically."

Chief Vance nodded slowly, his gaze distant for a moment. "My great-grandfather negotiated with the US government over water rights. He fought them in their own courts, using their own laws against them to protect our people. He understood that our sovereignty was not a gift from them, but a right we had always possessed. He taught us to be resilient, to adapt and find new ways to secure our future."

He turned back to Lynn, a look of profound, historical weight in his eyes. "We see this partnership in the same light. This is not about siding with one corporation against another. This is about ensuring our Nation's economic independence for the generations to come. Your company's conflict with the federal government and the old shipping cartels is… an opportunity. It allows us to leverage our sovereignty in a way my ancestors could only dream of. We are not just a landlord, Ms. Lynn. We are your most steadfast ally. Your independence ensures our prosperity."

Lynn was silent for a moment, humbled by the depth of his perspective. This wasn't simply a strategic loophole. It was a partnership rooted in a shared desire for self-determination against powerful, centralized forces. TTC and the Cherokee Nation, two vastly different entities, were united in their fight to operate free from the chokehold of the past. The very ground beneath their feet had become the frontline in the teleportation battle.

Ren also spoke with Bruce about the challenges of integrating with existing infrastructure and dealing with resistance from legacy industries.

"The ports are fighting us, Ren," Bruce admitted. "They see the decline in ship traffic, and they're pushing back on our integration plans. Lobbying port authorities, trying to impose new fees, complicating access for our ground vehicles."

"We anticipated this," Ren said, though the relentless nature of the opposition was frustrating. "They're protecting their legacy. But the economic logic is undeniable. The faster, cleaner method will prevail. Our focus needs to be on demonstrating the value, even within their systems, while building our own independent infrastructure where possible, like the tribal sites."

She looked at Terri. "Are there any technical vulnerabilities they could exploit at the port integration points? Any way they could interfere with the ground MTUs or the link to the orbital arrays?"

Terri's expression became intensely focused, the technical

challenge overriding everything else. "Our core systems are secure, Ren. The link to the orbital array is quantum encrypted. But the physical environment of a traditional port is… complex. Layers of legacy systems, wireless signals, potential physical access points that are outside our immediate control. We're adding layers of local perimeter defense and signal integrity checks, but it's not as controlled as our own dedicated sites."

This was a constant source of concern for Terri – external factors influencing system integrity.

Their conversations would often drift from the technical to the theoretical, exploring the limits of what they were building.

"Are there any blind spots in the network, Terri?" Ren asked one night, standing with her in the control room, looking at the glowing map, the vast dark blue areas of the oceans. "Any places we can't reach, or where our signal is weak?"

Terri followed her gaze to the ocean. "Our coverage is global now, for surface-to-surface. But underwater… that remains a hard limit, as you know.

Terri placed a hand lightly on Ren's arm, a brief, comforting touch that spoke volumes about their shared commitment and the weight they carried. "We are, Ren. Sharpa is making progress on the theoretical models. It's incredibly complex, but we're pushing the boundaries." Her touch lingered for a moment longer than strictly professional, a silent acknowledgment of the immense pressure Ren was under and Terri's support, both technical and personal. Ren found herself leaning into the touch for a brief second, drawing strength from it.

The foundation had shifted, and the forces of reaction were gathering, ready to fight to reclaim the ground Ren had so quickly transformed, using every means at their disposal, from lobbying to exploitation, to the subtle, terrifying possibility of technical sabotage.

But building a new world inevitably disrupts the old one. The efficiency, speed, and environmental cleanliness of the TTC network were directly dismantling industries built on delay, distance, and pollution. The ships rusting in harbors, the silent cargo planes, the choked highways now carrying fewer long-haul trucks – these were the visible signs of the old arteries hardening, replaced by the invisible conduits of quantum entanglement. And the entities that controlled those old arteries, that had grown immensely wealthy and powerful from their chokehold on global logistics, were watching Ren's map with growing alarm and fury. But its very success was creating the conditions for a backlash that would test its resilience in ways Ren had anticipated but not fully comprehended.

5 THE BATTLE FOR THE GROUND

The network, expanding relentlessly across continents and oceans, was more than just a collection of physical hubs and orbiting satellites; it was a fundamental challenge to the established order, particularly impacting industries built on the friction of distance. The traditional shipping industry, the cargo airlines, the vast logistics and freight companies, even elements of the fossil fuel sector and the construction industry – all watched with growing alarm as their market share eroded, their assets became obsolete, and their deeply ingrained business models faced extinction. Their response was not passive acceptance, but aggressive, coordinated resistance, leveraging their immense wealth, political connections, and control over information channels.

The initial skirmishes were waged in the media, a battle for the narrative, for the hearts and minds of the public. Not all media, certainly. Independent news outlets, technological blogs, and publications focused on sustainability or humanitarian aid often covered TTC positively, highlighting its efficiency, environmental benefits, and role in disaster relief (like the burgeoning, though not yet public, aid operations). But the most powerful, widely consumed "conservative" corporate media spearheaded a relentless, highly coordinated campaign of fear, doubt, and resentment.

Ren stood in the glare of studio lights at Global News' New York headquarters, having been assured this would be a technology segment about quantum physics applications. The host, Robert Sterlingson, smiled warmly as the cameras rolled.

"Dr. Franco, thank you for joining us. Let's start with the human cost of your technology." His smile sharpened. "We have Maria Santos on the line from Port Elizabeth. Maria?"

The screen split, showing a tearful woman in a small apartment. "Dr. Franco, my husband worked the docks for twenty years. Now he's unemployed, depressed. How do you sleep at night knowing you've destroyed our lives?"

Ren's jaw tightened. "I'm sorry for your family's difficulties, but—"

"But nothing!" Maria's voice cracked. "You sit in your ivory tower playing with physics while real families starve!"

Sterlingson leaned forward. "We also have evidence that your company has been buying homes under false names, forcing elderly residents from their communities."

"That's categorically false," Ren said, her voice steady despite her racing pulse. "We've documented multiple cases of impersonation—"

"Yet the victims all say 'TTC' contacted them." Sterlingson produced a stack of papers. "Signed affidavits from seventeen families. Are they all lying, Dr. Franco?"

"Someone is using our name—"

"How convenient." Sterlingson turned to camera two. "After the break, we'll hear from Senator Morrison about why The Teleport Company might be the greatest threat to American workers since automation."

The red recording light went off. Sterlingson's warm demeanor vanished. "Nothing personal, Dr. Franco. But my viewers need someone to blame for their problems, and you've painted a pretty big target on yourself."

Ren stood, removing her microphone. "Your viewers deserve truth, not manufactured outrage."

"Truth doesn't pay for the network," Sterlingson replied. "Fear does. And right now, everyone's afraid of you."

As Ren left the studio, her phone buzzed with messages from

Lynn: "Don't watch the replay. Working on response. They edited your answers."

In the lobby, a young production assistant caught up with her. "Dr. Franco? I'm sorry about that ambush. Not all of us agree with it." She glanced around nervously. "My brother's a trucker. Lost his job last month. But he's retraining for MTU maintenance now. The future you're building... some of us see it."

The woman hurried away before Ren could respond, leaving her standing alone as tourists photographed the Global News logo, oblivious to the media onslaught being waged inside.

Ren looked down at their hands, then up at Terri's face, her usual analytical detachment softening. "How do you always know what I need to hear?"

"Because I know you," Terri said simply. "Better than you think."

The admission hung between them, charged with unspoken meaning. Ren didn't pull her hand away. Instead, she turned it over, her fingers intertwining with Terri's. "Sometimes I think you're the only one who does."

In the blue glow of the control room, surrounded by the technology that was changing the world, something shifted between them—a quiet acknowledgment of a connection that had been building for years, a foundation as solid as the quantum principles that powered their network.

Frustrated by their inability to get fair coverage, Bruce had secured a meeting with a top executive at one of the networks leading the charge, a man named Mark Rolte. They met in Rolte's polished, minimalist office overlooking Manhattan.

Bruce laid out his case with uncharacteristic restraint, presenting data, evidence of the fabricated pet story, and statistics on job creation in TTC-related fields. "Mark, you know this report about job losses in Port Penobscot is skewed. You're only interviewing the longshoremen, ignoring the new logistics jobs at the distribution hub that opened because of our MTU. You're stoking fear."

Rolte leaned back in his leather chair, a cynical smile playing on his lips. He steepled his fingers. "I'm going to be honest with you,

Bruce. Our viewers respond to emotional stories about real people, real struggles. It resonates. A longshoreman who has lost the job his father and grandfather did? That's a powerful story. A tech startup hiring programmers for 'quantum logistics'? That's abstract. People don't even know what it means. It doesn't sell."

"But it's the truth!" Bruce insisted.

"Truth is… contextual," Rolte said, his smile never faltering. "And our advertisers—the shipping lines, the aerospace companies, the trucking unions—they have a vested interest in the existing infrastructure. Their advertising dollars keep this network on the air. It's not personal, Bruce. It's just business." He spread his hands in a gesture of faux helplessness, the very picture of cynical pragmatism. Bruce left the meeting fuming, the executive's cold dismissal a stark reminder of the financial forces fueling the media war against them.

Katya, ever analytical, pointed to a graph showing advertising spending by the major players in traditional logistics and manufacturing over the past two years.

"The major shipping lines, the aerospace manufacturers, the large construction conglomerates… their advertising budgets are being redirected on a massive scale. Less on promoting their services, more on influencing public opinion against us. They are funding think tanks, lobbying groups, and sophisticated media campaigns. It's a coordinated financial and informational attack. They're weaponizing public fear to protect their bottom line." She showed examples of 'independent studies' published by think tanks with undisclosed ties to the transportation industry, highlighting only job losses and downplaying environmental benefits or cost savings, framed as objective analysis to mislead the public and policymakers.

The construction sector felt the impact acutely, particularly as the Homes and Buildings division expanded its reach across the network, delivering modular units and enabling home relocation. Why wait months for materials to be manufactured and shipped across continents or states, dealing with delays, damage, and fluctuating costs, when a complete, pre-fabricated kit for a house or an entire apartment building could arrive instantly at the building site, ready for assembly?

Inside a bustling, but tense, construction union hall in Chicago. Workers sit on folding chairs, listening intently to their union representative, a man named Tony Moretti, known for his fiery speeches and fierce protection of his members' jobs. "They're bringing in houses ready-made now!" Tony bellowed, slapping a newspaper on the podium, a picture of a teleported modular unit prominent on the front page. "Or shipping entire apartment buildings like LEGO sets! What about our plasterers? Our bricklayers? Our farmers? Our truck drivers who used to bring in the lumber and the drywall? This isn't building; this is… assembly work! And they're paying less for it! These aren't the skilled trades our fathers taught us! Our livelihoods are disappearing!"

In the back, a 55-year-old carpenter named Frank listened, his heart heavy. Frank had been swinging a hammer for thirty-five years. He could frame a house blindfolded, his hands reading the wood, his skill a source of deep, quiet pride. His father had taught him the trade, the scent of sawdust, a kind of family perfume. Now, his contracting company was struggling, losing bids to modular builders.

Last week, desperate for work, he had taken a short-term job on a modular assembly site. The experience had been soul-crushing. Instead of blueprints, he was given a tablet with a 3D animated model. Instead of measuring and cutting lumber, he was told to snap pre-fabricated, polymer-composite panels into a steel frame. There was no craft, no skill, just following a sequence like a factory worker. His younger crew members, kids who had grown up with tablets, adapted quickly. Frank felt slow, clumsy, his decades of expertise rendered obsolete.

The tension on the site was palpable. The first day, a conflict erupted between Frank's crew of traditional carpenters and the younger, TTC-trained modular technicians.

"You call that building?" a grizzled electrician from Frank's crew spat at a young tech. "You're not building anything! You're just snapping pieces together like a bunch of kids with a LEGO set. Where's the craftsmanship? The pride?"

The tech, a woman in her late twenties with a sharp haircut and a confident smirk, didn't miss a beat. "We're building faster, cheaper, more efficiently, and with a tenth of the on-site accidents. The 'craftsmanship' is in the factory, where these components are manufactured to a millimeter's precision. You're just afraid of change." The electrician had to be physically restrained. Frank didn't join the argument, but he felt the sting of the young woman's words. It wasn't that he was afraid of change; he was afraid of a world that no longer had a place for him in it.

At a traditional building supply company, lumber sat aging in the yard, wrapped in plastic. Warehouse shelves were stocked with drywall, insulation, and roofing materials, gathering dust. The owner, a man named Bob, talked on the phone, frustration and desperation in his voice.

"Another contractor switching to modular, says it's cheaper with the teleport delivery. Doesn't need our two-by-fours anymore, doesn't need our shingles, doesn't need our cement. What am I supposed to do with this inventory? What about my employees? Become a kit unpacker? This is killing our business!" The industry was fracturing, some companies trying to pivot, retraining workers in modular assembly or specialized site preparation for teleported homes, others simply facing bankruptcy, their struggle adding potent visual examples to the media firestorm about job losses.

The housing market disruption went deeper than just individual anecdotes, as the expanded network made 'teleport-ready' properties visible and accessible to a global market. For generations, a house's worth was primarily determined by its location and the prevailing real estate conditions of that specific town or city – proximity to jobs, quality of schools, safety of neighborhoods. TTC changed that equation fundamentally. A charming, but cheap, house in a declining rural town, now suddenly connected to the world via a nearby tribal MTU or a newly established regional hub, became visible – and accessible – to buyers in booming distant cities or even other countries. Its market value was no longer capped by local demand or the value of surrounding properties; it was set by a global pool of potential buyers willing to pay the teleportation fee, which, while significant, was often still less than the difference in property values between the origin and destination. Global property listings, once a niche luxury, became a mainstream reality for any home owner willing to consider a move – not just of themselves, but of their entire residence.

A town council meeting in that Pennsylvania town, held in a drafty old municipal building. The room is packed, citizens are agitated, voices raised in frustration and fear. The town treasurer, a mild-mannered man named Mr. Henderson, gestures nervously at a projection showing declining property tax revenue over the past year. "Another fifteen properties designated 'Teleport-Ready' this quarter. Six have sold and been physically removed from our tax rolls this month. Those six properties alone were paying over $50,000 in annual property taxes! If this continues, our property tax base will shrink by twenty percent in eighteen months. We can't fund the school district next year. We can't maintain the roads. We can't pay the police force. We are facing municipal bankruptcy."

An elderly man in overalls shouted from the back. "My family's lived here a hundred years! Why should my land taxes go up just because some rich city folk are buying up our history and beaming it away?"

The meeting descended into chaos. But then a different voice cut through the noise. A young woman named Chloe, who had moved back to the town a few years ago after a failed attempt to make it in the city, stood up.

"Maybe… maybe we're looking at this the wrong way," she said, her voice hesitant at first, then gaining strength. "Yes, we're losing the old houses. But we're left with the land. And we're seeing new people moving into the area as well because of that land. They need services. I just started a small business specializing in site-prep and landscaping for teleported homes. I've hired three people who were laid off from the old lumber yard. Maybe this is an opportunity to reinvent ourselves, to offer something new, instead of just trying to hold onto what's leaving."

Her words didn't magically solve the town's budget crisis, but they introduced a flicker of hope, a different perspective into a room consumed by fear of the unknown. The mayor, a pragmatic woman named Janice, listened intently. The dilemma she faced was excruciating. If she embraced TTC and the change it brought, she risked alienating the older, more established residents and the few remaining traditional businesses. She'd be seen as a traitor to the town's heritage. But if she opposed them, if she joined the chorus of condemnation, she might be signing the town's death warrant, ensuring it became a forgotten backwater, a ghost town left behind by the march of progress. Chloe's small business was a fragile green shoot in a dying forest, but it was a start. Janice knew she had to find a way to nurture more like it.

This was the core of the local government crisis. Their primary, predictable revenue source was becoming volatile, literally disappearing. Cities and towns, already struggling with stagnant economies or rising costs for services, saw their financial foundations crumbling. Their response was immediate and visceral. Town councils passed resolutions condemning TTC, declaring it a threat to community stability, demanding state and federal intervention. Mayors lobbied state representatives, begging for solutions. The focus quickly shifted to the only immobile asset: land. The debate over land value tax, previously an academic discussion among economists, became an urgent, politically charged necessity.

At a state legislative hearing room, packed with lobbyists, town officials, and media, the air thick with tension. A rural mayor testifies, voice trembling with anger and desperation. "This company is gutting our towns! They're taking our homes, our history, our very identity! Our tax base! They profit from our decline! We need to stop this or find a new way to survive! We need legislation to protect our communities!"

A state senator, clearly coached by lobbyists from the development and construction industries, asked leading questions designed to elicit emotionally resonant answers, steering the testimony toward the negative impacts. "So you believe a tax based solely on land value, potentially raising taxes for those who haven't moved their homes but now own valuable land, is necessary to prevent the collapse of municipal services?"

"We need something!" the mayor insists, pounding the table, his frustration absolute. "This company offers no solution for the communities they destroy, only for the people who leave them behind!"

In a lavish office suite in Washington D.C., far from the public hearing rooms, the air was thick with the scent of power and expensive cologne. Senior executives from a major shipping corporation, a large aerospace company, and a national construction conglomerate met with their chief lobbyist, Mr. Thompson. Holographic displays showed graphs of plummeting profits in their respective sectors and TTC's rapidly expanding network, specifically highlighting the growth of the Homes division and the new hubs in the interior of the country and on tribal lands .

"We've got the media drumming up public fear about unstable houses and disappearing neighborhoods, linking it to the drug crisis and national security," the shipping exec said, a grim smile on his face. "The local governments are in chaos, adding pressure on their state reps, who are calling their congressmen, screaming about lost tax revenue. Now we push the federal hammer. This 'Secure Ports Act' is our best chance to stop them expanding inland and confine them where we can control the access."

The lobbyist, Mr. Thompson, nodded, reviewing notes on his tablet. "President Flores is fully aligned. The bill is drafted, positioned as essential for national security, infrastructure integrity, and regulatory oversight of a novel technology. It leverages all the public fear we've generated about instability, drugs, and lack of control. It's packaged as protecting American communities and American jobs from an unregulated foreign company." He paused, a look of satisfaction on his face. "But the core mandate is designed specifically to limit TTC's geographic reach. No TTC operations or receiving sites anywhere in the US except existing, federally controlled ports – specifically, major international airports and seaports. That's it. We choke off their interior access."

"It effectively neuters them inland," the construction exec grunted, his voice heavy with satisfaction. "Keeps our territories safe. They can dump containers on the docks, but they can't teleport a house to a suburban lot in Ohio, or components directly to a rural construction site in Georgia. Makes their Homes division irrelevant for most of the market where people actually want to live or build. It protects our members and our businesses."

Bora, who had been listening silently, finally spoke. His voice was calm, measured, carrying an authority that silenced the others.

"The strategy is sound for the short term," he said, his gaze sharp and analytical. "Restrict their physical footprint, leverage the existing infrastructure we control, use the media and political pressure to generate public fear and regulatory mandates."

A junior executive, new to this inner circle, cleared his throat. "But, sir, what if this backfires? Restricting them could push them to develop more independent infrastructure, like those tribal hubs. It might make them stronger in the long run."

Bora's gaze turned to the young man, a look so cold and dismissive it made him shrink in his chair. "That's a risk we're willing to take. Control is paramount. An untamed technology must be caged. If it breaks the cage, you build a stronger one. You do not let it roam free." His eyes flickered to his secure tablet. A cryptic, single-line message glowed on the screen for a moment before he dismissed it: "Phase Two authorization pending. 'The Ghost' is ready for initial testing." He looked up, his expression unreadable. "Besides," he added, his voice dropping slightly, "legislation is not the only tool at our disposal. There are... technical avenues to explore. Methods of disruption that go beyond the political. One must understand the system itself to find its inherent weaknesses." His words were a chilling hint of a deeper, more sophisticated plan, a suggestion that their opposition extended far beyond lobbying and media campaigns. This was not just a business fight; it was becoming a war on multiple fronts, including one fought in the invisible realm of technology itself.

"And forces anyone using them to rely on our planes, our trucks, and our rail lines for onward travel from the port," the aerospace executive added with satisfaction. "We get our piece of the pie back. And we tie their technology, which bypasses distance, back into the slow, bottlenecked infrastructure we still control. We make their speed dependent on our delays. We regain control of the supply chain, even the last mile."

Bora finally spoke, his voice calm, measured, carrying an understated authority that immediately silenced the others. "The strategy is sound for the short term," his gaze sharp and analytical. "Restrict their physical footprint, leverage the existing infrastructure we control, use the media and political pressure to generate public fear and regulatory mandates. But we must also explore other avenues. Technical vulnerabilities. Methods of disruption that go beyond legislation. Understanding the system itself is key. Obtaining several of the MTUs is not out of the question. How does it truly work? Where are its inherent weaknesses, beyond what they publicly present?"

His questions were precise, chillingly insightful, hinting at a mind that understood not just business strategy, but the underlying technology itself.

Later that evening, Bora stood alone in his penthouse, staring out at the harbor where his father's ships once docked. He removed his perfect suit jacket, carefully hanging it up—a habit from childhood when even a single wrinkle would earn his father's disapproval. On his desk sat a faded photograph: a younger Bora standing proudly beside his father on the bridge of a container ship, both in uniform, the only time his father had ever put his arm around him.

He poured himself a drink, not touching it. "I'm finishing what you started, Father," he whispered to the empty room. "They took your dignity. I'll take their future." His phone buzzed—another update on the Ghost project. He straightened his shoulders, the moment of vulnerability vanishing as quickly as it had appeared. The business of revenge required perfect composure.

This was a new level of adversary, Ren and her team would soon realize. Not just businessmen protecting their interests, but someone with the strategic vision and potentially the technical understanding to attack TTC on multiple, deeper fronts.

This was the core of the Flores Administration's proposed legislation. Officially, it was about security, customs control, and ensuring fair competition and safety standards for a new technology. In reality, as Lynn's team had meticulously documented, it was a transparent protectionist measure, drafted by industry lobbyists, designed to use government power to stifle innovation and protect obsolete industries by restricting TTC's operational footprint to areas where they were least disruptive to traditional transport. It would confine TTC to a handful of coastal and airport locations, severely limiting its reach and undermining its core value proposition of point-to-point instantaneous transfer, especially for something as location-sensitive as a home or critical

Just-In-Time components for inland manufacturing. It was a direct attempt to use state power to maintain the old economic structures against the force of technological change.

Lynn and her legal team were already dissecting the bill the moment it was leaked. They identified every loophole, every potential constitutional challenge (arguing it unfairly targeted one company and restricted interstate commerce), every point of weakness in its security rationale (contrasting it with TTC's own robust, if recently tested, security protocols). They prepared to fight it in court, lobby sympathetic legislators (emphasizing the bill's true protectionist nature and its negative economic impacts), and present compelling data on the economic and social benefits of TTC, directly challenging the cartel's narrative point by point.

But even in this legislative battle, an unexpected avenue opened, leveraging a unique aspect of the political landscape Ren and Lynn had the foresight to explore years earlier during the initial network planning.

"The Native American Nations," Lynn said, a flicker of grim hope in her voice during a strategy meeting, bringing up a map of the United States overlaid with the boundaries of federally recognized reservations. "Their reservations are sovereign territory, with their own governmental structures and legal systems. While the federal government has authority over certain matters through treaties and statutes, the reach of a bill like the Secure Ports Act, intended to regulate commerce and infrastructure on federal land or within standard state jurisdiction, is questionable, perhaps even non-existent, on tribal lands, depending on how it's drafted and challenged."

Lynn revealed she had been quietly solidifying partnerships with several tribal governments across the United States, leveraging the relationships Bruce had initiated during Phase Two rollout. These were tribes whose lands were strategically located to fill gaps in the network, often near major population centers or freight corridors but distant from existing ports. She had found keen interest not just in the economic benefits (lease revenue, jobs, access to global markets, affordable housing for their members via teleported modular units, preserving their culture by relocating historical structures onto tribal land) but in the political leverage the partnership offered – a way to assert their sovereignty through economic power and independence from federal overreach and the control of external corporations.

The tribal council chamber blended modern function with sacred tradition. Sunlight streamed through high windows of energy-efficient glass, casting patterns across walls adorned with intricate tapestries depicting the Nation's history. The council table—a massive, polished slab of local oak—had been carved by hand decades ago, each panel telling a story of the tribe's journey. State-of-the-art holographic projectors sat inconspicuously beside traditional talking sticks and ceremonial items, a visual representation of the Nation's philosophy: honor the past while embracing the future.

Chief Standing Bear reviewed security footage on his tablet. "This man, Frank Kowalski, was identified approaching our perimeter yesterday. Former carpenter, now connected to the Denver theft."

Alayna studied the image. "He's desperate, not evil. The system failed him before we disrupted it."

"Perhaps," the Chief said. "But desperation makes people dangerous. Double our security. And Alayna? Reach out through the construction unions. Offer retraining programs. We can't save everyone, but we can try to convert enemies into allies."

Outside, the proposed MTU site was visible in the distance—a stretch of red earth bordered by ancient cottonwoods, their leaves shimmering silver in the breeze. The land had once been considered worthless by government surveyors, too far from water and roads to be valuable. Now, ironically, its very isolation from federal infrastructure made it perfect for TTC's needs.

As Lynn and Bruce entered, they noticed council members weren't seated by rank or age, but in a circle where all voices held equal weight—a governance structure that predated European democracy by centuries.

Bruce and Lynn are meeting with the Intertribal Consortium in the US Southwest, presenting refined plans for a major MTU facility on tribal land.

"This facility," Lynn explained, pointing to the proposed site on a holographic map, "would operate under the Nation's laws. It would be a global gateway, connected directly to Europe, Asia, South America, via our satellite network. It would handle cargo, modular housing components, eventually even people, entirely bypassing the federal port system envisioned by the Secure Ports Act."

Chief Standing Bear, listened intently, his face thoughtful, stroking his chin. "And this proposed federal law? This 'Secure Ports Act'? How does it affect us? Will it force us to choose?"

"If it passes as written, it restricts our operations on federal and state land," Lynn confirmed. "But your sovereign territory provides a sanctuary. A place where we can operate, and where you gain direct access to the global network, free from that specific federal overreach. It makes your Nation a vital hub, both economically and strategically, in the new landscape of teleportation."

"For generations," Chief Standing Bear continued, his weathered hands resting on the ancient wooden table that had hosted tribal councils for over a century, "we have existed in a paradox. Sovereign on paper, dependent in practice. Every resource we needed—food, medicine, building materials—had to pass through systems controlled by others, on roads that cut through our lands but weren't ours to govern."

He gestured to the holographic display of the proposed MTU facility. "This technology doesn't just offer jobs or lease revenue. It offers true sovereignty—the ability to connect directly with the world on our terms, not as an afterthought on someone else's supply chain."

An elder council member, Clara Whitefeather, who had been silent until now, leaned forward. "My grandmother told stories of government agents who would withhold food deliveries if our children didn't attend their schools, didn't speak their language. Control of what moves in and out of our land has always been about power, about forcing us to assimilate or starve."

Lynn nodded, understanding the historical weight behind their considerations. "That's precisely why we believe this partnership transcends business. It's about self-determination in its most practical form."

"And when the federal government pushes back?" Clara asked, her eyes sharp with generations of justified suspicion. "When they see us helping you bypass their control?"

"Then we stand together," Bruce said, the usual sales pitch absent from his voice. "Our legal team has already prepared briefs defending tribal sovereignty in commerce. We're not just building on your land—we're investing in your right to determine your own economic future."

The partnerships were solidified. MTU ports on reservation lands became a key element of TTC's strategy for the US market, creating a parallel network within the United States, a series of sovereign economic zones immune to the restrictions of the Secure Ports Act if it passed. For the Native American Nations, it offered a path to economic independence and leverage, a chance to become key players in the new global economy rather than being left behind. It was an alliance born of necessity and mutual interest, a testament to the unpredictable ways disruptive technology could redraw lines of power and forge new partnerships, using the very ground beneath their feet as a new kind of economic and political leverage against centralized control.

By the time the Secure Ports Act was formally introduced in Congress, framed by the Flores Administration as vital legislation for national security and fair trade and backed by a tidal wave of industry lobbying and media fear-mongering, TTC had already laid the groundwork for its counter-strategy. The media war raged, the construction sector scrambled, local governments panicked, and the transportation cartels felt confident in their impending legislative victory.

The MTU transport convoy moved through the Colorado mountains at dawn, two escort vehicles flanking the specialized truck carrying a small cargo MTU unit destined for the Denver distribution center. Elena Rodriguez monitored the route from her tablet in the lead vehicle.

"Mountain pass coming up," her driver noted. "Narrow section for about three miles."

Elena's security chief, Markus Webb, spoke through the comm.

"Drone surveillance shows clear roads ahead. No traffic for—wait." His voice sharpened. "Vehicle approaching fast from behind. Not showing on traffic management systems."

Elena pulled up the drone feed. A black semi-truck, no plates, gaining rapidly. "That's not random. Alert Denver, initiate Protocol Seven."

The semi suddenly accelerated, ramming the rear escort vehicle and sending it spinning into the guardrail. Elena's driver swerved as another vehicle—a modified pickup—came from a hidden turnout ahead.

"Boxed in!" the driver shouted.

The MTU transport lurched to a stop. Figures in ski masks emerged from both vehicles, moving with military precision. No weapons visible, but they carried industrial cutting equipment and signal jammers.

"They're not trying to hurt anyone," Marcus observed. "They want the unit intact."

Elena watched helplessly as the thieves efficiently cut through the transport's security locks. Within minutes, they'd transferred the MTU to their semi using a mobile crane they'd clearly brought for this purpose.

"Tracking beacon?" she asked.

"Already disabled. They knew exactly where it was." Marcus's face was grim. "Inside knowledge."

As quickly as they'd appeared, the thieves vanished, leaving the convoy stranded but unharmed. Elena immediately called Ren.

"They took it," she reported. "Professionally executed. They'll reverse-engineer it within days."

"They'll try," Ren replied. "But without the quantum encryption keys and satellite authorization, it's an expensive paperweight."

"Unless they have someone inside who can provide those."

A pause. "Double security rotation immediately. And Elena? This wasn't random. Someone's building their own network."

Later, in a warehouse outside Denver, Frank the carpenter supervised as the stolen MTU was unloaded. His hands, which once crafted homes with pride, now trembled as he connected diagnostic equipment.

"You sure about this?" asked Tommy, a younger construction

worker he'd recruited.

Frank thought about his empty bank account, his wife's medical bills, the promise of enough money to start over. "TTC destroyed our livelihoods. Now we return the favor."

His phone buzzed. A text from an unknown number: "Good work. Payment transferred. Await further instructions. - B"

Frank stared at the yellow frame, wondering if he'd just traded his soul for revenge.

The Senate Commerce Committee hearing room buzzed with hostile energy. C-SPAN cameras captured every moment as Ren took her seat at the witness table, facing a panel of senators whose campaigns had been generously funded by shipping, trucking, and aviation interests.

Senator Morrison from Alabama launched the first attack. "Dr. Franco, my state has lost twelve thousand transportation jobs in six months. These are good, honest Americans who can't feed their families because of your technology. What do you say to them?"

Ren leaned toward the microphone. "Senator, I would note that Alabama has also gained eight thousand jobs in renewable energy, MTU maintenance, and quantum logistics. The transition—"

"Transition?" Senator Morrison's voice rose. "You call destroying entire communities a 'transition'? My constituents call it economic warfare."

Senator Kim from California interjected, her tone deceptively mild. "Dr. Franco, can you guarantee that your technology can't be used to transport illegal drugs or weapons?"

"Our scanning protocols are more thorough than any existing inspection system—"

"That wasn't my question. Yes or no—can you guarantee zero illegal usage?"

Ren paused. "No technology can guarantee—"

"So you admit your system could be exploited by cartels and terrorists?" Senator Kim smiled coldly. "Let the record show the witness admits her technology poses a national security threat."

"That's a mischaracterization—"

Senator Thompson from Texas cut her off. "Let's discuss your so-called tribal partnerships. You're exploiting sovereign land to avoid federal oversight, aren't you?"

"We're partnering with Native American nations to bring economic opportunity—"

"You're using them as a loophole!" Thompson slammed his hand on the desk. "Hiding behind their sovereignty while destroying American jobs!"

From the gallery, Ren could see Bora watching, a slight smile playing on his lips. He'd orchestrated this perfectly.

Senator Roberts from Mississippi, the committee chair, gaveled for order. "Dr. Franco, the Secure Ports Act would simply ensure proper oversight of your operations. Why do you oppose common-sense regulation?"

"Because it's not regulation—it's strangulation," Ren replied, her composure finally cracking. "You're trying to force us into bottlenecks controlled by the very industries we're disrupting. It's protectionism disguised as security."

"That's quite an accusation," Roberts said coldly. "Are you suggesting this committee has been compromised?"

Lynn stood up in the gallery, ready to intervene, but Ren continued. "I'm stating that the Secure Ports Act was written by shipping industry lobbyists, not security experts. Page forty-seven contains language lifted verbatim from a Bernheimer Logistics internal memo."

Gasps rippled through the gallery. Roberts face reddened. "How did you obtain private corporate communications?"

"They were filed publicly in an unrelated lawsuit last year. Perhaps the committee should read its own legislation more carefully."

The hearing devolved into shouting. Roberts gaveled repeatedly. "This hearing is adjourned! Dr. Franco, you've shown contempt for this institution!"

As Ren left, surrounded by Lynn's legal team, a reporter shouted, "Dr. Franco! Any response to accusations you're a threat to national security?"

"The only threat is to monopolies that have controlled global trade for too long," Ren replied. "The future doesn't need their permission to arrive."

That night, the edited clips played endlessly on cable news: Ren "admitting" security vulnerabilities, "attacking" the Senate, "showing contempt" for American workers. The war for public opinion was being lost, one soundbite at a time.

Halfway across the world, in a windowless room filled with cutting-edge equipment, a figure known only as "The Ghost" removed specialized interface gloves and smiled at the data streaming across multiple screens. The intrusion had been brief but successful—a test probe that had touched the edge of TTC's quantum network and retreated without detection.

"Phase Two entry point confirmed," The Ghost said into a secure comm link. "Their satellite defenses can be breached."

Bora's voice came through, cool and satisfied. "How soon until we can implement the full protocol?"

The Ghost studied the complex quantum encryption patterns captured during the brief intrusion. "Two weeks. Maybe less."

"Proceed," Bora ordered. "And remember—we don't want to destroy their network. We want to control it."

As the connection ended, The Ghost turned back to the screens, fingers dancing across holographic interfaces, probing deeper into the quantum architecture that Ren had spent years perfecting, looking for any vulnerability that would turn her revolutionary technology into a weapon against her. He only needed to find one.

Frank sat in his empty house, the stolen MTU diagnostic data spread across his laptop. His wife slept upstairs, unaware of what he'd done. The money would cover her treatments, give them a fresh start.

His phone rang. Unknown number.

"Mr. Kowalski," the voice was cultured, cold. "You've proven useful. How would you like to do more than steal equipment? How would you like to shut down their entire network?"

"Who is this?"

"Someone who understands your anger. The Ghost will be in touch with instructions."

The line went dead. Frank stared at his hands—hands that once built homes, now tools of destruction. Outside, a TTC truck drove past, carrying modular housing components to families who could finally afford homes.

He closed the laptop, decision made. Tomorrow, he'd call the FBI. Whatever he'd started, it had gone too far. But tonight, he'd hold his wife and pretend the world hadn't changed beyond recognition.

In Montreal, Bora reviewed The Ghost's report. "Kowalski is having second thoughts."

"Then we activate our contingency," The Ghost replied. "His wife's medical bills provide excellent leverage."

The war for the ground had found its unwilling soldiers.

6 THE SICHUAN RESPONSE

On a Tuesday afternoon in the late spring 2063, the planet held its breath, watching live feeds of unimaginable destruction. A seismic event of terrifying magnitude – a 9.8 earthquake – ripped through the densely populated province of Sichuan in southwestern China. The earth did not just shake; it tore itself apart with a primal force. Mountains crumbled into avalanches of dust, rivers were rerouted by torrential landslides, entire cities were reduced to rubble in seconds, their skylines collapsing like sandcastles. The ground ripped open, swallowing homes and people. The sheer, raw power of the natural world asserted itself with brutal, indifferent finality.

The news feeds showed sweeping aerial shots of collapsed cities, but on the ground, in a small, nameless village nestled in a mountain valley, the apocalypse was intimate and brutal. One moment, Mingxia was hanging laundry in her small courtyard, the sun warm on her face. Next, the world was a roaring chaos. The ground heaved, throwing her against a stone wall. Her house, the house her grandfather had built, folded in on itself with a sound like a giant's sigh.

When the shaking finally subsided, a thick, choking dust filled the air, turning the bright afternoon into a grey twilight. The silence that followed was more terrifying than the noise. Mingxia, her arm broken and bleeding, frantically clawed at the rubble where her home had been, her voice a raw, desperate scream. "Wei! An! Where

100

are you?" Her two young sons had been inside, playing a game.

Around her, the scene was one of Dantean horror. An old man, the village elder, sat amid the wreckage of the teahouse, rocking back and forth, muttering prayers, his eyes vacant. A group of neighbors worked together, using their bare hands to lift a concrete beam that had pinned a young woman. The air was thick with the smell of broken earth, gas from ruptured lines, and something acrid and organic that Mingxia didn't want to identify.

A few hours later, a team of local first responders, their uniforms covered in dust, finally made it to the village on foot, their vehicles abandoned miles away on a road that no longer existed. Their faces were grim masks of exhaustion and despair. The team leader, a hardened veteran named Captain Chen, knelt beside a frantic man pointing toward a collapsed schoolhouse.

"We have reports of hundreds trapped in there," the man pleaded. "Mostly children! But the main support beams have shifted. The whole structure could come down if we move the wrong piece."

Chen's radio crackled. "We have multiple reports of survivors in the residential areas to the east," a voice said. "But access is cut off. We need heavy equipment."

"There is no heavy equipment," Chen muttered, his voice raw. He looked at the school, then at the desperate faces around him. He had a team of twenty rescuers, a few crowbars, and a handful of medical kits. It was a triage situation from hell. "We focus on those we can reach now," he said, his voice cracking with the unbearable weight of the decision. "Surface survivors first. The school…we need to assess the structural integrity before we send anyone in. We go where there's the highest chance of saving lives right now."

In Beijing, an emergency session of the Central Military Commission convened in a secure bunker. General Zheng, commander of the Western Theater, spoke forcefully to the assembled officials via encrypted link.

"Foreign technology operating on Chinese soil without oversight? Absolutely not. We have our own relief capabilities."

Vice Minister Zhang nodded. "The People's Liberation Army has deployed thirty thousand troops. We don't need—"

"Sir," an aide interrupted, "Mianyang hospital reports they have six hours of antibiotics remaining. The roads won't be cleared for days."

Zhang's jaw tightened. "We maintain control. Any foreign assistance goes through military channels."

General Wei added, "And this TTC... their technology could be weaponized. Bringing it onto our soil during a crisis, when our defenses are stretched—it's a security risk we cannot accept."

"Then people die," the aide said quietly, immediately regretting his boldness.

The room fell silent. Zhang finally spoke: "One test. Military supervised. Limited scope. If anything seems suspicious, we shut it down immediately."

The infrastructure of the region, the very arteries that connected cities and communities and enabled aid delivery, was utterly obliterated. Airports, vital for bringing in international aid and rescue teams, saw runways buckle into unusable waves of tarmac and concrete, control towers topple, and terminals collapse. Highways, the traditional lifeline for ground transport and emergency convoys, fractured into impassable canyons, were buried under rockslides hundreds of meters deep, or simply vanished into newly opened fissures in the earth. Rail lines twisted into abstract sculptures of useless metal, bridges collapsed into rivers, their spans sheared away.

The global response was immediate, heartfelt, and frustratingly impotent against the physical barriers the earthquake had erected. Nations pledged aid with solemn declarations, rescue teams mobilized with desperate urgency, tons of essential supplies – tents, medical kits, food, water purification equipment, heavy machinery for clearing rubble – were gathered in warehouses and logistics hubs worldwide. But the physical reality was unyielding. Cargo planes sat on tarmacs in neighboring countries, their precious cargo unable to fly into non-existent or damaged airports. Ships carrying heavy machinery and bulk supplies rerouted toward the nearest coastal ports, knowing they faced weeks of sailing only to arrive at docks potentially damaged themselves or facing overland journeys of hundreds of kilometers through a landscape of collapsed roads and impassable terrain. Ground convoys were planned, aid trucks loaded and ready, but the sheer scale of the infrastructure damage meant routes were not just difficult, but utterly impassable, requiring days, even weeks, of arduous, dangerous work just to clear minimal paths for limited access. The traditional methods of global humanitarian response, built on planes, ships, trucks, and navigable infrastructure, were rendered tragically useless by the sheer, unyielding reality of a broken physical world.

The silence from the devastated region was punctuated only by the frantic, fragmented reports that managed to filter out via satellite phones and overwhelmed emergency frequencies – desperate pleas for help that the world seemed unable to deliver. Aid sat in warehouses, rescue workers stood ready, but the physical reality of the shattered landscape created an insurmountable barrier. The traditional methods, the very systems the cartels championed as 'reliable' and 'accountable,' had utterly failed in the face of a truly catastrophic natural event.

"But," Terri continued, her expression growing more concerned as she studied the data, "the seismic aftershocks are creating significant ground instability. Our quantum field requires precise spatial coordinates to rematerialize objects safely. If the ground shifts during transfer..." She didn't need to finish the thought.

"Solutions?" Ren asked, her tone clipped but not impatient.

Terri's fingers flew across her console. "We'll need to modify the anchor units to compensate for ground movement in real-time. I'm thinking a network of micro-seismic sensors deployed with each unit, feeding continuous spatial recalibration data." She looked up at Ren. "It's never been tested in field conditions this extreme."

"Can your team make it work?"

"Yes," Terri said without hesitation. "But we'll need to divert processing power from the commercial network. And the first deployments will be risky."

On the screens showing the Mianyang receiving point, they watched as a container of medical supplies materialized—slightly askew, one corner partially embedded in the ground where it had shifted—but intact. The aid workers rushed forward, already prying it open.

Terri exhaled slowly. "That was too close. We need to implement the adaptive field algorithms immediately. And we need more ground stabilization at the receiving points."

"This is it," Ren said, her voice quiet but carrying absolute conviction, cutting through the low hum of the fusion reactor and the distant sounds of the Atlantic weather. She rarely spoke with such overt emotion, but the scale of the suffering on the screen moved her deeply. "Everything we built, everything we risked, the fight we are in… this is the validation. This is why." She gestured to the screen, the image of a collapsed city a stark, horrifying visual reminder of the stakes. "They are cut off. Every minute matters. Every life. We can move aid faster, more reliably, than anything that's ever existed. Without roads, without runways, without ships. Without needing the old system that has failed them."

There was no debate, no hesitation among the team. The media attacks, the political pressure, the economic warfare, the investigations into the 'ghost', the frustration of seeing their technology maligned – all faded into insignificance against the scale of the human suffering on the screen. Their technology, which had been portrayed as destructive and dangerous, had the potential to be a unique force for salvation in this moment, precisely because it bypassed the broken physical world.

Ren turned to Terri, her gaze seeking out her technical partner. "Terri, can we establish temporary receiving fields in the zone? Remote deployment? Is the satellite coverage sufficient over Sichuan?"

Terri was already pulling up the data. "Satellite coverage is sufficient, Ren. Alpha and Beta arrays have direct line of sight.

Establishing temporary receiving fields... it's technically challenging given the seismic instability and atmospheric dust, but yes, it's possible. We have rapidly deployable MTU anchor units, designed for harsh environments. We can adapt protocols for unstable ground." Her focus was absolute, already calculating energy requirements, signal stability, potential interference.

"How quickly can we get anchor units on the ground?" Ren asked.

"Small drones carrying the units can be teleported to the fringes of the zone and fly in," Terri explained. "Or small, specialized security teams can carry them in via helicopter. We need ground confirmation and activation, even for a temporary field."

Ren nodded, already planning. "Lynn, coordinate with aid agencies and any remaining contacts on the ground. We need precise GPS coordinates for safe drop zones. Open areas, stable ground if possible. We need confirmation that they can secure the site immediately post-arrival to prevent chaos."

Lynn, already on her secure comms, faced immediate skepticism. Lynn had been on calls for three straight hours, her voice hoarse. Each Chinese official passed her to another department, each with new requirements.

"We need technical specifications for your quantum encryption," demanded Colonel Chen from Military Intelligence.

"That's proprietary—"

"Then no authorization."

Lynn muted herself, turning to Ren on another screen. "They want our encryption protocols."

"Absolutely not," Ren said flatly. "That compromises our entire network."

"People are dying."

"And if we give them our protocols, Bora's network will have them within hours. Then everyone dies when they corrupt our transfers."

Lynn unmuted. "Colonel, we can provide operational parameters without revealing proprietary methods. We'll demonstrate complete scanning protocols, show contamination detection, but the quantum signatures must remain secured."

"Unacceptable. No transparency, no access."

From another monitor, Bruce interjected: "What if we offer limited access? One Chinese military observer in our control room during transfers?"

Ren's expression hardened. "That's—"

"That's five thousand lives," Lynn interrupted, surprising herself with her firmness toward Ren. "Minimum."

A long pause. Ren finally nodded. "One observer. No recording devices. They see operations, not architecture."

Lynn relayed the offer. After an agonizing pause, Colonel Chen responded: "Standby for instructions."

Meanwhile, a tense diplomatic dance was unfolding. On a secure video call, Lynn faced a panel of stern-faced Chinese officials, led by Vice Minister Zhang of the Emergency Management Ministry.

"This is an internal Chinese matter," Zhang stated flatly. "Foreign intervention must follow proper protocols. Your company cannot simply... beam things into our sovereign territory."

Lynn kept her expression respectful but firm. "Vice Minister, we understand your concerns completely. That's why we're seeking your explicit permission and coordination. But conventional aid routes are completely cut off. People are dying waiting for help that cannot reach them through traditional means."

"And who would control these... appearing supplies? Who would distribute them? China has its own systems."

"Your systems, your control," Lynn assured him. "We provide the delivery method only. Your emergency services determine what goes where, based on your assessment of needs. We're offering a tool, not taking over the response."

Zhang conferred quietly with his colleagues. After a moment, he turned back to Lynn. "A test. One delivery to coordinates we specify, under military supervision. If successful, we will consider broader authorization."

Lynn nodded, knowing this was the best they could hope for. "Agreed. Send the coordinates. We'll be ready in thirty minutes."

Lynn was then on a video call with Dr. Thorne, the grim-faced European director of a major international medical aid organization, Global Health Response.

"Teleportation?" Thorne said, his voice weary and dismissive. He was in a chaotic staging area in Chengdu, surrounded by mountains of medical supplies they couldn't move. "Ms. Lynn, with all due respect, I don't have time for science fiction. My teams are on the ground, and people are dying. We need reliable transport—helicopters, trucks—not some unproven, magical technology."

Lynn met his gaze without flinching, her voice calm and firm. "Dr. Thorne, I understand your skepticism completely. But your helicopters can't land because the landing zones don't exist, and your trucks are sitting on a highway that's a hundred kilometers from a landslide the size of a small city. The traditional routes are impassable. We can deliver your supplies—these very supplies I see behind you—directly to the coordinates of your field hospitals in the next ten minutes. We can bypass the damage entirely."

She shared her screen, showing him live satellite imagery of the impassable roads he was referring to. "Isn't that worth a try? Give me the coordinates for one field clinic. Let us send one container of sterile bandages. If it doesn't arrive in five minutes, I will never bother you again."

Thorne hesitated, then looked at the desperate faces of the wounded being brought into his chaotic field hospital. He was out of options. "Fine," he grumbled. "One container. Here are the coordinates for our makeshift clinic in Mianyang." He read them off, his tone still thick with disbelief. Lynn relayed them to the control room.

Five minutes later, a frantic voice from one of Thorne's field medics crackled over his radio. "Sir! You're not going to believe this! A shipping container… it just appeared! In the town square! It's full of bandages and antibiotics!" Thorne stared at his comms device, then back at Lynn on the video screen, his skepticism replaced by stunned, dawning hope. "Send it all," he said, his voice barely a whisper. "Send everything you have."

Meanwhile, Katya was waging her own war on the logistical front. She was on a secure call with a major pharmaceutical supplier in India, her voice cold and hard as steel.

"I need your entire stock of broad-spectrum antibiotics and tetanus vaccines," she stated, her tone leaving no room for negotiation. "Yes, all of it."

The supplier stammered. "But, Ms., that's millions of dollars of inventory! We have existing contracts, shipping schedules…"

"TTC will wire the full payment, plus a fifteen percent premium for immediate reallocation, into your account in the next sixty seconds," Katya interrupted, her fingers already authorizing the transfer. "Cancel your other shipments. Lives are at stake. Get it to our MTU facility in Mumbai within the hour. We will handle transport from there. Do not make me call your competitor." The supplier, faced with the combination of immense financial incentive and undeniable moral urgency, quickly agreed. Katya moved on to the next call, a master of applying financial leverage for humanitarian ends.

Within hours of the initial, high-level contact with aid agencies and Ren's decisive commitment of TTC's full resources, the first aid shipments began. Not trickling in by air or sea, facing days or weeks of transit and the monumental task of navigating shattered infrastructure, but appearing in the designated zones. From TTC facilities and partner supplier warehouses around the world, vast quantities of vital supplies were loaded into MTUs, flagged as the highest priority. The orbital satellites, TTC's silent workhorses, redirected energy and processing power, pulsing with energy, beaming the quantum data streams down to Sichuan.

In an overcrowded, makeshift clinic in a relatively less damaged town square outside the immediate impact zone. Doctors and nurses, many of them local survivors, work tirelessly with dwindling supplies. A foreign aid worker, who managed to reach the area days later on a difficult helicopter journey, looks at the grim scene. They have antiseptic, but no antibiotics. Bandages, but no painkillers. They are treating fractures with makeshift splints, unable to perform necessary surgeries because equipment couldn't be brought in. People are dying of preventable infections, of treatable injuries, simply because the aid is stuck outside the ring of devastation. The frustration and heartbreak are palpable. Messages pleading for medical supplies, for water purification tablets, for food, are sent out via satellite phones, reaching the outside world like desperate cries in the wilderness.

It was in this moment of desperate need, when conventional logistics failed utterly, when the gap between willingness to help and the ability to deliver help felt like an unbridgeable chasm, that the world turned, tentatively at first, then with growing urgency, to The Teleport Company. The calls came not through formal, bureaucratic channels initially, which were themselves overwhelmed and struggling to coordinate, but as desperate pleas from NGOs on the ground whose supply networks had collapsed, from overwhelmed provincial and national governments scrambling for any solution, from international aid agencies paralyzed by their inability to reach the affected populations. They knew about TTC, about the company that could make things disappear here and reappear there. They had heard the whispers, seen the limited news reports about instant cargo. Could they do the impossible? Could they bypass the broken world and deliver hope directly?

TTC absorbed the vast majority of the costs – the cost of the aid itself, the energy expenditure for transfers, the operational expenses. Prioritizing speed and saving lives became the sole focus, overriding profit margins or even long-term financial stability in the face of such immense human suffering. The sheer volume of aid moved in the first 24 hours, then 48, then 72, exceeded what traditional methods could have delivered in weeks, perhaps even months, given the scale of the infrastructure failure.

In the Chengdu temporary distribution center, Chinese Army Captain Liu supervised the unloading of medical supplies from an MTU that had just received them from Mumbai. The building shook—another aftershock.

"Secure the antibiotics!" he shouted.

Three trucks rolled up outside—military vehicles with proper identification. Soldiers in PLA uniforms emerged.

"Emergency redeployment," the lead 'soldier' announced, presenting orders. "These supplies are needed in Dujiangyan immediately."

Captain Liu frowned. "I wasn't notified—"

"Aftershocks damaged their storage. They need immediate resupply." The man's Mandarin was perfect, his uniform authentic.

As Liu reached for his radio to confirm, the man struck him. Liu collapsed. The fake soldiers efficiently loaded half the medical supplies into their trucks.

Fifteen minutes later, when Liu regained consciousness, the trucks were gone. So were antibiotics meant for ten thousand people.

In Montreal, Bora received confirmation. "Phase Two

successful. Medical supplies secured."

"Ensure they surface on the black market with TTC tracking codes visible," he instructed. "Make it look like internal theft."

The Ghost added, "The neural disruptor left traces. If they scan, they'll find quantum signatures matching TTC's frequency."

"Perfect. They'll suspect insider corruption."

In the midst of coordinating another wave of aid deliveries, Terri noticed something odd on her monitor—a brief fluctuation in the quantum field stability of Satellite Beta, similar to the anomaly she'd observed days earlier but had attributed to routine power variance.

"That's strange," she muttered, pulling up the diagnostic data.

"Problem?" Ren asked, looking up from her own work.

Terri hesitated. "Probably nothing. Just another field fluctuation. The system's under unprecedented stress with all these emergency transfers."

"But?" Ren prompted, knowing Terri well enough to sense her uncertainty.

"But the pattern is... unusual. Not consistent with power fluctuations or environmental interference." She shook her head. "I'll have the security team run a deep scan when things calm down. Right now, we need to focus on the aid deliveries."

What neither of them knew was that while their attention was fixed on the humanitarian crisis, The Ghost was using the opportunity to probe deeper into their systems, exploiting their diverted resources and attention to map the quantum architecture of TTC's network. The fluctuation Terri had noticed wasn't a system strain—it was a deliberate intrusion, testing how far into the system The Ghost could penetrate before being detected.

"We have a problem," Katya announced, looking up from her tablet during an emergency coordination meeting. "The MTU in Mumbai can only handle three more transfers today before it needs maintenance. We have two shipments ready: vaccines for a field hospital in Chengdu serving thousands of injured, and food supplies for isolated mountain villages where people haven't eaten in days."

"Send both," Bruce said immediately.

"We can't," Terri replied, shaking her head. "The power

requirements would overload the system. We'd risk losing both shipments."

Ren studied the data silently, her face a mask of concentration. Lives hung in the balance of her decision. "What's the timeline for each need?"

"The vaccines will save more lives immediately," Lynn said, reviewing reports from the ground. "But the mountain villages... they might not survive another 24 hours without food and water."

"The Chinese authorities are requesting the vaccines as top priority," Katya added. "They're focusing resources on the urban centers first."

Ren looked around the table, the weight of the decision visible in her eyes. "We send the food to the villages," she said finally. "The hospitals have at least some supplies. The isolated villages have nothing. And..." she hesitated, "we don't just follow government priorities if they conflict with the greatest need."

"The Chinese government won't be pleased," Lynn warned. "We're operating there at their discretion."

At the Mianyang receiving site, Elena Rodriguez and a small TTC team worked alongside Chinese military to establish a secure receiving zone. The ground was unstable, buildings nearby groaned with each aftershock.

"Elena, we need to move the MTU back," called James Chienga, one of their field engineers. "This building could come down."

"Five more minutes," Elena insisted, monitoring an incoming transfer of surgical equipment. "The field hospital needs—"

The aftershock hit without warning. The partially collapsed building adjacent to their position finally gave way. James shoved Elena clear as tons of concrete crashed down.

"James!" Elena scrambled toward the rubble where he'd been standing. His leg was visible, twisted at an unnatural angle, the rest of him buried.

Chinese soldiers rushed to help, frantically pulling debris. Elena could hear James screaming, then worse—silence.

"He's breathing!" a soldier shouted in Mandarin. "But his spine—don't move him!"

Elena's hands shook as she called St. John's. "Medical emergency. James is critical. Spinal injury, possible internal bleeding."

Terri's voice came through: "The nearest trauma center is—"

"Sixty kilometers of destroyed roads away," Elena finished. "He needs immediate surgery or he's paralyzed. Maybe worse."

In the control room, Ren made a cold calculation. "Can he be stabilized for transport?"

"Ren!" Terri turned on her, shocked. "He's one of ours!"

"And thousands are dying. We can't redirect medical supplies for one person."

"We can do both," Terri shot back, her usual deference gone. "Or are we only humanitarians when it's convenient?"

The control room went silent. Everyone watched Ren wrestle with the decision.

"Route the next surgical kit to Elena's position," Ren finally ordered. "Include a spine stabilization unit. The Chinese military surgeons can operate on-site."

Elena coordinated with the Chinese medics, using TTC's supplies to save James's life in a makeshift surgical tent while aftershocks continued. The successful surgery would save James but leave him with months of recovery ahead—and Elena with survivor's guilt that would complicate her future risk assessments.

The global media, previously focused on the economic disruption caused by TTC, suddenly had a different story to tell, one far more compelling and far less easy for the cartels and their allies to manipulate. Live feeds from Sichuan, captured by overwhelmed news crews who had managed to reach the fringes of the disaster zone, showed aid workers, their faces streaked with dust and exhaustion, rushing to receive pallets materializing out of thin air (or rather, appearing within the visible energy field of the temporary MTU units). Survivors, previously unreachable, their fate uncertain, their needs unmet, suddenly had access to food, water, medical care, and shelter.

The images of tangible aid appearing where before there was only despair spoke louder than any manufactured headline about job losses or economic disruption. They showed a child receiving a blanket that had been in a warehouse in Canada hours before. They showed a doctor receiving antibiotics that had just appeared from a facility in India. They showed families huddling under tents that materialized in a flattened village square.

Governments that had been wary, influenced by the powerful lobbies of the legacy industries, became cautiously supportive, even overtly grateful. International bodies that had debated regulating or restricting TTC found themselves coordinating with the company, facilitating logistics on the periphery of the disaster zone, and acknowledging that in this crisis, TTC had provided the only viable lifeline.

The transformation was particularly striking on Global News, where anchor Veronica Yancey—who had previously led the charge against TTC with emotional stories of displaced workers—now stood in the network's New York studio, her tone markedly different.

"The images coming from China tonight are nothing short of miraculous," she said, as footage played of aid materializing in devastated areas. "TTC's technology, which has been the subject of intense debate and criticism—including on this very network—is now providing a lifeline where traditional methods have failed completely."

The camera cut to a split screen with Franklin Rossmon, Global News' senior business analyst and a vocal critic of TTC. "Franklin, you've expressed concerns about this technology's economic impact. Does this change your assessment?"

Rossmon shifted uncomfortably. "The humanitarian application is... undeniably impressive, Veronica. I still have serious concerns about the long-term economic disruption, but..." He paused, choosing his words carefully. "In this specific context, it's saving lives that would otherwise be lost. That can't be dismissed."

Later that evening, in a more pointed exchange, Global News' panel discussion turned heated when Rossmon attempted to pivot back to economic concerns.

"While acknowledging the current benefits," he began, "we must still consider—"

"Consider what?" interrupted Dr. Patel, a humanitarian aid expert. "Consider that thousands would be dead without this technology? That children would be orphaned, families destroyed? At what point do we admit that protecting outdated industries doesn't justify human suffering?"

The conversation marked a subtle but significant shift. The media narrative hadn't completely transformed—concerns about jobs and economic disruption remained—but they were now balanced against tangible evidence of lives saved, creating a more nuanced public conversation that the cartels could no longer easily control.

Ren watched the news reports from the control room, surrounded by her team, the feeds showing the impact of their work. The stoic façade she usually presented cracked slightly. She saw faces, not just statistics – the relief, the hope sparked by the sudden, miraculous arrival of help. She saw her technology, her life's work, bypassing the brokenness of the world to deliver salvation. This was the 'better world for everyone' she had dreamed of, the vision that had driven her through years of doubt, secrecy, and relentless work. For a brief, intense period, the economic battles, the corporate resistance, the legal challenges – they didn't disappear, but they faded into the background, muted by the overwhelming imperative of saving lives. All that mattered was the aid, the silent, powerful act of bringing salvation from here, to there, instantaneously.

The Sichuan earthquake had shaken the earth itself, reshaping its physical contours with brutal force. But TTC, by bypassing that shattered physical reality to deliver aid, had shaken the foundations of global humanitarian response, proving that in a world facing increasingly severe and unpredictable disasters, the ability to convey resources independent of traditional, vulnerable infrastructure was not a luxury, but a necessity. The crisis became a powerful, unsolicited demonstration of TTC's potential, a moment of grace in the ongoing battle for its future, a stark contrast to the negative portrayal by its enemies. It provided a powerful, real-world counter-argument that no amount of lobbying or media manipulation could easily dismiss.

Late that night, after the first full day of aid deliveries had been successfully completed, an exhausted quiet fell over the control room. Elena sat beside James's medical cot in the field hospital, watching the IV drip antibiotics into his arm—antibiotics that could have gone to dozens of others. His spine was stabilized, but he'd never run again. Might never walk without assistance.

"Stop," James whispered, his voice rough. "I can see you calculating how many people my medical supplies could have saved."

"James, I—"

"You made the right call. Both of you did." He managed a weak smile. "Besides, now I get to redesign our field safety protocols from a wheelchair. Silver lining?"

Elena squeezed his hand, unable to speak past the guilt.

Her tablet chimed—a message from Ren: "James's medical expenses covered. Full salary during recovery. Tell him his sacrifice saved the program. The Chinese military cited our caring for wounded personnel as evidence we could be trusted."

"See?" James said, reading over her shoulder. "Even Dr. Franco knows—sometimes the human choice is the strategic choice."

7 THE SHADOW CAMPAIGN

The alert came at 7:05 AM, piercing through the control room's normal hum. Terri was already there, monitoring a routine transfer of agricultural equipment from Brazil to Kenya.

"Hold on," Chen Li said from his station, frowning at his screen. "I'm getting anomalous density readings in container seven."

Terri moved to his console, studying the quantum signature analysis. The pattern was subtle but unmistakable—organic compounds that didn't match the manifest. Her stomach dropped.

"Run the narcotic signature comparison," she ordered quietly.

The results confirmed her fear: cocaine, professionally concealed within legitimate cargo. The containers had already materialized at the Nairobi MTU.

"Lock down the receiving area," Terri commanded, hitting the emergency protocol. "No one moves those containers." She grabbed her secure phone. "Get me the Kenyan National Police, priority line."

Within minutes, she had Inspector Kamau on the line. "Inspector, we've detected contraband in a shipment that just arrived at our Nairobi facility. Containers are secured, but we need immediate intervention."

"How long can you hold them?" Kamau asked.

"Our security can maintain the lockdown, but the recipients are already arriving. They have valid pickup documentation."

"We're fifteen minutes out."

Terri watched the security feeds as three vans pulled up to the facility. Men emerged, presenting paperwork to the guards. Professional, organized, expecting no resistance.

"Stall them," Terri told the security chief. "Technical difficulties with the release mechanism."

The next fourteen minutes stretched like hours. On the feed, the men grew agitated, making phone calls. One approached the MTU directly, examining it with unsettling familiarity.

When the police arrived, the arrests were swift but tense. Terri watched as Inspector Kamau personally supervised the container inspection, confirming the drugs.

"Dr. Simmons," Kamau said over the phone afterward, "these men had inside knowledge. They knew exactly which containers, exactly when they'd arrive."

"Send us everything," Terri replied. "We're tracking this network."

The transfer stream from Brazil to Miami showed normal readings for nineteen containers. Then container twenty's data stream fractured on her screen like breaking glass.

"What the hell?" Terri rushed to the console as alarms blared.

The quantum signature split in real-time, one portion completing the transfer to Miami, the other veering off, materializing somewhere else entirely. Istanbul, according to the emergency locator beacon.

"Shut it down!" Terri commanded.

"It's already complete," Chen Li reported, his face pale. "Nineteen successful, one... split."

Terri's hands flew across the controls, pulling up every diagnostic available. No power fluctuation. No system error. The infrastructure was perfect, but something had reached into the quantum stream itself and torn it apart.

"Get me satellite telemetry for the exact moment of the split," she ordered. "Every sensor reading, every energy signature within a thousand kilometers."

As data flooded in, a pattern emerged—a brief spike in localized electromagnetic activity, but not from their equipment. External. Targeted. Precise.

"Someone did this," Terri breathed. "Someone interfered with an active transfer."

She immediately called Ren. "We've been attacked. Not hacked—physically attacked at the quantum level."

An official, gold-embossed invitation arrived for the International Transportation Innovation Summit in Dubai. Katya argued fiercely for attending. "We cannot afford to be seen as hiding. Our absence would be interpreted as weakness. The financial markets are watching. Governments are watching. We must project strength, confidence, and control." Her logic was impeccable, framing the conference not as a risk, but as a strategic necessity. Reluctantly, Ren agreed.

Ren decided on a small, focused team: herself as founder, Lynn to handle legal ambushes, and Terri as chief technologist. Katya would remain in St. John's managing the financial front, while Bruce would coordinate media strategy from afar.

At the opening reception, a German shipping magnate, a portly man named Klaus Bernheimer, cornered Ren. "Your... machines... have put my family's company, a company that has been building ships for a hundred years, on the verge of bankruptcy," he slurred, his face flushed with champagne and anger. "You speak of progress. I see only destruction."

It was at that same reception that they formally met Bora. He moved through the crowd with an effortless, predatory grace, a stark contrast to the blustering anger of men like Bernheimer. He was impeccably dressed in a tailored suit of a material Ren didn't recognize, his presence both captivating and deeply unsettling. Bruce, who had arrived separately to manage the on-the-ground media, introduced them.

"Ren Franco, I'd like you to meet Bora," Bruce said, forcing a cheerful tone. "Bora is a leading consultant in... well, in strategic futures and bespoke architecture."

Bora extended a hand. His grip was firm, his eyes analytical and cold. "Ren-san," he said, his voice a smooth, cultured baritone. "An honor. Your work is profoundly disruptive. I admire the audacity." There was no warmth in his words, only a chilling, professional assessment.

He turned his attention to Terri. "Doctor, I've read your papers on quantum coherence. Quite fascinating. Maintaining the integrity of a quantum state over such distances... the technical challenges must be immense. Especially with external interference." His words were casual, but the implication was clear. He knew about their problems. He might even be the source of them.

"Business is like any other ecosystem, Ren-san," Bora continued, his gaze returning to Ren. "It requires balance. Regulation. Predictability. Your technology introduces a level of chaos that established systems cannot tolerate. Governments are becoming... nervous. A nervous government is a regulating government. It would be a shame to see such a brilliant innovation... caged." His words were a veiled threat, a warning wrapped in the language of business consulting. At that moment, Ren knew she wasn't talking to a consultant. She was talking to a key strategist, perhaps even the leader, of the opposition.

The next day, Ren delivered her keynote address. The hall was packed, the audience silent and hostile. She spoke not of profit, but of a cleaner planet, of connecting humanity, of the ethical responsibility that came with their power. The question and answer session was brutal.

"Dr. Franco," a journalist from a major financial network asked, his voice dripping with condescension, "given the recent security breaches that have allowed vast quantities of illegal narcotics to be transported via your network, how can you possibly claim your system is secure? Aren't you simply a high-tech drug mule for the world's criminals?"

Lynn stepped in, her voice calm and cutting. "Our system's internal security protocols were the very thing that detected the illicit cargo, a feat that would be impossible with traditional shipping containers that can sit unchecked for weeks. We are cooperating fully with international law enforcement to..."

But the narrative was set. The questions were relentless, all focused on fear, instability, and crime. Throughout the ordeal, Terri sat in the front row, her gaze locked on Ren, a silent beacon of support. As Ren walked off the stage, exhausted and battered, Terri was the first person she sought out.

"They're not listening," Ren murmured, her voice low with frustration.

"It doesn't matter," Terri replied, her hand finding Ren's and giving it a quick, firm squeeze. "We know the truth. We just have to keep speaking it." Her unwavering belief was the only thing that kept Ren from feeling completely isolated.

The conference room at the Dubai International Transportation Innovation Summit was a monument to old money—mahogany panels, Persian carpets, and windows offering a panoramic view of the city's skyline. It had been designed to intimidate, to remind visitors of the established order's permanence. Today, it would host what the organizers euphemistically called a "dialogue session" between TTC and traditional shipping interests.

Ren entered flanked by Lynn and Terri, their footsteps muffled by the thick carpet. Across the massive table sat five executives from the world's largest shipping conglomerates. Klaus Bernheimer was there, his face already flushed despite the early hour. Victoria Henryson from Oceanic Maritime Alliance sat rigid, her expression carved from ice. Three others Ren recognized from their companies' aggressive anti-TTC campaigns. One she had seen, but who was never introduced was Bora. Present in so many anti-TTC photos but never interviewed, almost as if the coordinator.

"Dr. Franco," Bernheimer began without preamble, his German accent thickening with barely contained anger. "Your technology has cost my family's company—a company that has operated for over a century—nearly forty percent of its value."

"Your company's devaluation isn't my responsibility," Ren replied evenly, taking her seat. "Markets respond to innovation. They always have."

"Innovation?" Henryson's voice dripped with contempt. "You call destroying millions of jobs innovation? Entire port cities are facing economic collapse because of your... apparatus."

Lynn leaned forward, her legal training evident in her measured tone. "The Teleport Company has created thousands of new jobs in thousands of locations in quantum engineering, sustainable logistics, and humanitarian aid coordination. Economic transition is not the same as economic destruction."

"Pretty words," spat one of the other executives, a weathered American named Thompson who ran Gulf Logistics. "Tell that to the longshoremen's families who can't put food on the table. Tell that to the ship crews stranded without work."

"The same argument was made against automobiles, aircraft, and computers," Terri interjected, her voice calm but firm. "Progress doesn't stop because change is uncomfortable."

Bernheimer slammed his hand on the table. "This isn't progress! It's chaos! Drug shipments appearing from nowhere, cargo vanishing mid-transport, no oversight, no control—"

"Every incident you're referring to was detected by our security protocols," Ren interrupted, her voice sharpening. "Which is more than can be said for the tons of contraband that move through traditional shipping every day, hidden in containers that go uninspected for weeks."

"At least our containers can be tracked!" Thompson shot back. "They follow routes, pass through customs, and have documentation trails. Your system is a black box—literally! Cargo disappears in one place and appears in another with no accountability for what happens in between."

"Our quantum signature verification provides more accountability than any physical inspection," Terri responded. "Every atom is catalogued, every molecule tracked. The integrity of our transport—"

"Your 'integrity' allowed a shipment to split in half!" Henryson cut in. "Twenty containers became debris. How do we know that won't happen to oil? Chemicals? Nuclear materials?"

Lynn pulled out her tablet. "The single split-shipment incident represents a 0.0001% failure rate compared to the 2.3% loss rate in maritime shipping from storms, piracy, and container loss. Your industry loses over 1,000 containers at sea every year."

"Those are acts of God or criminals," Bernheimer countered. "Not fundamental flaws in physics that we don't understand!"

"You're right," Ren said quietly, drawing all eyes to her. "You don't understand it. And that terrifies you. Not because it's dangerous, but because it makes you obsolete."

The room went silent for a moment, the tension palpable.

Victoria Henryson stood slowly, her movements deliberate. "Dr. Franco, let me be clear. The global shipping industry moves ninety percent of world trade. We employ millions directly and support billions indirectly. We are not some antiquated system waiting to be discarded. We are the circulatory system of global civilization."

"A circulatory system that's clogging the planet with carbon emissions," Ren stood as well, meeting Henryson's gaze. "Killing our oceans with bunker fuel, creating maritime graveyards of abandoned ships. You had a century to innovate, to clean up your industry. You chose profits over progress."

"And you chose to play God!" Bernheimer was on his feet now too. "Moving matter through space like some sci-fi fantasy, with no thought to the consequences!"

"The consequences?" Ren's voice rose for the first time. "The consequence is that aid reaches disaster zones in minutes instead of weeks. The consequence is that landlocked nations can participate in global trade without paying your extortionate inland transport fees. The consequence is a world where distance doesn't determine destiny."

Thompson laughed bitterly. "Beautiful speech. But who controls this miracle technology? One company. Your company. You talk about democratizing trade while building a monopoly that would make the old railroad barons jealous."

"We've offered to license our technology—" Lynn began.

"At impossible prices with restrictions that would make us your vassals," Henryson interrupted. "You're not offering partnership, you're demanding surrender."

"Because you'd use it to maintain the same broken system," Terri said, standing as well. "You'd find ways to add delays, create artificial scarcity, maintain your profit margins at the expense of efficiency."

"Efficiency." Bernheimer said the word like a curse. "Your efficiency is built on technology you can't fully control. What happens when someone hacks your quantum network? When terrorists figure out how to teleport bombs? When criminals realize they can move anything, anywhere, instantly?"

"The same fears were raised about the internet," Lynn countered. "Yet here we are, having adapted, having built safeguards—"

"The internet doesn't move physical matter!" Thompson slammed his fist on the table. "It can't materialize a weapon in the heart of a city!"

"Neither can we," Ren said firmly. "Every transfer requires paired MTUs, preparation, scanning—"

"For now," Henryson interrupted. "But technology evolves. What you've controlled today could be weaponized tomorrow. And unlike ships, which we can track and intercept, your system operates outside conventional oversight."

"You mean outside your control," Ren said coldly. "That's what this is really about. Not safety, not jobs, not even profit. Control. For a century, you've controlled what moves and when. You've decided which nations prosper and which stagnate based on their access to ports and shipping lanes. That's the power you're losing."

Bernheimer's face was purple now. "And what gives you the right to take it? One woman, one company, deciding the fate of global trade?"

"What gave you the right to hold it?" Ren shot back. "Historical accident? The fact that your great-grandfather bought ships before others did? At least our technology is based on merit, on innovation, on solving real problems—"

"Your technology is based on arrogance!" Thompson roared. "The arrogance to believe you can reshape the world without consequences, without oversight, without—"

"Without your permission," Terri finished for him. "That's what really bothers you. We didn't ask for your blessing. We didn't integrate into your cartels and committees. We just built something better."

The room fell silent again, but this time it was the silence before a storm.

Henryson gathered her materials with deliberate calm. "This conversation has clarified something important, Dr. Franco. You're not interested in coexistence. You're interested in conquest."

"I'm interested in progress," Ren replied. "If you can't adapt to that—"

"We'll see who adapts to whom," Bernheimer interrupted, his voice low and threatening. "You think you're untouchable because of your technology. But technology is only as strong as the infrastructure it depends on. Satellites can fail. Power grids can be regulated. Governments can be influenced."

"Is that a threat?" Lynn asked, her hand moving to her phone to record.

"It's a prediction," Thompson said, standing to leave. "You've declared war on an industry that's survived pirates, wars, and economic collapses. We're not going to simply fade away because you've invented a magic trick."

As the shipping executives filed out, Henryson paused at the door, turning back to Ren. "You know, Dr. Franco, there's an old maritime saying: 'The sea is patient, but it always wins in the end.' You might want to remember that."

After they left, Ren, Lynn, and Terri stood in the empty conference room, the weight of the confrontation settling over them.

"That went about as well as expected," Lynn said dryly.

"They're scared," Terri observed. "Cornered animals are dangerous."

Ren walked to the window, looking out at Dubai's port in the distance, its cranes and containers looking like toys from this height. "They're right about one thing. This is a war. But it's not one we started—it's one they've been waging against progress for decades. We're just the first ones with weapons they can't match."

"Let's hope that's enough," Lynn murmured.

As they prepared to leave, none of them noticed the small device attached under the conference table, its red light blinking steadily, transmitting every word to a yacht anchored in Dubai's harbor where Bora sat, reviewing the conversation with a cold, calculating smile.

"Arrogant, Dr. Franco," he murmured to himself. "But admirably so. You've just told me exactly how to destroy you—through the very infrastructure you depend on but don't control."

The spider's web grew tighter.

That night, at the conference's opulent closing gala, a black-tie affair held in a ballroom with a view of the entire glittering Dubai skyline, Ren found herself cornered by the pressures of a world she had never sought to join. She stood on a balcony, the noise of the party a distant murmur, staring at the city lights. Katya joined her, a glass of sparkling water in her hand.

"They're like wolves, Ren," Katya said quietly, following her gaze. "They smell blood. Our financial partners are getting cold feet. The constant negative press, the threat of regulation… it's making them nervous. I'm fighting fires on a dozen fronts just to keep our credit lines open."

"I'm an engineer, Katya," Ren confessed, a rare moment of vulnerability in her voice. "A physicist. I understand data, systems, algorithms. This world of politics, of public perception, of smiling while people lie to your face… it's a language I don't speak."

Katya placed a reassuring hand on her arm. "You don't have to speak it. You have to lead us through it. Your clarity, your focus on the mission, that is what grounds us. Bruce handles the media, Lynn handles the law, and I handle the money. Your job is to keep being the person who can see the future through all this noise. We trust your vision, Ren. That is why we are all here." Her words, delivered with her characteristic quiet authority, were a powerful reassurance, a reminder of the team's loyalty and shared purpose.

The diagnostics lab was their sanctuary, a world of pure data, insulated from the messy human drama unfolding in Dubai. The walls were covered in holographic displays showing complex quantum waveforms and transfer stream simulations. They were searching for the fingerprint of the intruder, the subtle signature of the external interference that had caused the split shipment.

"It's like looking for a ghost," Dr. Sharpa sighed, pushing her glasses up her nose. "The energy signature of the interference is almost indistinguishable from background quantum fluctuations. It's elegant in its subtlety. And terrifying."

"They're not using brute force," Terri said, pacing in front of a data stream model. "They're not trying to break the encryption. They seem to be nudging it. Exploiting a subtle loophole in the quantum state transfer itself. But we can't replicate it. We can't find the vulnerability they're using."

Late one night, Terri was on a secure video call with Ren, who was back in her hotel room in Dubai. They were thousands of miles apart, but in that moment, the connection felt immediate and profound.

"Still no luck," Terri reported, her voice tired. "It's like our adversary understands physics on a level we didn't anticipate. Or they're using a technology we don't know exists."

Ren was silent for a moment, her own weariness evident even through the screen. "Keep looking, Terri. I know you'll find it. You are the best at what you do." The praise, simple and direct, meant more to Terri than any official commendation. In his eyes, she saw not just a CEO, but the brilliant, driven woman she admired, struggling under an immense weight. She felt an overwhelming urge to reach through the screen, to offer some comfort, some personal connection beyond the professional crisis that consumed them.

The Dubai conference concluded. On the surface, it had been a public relations disaster. But beneath the surface, something had shifted. Katya's meetings had secured a tentative line of credit from a progressive Middle Eastern sovereign wealth fund, one that saw beyond the current turmoil to the long-term potential of TTC. Lynn had made inroads with several smaller nations who were tired of the dominance of the old shipping cartels and saw TTC as a potential partner for economic independence.

"We found it," Terri's voice crackled with excitement over a secure line to Ren's jet as she flew back from Dubai. "A temporal anomaly. In the split shipment data. For a picosecond, the quantum stream's internal clock was out of sync with our satellite's master clock. It's an impossibly small window, but it's the only time an external command could have been injected without triggering our integrity alarms."

"They can manipulate time-space on a localized, microscopic level," Ren murmured, her mind reeling with the implications. It was a level of technological sophistication that was terrifying, but it was also a vulnerability they could now look for, a signature they could hunt. It was a glimmer of hope.

The blow came not through a political decree or another media smear about job losses, though those continued in the background. It came from within the network itself, a subtle, insidious corruption of the system's integrity, leveraging the very speed and discretion that made it revolutionary. The first warning signs appeared not as dramatic failures, but as faint red flags in the complex, constantly flowing data streams monitored 24/7 by

Terri's technical division. These streams represented the quantum blueprints of every item moving through the network, verified against their manifests.

Dr. Chen Li, the senior quantum diagnostics engineer on Terri's team, was performing routine post-transfer integrity checks late one night. His focus was on a large, multi-container shipment manifested as processed food – canned goods and dry staples – originating from a major logistics hub in Europe and destined for a regional distribution hub in North Africa. These checks, a standard part of TTC's rigorous protocol, used advanced quantum signature analysis to verify that the cargo arriving at the destination was a perfect, untampered replica of the cargo scanned at the origin. The system was designed with multiple layers of verification, capable of detecting even minor discrepancies – a container seal broken mid-transfer, a single item missing, an added foreign object, or a deviation in material composition.

The primary integrity check passed without incident. The total mass of the containers, their external dimensions, and the overall quantum signature of the declared cargo matched the manifest perfectly. Everything appeared normal on the surface. But Li had implemented a new, experimental protocol – a tertiary, high-resolution spectral analysis that probed deeper into the layered quantum signatures, looking for anomalies within the bulk of the declared contents, below the surface level. This was the digital equivalent of an X-ray or MRI, but far more detailed and operating at the atomic level.

"Tertiary scan initiated," Li murmured, adjusting the parameters on his console, his fingers flying across the holographic interface. The scan delved into the complex data structures representing the cargo, attempting to identify the specific materials and their arrangement within the container without physically opening it – the digital equivalent of an x-ray, but far more detailed and operating at the atomic level.

The results flickered across Li's screen, initially presenting as complex data points, then resolving into a complex heatmap overlaid on a schematic of the container's contents. Certain areas within specific crates of canned goods showed energy signatures inconsistent with preserved food, packaging materials, or the container itself. They were distinct, high concentrations of specific, complex organic compounds – molecules that did not match the known chemical profiles of steel, tin, water, vegetables, preservatives, or cardboard. Li's heart gave a jolt. He cross-referenced the signatures against a database of known substances, including materials used in manufacturing, industrial chemicals, and, as a necessary security measure, known contraband signatures. His eyes widened slightly. The pattern was unmistakable.

He immediately flagged the anomaly internally, escalating it directly to Terri's dashboard. "Potential cargo discrepancy detected," his urgent report read. "Manifest ID AP2-CAN6-0127, Container ID CAN-241-931. Suspected presence of undeclared organic compounds within legitimate cargo. There's a high probability match to narcotics signatures."

Terri received the alert instantly in the control room, a late-night shift for her, as usual. Her usual calm, scientific focus was absolute, but an internal alarm bell began to ring, loud and insistent. "Undefined organics? In a food shipment? High probability match to narcotics?" She accessed Li's report, reviewing the signature analysis herself, zooming in on the spectral data. The data was unambiguous, chillingly clear. It wasn't just a random contaminant; it was a deliberate, concealed payload. "Cross-reference with known contraband signatures, including processing agents and masking materials."

The system ran the comparison, accessing restricted law enforcement databases. The results confirmed her growing suspicion. The energy signatures matched not just raw narcotics, but processed illegal drugs – specifically, high-purity cocaine and heroin, cleverly concealed and possibly treated with masking agents or layered within the bulk of the legitimate cargo in a way designed to evade standard volumetric scans at the origin.

A tense silence fell over the control room as Terri initiated a secure, high-priority call to Ren. She didn't hesitate; some things couldn't wait for a morning brief. Ren was in her private quarters within the complex, but instantly alert at the sound of Terri's voice and the priority alert code. "Ren, it's Terri. We have a confirmed Level 2 cargo anomaly." Level 2 wasn't as critical as the Level 1 split shipment, which indicated a potential system failure, but it represented a severe security breach involving illicit cargo. "Routine deep scan on a food shipment flagged anomalies. We detected high concentrations of illegal narcotics hidden within several containers in that shipment. The signatures are confirmed."

Ren was in the control room within minutes, pulling on a jacket over her sleep clothes, her face grim, her mind already running through the implications. "How did they get in, Terri? Our origin scans should detect hidden cargo during loading. The system takes a full quantum snapshot before transfer."

"That's what we're investigating, Ren," Terri replied, pulling up the logs and scanning data for the origin MTU in Europe. "It's the baffling part. The manifests were clean. The initial, standard volume scans at the source MTU during the loading process showed no anomalies – passed all integrity checks for the declared cargo. The discrepancy detection occurred either mid-transfer – though the data transfer integrity remained high, indicating no disruption of the stream itself – or, more likely, upon arrival verification after the container rematerialized at the destination MTU in North Africa. Dr. Li's deep scan protocol is what caught it, a protocol that runs as a secondary check after a successful primary transfer validation. The analysis is picking up residual traces, subtle deviations in the expected quantum state, almost like a ghost imprint of the illicit substance, even after the substance itself had been rapidly extracted from the container at the destination."

"Extracted?" Ren echoed, a knot forming in her stomach. The speed implied coordination.

"The containers arrived at the destination MTU as scheduled," Terri explained, pulling up the logs and any available, grainy security footage from the North African facility's external cameras. "Our on-site verification protocols, triggered by the initial anomaly flag from Dr. Li's deep scan, flagged the discrepancy. However, by the time the local security team was alerted by the system and could physically inspect the containers, they had already been moved from the receiving field by the designated recipients. Standard protocol, designed for efficiency, allows recipients with confirmed manifests and validated identities to pick up cargo promptly from the receiving field to prevent congestion."

Lynn, who had joined the briefing via secure link from her St.

John's office, saw the implications instantly, her legal mind already calculating the potential damage and liability. "They knew exactly which containers contained the hidden cargo, exactly when they would arrive, and had people in place with seemingly legitimate credentials and vehicles to pick them up immediately upon materialization. This wasn't random smuggling. This was a precise, coordinated exploitation of our system and our protocols. They bypassed the source scan and leveraged the destination pickup process with military-like precision."

Ren's mind raced, connecting this to the split shipment. That was potentially an attack on the network mechanism. The drug shipments were an attack on the network's purpose and reputation, leveraging its speed and efficiency for criminal ends. Who had the motive? The resources? And, most disturbingly, the potential insight into TTC's proprietary scanning and transfer protocols required to bypass the initial detection at the source, and the on-the-ground coordination to facilitate such rapid, targeted pickups? The conversation with Bora, her quiet understanding of his disruptive impact, and her connection to the "distressed" transportation cartels all clicked into place with a sickening certainty. This was her. Or her network.

"This is them," Ren stated, her voice low and cold, recognizing the pattern of deliberate, targeted action. "The cartels. Or what's left of them, under new guidance. They couldn't beat us on efficiency, environmental impact, or humanitarian response after Sichuan. They're going to try and frame us as a tool for criminals. Associate teleportation with illegal activity on a massive scale and paint us as unstable, dangerous, out of control. They'll use public fear against us."

"We need to identify the source, the recipients, the entire chain, and gather irrefutable evidence," Katya said, her financial background making her focus on the paper trail, the money laundering that must be involved. "And we need to do it quietly. Apprehend the perpetrators through law enforcement before the media gets hold of this."

Ren arrived, alerted by the Tier 1 flag, stepping into the charged atmosphere of the control room. She took in the display, the red line split with amber, the grim faces of her team. "A glitch?" she asked, though her tone held no real question, only a challenge to the apparent reality. Her creation, flawed at its core?

"No, Ren," Terri said, shaking her head slowly, the word insufficient. "The system diagnostics ran a full self-check. No internal error. It's... external interference. Targeted. Surgical. Something interacted with the transfer stream mid-propagation."

Ren's eyes narrowed, the intellectual puzzle warring with the terrifying implications. "Sabotage?"

"It's the only explanation that fits the data," Terri confirmed grimly. "Someone is capable of manipulating quantum streams in transit. Violating the rules of teleportation."

This was a terrifying escalation. The drug shipments were destroyed after arrival. The split shipment was an attack on the process itself. It struck at the heart of TTC's credibility. Who would trust their system if it could be manipulated like this?

Ren convened the core team immediately, their faces stark with exhaustion and shock. Bruce was struggling to process the operational disaster – lost cargo, irate clients, the sheer absurdity of a split shipment. Katya's mind immediately went to the financial implications – insurance claims, regulatory fines, the inevitable tightening of capital access by wary banks, and the cartels' allies. Lynn was already anticipating the legal storm – lawsuits for cargo loss, inquiries into the technology's fundamental safety.

"Twenty containers of electronics, gone or split," Bruce reported, running a hand through his hair in frustration. "Miami is demanding answers, Istanbul is demanding explanations. The client is threatening to sue us into oblivion. This makes us look like amateurs, Ren. Unreliable."

"It's worse than that, Bruce," Katya said, her voice tight. "This isn't just unreliable. This is terrifying. If the system can be manipulated in transit, what else can be done? The financial world is risk-averse, and this incident will only solidify the narrative that TTC is a dangerous, unpredictable liability. They'll freeze our assets if they can, choke off our funding."

"And legally," Lynn added, her expression grim, "proponents of the Secure Ports Act will use this as definitive proof that we are a threat. 'Untraceable, uncontrollable, unstable,' that's their argument. A system that can rip cargo apart in transit cannot be trusted with national security, let alone human lives." She looked at Ren, acknowledging the chilling implications for the Life MTU R&D.

Ren listened, her gaze sweeping over her team, the weight of their fear and the crisis pressing down. "We need to understand how this happened," she said, her voice resolute. "Who is capable of manipulating a quantum stream? This wasn't random. This was targeted. Surgical. It points back to the adversary behind the drug shipments, the aid destruction. Someone who knows our system." She thought of Bora, the strategist for the legacy industries, his interest in technology, and his presence on the yacht. Could he be behind this?

"The ghost in the machine." That was the term the technicians began using in hushed tones, capturing the elusive, unsettling nature of the adversary. Not a simple malfunction, but an intelligent, malicious presence operating within or alongside their network, violating the fundamental rules of physics they had engineered. An adversary who seemed to be escalating their attacks from exploitation to direct technical sabotage, striking at the core of TTC's existence, at Ren's life's work.

Ren stepped back into the technical investigation with renewed intensity, working side-by-side with Terri, Dr. Sharpa, and the team, fueled by caffeine and a desperate need to understand. Days bled into nights. The lab became their world, their battleground against the unseen enemy. They analyzed the corrupted data stream, searching for any trace of the injected command, any anomaly in the energy profile of the transfer that wasn't accounted for by the standard physics. They ran countless simulations, attempting to replicate the conditions, to understand how an external force could inject commands or manipulate the quantum entanglement stream without being immediately detected by the system's robust internal monitors.

"The signature is so faint, Ren," Terri murmurs late one night, alone with Ren in the lab, the only sounds being the hum of equipment and the soft click of data pads. "It's like trying to find a single photon in a supernova. It barely registers above the normal transfer energy flux, and then it vanishes."

"But it was precise," Ren counters, looking at the data on her pad. "Timed to coincide with the stream propagation. It wasn't random noise. It was... surgical. It violated the coherence integrity at a specific point in the transfer." She looked at Terri, their gazes meeting across the dimly lit space. "Could it be leveraging a vulnerability in the satellite hardware itself? Something physical, not just software? Or in the ground MTUs' uplink?"

Terri shakes her head. "We ran full diagnostics on Satellite Alpha immediately. No sign of external physical tampering, no unexpected energy drains on its systems. The transfer completed normally from the satellite's perspective for 19 containers. It's the 20th stream that was diverted before or during processing."

"So the interference happened before or during the stream handoff to the satellite, or maybe as it was being processed," Ren hypothesized, thinking aloud, working through the problem with Terri, who could keep pace with her rapid-fire technical reasoning, adding her own insights and questions. "Or maybe it's not about the satellite or the ground MTU itself, but the uplink/downlink process through the atmospheric layer? Or the interaction with other ambient signals? Cosmic radiation maybe? The vulnerability is in the space between the origin and the satellite?"

They explore theoretical possibilities, bouncing ideas off each other, their technical language dense and rapid, their minds working in perfect sync. Could it be a localized energy field generator? A quantum computer specifically designed to interact with propagating entanglement streams? A new form of electronic warfare operating at the quantum level, invisible to traditional detection? Could Bora's interest in "bespoke mobile architecture" and his probing questions on the yacht about technical details be related to developing this capability? The possibility added a chilling layer to Ren's suspicion.

Before Ren could even formulate a comprehensive plan to investigate the issue internally, gather more evidence, and apprehend the perpetrators through discreet cooperation with international law enforcement, leveraging their network of trusted contacts (something they had done successfully, albeit quietly, with the initial, smaller incidents), the corporate media machine, previously primed by the cartels' lobbying efforts and now perhaps directly supplied with information from Bora's network, roared to life. Fueled by what felt like a perfectly orchestrated, high-speed leak of selective, incriminating information, news broke across every major network, newspaper, and digital platform controlled by or aligned with the legacy industries.

While the media firestorm raged, Terri's team worked around the clock, delving deeper into the data, fueled by anger and a desperate need to understand how their system had been compromised and who was behind it. They cross-referenced manifests, analyzed recipient identities (discovering layers of shell corporations, stolen IDs, and fraudulent documentation), traced payment methods (often utilizing complex, rapidly shifting cryptocurrencies and offshore accounts), and looked for patterns across the global network. The patterns were chillingly clear and pointed to a sophisticated, highly organized operation, carefully selecting routes and timing to maximize impact and minimize interception. Multiple shipments over several months, originating from different continents, often from locations with lax oversight or high rates of corruption, destined for seemingly unrelated hubs in various countries with known high rates of narcotics consumption or distribution – North Africa, Eastern Europe, parts of Southeast Asia. And the recipients were consistently individuals or entities with no legitimate business in the sector, many with confirmed ties to organized crime groups flagged by international law enforcement databases.

Reports filtered back to Ren from her discreet security network, confirming physical anomalies associated with some of these suspicious shipments at the receiving sites. Surveillance footage (acquired discreetly by TTC's own security contractors, operating outside the compromised public view) showed rapid, almost paramilitary-style pickups of the containers at destination MTUs, often by individuals who matched profiles of known criminal enforcers rather than logistics workers. There were even reports of secondary, off-site transfers occurring almost immediately after pickup, using vans or trucks designed for quick loading, suggesting the containers were moved to hidden locations where the drugs were quickly extracted before law enforcement, even if notified by TTC, could arrive.

Then came disturbing news from Romania and Hungary. Medical supplies sent through TTC's humanitarian program had been destroyed—vaccines spoiled, medicines shattered, equipment crushed. Security footage showed coordinated raids by the same criminal networks receiving drug shipments. The message was clear: turn TTC's humanitarian victories into defeats. Images of destroyed aid next to yellow MTUs went viral, carefully orchestrated propaganda that erased Sichuan's goodwill overnight.

The corporate media machine, already in overdrive, amplified these incidents to devastating effect. Photos of smashed medical supplies next to a yellow TTC MTU unit became viral symbols of the perceived danger and instability of quantum technology. The narrative solidified, repeated endlessly across screens and headlines: teleportation brought drugs and destroyed aid, while traditional shipping, for all its faults, was stable, accountable, and controllable. The nuance of TTC detecting the drugs after the transfer, or the destruction being caused by external criminal forces actively exploiting the network after arrival, was deliberately omitted, downplayed, or dismissed as TTC trying to deflect blame.

Representatives from the world's largest ship and aircraft manufacturers, sensing their moment and perhaps guided by the strategic mind behind the attacks, went public with unified, forceful demands. They took out full-page ads in major newspapers, went on so-called news shows, and intensified their lobbying efforts in national capitals and international bodies.

At a televised press conference, the CEO of a major shipbuilding corporation addresses a crowd of reporters, his voice ringing with indignation. "The events of the past weeks demonstrate, unequivocally, the inherent dangers of this unregulated teleportation technology," he declared, his voice resonating with feigned authority and concern. "It is being used by criminal syndicates to traffic narcotics on an unprecedented scale, flooding our streets with drugs and fueling violence. It is enabling the destruction of humanitarian aid, causing immense suffering to innocent people. While our industries face challenging transitions, which are often made more difficult by unfair competition, we provide jobs, stability, and security. Our cargo is tracked, our vessels are regulated, our planes are controlled, and our supply chains are transparent and accountable. This… this is chaos. It is a threat to global security and public health." He gestured dramatically at a screen showing images of the destroyed aid. "We call upon governments worldwide to immediately implement a moratorium on all TTC operations, or ideally, shut down this dangerous network entirely, until its fundamental security flaws can be addressed and it can operate with the same level of safety and accountability as traditional methods."

Their message was simple, powerful, and leveraged the fear and uncertainty the incidents had created: their industries might be polluters, they might be slow, but they were safe and accountable; TTC was neither. The implication was clear: return to the old ways, the 'secure' ways, before this unpredictable technology caused irreparable harm.

Adding a layer of chilling confirmation to Ren's suspicions, she continued receiving encrypted messages through the complex, untraceable dead-drop email system she had discovered weeks earlier. It wasn't email, not standard messaging. It was a series of encrypted packets appearing in obscure data caches online, accessible only via a tortuously complicated decryption process using rotating keys and anonymized servers – a method designed to be virtually impossible to trace back to the sender, requiring immense technical skill to implement and manage. Ren, with her deep knowledge of encryption and network security, recognized the sophistication. This wasn't a random hacker; this was someone who knew exactly what they were doing, someone operating with intent, high-level technical skill, and a personal connection to the unfolding events – a connection that felt increasingly tied to Bora.

The messages weren't threats or demands for money. They were taunts, observations, critiques, almost… artistic critiques of TTC's vulnerabilities and Ren's efforts, crafted with a cold, detached intelligence that was uniquely hers.

It was another late night for Ren in her private office within the secure complex, the only light coming from her encrypted terminal. Lines of seemingly random data fill the screen. She runs a decryption script she wrote herself. Text appears, stark and unsettling, each word chosen with precise intent, revealing a chillingly strategic mind at work.

Subject: The Fragility of Good Intentions.

"Aid is sentimental, Ren-san. A noble concept. Profit is concrete. Power is absolute. Your system moves both with equal efficiency. Pity its design does not adequately protect the ephemeral from the pragmatic. A shame about the medicine. Such delicate packaging. Did you truly believe sentimentality was a sufficient defense against those who understand the value of disruption? Perhaps a demonstration was required."

The signature on the messages was cloaked, bouncing through layers of anonymized proxies, impossible to trace directly. But the style, the cold, detached tone, the subtle allusions to design, to elegance in disruption, the knowing quality that hinted at an intimate understanding of TTC's internal struggles, technical details, and even Ren's personal motivations... it screamed one name: Bora. He was actively, intelligently, maliciously involved, orchestrating the campaign of chaos and disinformation from the shadows, using TTC's own technology as both a stage and a weapon against her.

The Red Pills weren't just cargo; they were weapons in an information war. The violence wasn't random; it was a consequence of the shipping cartels' new, untraceable supply lines disrupting existing criminal markets. The aid destruction wasn't senseless vandalism; it was calculated propaganda designed to generate specific, devastating images for the media, directly countering the positive images from Sichuan. The media frenzy wasn't independent reporting; it was an orchestrated campaign of disinformation. And at the center of it, pulling the strings, taunting her with chilling elegance through the digital ether, was Bora.

Lynn burst into Ren's office without knocking, her face pale. "We found our leak."

Ren looked up from Bora's latest message. "Who?"

"Marcus Chen, logistics coordinator in the Singapore hub. Financial forensics turned up cryptocurrency payments matching the timing of the compromised shipments."

Within an hour, Ren was on a secure video call with Marcus, who sat in a Singapore police station, his face drawn.

"Why?" Ren asked simply.

Marcus couldn't meet her eyes through the screen. "They threatened my family first. Then they offered money—more than I'd make in ten years. They knew things about our protocols, our schedules. They said they just wanted to move some packages, nothing harmful."

"Nothing harmful?" Ren's voice was ice. "Those drugs are destroying communities. That aid you helped them target was for dying children."

"I didn't know about the aid," Marcus whispered. "I swear, I thought—"

"You thought you could profit from betraying everything we built." Ren leaned forward. "Who contacted you? How?"

"I never met them. Everything was encrypted, anonymous. But..." Marcus hesitated. "They mentioned someone called 'the architect.' Said he understood systems better than their builders."

Ren's blood ran cold. Bora.

"You're going to tell the authorities everything," Ren said. "Every contact, every payment, every protocol you shared. And Marcus? We trusted you. I trusted you. That trust built this network. Your betrayal hasn't just hurt the company—it's hurt every person we could have helped."

After the call ended, Ren sat in silence before calling Lynn. "How many more?"

"We're investigating three other suspects. All recent hires, all with financial anomalies."

"Purge them. Prosecute them. Make it public that we found them ourselves and turned them over."

Back in the control room, the core team gathered, bone-tired, fueled by caffeine and determination. The screens show overlapping maps – the TTC network, overlaid with locations of suspicious shipments, areas of violence, and points where aid was destroyed. It's a grim picture of a network under attack. Ren stands at the main console, her face weary but resolute.

"They're hitting us everywhere," Bruce said, running a hand over his face, looking at the screens showing negative news reports and declining public sentiment metrics. "Media, politics, finance, even... even on the ground, physically destroying things we sent to help people. Making us look like we bring drugs and chaos. Using every angle."

"And using our own system to do it," Terri added, her voice weary, rubbing her temples, her gaze fixed on the diagnostics showing subtle network anomalies. "Exploiting its speed, its inherent trust in a validated manifest. Finding ways to bypass our detection, or at least, to act faster than we can react, it's like they're inside our heads, anticipating our moves. It suggests an intimate knowledge of our protocols and vulnerabilities."

Ren looked at them, her team. The brilliant, dedicated individuals who had helped her build the impossible. She saw their exhaustion, their fear, but also their unwavering resolve. They wouldn't give up. She wouldn't give up. Bora's taunts, her actions had clarified the enemy. They weren't just fighting a business rival; they were fighting a philosophy of control, a willingness to inflict chaos and suffering for power. They were fighting an intelligent, sophisticated adversary who understood that in the 21st century, the battle for reality was fought not just with physical force, but with information, perception, and leveraging the very technology they sought to control.

"They want to make the world afraid of us," Ren said, her voice calm despite the internal turmoil, the cold fury building within her. "They want to prove that traditional systems, for all their faults, are necessary because our technology is unpredictable and dangerous. They're using criminality and chaos to justify maintaining the old world order built on distance and delay."

She didn't mention Bora's messages explicitly to the full team yet, though she had shared aspects of the sophistication of the attacks with Terri and Lynn. That was her burden to carry, the knowledge that their adversary wasn't just a faceless corporation, but a brilliant, malicious individual who seemed to be enjoying the game, testing her limits, pushing her to respond. The quiet war had just turned terrifyingly personal, technically intricate, and morally abhorrent. The Red Pills had opened a dark new chapter, and Ren knew that to survive, they had to confront the source of the shadow campaign, not just the symptoms. The question was, how do you fight an enemy who can move in the shadows.

The video from Chief Vance arrived during the morning briefing. The team watched as armed figures set up what looked like a TTC MTU in the desert—yellow casing, similar dimensions, even bearing counterfeit TTC logos.

"That's one of ours?" Bruce asked, confused.

"No," Terri said, zooming in on the image. "Look at the panel configuration. It's wrong. The quantum stabilizer housing is just... decorative. This is a shell, a fake."

The video continued. The armed men placed explosive devices inside the fake MTU, then retreated. Minutes later, vehicles arrived—local law enforcement responding to an anonymous tip about illegal teleportation activity on tribal lands. As they approached the device, it detonated.

The room went silent. The explosion was massive, designed to kill.

"Three officers injured," Chief Vance's voice came through the speaker. "One critical. The media is already reporting it as a TTC equipment explosion."

"But it's not our equipment," Lynn protested.

"Doesn't matter," Vance replied grimly. "It looks like your equipment. Yellow casing, your logo. The photos are already circulating. 'TTC Unit Explodes, Officers Injured.'"

Ren studied the footage again. "This is Bora. He's not trying to copy our technology—he's creating fake units to stage attacks and blame us."

Terri pulled up inventory reports. "We've had seven MTU casings reported damaged beyond repair during shipping over the last six months. Standard procedure is to destroy them, but if someone intercepted them before disposal..."

"They could create convincing fakes," Lynn finished. "Plant them anywhere, fill them with explosives or contraband, and when they're discovered or detonated, we take the blame."

Another video file arrived from Vance. This one showed the aftermath—investigators finding drug packages scattered around the blast site, strategically placed to survive the explosion.

"They're framing this as a drug teleportation site that exploded," Vance explained. "The narrative writes itself—TTC equipment used for drug running, destroys itself and nearly kills cops."

"How many more fake units are out there?" Ren asked quietly.

"Based on the missing casings, they could have built at least six more," Terri calculated. "Empty shells that look like MTUs but are just containers for whatever horror they want to stage."

Lynn was already on her phone. "I'm alerting all our sites to document every real MTU with serial numbers, GPS tags, and live feeds. When the next fake appears, we need to prove immediately it's not ours."

"They won't care about proof," Ren said. "The image is what matters. Yellow casing, our logo, an explosion. That's what people will remember."

Terri pulled up a map, marking locations where casings had gone missing. "If I were Bora, I'd place the next fake somewhere with maximum media coverage. A major city, during a public event."

"Or multiple fakes at once," Ren added darkly. "Coordinated explosions, all blamed on malfunctioning TTC equipment. He doesn't need working teleportation. He just needs fear."

The screen showed news coverage already beginning—images of the fake MTU before the explosion, looking identical to their real units from a distance. The reporters were calling it a "teleportation disaster," questioning the safety of all TTC installations.

"He's weaponized our own image against us," Katya said from the speakers, watching the same feeds from St. John's. "Every yellow container is now a potential bomb in the public's mind."

"Then we change the game," Ren decided. "Lynn, I want legal action against anyone distributing these fakes. Terri, can we create a verification system? Something that proves definitively whether a unit is ours?"

"I can embed quantum signatures in our real casings that can be read by a simple scanner app," Terri suggested. "Make it publicly available. 'Verify Real TTC Equipment' or something."

"Do it. And Chief Vance?" Ren addressed the speaker. "Thank

you for the warning. Please send our condolences to the injured officers. We'll cover all medical expenses."

"Appreciated, but Ren—be careful. Whoever's doing this isn't just trying to destroy your business. They're trying to create actual casualties and blame you for them. This is terrorism using your brand as the weapon."

After the call ended, Ren turned to her team. "Bora's escalating. He's moved from corporate sabotage to actual terrorism, using our image as cover. Every fake MTU that explodes, every person hurt, will be blamed on us."

"We need to find these fakes before they're deployed," Lynn said.

"And we need to find Bora," Ren added coldly. "This ends now."

It was well past midnight when Terri knocked on Ren's apartment door within the complex. Ren answered, surprised to find Terri holding a tablet, her face flushed.

"We need to talk," Terri said. "About the photos."

Ren's expression didn't change, but her grip on the door tightened. "What photos?"

"Don't," Terri said softly. "I know you saw them. The backup system logs show you accessed that folder after I deleted it from the main server."

Ren stepped aside, letting Terri in. The apartment was sparse but comfortable, dominated by technical manuals and a wall of monitors showing various TTC operations.

"I didn't mean to invade your privacy," Ren began.

"But you kept them." It wasn't a question.

Ren moved to her desk, pulling up a secure folder on her personal system. Inside were the photos—Terri in various poses, intimate but artistic, clearly taken during a rare moment of personal freedom.

"I should have deleted them immediately," Ren admitted. "But I..." she paused, struggling with the words. "They showed a side of you I'd never seen. Confident in a different way. Beautiful."

Terri moved closer, studying Ren's face. "You've looked at them

142

since?"

"Yes."

"Often?"

"Yes."

Terri set down her tablet, then slowly reached up to unpin her hair, letting it fall loose around her shoulders. "The photos were from two years ago. A relationship that ended badly. I uploaded them by accident when transferring personal files to the new secure server."

"I know," Ren said quietly. "The metadata showed the date."

"Always the engineer," Terri said with a small smile. Then, more seriously, "But you're not just looking at them as data, are you?"

"No," Ren admitted. "I'm looking at them as... you. The you that exists outside of crisis management and quantum physics. The you that dances alone in her apartment, that takes photos by candlelight, that—"

Terri silenced her with a finger to her lips. "That you is right here, Ren. Has been for months. You just needed to see her."

She stepped back, unbuttoning her jacket slowly. "The photos were static. Past tense. But I'm here now. Present tense." She draped the jacket over a chair. "Would you like to see the current version? No camera needed."

Ren's breath caught. "Terri, we're in the middle of a crisis—"

"We're always in the middle of a crisis," Terri interrupted. "That's our life now. But this, us—this is real too. Maybe more real than anything else."

She moved to the window, moonlight outlining her silhouette. "In the photos, I was performing for someone else's gaze. Tonight, I'm just being. For you. With you."

Ren stood, moving toward her slowly. "I don't know how to do this. Balance the personal with everything else."

"Neither do I," Terri admitted, turning to face her. "But I know that when I kiss you in the lab, when I touch your hand during briefings, when I see you fighting for our vision—that's when I feel most alive. Most myself."

They stood inches apart now. Ren reached up, touching Terri's face gently. "The photos were beautiful. But this—you, here, real— is extraordinary."

Terri leaned into her touch. "Then stop looking at old photos and start making new memories."

Their lips met, soft at first, then with growing passion. Unlike the brief kiss in the lab, this was unhurried, deep, a conversation without words. When they finally pulled apart, both were breathing heavily.

"Stay," Ren whispered.

"There's nowhere else I want to be," Terri replied.

They moved to the couch, Terri curled against Ren's side, the tablet forgotten on the coffee table. For the first time in weeks, the monitors showing TTC operations weren't the focus of Ren's attention.

"The photos," Terri murmured against Ren's shoulder, "you can keep them if you want. But I'd rather give you new ones. Ones meant for you."

"I'd rather have you," Ren replied, pressing a kiss to her forehead. "Present tense. Future tense. All the tenses."

They stayed like that for hours, talking quietly about everything except the crisis—childhood memories, favorite books, dreams deferred. When dawn approached, neither had slept, but both felt more rested than they had in months.

"We should probably check the overnight reports," Terri said reluctantly.

"In a minute," Ren replied, holding her closer. "The world can wait one more minute."

8 THE GHOST IN THE MACHINE

The explosion at Rotterdam port lit up the pre-dawn darkness like a second sunrise.

Terri was already at her console when the emergency feeds came through. "Ren! We have a situation at Rotterdam MTU!"

The main display showed security footage: smoke billowing from the TTC facility, emergency vehicles racing toward the scene. The timestamp read 04:47 local time.

"Casualties?" Ren's voice was tight.

"Three TTC technicians injured, two port workers. The MTU itself..." Kenji pulled up structural diagnostics. "Significant damage to the receiving bay. Someone planted explosives timed to detonate during a major pharmaceutical shipment."

Lynn's phone buzzed. "Port authority says they found components matching Bora's fake MTU designs in the debris. He's not just bypassing our systems—he's actively destroying them."

Bruce looked pale. "The media will crucify us. They'll say we can't protect our own facilities."

"We need someone on the ground," Ren said. "Terri, can you—"

"Already packing," Terri interrupted, grabbing her field kit. "I'll take the next flight."

Ren caught her arm. "Be careful. If Bora's escalating to physical attacks—"

"I have to go." Terri's jaw set with determination. "You need this evidence."

Ren recognized the look—Terri taking unnecessary risks to prove herself, to protect what they'd built. "Promise me you won't do anything reckless."

Terri's smile didn't reach her eyes. "I promise I'll get what we need."

Six hours after Terri left for Rotterdam, Lynn had assembled a different kind of team in the secure conference room.

"We're going on offense," she announced to the small group of TTC's best security analysts. "Marcus here used to work for Interpol's cybercrime division. Sarah has contacts in shipping security across Europe. We're going to find where Bora's fake MTUs are being manufactured."

Marcus pulled up a map dotted with red markers. "These are facilities that have ordered the specific rare earth metals needed for MTU construction but aren't registered TTC suppliers. Cross-referencing with shell companies linked to legacy shipping interests..."

"There." Sarah pointed to a cluster near Hamburg. "Three purchases in the last month, all from companies registered in the past year."

Lynn nodded. "We infiltrate their systems tonight. Quietly. We need proof before we can move."

The night shift supervisor, a sharp young physicist named Kenji Tanaka, stood rigidly at his station, eyes wide with a mixture of disbelief, professional dread, and a hint of fear – a feeling echoed on the faces of the few technicians present. Alarms weren't blaring, the facility wasn't in lockdown, but the silence felt heavy, charged with unspoken questions and the oppressive weight of a system anomaly they couldn't explain.

"Dr. Franco, thank God," Tanaka said, his voice strained, cracking slightly as she approached. "We have… we have a Level 1 event. A major one. On a cargo transfer. It just completed."

Ren strode to the main display, the holographic map of the globe glowing ominously, a thick red line connected a node in Brazil

146

(specifically, an MTU facility near the port of Santos) to a node in the United States (the Miami Port MTU). But emanating from that red line, branching off midway over the Atlantic, was a thinner, pulsating amber line that arced toward... Turkey. Istanbul. The visual representation of the transfer stream was corrupted, split, leading to two unintended destinations, a single transfer violating the fundamental rule of one origin, one destination. It was impossible.

"Explain," Ren said, her voice tight, forcing calm despite the alarm screaming in her mind. Had a satellite malfunctioned? Was there a solar flare? Was this related to the interference they'd suspected with the drug shipments?

"Manifest ID BX7-USA9-0412," Tanaka reported, his fingers flying across his console, pulling up the raw data stream, the transfer logs, and the diagnostic readouts.

"Standard cargo manifest: twenty containers of manufactured goods, high-end electronics components, specifically computer processors and memory modules. Origin: Santos, Brazil. Destination: United States, Port of Miami MTU. Transfer initiated at 03:17 UTC. Quantum signature lock established, origin scan verified, energy expenditure initiated, spatial coordinates locked for Miami."

He swallowed hard, gesturing at the display.

"Nineteen containers... nineteen containers completed transfer successfully, validated arrival at Miami MTU, logs confirmed. All integrity checks passed. Perfect transfers. Standard procedure."

Ren's gaze snapped to the amber line leading to Istanbul. "And the twentieth?"

Tanaka hesitated, running a diagnostic again, as if hoping the data had changed in the last five minutes, that it was just a system error that could be reset, a misread sensor.

"That's... that's the anomaly, Doctor. The twentieth container. The primary data stream was routed normally toward Satellite Alpha for the Brazil-US transfer. But something happened during transit. Our system registered a severe divergence. The quantum signature for the twentieth container... it fractured."

He brought up a complex diagnostic overlay, zooming in on the transfer sequence for the twentieth container as it passed through the mid-point of its journey toward the orbital network. It showed the initial decoherence at the Brazilian origin – the container dissolving into a stream of quantum information and energy. Then, midway through the process, while the stream was propagating toward the designated satellite, a brief, almost imperceptible fluctuation in the stream – a fraction of a second where the signal became distorted, layered, as if overlaid with another signal, another instruction. The bulk of the stream continued its trajectory toward Satellite Alpha, eventually beaming down to Miami, consistent with the original manifest. But a smaller, significant portion of the container's quantum signature data had branched off, seemingly re-routed by a secondary, external coordinate injected into the stream, transmitting toward a different satellite entirely, one positioned over the Middle East (Satellite Beta or Gamma), before being beamed down to Istanbul.

"The data confirms partial arrival," Tanaka continued, looking physically ill, the scientific detachment breaking under the sheer impossibility of the event. "At the Miami MTU, our receiving diagnostics detected... fragments. Dispersed particles, residual energy signatures consistent with a small portion of the container materializing. Less than five percent by mass. Junk data. Useless debris." He gestured to the amber line ending in Istanbul. "And our system detected the remainder of the quantum signature data resolving... at the Istanbul MTU, seventy-two milliseconds later. The bulk of the container, intact, but at the wrong destination, with no record of the Istanbul destination in the original manifest or transfer command in our logs."

Silence descended over the control room, heavier than the North Atlantic night outside, broken only by the low, steady hum of the facility and the frantic beeping of diagnostic alerts on consoles confirming the anomaly, running system-wide checks.

"This isn't random," Ren said, staring at the data. "The precision required... wait." She pulled up her old university files. "Terri, look at this quantum signature pattern."

The waveform on screen matched one from fifteen years ago—a paper she'd co-authored with a brilliant but unstable colleague named Adrian Reeves.

"Adrian specialized in quantum interference patterns," Ren's voice was hollow. "He always said teleportation could be weaponized if you could insert noise at the right frequency. I thought it was theoretical."

"Where is he now?" Terri asked.

Kenji was already searching. "Dr. Adrian Reeves... left academia eight years ago. Current employer..." He paled. "Europort Logistics. One of Bora's shell companies."

Ren felt sick. "He's using my own research partner against me."

This was a terrifying escalation, a stark contrast to the drug shipments. The drug shipments, while criminal and damaging to their reputation, were an exploitation of the use of the network, leveraging its speed and discretion after the transfer was complete. The split shipment was an attack on the functionality of the network itself, on the very act of teleportation. It demonstrated that the system, the supposedly infallible system built on the bedrock of quantum physics, was vulnerable to external manipulation at its core. Who would trust their critical supplies, their sensitive data, or potentially even themselves (if the Life division ever went public), to a system that could misdirect or fragment cargo? The integrity of every future shipment, the perceived reliability of the technology itself, was implicitly questioned by this one, horrifying event. It struck at the heart of TTC's value proposition: guaranteed, instantaneous delivery. It fueled every fear the cartels were propagating.

The office team threw themselves into the investigation with a renewed sense of urgency and dread. While Ren, working closely with Terri and her team, focused on the technical puzzle, the other executives grappled with the immediate, messy fallout.

In Miami, the consignee of the split shipment, a major electronics distributor, was livid. Their CEO paced his office, shouting into his phone.

"Fragments? What do you mean fragments? I paid for a complete shipment, delivered instantly. Not some high-tech jigsaw puzzle!" He slammed his fist into his desk. "I want a full investigation. Every piece accounted for. And you can expect our legal team to be in touch."

Across the Atlantic, in Istanbul, confusion reigned. Customs officials stared at the unexpected container, checking and rechecking manifests.

Zeynep Koçak, the port director, rubbed her temples. "It just...appeared? Out of thin air? That's not possible." She turned to her assistant. "Get TTC on the line. I want an explanation. And contact the Ministry of Trade. They need to be aware of this...anomaly."

In the global media, the story exploded. News anchors delivered breathless reports, their tone a mix of fascination and fear.

"In an unprecedented event, a TeleTransport Container shipment from Brazil to the United States appears to have been...split in transit, with the majority of the cargo materializing in Istanbul, Turkey, thousands of miles off course. Experts are baffled, and concerns are mounting about the stability and security of TTC's quantum teleportation network."

On social media, speculation ran rampant. Conspiracy theories flourished, and TTC's competitors seized the opportunity to sow doubt.

@SecureShip: "This is what happens when you trust unproven tech. Stick with reliable, traditional shipping. #TTCfail #SplitShipmentScandal"

In the financial world, the reaction was swift and brutal. Katya found herself in a tense video call with a group of grim-faced bankers.

"Ms. Volkov, in light of recent events, we have concerns about TTC's technical stability. We're reviewing our credit arrangements and considering our options."

Katya fought to keep her composure. "This is an isolated incident. We're investigating fully and..."

The lead banker cut her off. "Investigate quickly, Ms. Volkov. Time is money, and right now, your company is looking like a very risky investment."

After the call, Katya slumped in her chair, exhaustion and worry etched on her face. A soft knock on her door made her look up. Terri stood there, two steaming mugs in hand.

"Thought you could use a pick-me-up," Terri said, offering a mug to Katya. "It's been a hell of a day."

Katya accepted the mug gratefully, inhaling the rich aroma of coffee. "That's an understatement. The banks are circling like sharks. They smell blood in the water."

Terri sat down across from Katya. "We'll figure this out, Katya. Ren and I, the whole technical team, we're working around the clock. We'll find the cause and fix it."

Katya sighed. "I know you will. But can we do it before the financial rug gets pulled out from under us? Every minute counts."

Terri reached across the desk, squeezing Katya's hand. "We won't let that happen. TTC is more than a company. It's a vision. A better future. We'll fight for that."

Katya managed a tired smile. "Thanks, Terri. For the coffee and the pep talk. I needed both."

Terri grinned. "Anytime. We're in this together. All of us."

In a tense meeting room, Ren stood before her exhausted but determined team. The wall screens were filled with data readouts, anomaly reports, and network diagrams.

"We're dealing with an adversary of unprecedented sophistication," Ren began, her voice steady despite the strain. "They've demonstrated the ability to manipulate our quantum streams in a way we thought impossible. Our task now is to understand how and why."

She gestured to the screens. "We're setting up new monitoring protocols on every node and satellite. Any anomaly, no matter how small, gets flagged and analyzed."

Dr. Sharpa nodded. "We're looking for patterns, any consistencies in the interference. If we can characterize the method, we can develop countermeasures."

Terri spoke up. "I'm running simulations on potential attack vectors. Quantum level intrusions, exotic physics, anything that could explain the precision and subtlety of the manipulation."

Ren met Terri's eyes, a flicker of gratitude and something deeper passing between them. "Good. We leave no theoretical stone unturned. This is a puzzle, and we will solve it."

She turned back to the group. "Bruce, I need you to handle the PR front. Emphasize our commitment to understanding and resolving this issue. Transparency and confidence."

Bruce nodded, his usual charm replaced by grim determination.

"Katya, keep the financial wolves at bay. Reassure our partners, but be honest about the gravity of the situation."

Katya's jaw tightened, but she nodded.

"Lynn, prepare for legal battles. Coordinate with the technical team. We need to be ready to defend our systems and our actions."

Lynn's eyes glinted with steely resolve.

Ren surveyed her team, pride and worry warring in her chest. "We're in uncharted territory. But if anyone can navigate this, it's us. Let's get to work."

Ren, Terri, Dr. Sharpa, and Kenji Tanaka are hunched over screens, analyzing the data from the split shipment. The room is filled with complex equations, waveform displays, and holographic models of the transfer stream. They are looking for the fingerprint of the intruder.

"The energy signature of the interference was incredibly weak, Ren," Dr. Sharpa explained, pointing to a complex waveform on a screen, zooming in on the almost imperceptible blip in the data stream. "Almost below our detection threshold for anomalous energy spikes. It was like a whisper in a hurricane of energy. But it was precise. Timed perfectly to coincide with the transition phase of that specific container's data stream as it propagated toward the satellite. It wasn't random noise; it was targeted."

"Remember that first quantum entanglement test?" Terri said, breaking the tense silence. "When the power grid failed mid-experiment?"

A ghost of a smile touches Ren's lips. "And we had to recalculate everything by hand, using that ridiculous red flashlight of yours."

"Hey, Mr. Blinky saved the day."

"Mr. Blinky?"

"That's what I named the flashlight. He has many uses." Terri admits with a self-deprecating smile.

Ren's laugh is brief but genuine. "I never knew that."

"Some things are too embarrassing to share."

"Not anymore, apparently."

Terri added, "It's like they didn't inject a virus, but used a precise, undetectable force field to subtly nudge the quantum state, influencing the destination encoding process. We're looking at exotic physics possibilities. Maybe manipulating the zero-point energy field locally? Or resonant frequency interference?"

Ren stared at the data, her mind processing the implications, comparing it to what they knew about the adversary. "Precise timing, minimal energy signature... suggests a deep understanding of our internal architecture. Not just brute force interference, but leveraging existing pathways or vulnerabilities we didn't know we had. Or... using a method of manipulating quantum states we haven't considered possible for an external entity. Someone who knows our system intimately. Someone who might have had access or deep knowledge."

Terri leans over Ren's shoulder to point at something on the screen, her breath warm against Ren's ear. "Look at this energy signature. It's almost like..."

"A fingerprint," Ren finishes, acutely aware of Terri's proximity, the subtle scent of everything Terri. Neither moves away, the closeness feeling both natural and charged.

"Exactly," Terri said, her voice dropping slightly. "Unique to whoever did this."

When she finally straightens up, Ren feels the absence of her warmth like a physical thing.

Her thoughts immediately went to Bora and his connection to the legacy industries. Could he possess this kind of technical understanding or have access to those who did? The possibility was chilling.

"Could they have used the data from the source scan?" Ren mused aloud, thinking of the initial scan bypasses for the drug shipments. "If they could somehow intercept or analyze the quantum signature data during the source scan, could they use that information to predict the stream structure during propagation and target it?"

"The source scan data is encrypted and transmitted immediately," Terri countered. "Intercepting and decrypting it in real-time would require breaking our quantum encryption, which is theoretically impossible with current computational power." She paused, a flicker of doubt crossing her face. "Unless... their method of interference is a way to circumvent quantum encryption itself. An entirely new form of information access."

The ghost in the machine. An adversary who could violate the fundamental rules of their engineered reality. An adversary who seemed to be escalating their attacks from exploitation to direct technical sabotage.

Late at night in the lab Ren walked in to join Terri.

"I keep thinking about all those people who depend on us," Ren said quietly, her usual composure slipping. "If we can't solve this..."

Terri moved closer, her voice gentle. "You don't have to carry this alone, Ren. That's why we're here—why I'm here."

"But I designed it. The system, the network... if it fails, that's on me."

"No," Terri said firmly, surprising them both with her intensity. "That's on us. Your vision, my implementation. We built this together." She hesitated, then added, "And we'll fix it together."

Ren looks up, the rare vulnerability in her eyes making her seem younger, more human. "Promise?"

"Promise."

"What if we can't stop them?" Ren asked, the question she wouldn't dare voice to anyone else. "What if they take everything we've built?"

Terri sits beside her, close enough that their shoulders touch. "Then we start again. Together."

"It took years, Terri. Everything I had—"

"Everything we had," Terri corrects gently. "And yes, it would be devastating. But your mind, your vision—those can't be taken. As long as we have those, we can rebuild."

Ren looks at her, really looks at her. "How do you always know what to say?"

"I don't," Terri admits. "I just know you."

Ren stepped away from the console for a moment, walking to the large window overlooking the stormy ocean, trying to clear her head. The technical mystery was overwhelming, but the practical consequences were immediate and severe.

Bruce entered the lab, looking stressed, his usual energy subdued. "Twenty containers of electronics components. High-value. Destined for a major distributor in Miami. Nineteen arrived perfectly. One... mostly didn't, and the rest ended up across the world in Istanbul. The consignee is... understandably furious, threatening lawsuits that could cripple us."

Bruce launches into another anxious scenario about public reaction. Ren catches Terri's eye across the table. A slight raise of her eyebrow, the barest tilt of her head.

Terri nods almost imperceptibly and smoothly interrupts. "Bruce, we need to focus on the technical solution first. The PR strategy depends on what we discover."

"Exactly," Ren said, the word carrying a weight of gratitude only Terri would recognize.

Later, Terri explains to Lynn: "She needed the conversation redirected. Bruce's anxiety was making it harder for her to think."

He ran a hand through his hair. "The authorities in Istanbul are confused, to say the least, by a partial container of electronics materializing at their MTU with no manifest. The authorities in Miami are demanding explanations for the fragments. The media… it's a feeding frenzy. They're saying the technology is fundamentally unstable, that this proves it can't be trusted with valuable cargo, let alone anything critical. Or… or people."

Katya joined them, her face drawn, having just finished a difficult call. "The financial pressure is mounting exponentially, Ren. Banks are citing 'unforeseen technical risks' and 'asset instability.' This incident gives the cartels' allies in the financial sector all the justification they need to make our lives impossible. Credit lines are being reviewed, transactions are being stalled. They're leveraging this to strangle us financially." She sat down heavily on a stool, looking exhausted.

Lynn arrived, holding a stack of legal documents. "The lawsuits have started. Breach of contract, negligence, technological failure. And regulatory bodies worldwide are requesting detailed reports, questioning the safety and reliability of the system. The Secure Ports Act proponents are using this as definitive proof that we are too risky to operate inland. This single incident undermines months of work building trust."

Ren listened, feeling the weight of it all. The technical mystery was overwhelming, but the practical consequences were immediate and severe. Their adversary had found a way to inflict maximum damage with a single, targeted attack, striking at the heart of their credibility and reliability.

Terri returned to Ren's side, her gaze meeting Ren's again, a silent offer of support passing between them. "We need to understand how they did this, Ren," she said, her voice low and urgent. "Not just to fix it, but to identify who is capable of this. This is beyond anything we've seen. It might point to the 'ghost's' true nature, or the capabilities of the network Bora might control."

Ren nodded, turning from the window, her focus hardening, the weariness replaced by resolve. "Then we find the signature. We find the vulnerability they exploited. If it's based on physics, we can understand it. If it's based on our architecture, we can find the backdoor." She looked at her team, gathered in the lab, exhausted but determined. "We track every anomaly in every transfer stream from that window. We look for any correlation, any pattern, any subtle deviation that doesn't fit. We throw every processing cycle we have at simulating potential interference methods. If someone can manipulate quantum states in transit, we need to know how, and we need to find a way to detect it in real-time."

In the depths of the TTC labs, Ren, Terri, and Dr. Sharpa huddled around a console, eyes strained from hours staring at screens. The room was a chaos of equations, diagrams, and flickering data streams.

"It's like trying to catch smoke," Terri muttered, frustration evident in her voice. "Every time we think we've found the interference signature, it slips away."

Dr. Sharpa rubbed his chin thoughtfully. "It's almost as if it's adapting to our detection methods. Evolving."

Ren's brow furrowed. "Or perhaps we're looking at it wrong. What if it's not a brute force intrusion, but something more subtle? A manipulation of the underlying quantum states?"

Terri's eyes widened. "Like a resonance effect? Inducing changes in the stream without direct interference?"

Ren nodded, excitement kindling in her eyes. "Precisely. It would explain the difficulty in detection. We need to adjust our models, look for ripple effects rather than direct tampering."

Dr. Sharpa was already typing, adjusting the simulation parameters. "On it. If we can identify the resonance pattern, we might be able to trace it back to the source."

As they worked, a thought nagged at the back of Ren's mind. The precision, the adaptability, the deep understanding of their systems required for such an attack... It suggested an intimate familiarity with TTC's technology. An insider's knowledge.

She glanced at Terri, seeing the same troubled realization in her eyes. They had always known their technology would be a target. But this felt different. Personal. As if the attacker knew them, knew their work, their minds.

A chill ran down Ren's spine. They were hunting a ghost in the machine. But perhaps the most troubling question was not how the ghost was attacking them, but why. And what it wanted.

In the quiet hours of the night, the TTC headquarters took on a different character. The bustle of the day gave way to the hum of servers and the soft glow of screens. In a dimly lit lab, Ren and Terri sat side by side, nursing cups of long-cold coffee, eyes fixed on the data streams before them.

"It's personal, isn't it?" Terri said softly, breaking the companionable silence. "This attack. It feels targeted. Not just at TTC, but at you."

Ren sighed, leaning back in her chair. "I can't help but feel that way. The precision, the timing. As if they know how I think, how I work."

Terri reached over, placing a hand on Ren's arm. A simple gesture, but one filled with understanding and support. "You're not in this alone, Ren. We're all behind you. I'm behind you."

Ren covered Terri's hand with her own, a rare moment of vulnerability. "I know. And I'm grateful. More than I can say." She paused, gathering her thoughts. "But I also know the weight of responsibility. If we can't stop this, if we can't protect the integrity of the network..."

"We will," Terri said firmly, her grip tightening. "We will find a way. Because what we've built here, what you've built, it's too important to let someone tear it down."

Ren met Terri's eyes, seeing the fierce determination there. The unshakable belief. In TTC. In their work. In her. It was a lifeline in the chaos, a beacon in the uncertainty.

She let herself lean into that support, just for a moment. Let herself feel the warmth of Terri's touch, the steadiness of her presence. In the face of an enemy they couldn't see, a threat they couldn't yet fully comprehend, these moments of human connection were more precious than ever.

"Thank you," Ren whispered, the words inadequate but

heartfelt.

Terri smiled softly. "Anytime. Now, let's find this ghost and show them what happens when they mess with the best minds in the business."

Ren returned the smile, renewed determination settling over her. They had a long fight ahead. But they would face it together.

In the control room, a new sense of purpose took hold as the team implemented their anomaly tracking protocols. Every screen displayed a different facet of the global network, each data point a potential clue.

Lina, the young technician who had first spotted the energy blip, called out from her station. "I've got something. A series of micro-fluctuations in the quantum coherence of several streams. They're small, barely detectable, but they form a pattern."

Ren and Terri hurried over, studying the readouts. Sure enough, there was a consistency to the fluctuations. A rhythm almost, a subtle pulsing that didn't match the normal flow of data.

"Can we isolate the affected streams?" Ren asked, mind racing.

Lina's fingers flew over her keyboard. "Working on it. They're spread out, different origins and destinations. But..." Her eyes widened. "They all passed through the same satellite node. Satellite Gamma, over the Indian Ocean."

Terri frowned. "That's one of our oldest satellites. Due for an upgrade next quarter."

Ren's eyes narrowed. "Or perhaps it's been compromised. The adversary exploiting a weakness in the older hardware?"

Dr. Sharpa spoke up from his station. "I'm not seeing any signs of physical tampering or unauthorized access to Satellite Gamma's systems. But the quantum signature of these anomalies... It's similar to the split shipment. A resonance pattern."

Ren felt a mix of excitement and dread. A lead, but one that confirmed the scale and sophistication of their enemy. "Dig deeper. I want every byte of data from Satellite Gamma analyzed. If there's a vulnerability, we need to find it."

As the team worked, a chilling thought crept into Ren's mind. They were making progress, but it was reactive. Catching glimpses of their adversary's handiwork after the fact. To truly counter this threat, they needed to get ahead of it. Anticipate the next move.

But how did you predict the actions of a ghost? Especially one that seemed to know your every step before you took it?

In the data lab, Ren and Terri pored over the anomaly readouts, searching for the elusive pattern that could crack the case. Dr. Sharpa joined them, his brow furrowed in concentration.

"There," he said suddenly, pointing to a series of spikes on the screen. "Those micro-fluctuations in the quantum coherence. They're not random. There's a periodicity to them."

Terri leaned in, studying the data. "You're right. It's subtle, but it's there. A recurring signature, hidden in the noise."

Ren's mind raced. "A signature. Like a fingerprint. If we can isolate it, match it to known patterns..."

"We might be able to trace it back to the source," Terri finished, excitement building in her voice.

They set to work, refining their algorithms, filtering out the background noise. Slowly, a picture began to emerge. A distinct waveform, repeating across multiple anomalies.

Dr. Sharpa sat back, a look of realization on his face. "This pattern, the way it's interacting with our quantum streams... It's not just interference. It's manipulation."

Ren's eyes widened. "Manipulation? You mean..."

"The adversary isn't just disrupting our streams. They're controlling them. Steering them." Dr. Sharpa's voice was grave. "This is beyond anything we've seen. The level of precision, the ability to influence quantum states..."

A chill settled over the room. The implications were staggering. An adversary with the power to control their network, to bend the very fabric of their teleportation system to their will.

Terri broke the silence. "But who has that kind of capability? A rival company? A government?"

Ren shook her head. "I don't know. But whoever they are, they're not just technologically advanced. They're strategically smart. Targeting our weaknesses, exploiting our blind spots."

Dr. Sharpa frowned. "Could it be a group? A collaboration between multiple entities?"

"Or a single mastermind," Terri countered. "Someone with the resources and the brilliance to pull this off alone."

Ren's thoughts turned inward. A single mastermind. Someone

brilliant, resourceful, and ruthless. Someone who knew TTC inside and out. The specter of Bora rose in her mind again, but she pushed it aside. She needed proof, not suspicions.

"We need to keep digging," she said finally. "Analyze this signature from every angle. Trace every lead. We're close, I can feel it. Close to unmasking our ghost."

The team nodded, a new sense of purpose taking hold. They had a trail now, a glimmer of insight into their adversary. It was a start.

Alone in her office, Ren stared at the data readouts, her mind turning over the implications of the latest findings. The subtle patterns, the exploitation of older systems. It spoke to an adversary with intimate knowledge of TTC's infrastructure.

She pulled up the personnel files, scrolling through the faces of her team. People she trusted, people she had worked with for years. The idea that one of them could be involved, could be working against them, made her stomach turn.

But she couldn't ignore the possibility. The attacks were too precise, too tailored to their specific vulnerabilities. She needed to consider every angle, no matter how painful.

Her gaze lingered on one face in particular. Bora. The brilliant engineer who had been with her from the start, who had helped build TTC from the ground up. But also the man who had left under a cloud, who had made no secret of his disagreement with the direction of the company.

Could he be involved? Using his knowledge against them? The thought made Ren's heart ache. She had trusted him, valued his insights. The idea of that trust being betrayed...

She shook her head. She couldn't jump to conclusions. But she couldn't ignore the possibility either. She made a note to dig deeper into Bora's recent activities. If there was a connection, she needed to know.

A knock at her door startled her out of her thoughts. Terri poked her head in, concern etched on her face.

"Everything okay? You look like you've seen a ghost."

Ren managed a tight smile. "Just considering all the angles. Including some I'd rather not."

Terri stepped into the office, closing the door behind her. "The inside job theory?"

Ren nodded. "I hate to think it, but it's something we must consider."

Terri sighed, sinking into a chair. "I know. It's a bitter pill. But if it's true, we need to know. We can't fight an enemy in our own ranks."

Ren met Terri's gaze, seeing the same mix of determination and worry in her own. A silent understanding passed between them. They were in this together, no matter where the truth led.

Ren sat in her darkened office, the only light coming from the glow of her computer screen. Data readouts and anomaly reports scrolled by, but she barely saw them. Her mind was elsewhere, lost in the weight of responsibility and the gnawing fear of failure.

She had always prided herself on her strength, her ability to shoulder any burden. But this... This felt different. The stakes were higher than ever. Not just the fate of TTC, but the trust of the entire world in the promise of quantum teleportation.

If she failed, if she couldn't stop this adversary, it wouldn't just be the end of her company. It would be the end of a dream, a vision of a better future.

A soft knock at the door broke her spiraling thoughts. Terri stood in the doorway, two steaming mugs in hand.

"Thought you could use a pick-me-up," she said softly, setting one of the mugs in front of Ren. "You've been here all night."

Ren managed a tired smile. "Thanks. Sleep seems like a luxury these days."

Terri settled into the chair across from Ren, her eyes filled with understanding. "You're carrying a heavy load, Ren. But you don't have to carry it alone."

Ren sighed, wrapping her hands around the warm mug. "I know. But it's hard not to feel isolated. Like the whole world is watching, waiting for me to fail."

Terri reached across the desk, covering Ren's hand with her own. "The world is watching, yes. But not waiting for you to fail. They're hoping for you to succeed. We all are."

Ren met Terri's gaze, seeing the unwavering support there. The belief in her, in their mission. It was a lifeline in the darkness, a reminder that she wasn't alone.

"I don't know what I'd do without you, Terri," she said softly, the words heavy with unspoken emotion. "You've been my rock through all of this."

Terri smiled, her thumb brushing gently over Ren's knuckles. "And I always will be. We're in this together, Ren. No matter what comes."

For a moment, the world fell away. The crisis, the adversary, the weight of responsibility. All that existed was this connection, this moment of understanding and comfort.

Ren let herself lean into it, drawing strength from Terri's presence. Tomorrow, they would dive back into the fight. They'd chase down leads, unravel mysteries, and face whatever challenges their ghost threw at them.

But tonight, in the quiet of her office, with Terri's hand in hers, Ren allowed herself a moment of serenity. A moment to just breathe, to remember what she was fighting for. Not just a company, but a connection. A bond forged in the crucible of crisis, but one that would endure long after the battle was won.

With Terri by her side, Ren knew she could face anything. Even a ghost in the machine.

Lynn's team struck digital gold.

"We're in," Marcus announced in a sarcastic hacker voice. "The Hamburg facility is producing fake MTUs—they look identical to ours but are rigged with explosives. They're planning simultaneous attacks on five major ports next week."

"Can we stop them?" Ren asked.

"Better. We can turn their own weapon against them." Sarah pulled up shipping manifests. "They're using our logistics protocols to hide the fake units. But if we alter the delivery coordinates..."

"We can have them all delivered to a single, controlled location," Lynn finished. "Let the authorities find their entire arsenal."

Ren made the call. "Do it. And leak just enough information to make Bora panic. Force him to make a mistake."

As her team worked, Ren's phone buzzed. A text from the Rotterdam team: "Found something in the debris. Adrian Reeves' fingerprints, literally. He was here supervising. We have him."

The ghost had a face. The attacks had evidence. And somewhere in Rotterdam, medicated and brave, the woman Ren loved had just given them their first real victory.

The war with Bora was escalating, but for the first time, TTC was fighting back.

A small explosion at the TTC campus perimeter sent everyone scrambling. Terri had been examining suspicious equipment near the delivery gate when the device detonated.

In the medical bay, as Dr. Patel cleaned her cuts, the pain medication loosened Terri's usual control.

"Just debris cuts," Dr. Patel assured Ren, who'd rushed in moments after the blast. "The medication will make her a bit loopy for the next hour."

Ren pulled a chair close to Terri's bed. "What were you thinking, going out there alone?"

"Had to check." Terri's words were slightly slurred. "The delivery manifest didn't match. Fake MTU components. Got photos before it..." She gestured vaguely at her bandaged arm.

"You could have waited for security—"

"Ren." Terri's eyes were unfocused but intense. "When that blast knocked me down... all I could think was that I never told you. Never showed you."

"Terri, you're medicated—"

"I want to kiss you until neither of us can breathe. Want to trace every line of your body with my hands, my mouth. Want to make you forget everything but my name." The medication had stripped away her filters. "God, Ren, I dream about you. About us. About finally—"

"Terri." Ren's voice was rough. "Tell me when you're not on painkillers. When you can remember saying it."

Terri smiled drowsily, reaching for Ren's hand. "I'll remember. And I'll still mean it. The way you look at me when you think I'm not watching... you feel it too."

Dr. Patel returned with discharge papers. "She'll be fine by morning. Someone should stay with her tonight, though."

"I will," Ren said immediately.

As Terri drifted into medicated sleep, still holding Ren's hand, her phone buzzed with a message from Lynn: "We found Adrian

Reeves in the security footage. He planted the device himself. We have him."

The ghost had a face. The woman she was falling for had just risked everything for evidence. And somewhere in Hamburg, their enemy was about to discover that TTC was no longer playing defense.

9 ICE AND INTROSPECTION

The control room in St. John's no longer felt like the command center of a revolutionary company. It felt like a bunker—the last defensive position of a besieged army. Ren stood before the main display, shoulders rigid as she studied the latest attack metrics, the harsh blue light casting deep shadows across her face. Her eyes burned from hours of staring at scrolling data, each line representing another potential vulnerability in their system. The room hummed with the sound of cooling fans and nervous energy as technicians worked feverishly at their stations.

"Another hit piece," Bruce said, flicking a news headline onto the shared screen with a gesture that betrayed his frustration. The article splashed across the display in bold, accusatory text. "This one's claiming our network was designed specifically to enable drug trafficking. They're getting more creative with their smear campaign."

Lynn snorted without looking up from her legal briefs, papers scattered around her in organized chaos. "Because traditional shipping methods have been so effective at preventing that," she remarked sarcastically, adjusting her reading glasses. "Apparently creating an efficient, transparent logistics system is now equivalent to running a cartel."

The tension in the room was palpable, hanging heavy like an invisible fog. Everyone moved with the cautious efficiency of people who hadn't properly slept in days. Coffee cups littered workstations, and the recycling bin overflowed with energy drink cans.

Bruce's phone buzzed with an encrypted message. He glanced at it, and his face went pale, the color draining as if someone had opened a valve. "We need to talk. Privately. Now." His voice carried an urgency that cut through the ambient noise.

In the secure conference room, a windowless box lined with signal-blocking mesh, Bruce pulled up security footage on his tablet. The timestamp showed 3:00 AM, three days prior. "Someone accessed our emergency evacuation protocols. The yacht contingency, safe house locations, transportation routes, security rotations—everything."

"Who?" Ren's voice was sharp enough to cut glass.

"The access came from Marcus Chen's terminal in logistics. But Marcus has been on medical leave for two weeks—burst appendix." Bruce's jaw tightened visibly. "Someone cloned his credentials."

"Wait," Terri said, pulling up her tablet with sudden urgency. "If they cloned Marcus's credentials three days ago, they've had access to our internal systems since then." Her fingers flew across the screen, lines of code reflecting in her glasses. "I can track every query from his account."

"What did they access?" Ren asked, moving to look over Terri's shoulder, close enough to feel the tension radiating from her.

"Personnel files, home addresses, security protocols..." Terri's face paled as she scrolled through the access logs. "And our MTU deployment schedules. They know exactly which units are operational and which are still being installed. They can see our entire expansion timeline."

"Could they compromise the MTUs?" Katya asked, her usually calm voice tight with concern.

"No," Ren said firmly, though her mind was racing through possibilities. "The quantum encryption is hardcoded at the hardware level. Each unit's quantum signature is unique and uncloneable. But they know our expansion timeline, where we're vulnerable, which routes are fully operational versus still in testing."

Bruce's phone buzzed again. He read the message, his expression darkening further. "Security just found something.

Marcus's keycard was used to enter the building at 1:33 this morning. Forty minutes before the fire alarm at the residential complex."

"Someone's still using it," Lynn said, her legal mind immediately grasping the implications. "They're inside. Right now."

"Lockdown," Ren ordered, her voice cutting through the rising panic. "No one in or out until security sweeps every floor. Seal the MTU chambers first—if they're trying to physically access the units—"

Terri's screen flashed red, an urgent alert overriding her investigation. "Too late. Marcus's credentials just accessed the executive elevator. Someone's coming up. They'll be here in thirty seconds."

Bruce moved toward the door, hand reaching for his concealed weapon. "Sarah's team is three minutes out. Everyone stay calm."

The elevator chimed, a sound that seemed to echo in the sudden silence. Everyone tensed, unconsciously moving away from the door.

The doors opened to reveal Dr. James Harrison from the logistics department, his hands raised, holding a USB drive. His face was haggard, sweat beading on his forehead despite the cool temperature. "Please don't shoot. I need to talk to Ren. They made me do it. They have my son."

"Stay where you are," Bruce commanded, weapon drawn but pointed at the floor.

"They said they'd kill him if I didn't help," Harrison continued, his voice breaking. "They needed inside information—shipping schedules, MTU locations, security protocols. I'm sorry. I'm so sorry. But this," he held up the USB drive, "this is everything I gave them. And more. Evidence of who they are, what they're planning."

"Put it down slowly," Bruce instructed. "Kick it over here."

Harrison complied, the drive skittering across the polished floor. "My son—"

"We'll help," Ren said, though she kept her distance. "But you're going into custody. Terri, sandbox that drive. Maximum isolation protocols."

"Already on it," Terri said, using a completely isolated laptop to examine the drive's contents. "It's... wait. This is tracking malware.

Sophisticated, but definitely malicious."

Harrison's face crumbled. "No, they said... they promised..."

"Your son isn't kidnapped, is he?" Lynn asked, her voice cold as she pulled up information on her phone. "He's in Monaco. Enrolled at the International School. Tuition paid by accounts linked to Westport Allied Shipping."

The man's shoulders slumped in defeat. "They said you'd destroy the shipping industry. That millions would lose their jobs. They offered to secure my son's future, pay for his education, set us up for life. I just had to provide some information..."

"You betrayed us for money?" Katya's voice held a rare note of anger.

"I thought I was protecting the future," Harrison said weakly. "They made it sound like you were the threat."

Security arrived then, Sarah's team moving with military precision to secure Harrison. As they led him away, Ren turned to her core team.

"We need distance," Bruce announced without preamble, pushing himself away from his console. His usually immaculate appearance showed signs of strain—his collar unbuttoned, sleeves rolled unevenly. "Perspective. We're making mistakes because we're exhausted."

"Perspective?" Ren's voice was sharp, cutting through the ambient noise. She turned from the display, arms crossed defensively. "While our enemies are actively sabotaging our network? While they're dismantling everything we've built?"

"Especially then," Bruce countered, meeting her gaze with unexpected firmness. "We're reacting, not strategizing. We're playing their game by their rules. And now we know we've been compromised from the inside. We need to regroup somewhere secure."

The alarm cut through Bruce's next words, a piercing wail that instantly transformed the room's atmosphere from tense to electric. Lynn's phone buzzed simultaneously with Katya's, the discordant tones merging with the alarm. Then Terri's terminal lit up with urgent notifications, bathing her face in pulsing red light.

"Fire at the St. John's residential complex," Lynn read, her face going pale as she scrolled through the message. "Three TTC employee apartments. Everyone's okay, but the damage is extensive. Fire department says it was deliberate—accelerants used."

"My neighbor just texted," Terri interrupted, swiveling in her chair and showing her screen to the group. Her normally steady hands trembled slightly. "Someone spray-painted 'TRAITORS' on my building's lobby. Security footage shows masked individuals. They came at 3 AM when the night guard was doing rounds."

Katya stood abruptly, knocking her chair backward. "I need to call my daughter. If they know where we live—" Her voice caught, fear replacing her usual composed demeanor.

"They're escalating," Ren said flatly, the implications settling on her shoulders like a physical weight. "From digital attacks to physical intimidation. They accessed our evacuation protocols, knew we'd run, and they're making sure we do. Driving us toward their trap."

Bruce nodded grimly. "The yacht's still our best option. At least there, we control the environment to some degree. But we need to be smart about it."

"How do we know the yacht is secure?" Lynn demanded, gathering her papers with controlled urgency. "If they have our evacuation protocols—"

"Because I registered it through seven shell companies," Bruce said quietly. "But you're right. If they have our protocols, they know about it. We'll have to assume we're compromised and adapt."

"Then why go?" Terri asked.

"Because we'll change the game," Ren said suddenly, her strategic mind clicking into gear. "Bruce, tell me you have contingencies."

Bruce smiled grimly, pulling up his tablet. "Three vessels, all departing within hours of each other. The Meridian leaves from Boston in two hours, registered to a shell company that could be ours. The Northern Star departs Montreal tonight—similar profile, similar route. Both have security teams that, from a distance, could be mistaken for us."

"And we take the third option," Ren said, understanding the strategy immediately.

"The Arctic Endeavor. Halifax. Least obvious port, oldest vessel, but the most capable in ice." Bruce's fingers flew across his tablet, coordinating the deception. "Let them chase ghosts while we disappear."

"My security chief, Sarah, is already implementing the shell game," Bruce continued. "Three identical vehicle convoys will leave headquarters at staggered intervals. Each taking different routes."

Sarah's voice came through Bruce's encrypted phone, her Israeli accent clipped and professional. "Decoy one is mobile. Silver sedan convoy heading to Boston. Decoy two preparing for Montreal flight. Decoy three—that's us—will take a circuitous route to Halifax."

"What about digital traces?" Terri asked, already thinking through the technical challenges.

"I'm routing false signals through our personal devices," Bruce explained. "They'll stay in St. John's, pinging towers, making automated purchases, creating a pattern of us still being here. Your digital shadows will maintain your routines while we're gone."

Lynn was reviewing maritime law on her laptop, her fingers flying across the keyboard. "If we're intercepted in international waters?"

"That's why we have Sarah's team," Bruce said. "Eight former special forces, all with maritime combat experience. Plus the crew—all ex-military, all vetted."

"Eight against how many?" Katya asked, her financial mind calculating odds.

"Depends on how badly they want us," a compact woman said, entering the room. Sarah moved with the controlled economy of someone trained to be dangerous. Her eyes never stopped scanning, cataloging exits, angles, threats. "But in Arctic waters, in winter? Numbers matter less than preparation. And we're very prepared."

Terri looked up from her terminal, having run her own analysis. "I found something else. Marcus Chen has a brother—David Chen in our security department. Same terminal access patterns, same anomalous behavior over the past week."

"Christ," Bruce muttered, immediately pulling up security protocols. "He has access to—"

"Had access," Sarah corrected. "My team just detained him. He was trying to leave the building with a case full of hard drives."

"How deep does this go?" Lynn asked.

"Deep enough," Ren said. "We leave in two hours. Minimum personnel, maximum security. Terri, can you maintain our quantum encryption from the yacht?"

"Already configured a portable command center," Terri confirmed. "Full access to our network, completely isolated from any local interference."

Three days later, after successfully evading surveillance through Bruce's elaborate deception, they were boarding the Arctic Endeavor in Halifax harbor. The converted ocean tug looked exactly as Bruce had described—a working vessel transformed into something more capable. Its ice-breaking hull bore scars from numerous Arctic encounters, the reinforced superstructure designed to withstand the worst nature could offer.

Captain Eriksen, a weathered Norwegian whose face looked carved from weathered oak, greeted them with professional efficiency. "Welcome aboard. We're ready to depart on your word."

"My security chief, Sarah," Bruce made the formal introduction as the compact woman joined them on deck, her eyes never stopping their constant surveillance sweep.

Sarah's assessment was brief and clinical. "We have a six-hour window before anyone could reasonably track us here from St. John's. After that, assume we're visible. My team has swept the vessel twice—no trackers, no surveillance devices. But if they knew our original plan, they're already positioning assets."

As they departed Halifax harbor, the lights of the city fading into morning mist, Ren stood at the railing, watching the coast disappear. The salt spray was sharp and clean, each breath filling her lungs with something other than recycled air for the first time in weeks. Despite everything—the threat behind them, the uncertainty ahead—she felt her shoulders beginning to unknot.

The relief was short-lived.

"Contact on radar," Captain Eriksen's voice came over the intercom four hours later, his Norwegian accent clipped and professional. "Another vessel, two kilometers off our starboard.

They've been matching our course for the last two hours."

Bruce moved quickly to the bridge. When he returned, his expression was grim. "High-end yacht. The Carthage. Registry's hidden behind shells, but..." He pulled up an image on his tablet. "Look familiar?"

The sleek black vessel in the photo was unmistakable—the same one Bora had been photographed on at the Monaco conference.

"Six hours," Sarah said quietly, checking her watch. "He was already in position. That means he knew our route before we did."

"Or he got lucky," Lynn suggested without conviction.

"No," Ren said, studying the radar return, noting the precision of their shadow's movements. "He knew. The question is whether he knew our original plan or our revised one. If it's the latter, we have a deeper problem."

They journeyed north along the coast, the sea growing progressively colder. Ice began forming on the deck railings in delicate crystalline patterns that grew thicker with each passing hour. The Carthage maintained its distance with mechanical precision—never closer than two kilometers, never further than five. It was psychological warfare at its most basic and effective.

The northern seas were different from anything most of them had experienced. The water turned from Atlantic blue to something darker, more primitive. Ice floes began appearing, small at first, then larger, grinding against the reinforced hull with sounds like breaking bones.

Ren couldn't sleep. The proximity of the Carthage, combined with the rhythmic groaning of ice against the hull, made rest impossible. She found Sarah on the bridge, watching the radar with predatory focus.

"They're maintaining position perfectly," Sarah said without looking up. "Even with these seas, the ice. That takes exceptional seamanship or exceptional technology."

"Or both," Ren said, studying the display. The Carthage's radar signature hadn't deviated by more than ten meters in hours. "What do you know about Bora's operations?"

"More than I should, less than I need." Sarah's reflection in the window was alert, watchful. "He tried to recruit me once. Five years ago, after I left the service. Offered triple what Bruce pays."

"Why didn't you take it?"

"Because I research my employers. Bora's money comes from interesting sources. Shipping cartels, authoritarian governments, people who profit from the current system's inefficiencies." Sarah turned to face Ren directly. "Your network threatens trillions in hidden revenue streams. You understand that, yes?"

"I know we're making enemies."

"No, you're threatening an entire shadow economy. Drug routes that depend on paperwork confusion. Arms shipments that disappear in bureaucratic gaps. Human trafficking that exploits jurisdiction overlaps." Sarah's expression was grim. "Bora isn't just protecting shipping companies. He's protecting the dark corners where the real money lives."

"The fake MTUs," Ren said suddenly, the pieces clicking together. "He's not trying to copy our technology. He's going to use non-functional units to stage something, make it look like our network was involved in something illegal."

"That would be my assessment," Sarah agreed. "A high-profile incident, perhaps multiple incidents, that would justify shutting down your entire network."

A massive wave slammed the yacht suddenly, throwing them against the bulkhead. The lights flickered, emergency power kicking in briefly before main power restored.

"We should check the fuel situation," Sarah said, steadying herself. "These conditions are burning through our reserves faster than planned."

They made their way to the engine room, where Chief Engineer Morrison was checking gauges by flashlight, his face grim in the dim light.

"We're losing fuel," he confirmed, pointing to readings that showed steady depletion. "The port tank's compromised. Ice damage, but..." He showed them the puncture pattern on his tablet's diagnostic screen. "Too regular to be natural. See these marks? That's not random impact."

"Sabotage?" Ren asked, though she already knew the answer.

"Or designed to look like it," Morrison said carefully. "Could be storm damage that happens to look suspicious. No way to know without draining the tank and doing a full inspection."

"Which we can't do at sea," Sarah said. "How long do we have?"

"At current burn rate? Forty hours, maybe less if the temperature keeps dropping. We're having to run the heating at maximum to keep the electronics operational."

The weather system that had been building finally forced their hand. Captain Eriksen made the announcement with professional calm that didn't quite hide his concern.

"Storm front approaching from the northwest. We need shelter within six hours. Baxter Inlet is our only option—protected harbor, good holding ground for anchors."

Through the gathering mist and driving snow, they watched the Carthage adjust course to follow them, maintaining that precise two-kilometer distance.

"He's been herding us," Ren realized, studying the meteorological data. "He knew this storm was coming, knew where we'd have to go."

The inlet was a narrow passage between towering cliffs of black rock and ancient ice. It opened into a protected harbor dominated by the skeletal remains of an abandoned Cold War research station. Concrete structures slowly being reclaimed by ice, roofs collapsed under decades of snow. Antenna arrays reached toward the grey sky like frozen fingers.

Both yachts anchored in the relative calm, five hundred meters apart.

The storm hit that night with Arctic fury—fifty-knot winds driving ice horizontally across the deck. The yacht rolled and pitched at anchor, but the inlet provided enough protection to keep them safe. Through the driving snow, they could see the Carthage's lights, steady and patient.

The morning brought an eerie calm and unwelcome news.

"Captain's damage report," Bruce announced, entering the salon with a grim expression. "Storm drove ice into our port fuel tank. We're losing diesel faster than expected—maybe forty hours at current consumption."

"Forty hours?" Lynn's voice remained steady. "I calculated forty-eight minimum yesterday."

"Hull insulation's compromised," Captain Eriksen explained. "We're burning thirty percent extra fuel just to maintain cabin temperature."

The VHF radio crackled to life. "Good morning, Ren-san." Bora's voice cut through the static with perfect clarity. "I trust you weathered the storm adequately?"

Ren took the handset, noting Sarah's positioning near the door. "What do you want, Bora?"

"To understand the mind that would reshape global commerce. Did you think there wouldn't be consequences?"

"The fire at St. John's. That was you?"

"Enthusiastic locals. I prefer more elegant solutions. Like demonstrating how thin the ice beneath you really is. Tell me, have you checked your fuel tanks recently? Ice damage can be so unpredictable."

Through the window, figures emerged onto the Carthage's deck, setting up surveillance equipment despite the freezing conditions.

"Quantum encryption protects content," Bora continued, "but every transmission has a heartbeat. Size, frequency, duration. Your 11:12 PM burst—twelve seconds, high priority. The 6:22 exchange—someone needed reassurance? You've contacted headquarters seventeen times. Panic has its own signature."

Sarah moved closer to Ren. "My team's ready. We can disable their equipment."

"And then?" Ren asked quietly.

"Then they know we'll escalate. They return fire. We're outnumbered three to one. Out here, it's suicide."

"So we're lab rats in his Arctic maze," Lynn said, her tone cutting.

"Enjoy your isolation," Bora's voice carried mock sympathy. "When you're ready to discuss terms, I'll be here. I have provisions for a week."

The radio went dead.

"He's gathering intelligence," Ren said. "Every decision tells him how we think."

"So what do we do?" Lynn asked.

"Stop playing his game. Terri, can you create false transmission patterns?"

Terri's eyes lit up. "Flood him with noise. Hide real signals in false ones."

"Exactly. Make it look like our systems are degrading."

While Terri worked on the deception, Ren pulled Bruce and Sarah aside.

"We need to go on offense," Ren said quietly. "Bora's surveillance works both ways."

"What are you thinking?" Bruce asked.

"Track his transmissions. Who's he reporting to?"

Sarah nodded. "I have equipment for that. Won't break his encryption, but we can see the metadata."

"There's something else," Sarah added. "The abandoned research station. I've seen heat signatures—minimal but consistent."

"Bora's people?"

"Or locals. Either way, it's a variable."

Lynn joined them. "I've been researching the station. Baxter Inlet Research Facility, abandoned in 1991. But it was a joint Canadian-American signals intelligence post. The infrastructure for monitoring communications might still be there."

"Meaning whoever controls that station has a significant advantage," Ren said.

That night, Ren and Terri worked in the cramped communications room, shoulders touching as they constructed their deception.

"Pattern needs to look panicked but systematic," Terri explained, coding transmissions. "Like we're desperately coordinating but failing."

"Include partial encryptions," Ren suggested. "Make it look like quantum coherence is breaking down."

Through the porthole, the Carthage's lights glowed steadily.

"Ren," Terri said quietly. "If something happens—"

"Nothing's going to happen."

"But if it does." Terri's hand found Ren's. "These last two years, building the impossible... it's been everything."

Ren turned their joined hands over. "We're going to get through this."

"Together?"

"Together."

Sarah appeared. "Movement on the Carthage. They're launching a drone."

"Let them," Ren said. "Every move tells us something too."

"What does a drone tell us?"

"That they're impatient. That watching isn't enough." Ren kept typing. "Bora's on a timeline too."

Another alarm chimed—a real transmission hidden in twelve false ones. As Terri decoded it, her expression shifted from relief to alarm.

"Ren, you need to see this." She pulled up the decoded data. "They identified our ghost. It's not one person—it's a coordinated group. Three inside TTC, two in regulatory positions, one in Canadian intelligence."

"Names?"

"Dr. James Harrison in logistics—the one who claimed his son was kidnapped. That was a lie. His son is in Monaco, enrolled in an expensive boarding school paid for by accounts linked to Westport Allied."

"He played us," Bruce said.

"The USB drive he gave us?"

"Tracking malware," Terri confirmed. "I sandboxed it, but if I'd plugged it into our main system..."

"What about the other two inside TTC?"

"Maria Santos in procurement and David Chen in security. David is Marcus Chen's brother."

"Security itself was compromised," Lynn breathed.

"Was compromised," Bruce corrected. "Both are in custody. RCMP grabbed them an hour ago."

"There's more," Terri said quietly. "The ghost wasn't trying to steal data. It was mapping our MTU network, identifying which units are fully operational versus still in testing."

"Why?" Lynn asked.

"Because someone's planning to use that information," Ren said slowly. "Either to attack our functional units or..."

"Or to make it look like our units were used for something they weren't," Terri finished. "Bora's fake MTUs. He's going to stage something and blame it on our network."

Through the porthole, the Carthage sat in darkness, waiting. But now Ren understood—Bora wasn't just hunting them. He was waiting for confirmation that his plan was in motion.

"How long until our MTU network can detect and flag any unauthorized matter transmission attempts?" Ren asked.

"I can push an update in six hours," Terri said. "But it needs to propagate through the entire network. Full coverage in maybe eighteen hours."

"Do it," Ren ordered. "And create a backup protocol—if any unit detects an anomaly, it immediately broadcasts to all other units."

"That'll create noise," Terri warned. "Bora will know we're onto something."

"Let him know," Ren said. "It might force him to move before he's ready."

As dawn approached, painting the Arctic sky in shades of grey and pale blue, Ren made a decision that shocked everyone.

"We're going to invite Bora over," she announced.

"Are you insane?" Lynn asked.

"No. We're in a stalemate. He can't board us by force without causing an international incident. We can't leave without risking our fuel situation. So we change the game."

"How?" Bruce asked, though his expression suggested he was already thinking through security protocols.

"Breakfast. A civilized discussion between competitors." Ren's smile was sharp. "Sarah, can your team ensure he doesn't bring weapons?"

"I can ensure he doesn't bring functional weapons," Sarah corrected. "Ceramic knives, carbon fiber garrotes—there are things we can't detect."

"He won't risk physical violence," Ren said. "Not when he's winning the psychological game. But I want to see him, read him, understand what he really wants."

"It's risky," Katya warned.

"Everything we do now is risky. But sitting here, slowly running out of fuel while he gathers intelligence? That's not a strategy. It's a slow death."

Bruce was already on the radio. "Carthage, this is Arctic Endeavor. Dr. Franco would like to invite Bora for breakfast. 0800 hours. Neutral ground, civilized discussion."

The response came after a long pause. "Mr. Tanaka accepts. One companion each. No weapons."

"No weapons we can detect," Sarah muttered.

Ren looked at her team. "Terri, keep the false transmissions running. Make it look like I'm making this decision out of desperation. Bruce, you're with me. Sarah, position your team. If this goes wrong..."

"It won't," Sarah said. "I'll have snipers on him from the moment he leaves his yacht."

"Lynn, Katya—review everything we know about Bora's financial network. If breakfast goes badly, I want options for retaliation."

As the team dispersed to prepare, Terri caught Ren's arm. "Be careful. He's not just smart—he's patient. This could be what he's been waiting for."

"I know," Ren said. "But we're out of time. The ghost is identified, his network is exposed, and something's about to happen with those fake MTUs. We need to know what."

"What if he doesn't tell you?"

"Then I'll know by what he doesn't say." Ren squeezed Terri's hand. "Keep monitoring everything. The moment something changes—"

"I'll signal you," Terri promised.

Through the window, they could see movement on the Carthage. A launch was being prepared. The abandoned research station loomed over the inlet, its broken windows dark. Sarah had spotted movement there earlier—brief, purposeful, quickly hidden.

"The mouse is inviting the cat to breakfast," Lynn said, joining them at the window.

"Or the cat is about to learn the mouse has teeth," Ren replied.

The Arctic morning was crystal clear, the storm having passed in the night. Ice crystals hung in the air like frozen diamonds. In six hours, Terri's update would protect the MTU network. In eighteen hours, they'd either be sailing home in triumph or...

Ren didn't finish the thought. There was only forward now, into whatever trap or opportunity breakfast would bring.

The Carthage's launch pushed off, heading their way. Bora stood in the bow, elegant in a thick wool coat, looking every inch the confident predator.

But predators, Ren knew, could also be prey. It all depended on the terrain. And this was her ship, her rules, her choice of battlefield.

"Let's go spring a trap," she said to Bruce.

"Whose?" Bruce asked.

"That's what we're about to find out."

The Arctic darkness was lifting, but the real battle was just beginning. The Carthage sat in the growing light, watching. But for the first time, Ren wondered who was really studying whom. The trap Bora had so carefully constructed might just become a mirror, reflecting his own assumptions back at him.

Tomorrow would bring Bora's next move. But today, over breakfast in the Arctic wilderness, two adversaries would finally meet face to face. And only one would leave with the advantage.

10 POLES AND PILLS

"The connection's been severed for three hours," the Nigerian Minister of Infrastructure's voice crackled through the emergency videoconference, distortion fragmenting his words as satellite lag complicated an already tense situation. Behind him, Ren could see dozens of agitated protesters filling the frame, their handmade signs bobbing in the afternoon heat: "TTC LIED - AFRICA DENIED," "QUANTUM COLONIALISM," and "RETURN OUR MONEY."

Ren stared helplessly at the blank status indicators for seventeen MTU sites across Sub-Saharan Africa, each represented by a dead red dot on the global deployment map. The sites—strategically positioned in major population centers from Dakar to Maputo—had gone dark simultaneously at 0300 local time, as if someone had thrown a master switch. "Minister Adebayo, our satellites show the units are still physically present and intact. We're working to determine what's causing the disruption—"

"Present but utterly useless!" Adebayo interrupted, his jaw tight with barely contained fury. Sweat beaded on his forehead under the harsh fluorescent lights of his emergency command center. "We paid millions for infrastructure that doesn't work. My government is facing riots in three cities already. The opposition claims we were scammed by Western technology—again. Just like the water purification systems of 2031 that poisoned an entire region."

Terri pulled up enhanced satellite imagery on her tablet, pinch-zooming to show crowds gathering around the dead MTU sites in Lagos, Nairobi, and Johannesburg. Military vehicles were visible at the periphery of several locations. She paled as her system completed its diagnostic scan. "Ren, these aren't our units. The quantum signatures are completely wrong. The molecular verification fails at every checkpoint."

"What do you mean they're not ours?" Lynn asked, leaning forward, her coffee forgotten in her hand.

"Someone installed fake MTUs. Empty shells that look identical externally but have no transfer capability whatsoever. They're just... elaborate props." Terri's voice carried the hollow timbre of disbelief as she swiped through damning verification failures. "Whoever did this had access to our installation schedules, our security protocols, our shipping manifests—everything. This wasn't opportunistic; this was meticulously planned."

The implications hit Ren like a physical blow, a cold wave of nausea washing through her body. Someone had systematically intercepted their entire African expansion initiative, replacing real multi-million-dollar units with sophisticated fakes, pocketing the payments while simultaneously destroying TTC's reputation across an entire continent. Seventeen nations, hundreds of millions of people affected.

"Get me visual confirmation from every member of our installation teams," Ren ordered, her fingers trembling slightly as she typed commands. "Every site, every signature. I want retinal scans, quantum verification, the works."

Bruce was already on his phone, scrolling rapidly through social media feeds, his expression growing grimmer by the second. "Media's picking this up everywhere. 'TTC's African Scam' is trending globally. The major international new outlets—they're all running with it. They're saying we deliberately sold non-functional units to developing nations as some kind of elaborate fraud scheme."

"That's impossible," Katya said, but her voice wavered as she pulled up financial records. "The installation teams reported successful deployment at all locations. The payments cleared through our accounts—" She stopped abruptly, her face paling as she checked her screens and ran an urgent trace. "The payments. They were intercepted and rerouted through a series of shell companies. The money never actually reached our accounts. It was diverted somewhere else entirely."

"Inside job," Lynn said quietly, her expression hardening as the full scope of the betrayal became clear. "Someone embedded in our African deployment team orchestrated this entire disaster from within."

The thundering at the reinforced doors shattered the pre-dawn quiet. "RCMP! This is a lawful raid under the Controlled Substances Act!" The metallic boom echoed through the facility's corridors, followed by the synchronized footfalls of tactical boots on polished floors.

Ren had been in the control room for twenty hours straight, coordinating damage control from the African disaster. Her eyes burned from staring at screens, body running on nothing but black coffee and adrenaline. Now she watched in shock as tactical teams flooded through their security checkpoints, weapons drawn, their movements precise and practiced. Dark kevlar vests emblazoned with "POLICE" contrasted sharply against the sterile white of TTC's headquarters.

"Nobody move!" The lead officer's voice boomed through the facility, amplified by the building's own communication system they'd somehow accessed. "We have warrants for the arrest of James Chienga, Maria Vasquez, and Robert Singh on charges of conspiracy to traffic controlled substances."

Terri's hand found Ren's arm, her fingers digging in with unexpected force. "Those are all Quantum Division personnel. My people." Her voice contained a mixture of disbelief and betrayal, her usual composure cracking around the edges.

The accused were led out in handcuffs—Chen, who'd been with them since the beginning, his normally immaculate lab coat replaced by rumpled casual clothes; Vasquez, who'd helped design the cargo manifest system, her face a mask of defiance; Singh, who managed quantum signature verification, looking shell-shocked and pale.

Detective Inspector Morrison, a stern woman with calculating eyes and silver-streaked hair pulled into a tight bun, approached Ren. Her navy blazer bore no insignia, but her authority radiated from every measured step. "Ms. Franco, we've been monitoring unusual patterns in your cargo transfers for the past eight months. Shipments with altered manifests, deleted signature records, payments to known cartel accounts in Panama and Ecuador."

"That's impossible. Our system—" Ren began, her voice faltering as the implications crashed over her like ice water.

"Your system has been compromised from within." Morrison produced a tablet showing transaction logs, quantum signature modifications, and financial transfers highlighted in damning red. "Your employees were paid two million dollars each to facilitate drug shipments across international borders. They've been deleting the quantum signatures of narcotics, making them invisible to your security protocols while preserving the appearance of legitimate cargo."

Ren felt the ground shift beneath her. The control room's harsh lighting suddenly seemed to intensify, casting everything in an unforgiving glare. The enemy wasn't just attacking from outside—they'd corrupted her own people, turned trusted colleagues into accomplices.

"Furthermore," Morrison continued, swiping through additional evidence on her tablet with methodical precision, "we have evidence suggesting this operation was coordinated with the fake MTU installations in Africa. Same payment structures, same shell companies in the Cayman Islands and Singapore. This isn't coincidental."

Lynn stepped forward, her lawyer's instincts taking over despite the early hour and the shock rippling through the room. "We'll cooperate fully with your investigation, Inspector. But I'll need to see those warrants, and I'll be calling our legal team immediately."

As Morrison handed over the documents, bound together with official government seals, she fixed Ren with a hard stare that seemed to pierce through pretense. "Ms. Franco, either you're running the most sophisticated drug operation in history, or someone's using your company as their personal trafficking network. Either way, TTC is now under federal investigation, and all quantum transport operations are suspended effective immediately."

Marius Okonko had been with TTC for two years, recruited specifically to lead their African expansion. He sat across from Ren now, flanked by Lynn and two security officers, his designer suit still impeccable despite being pulled from his Toronto hotel at dawn. A thin sheen of sweat glistened on his forehead under the harsh interrogation lights, betraying the calm demeanor he struggled to maintain.

"The payments were legitimate," Marcus insisted, his Nigerian accent thickening with stress, fingers interlaced tightly on the table before him. "I supervised every installation personally. I checked documentation, verified equipment, followed every protocol in the manual."

Terri connected her tablet to the wall display with a sharp, efficient movement that reflected her mounting frustration. "Then explain this." She played security footage from the Lagos installation—timestamp three weeks ago. The high-definition video showed Marcus directing crews to install units, pointing at schematics, nodding approvingly as technicians worked. But then Terri overlaid it with quantum scanning data, the numbers and wavelength patterns glowing an accusatory red against the blue background. "These signatures are fake. The resonance patterns don't match our standard configurations. You knew you were installing non-functional units. They're broadcasting the right signals, but there's nothing behind them—hollow shells designed to pass superficial inspections."

Marcus's composure cracked slightly, a muscle twitching in his jaw as his shoulders slumped almost imperceptibly. "You don't understand the pressure—the impossible position they put me in."

"From whom?" Ren's voice was deadly quiet, each syllable precise as a surgical instrument. Her hands gripped the edge of the table, knuckles white.

"They have my family." The words came out in a rush, like water breaking through a dam. "My daughter at university in London, my parents in Lagos. They showed me pictures of them going about their daily lives—my daughter entering her dormitory, my father at his medical practice. They told me what would happen if I didn't cooperate. Graphic, detailed threats." His voice caught. "Things I cannot repeat."

"Who?" Lynn pressed, leaning forward, her legal pad already filled with meticulous notes. "Names, descriptions, any identifying information?"

"I don't know names. They contacted me through encrypted channels, always different voices, different accents. But they knew everything—our schedules, our protocols, which security officers would be on duty and when." Marcus's hands shook as he reached for the water glass before him. "They said it was just about slowing expansion, making TTC look unreliable in emerging markets. Creating doubt among investors and partner nations. I didn't know about the drugs. I swear on my daughter's life, I didn't know they were using our network for trafficking."

Ren stood abruptly, unable to contain her fury, her chair scraping harshly against the floor. "Seventeen countries trusted us. Millions of people were counting on that infrastructure. Hospitals waiting for medical supplies, remote villages expecting educational resources, businesses relying on our promises."

"They gave me a choice," Marcus said, meeting her eyes with unexpected steadiness. "My family or your reputation. My daughter's life or your business goals. What would you have chosen in my place? What would any parent choose?"

Before Ren could respond, Marcus's phone—supposedly confiscated during security processing—buzzed loudly in the breast pocket of his suit jacket. The unexpected sound cut through the tension like a knife. Security immediately lunged forward, an officer grabbing the device with practiced efficiency, but the message was already displaying clearly on the screen for everyone to see:

"48 hours until the main event. Your African failure was just the appetizer. - B"

Yet, even as they battled on multiple fronts, even as Ren wrestled with the implications of Bora's subtle probing and the mystery of the 'ghost,' the fundamental drive that had created TTC persisted: the relentless pursuit of technological advancement and the expansion of their capabilities. They couldn't simply stop or retreat; their enemies would win, and the world would be denied the potential benefits TTC could offer. They had to push forward, grow their network, enhance their capabilities; not just for future profitability or humanitarian impact, but for resilience against the very forces trying to dismantle them. The polar expansion was a technical manifestation of this drive – strengthening the network, making it harder to disrupt globally.

"Phase Three deployment is complete," Terri announced, her voice carrying quiet pride despite the chaos surrounding them.

She manipulated the holographic display showing Earth crisscrossed by glowing quantum pathways and dotted with MTU facilities. The original three massive geostationary arrays—Alpha, Beta, and Gamma—now anchored a more extensive network. Swarming around the poles were new constellations of smaller satellites, depicted as shimmering clouds in polar orbits.

"We now have full orbital coverage," Terri stated, "including dedicated arrays in Arctic and Antarctic regions."

She zoomed in on the poles, showing dense overlapping satellite fields—a stark contrast to previous sparse coverage. This wasn't about closing gaps; it was building resilience against external pressure, expanding into the planet's most challenging environments.

"Network redundancy increased thirty percent," she explained, highlighting interconnected backup relays. "Every major MTU site has primary, secondary, often tertiary orbital links. If arrays go down—maintenance, environmental factors, or malicious interference"—she glanced pointedly at Ren—"traffic reroutes instantly through alternative paths without service loss."

This redundancy was technological countermeasure against demonstrated vulnerability, making single stream isolation harder for the 'ghost.'

"Energy buffer capacity increased fifty percent," she continued, showing enhanced storage within arrays recharged by solar power and wireless beaming from ground stations. "Higher resilience for unforeseen demands, transfers, large deliveries—plus crucial backup if ground power is compromised."

Ren nodded, reviewing the technical specifications displayed on her data pad. "The increased redundancy is critical, Terri. Especially now. Does this help us triangulate the source of the interference from the split shipment? More eyes on the network?"

Terri's expression became grim. "We're hoping. More data points, more angles of observation. But the signature was so faint, Ren. Like a whisper. Sharpa's team is still analyzing terabytes of raw data from that specific transfer stream, looking for any anomaly that correlates across multiple satellite receivers. It's like finding a specific subatomic particle in a universe of noise."

Lynn interjected, "From a legal standpoint, this network expansion strengthens our position. It shows we're investing in reliable global coverage. It counters the narrative that we're unstable or limited. It makes us essential." She paused. "Are there any specific vulnerabilities tied to this polar coverage that our adversaries might target?"

"High-latitude atmospheric interference is more complex," Terri admitted. "Aurora activity, ionospheric disturbances. We've built in compensation protocols, but they add another layer of complexity. And the sheer remoteness of the ground sites requires robust local security." She glanced at Ren, then back at the display. "The strategic value outweighs the localized technical challenges, though. Access to resources, scientific missions..."

The expansion into the Arctic and Antarctic was particularly significant. These regions, long defined by their isolation, extreme conditions, and the formidable barrier of ice, were becoming critical players on the global stage, particularly in the context of climate change, resource exploration, and strategic geopolitics. Traditional logistics in these areas were incredibly difficult, expensive, hazardous, and environmentally impactful. Supply lines relied on specialized icebreaker ships capable of navigating frozen seas, often only for limited seasons, or highly limited air transport dependent on fleeting windows of favorable weather and dangerous ice runways. Teleportation changed that equation entirely, offering a clean, instantaneous alternative.

"Arctic coverage fundamentally changes operations in the high north," Terri explained, showing projected MTU sites appearing near remote research outposts, coastal settlements, mining operations, and proposed extraction sites for minerals and rare earth elements, resources becoming increasingly valuable globally. "Supplying these locations is no longer constrained by sea ice, landing strip availability, or darkness. Equipment, supplies, even personnel – once Life MTU is operational and publicly accepted – can be moved instantly, year-round, reliably, with minimal environmental disturbance from transit.

"Antarctic is primarily focused on facilitating scientific missions and upholding the principles of the Antarctic Treaty System," Terri continued, shifting the display to show the vast, frozen continent, rendered as a stark white mass surrounded by ice shelves.

"Teleporting equipment, supplies, and critical samples directly to research bases like McMurdo, Palmer Station, or even remote field camps on the polar plateau. This significantly reduces the logistical footprint and environmental impact compared to traditional transport via heavy-lift aircraft landing on ice runways or ice-strengthened ships breaking through pack ice."

The Antarctic Treaty System placed strict limitations on human activity and environmental disturbance, designating the continent as a scientific preserve. Traditional supply lines for major research bases involved establishing vast staging areas, building and maintaining hazardous ice runways (prone to cracking and requiring constant maintenance), and undertaking perilous voyages through the Southern Ocean, all of which carried environmental risks from fuel use, potential spills, and physical disturbance. TTC offered a non-intrusive alternative, minimizing physical presence and disturbance on the fragile continent. Research teams could request specialized equipment and have it appear at their remote field camp. Geological samples or ice cores could be teleported directly from collection sites on the polar plateau to labs thousands of miles away for immediate analysis, bypassing weeks of frozen storage and risky transport that could compromise sample integrity.

"We're allowing science to operate with unprecedented speed and efficiency in these critical, yet fragile environments," Terri stated, her voice holding a hint of the environmentalist within her, "thereby reducing the need for fuel drops, heavy vehicle traverses across sensitive landscapes, and large-scale infrastructure that can disturb the pristine environment. It's a powerful tool for climate research, environmental monitoring, and preserving sensitive samples."

She looked at Ren, her eyes shining with the potential of this. "Imagine the data we can gather and the research we can enable, free from the constraints of traditional logistics."

Bruce, ever the opportunist, saw the commercial potential beyond pure science, though he knew it was politically sensitive in regions with complex environmental regulations and international agreements.

"Resource exploration in the Arctic is becoming significantly more viable and potentially safer with instant logistics," he pointed out during a discussion on market applications, projecting data on untapped mineral reserves. "Minerals, rare earths, potentially even undersea resources, once we solve the pressure issue. Teleporting bulk raw materials from remote extraction sites to processing centers, or necessary heavy excavation equipment to a mining location, could transform the economics and, crucially, reduce the environmental risks associated with building long, polluting pipelines or undertaking massive shipping operations in icy waters. It's a way to access resources with a vastly lower environmental footprint during transit."

He acknowledged the environmental concerns about the end activity but argued that TTC's approach was a necessary improvement over the traditional transport methods needed to access these resources.

Lynn, however, was already anticipating the new legal and environmental challenges their polar expansion would invite, fueled by the backlash they were already experiencing elsewhere.

"Operating in the polar regions brings specific international treaties and overlapping national claims into play," she cautioned. "The Antarctic Treaty System, while prohibiting military activity and prioritizing science, still requires transparency and respect for environmental protocols. The Arctic Council framework involves multiple nations with competing interests and significant environmental concerns, particularly from Indigenous communities who have inhabited these regions for millennia. Our operations, while cleaner in terms of transport emissions, are still a physical presence, utilizing significant energy and potentially enabling activities like resource extraction that raise complex environmental, sovereignty, and ethical questions. We need to navigate these frameworks carefully, ensuring we are viewed as facilitating research, responsible development, and climate monitoring, not enabling unchecked exploitation or violating treaty obligations."

Her team was already engaging with international bodies and national governments with polar interests, preemptively addressing potential concerns and highlighting the environmental benefits of how TTC transported goods compared to the old methods, while being transparent about the energy requirements of the MTUs themselves.

Despite this significant expansion, the increased coverage, and the enhancement of their network's resilience and capacity, one persistent technical hurdle remained, a stubborn, fundamental limit to the reach of the quantum field they had mastered in almost every other environment: the underwater world.

Ren often found herself in the control room late at night, long after the others had tried to get some rest, staring at the glowing network map, searching for answers in the data. Terri was frequently there with her, quietly working at her console, a silent, comforting presence. The bond between them, intensified by the shared isolation of their work and the recent intimacy hinted at during the Arctic trip, was a source of quiet strength for Ren.

"Another article linking the housing moves to rising crime rates in destination cities," Ren murmured, swiping away a projected news report, the narrative twisted to suggest teleporting homes brought criminals. "It's relentless. Every division is a target."

Terri sighed, leaning back in her chair. "They're leveraging every angle, Ren. Job losses, environmental impact, and now criminality. They want to make the world afraid of what we do." She looked at Ren, her expression softening. "You should try and get some rest. You've been here for eighteen hours."

Ren shook her head. "Can't, Terri. Not while the ghost is still out there. Not while they're attacking us like this." She walked over to Terri's console, looking at the diagnostics. "Any new signatures? Anything related to the split shipment anomaly?"

Terri shook her head. "Nothing definitive. We're seeing faint, fleeting anomalies in the transfer streams, but no clear pattern, no source triangulation. It's like they test the defenses, then retreat. Or they're operating with incredibly low energy signatures that are hard to distinguish from background quantum noise." She lowered her voice. "It's terrifying, Ren. The thought that someone can interact with the network at that level violates the fundamental principles."

Ren nodded, her gaze distant. "I know. It feels personal. Like they're trying to break the physics itself, not just the company." She thought of Bora, the chilling intelligence in his eyes, his questions about control and consequences on the yacht. She hadn't shared the depth of her suspicion about him or the taunting messages with Terri yet, not fully. But the feeling that he was somehow connected to this technical adversary, to the 'ghost,' was growing stronger.

The team was eating together, trying to maintain some normalcy, but the crisis was the elephant in the room. Bruce was talking about the challenges of countering the negative media narrative. Katya was discussing the strain on their financial reserves from the continuous legal battles and the need to keep funding operations while access to capital was restricted. Lynn was outlining the frustrating lack of progress in identifying the source of the attacks legally.

"It's like fighting smoke," Bruce said, running a hand through his hair. "Every time we counter one false narrative, they launch two more. They have resources, they have connections, and they don't care one iota about the truth."

"Their messaging is highly coordinated," Katya added. "Across different media channels, different countries. It's expensive. Someone with significant resources is funding this."

Lynn leans forward, lowering her voice. "And we're seeing unusual activity behind the scenes. Shell corporations being formed, assets being moved, individuals with no clear links to the industry appearing in positions that might facilitate logistics or security... it's like they're building something else, in parallel."

Ren listens, processing the information, her mind connecting the dots. This wasn't a desperate reaction from failing companies. This was a strategic campaign, orchestrated and well-funded.

Terri catches Ren's eye across the table, a silent communication passing between them. They both know the technical side of the attack, the sophistication of the 'ghost', is part of this larger picture.

It's not just a business fight; it's a fight for control of the future, using every tool available.

The conversation lightens briefly, shifting to something mundane – the quality of the food tonight, a movie someone watched, a shared complaint about the perpetual North Atlantic weather. In these small moments of normalcy, the bond between the team is evident, a source of resilience.

Bruce, ever observant, catches a shared glance between Ren and Terri, a moment where their hands brush as they reach for something, a subtle energy in the space between them. He grins. "Are we back to analyzing quantum entanglement over dinner?" He winks at Katya. "Or is there... another kind of field establishing coherence at the table?"

Katya glances up, her expression shifting from worried to amused. She catches the subtle flush in Ren's cheeks, the slight tension in Terri's posture. "It does seem the network isn't the only thing experiencing... interesting energy fluctuations, Bruce."

Lynn smiles, her eyes sparkling with knowing amusement. "Perhaps the pressure of the crisis is leading to unexpected... bonding opportunities?"

Ren feels a blush rise, unused to being the subject of this kind of teasing, especially from her core team. Terri, typically more reserved, also blushes, looking down at her plate for a moment before meeting Ren's eyes, a shared look of mortification and... something else. The sexual tension, the attraction that has been building between them, is suddenly made visible, acknowledged by the others, even if indirectly.

The conversation moves on, but the tension remains, acknowledged and gently highlighted by the team.

Ren sat alone, staring at reports of the damage—financial, reputational, operational. The weight of it all pressed down on her shoulders. She didn't hear Terri enter until the other woman's hands gently rested on her shoulders.

"You need to stop," Terri said softly, beginning to massage the tension from Ren's muscles. "You've been at this for twenty-two hours."

"I can't. Every minute we waste, they're planning something worse." But Ren's protest lacked conviction as Terri's skilled fingers worked at a particularly tight knot.

"The team is handling the immediate fires. Lynn's with legal, Bruce is managing media, Katya's tracing the money." Terri's hands stilled. "Let me handle you."

The words hung in the air, loaded with meaning. Ren turned in her chair to look up at Terri, seeing the concern, the exhaustion, and something more—a fierce protectiveness and desire.

"Terri—"

"No." Terri moved around the chair, settling herself on Ren's lap with surprising boldness, her hands framing Ren's face. "We've been dancing around this for months. The world is literally attacking us, Ren. If not now, when?"

Their lips met, urgent and desperate, all the fear and tension of recent weeks transmuting into passionate need. Terri's fingers tangled in Ren's hair, pulling her closer, while Ren's arms wrapped around Terri's waist, anchoring her.

When they finally broke apart, both breathing heavily, Terri rested her forehead against Ren's. "I've wanted to do that since the day you showed me your first successful quantum transfer."

"Why now?" Ren asked, her voice rough.

"Because tomorrow isn't guaranteed anymore." Terri kissed her again, softer this time. "Because watching you carry this alone is killing me. Because I love—"

Another explosion.

The bomb had detonated in the nearby substation—close enough to shatter windows and trigger evacuation protocols, far enough to avoid casualties. A message, not a massacre. TTC had its own power and was using the substation to send excess power to the local grid.

In the emergency bunker, the team huddled around hastily relocated equipment. The phone rang with an unknown number.

"Speaker," Ren ordered.

The voice was cultured, calm—Bora. "I trust I have your attention."

"You're a terrorist," Ren said flatly.

"I'm a businessman protecting established interests." His tone remained conversational. "Your African setback and employee arrests were demonstrations. You have forty-eight hours to announce TTC's voluntary dissolution."

"Go to hell."

"The bombs at your minor facilities? The drug shipments? The corrupted employees? Child's play." His voice hardened. "In forty-eight hours, if TTC still operates, I will demonstrate what happens when you ignore market forces. Every major city with an MTU will experience simultaneous 'accidents.' The death toll will be in the thousands. And every corpse will be laid at TTC's feet."

"You're insane," Bruce interjected. "The authorities—"

"The authorities who just raided you for drug trafficking? Who are investigating you for fraud in Africa? They'll believe whatever narrative the evidence supports. And I've been very careful with the evidence."

Lynn was frantically gesturing to keep him talking while her team traced the call.

"What makes you think we won't find you in forty-eight hours?" Ren asked.

"Because you don't even know who I really am, Ms. Franco. To you, I'm smoke and shadows. But I know everything about you. I know Terri Simmons just entered your office twenty minutes before the explosion. I know what you were doing. I know every weakness in your network, every vulnerable employee, every pressure point."

Terri's face flushed, but her jaw set with determination.

"Forty-eight hours," Bora repeated. "Dissolve TTC, or watch the world burn and know you lit the match."

The line went dead.

The bunker's emergency lights cast harsh shadows as Ren's core team assembled. Beyond them, through reinforced screens, she could see the full scale of their operation—hundreds of employees working frantically, coordinating with security forces, analyzing data streams.

"Status report," Ren ordered.

Katya went first. "The African payments traced to seventeen

different shell companies, all registered in the past six months. Total theft: forty-three million dollars. But here's the interesting part— they all link back to accounts that received payments from traditional shipping companies in the past year."

"So the old guard is definitely funding this," Lynn confirmed. "But proving it legally is another matter. The paper trail is deliberately convoluted."

Bruce pulled up media feeds. "The narrative is devastating. We're either incompetent enough to be infiltrated by drug cartels or complicit in their operations. Stock markets open in six hours— we're expecting a forty percent drop minimum."

"Security status?" Ren asked.

The new head of security, Patterson, a former military intelligence officer hastily promoted after the arrests, responded. "Every MTU site is under heightened alert. We've coordinated with local law enforcement in all operating territories. But if he has bombs already planted, or people already in position..."

"He does," Terri said quietly. "The precision of these attacks, the inside knowledge—he's been preparing this for months, maybe since we first announced."

Ren stood, moving to the wall-mounted display showing their global network. Red markers indicated compromised sites, yellow showed those under investigation, green showed operational. There was too much red and yellow.

"Options?" she asked.

"We could announce a temporary suspension," Lynn suggested reluctantly. "Not dissolution, but a pause for security review. It might buy time."

"That's exactly what they want," Bruce countered. "Once we stop, restarting becomes politically impossible. The fear narrative wins."

Terri had been quietly working at her station. Now she looked up. "I might have something. The fake MTUs in Africa—they had to manufacture them somewhere. That's specialized equipment, specific materials. If we can trace the component suppliers..."

"Do it," Ren ordered. She turned to the team. "Forty-eight hours. We need to find Bora, expose the conspiracy, and prevent whatever he's planning. If we fail, TTC dies, and with it, the future we're building."

Marius Okonko's interrogation had revealed one crucial detail: his handlers always knew about schedule changes within hours. That meant someone else was still inside, still feeding information.

"There's still a mole," Ren said. "Someone senior enough to access everything. Until we find them, all strategic discussions stay in this room. No external communications."

Patterson nodded. "I'll initiate communication lockdown protocols. Nobody leaves the facility."

As the team dispersed to their tasks, Terri lingered. When they were alone, she took Ren's hand.

"That thing about knowing I was in your office—"

"He's trying to rattle us," Ren said. "Make us feel exposed, vulnerable."

"It's working." Terri squeezed her hand. "But I meant what I said earlier. Whatever happens in the next forty-eight hours, I'm not wasting any more time pretending this is just professional between us."

Ren pulled her close, holding her tightly. "When this is over—"

"We'll have all the time in the world," Terri finished. "But first, we save the company. And stop a terrorist."

Through the reinforced windows, dawn was breaking over the Atlantic, painting the sky the color of blood. Forty-seven hours and counting.

11 LOVE AND GHOSTS

The team was on the call, scattered across different secure locations within the vast St. John's complex, or in Lynn's case, a fortified apartment in St. John's, necessitated by legal work requiring closer proximity to traditional infrastructure. Ren was in her element, back in the control room, her focus absolute, the complex feelings stirred by Terri's presence seemingly compartmentalized, replaced by the familiar intensity of the engineer, the architect of the impossible. But the experience had subtly changed her, adding a layer of human weight to her technical drive, a deeper understanding of the stakes beyond just physics and profit.

The morning started with a crisis. Lynn burst into the control room, tablet in hand, her usual composure shattered.

"We have a problem," she announced, pulling up a news feed on the main display. "Someone photographed you two at the harbor last night."

The image filled the screen—Ren and Terri, clearly intimate, silhouetted against the St. John's waterfront. The headline read: "TTC CEOs' Secret Romance: Security Risk or Corporate Scandal?"

Terri's face drained of color. "How did they—"

"It gets worse," Lynn interrupted. "The photo's already circulating in Saudi Arabia, Russia, and several African nations where we have pending contracts. The religious authorities in Riyadh are calling for immediate suspension of all TTC operations."

Ren stood frozen, her worst fears materializing. Their relationship, which had felt like a private sanctuary, was now a weapon their enemies could wield.

"The Indonesian Defense Ministry just canceled tomorrow's meeting," Katya added, checking her phone. "They're citing 'concerns about corporate stability and values alignment.'"

Bruce paced frantically. "This is exactly what Hartley wanted— a scandal to distract from our technical achievements. We need damage control, now."

"No," Ren said quietly, her voice cutting through the panic. "We don't hide. We don't apologize." She looked at Terri, seeking agreement. "But we also can't let our relationship jeopardize what we've built."

Terri nodded slowly. "Then we need to be smarter. More careful. And we need to turn this vulnerability into strength somehow."

Lynn was already strategizing. "I'll draft a statement emphasizing TTC's commitment to diversity and inclusion. Frame it as part of our innovative culture. But you two need to maintain professional distance in public from now on."

"There's something else," Katya said grimly. "The timing of this leak isn't coincidental. Someone's been watching you, waiting for the right moment to maximize damage."

"Dr. Ligia Volkov," Katya announced, introducing the tall, silver-haired woman who stood ramrod straight beside her. "The world's foremost expert on polar telecommunications and atmospheric physics. She's agreed to join our Polar Expansion Initiative."

Terri manipulated the holographic display dominating the center of the conference table. It showed a detailed, dynamic map of the globe, crisscrossed by glowing lines representing TTC's quantum data pathways and dotted with the icons of ground-based MTU facilities. Orbiting the Earth were the representations of TTC's satellite arrays. The original three massive arrays, Alpha, Beta, and Gamma, positioned in geostationary orbit over the equator, now appeared as anchors for a more extensive, intricate network. Swarming around the higher latitudes, particularly toward the poles, were new constellations of smaller, more numerous satellites, depicted as a shimmering cloud of light in polar and highly inclined orbits.

Dr. Volkov pulled up a new set of data. "There is another issue we must address. The polar waters."

"What about them?" Ren asked.

"Your quantum field cannot penetrate more than three meters below the water's surface," Ligia stated bluntly. "The density differential and the water's molecular structure create an impenetrable barrier to your teleportation matrix."

Terri's eyes widened. "We've never tested underwater teleportation extensively. We assumed—"

"You assumed wrong," Ligia interrupted. "I've run the calculations. Any MTU placed underwater or attempting to teleport through water will fail. The quantum coherence collapses immediately upon contact with liquid water at depth."

"That's... a significant vulnerability," Ren admitted, her mind racing through the implications.

"More than that," Bruce interjected, having overheard. "If someone wanted to hide operations from us, underwater would be perfect. We couldn't teleport in, couldn't extract anything..."

"The abandoned oil rigs," Terri said suddenly. "There are dozens in the North Sea alone. If someone wanted to establish operations we couldn't reach..."

Ligia nodded grimly. "Precisely why I bring this up. The Norwegian intelligence services have been monitoring unusual activity around several decommissioned platforms. Semi-submerged stealth ships approaching at night, then leaving before dawn."

"Bora," Ren said, the name tasting bitter. "He's using our limitations against us."

"There's more," Terri added, her voice quiet but commanding attention. "The polar coverage doesn't just protect us from political interference. It creates redundancy against technical attacks as well."

She brought up the data from the split shipment incident. "If someone is attempting to interfere with our quantum streams, having multiple routing options through different orbital arrays means we can isolate and bypass any compromised pathways."

Ligia Volkov, who had been silently observing, spoke up. "There is another benefit you have not mentioned. The poles are where climate change is most visible, most devastating. Establishing a presence there positions your company to assist with critical climate research and emergency response when the inevitable disasters come."

Ren met Ligia's knowing gaze. "That's not a coincidence, Dr. Volkov. Environmental response has always been part of our long-term mission."

"Good," Ligia said simply. "Then we understand each other."

Ligia's piercing blue eyes surveyed the room with clinical precision. At sixty-two, her face was lined with the wisdom of decades spent in the harshest environments on Earth. When she spoke, her Russian accent was still present despite thirty years in various western universities.

"Your technology is revolutionary," she stated bluntly, "but the poles are unforgiving. They do not care about your brilliant theories or your quantum fields. They will destroy your equipment without hesitation if you underestimate them."

Ren appreciated the directness. "That's precisely why we need you, Dr. Volkov. We don't want to underestimate anything."

Ligia nodded curtly. "I have reviewed your preliminary designs. They are... adequate as a starting point. But your cooling systems will fail within seventy-two hours of deployment in Antarctica during winter conditions. And your northern array housing will not withstand the ice expansion cycles."

Instead of being offended, Terri leaned forward with interest.

"We'd love to hear your suggestions for modifications."

A ghost of a smile touched Ligia's stern features. "Good. You are willing to listen. This is why I agreed to come." She activated her tablet, projecting a series of complex schematics. "First, we must redesign the external housing using a flexible composite that responds to pressure rather than resisting it..."

As Ligia detailed her recommendations, Ren exchanged a glance with Terri. This woman's expertise might be exactly what they needed to ensure the polar network's survival against both natural elements and human adversaries.

"We now have full orbital coverage," Terri stated, emphasizing the word 'full'. "Including dedicated arrays strategically positioned to provide optimal reception and transfer points in the Arctic and Antarctic regions." She zoomed in on the polar areas, showing dense overlapping fields of influence from the new satellites, a stark contrast to the sparser coverage there previously.

This was not about closing inconvenient coverage gaps on a map; it was about building a robust, resilient network capable of withstanding external pressure and expanding TTC's operational envelope into some of the planet's most challenging, strategically significant, and environmentally sensitive environments. It was about removing any corner of the globe from the limitations of traditional transport, making their network truly global and ubiquitous.

"This deployment increases our overall network redundancy by thirty percent," she explained, highlighting the complex web of interconnected pathways and backup relays now available. "Every major MTU ground site now has primary and secondary orbital links, and in many cases, tertiary as well. If a satellite array is temporarily unavailable – for maintenance, environmental factors, or as a result of... malicious interference," she allowed herself a pointed look at Ren, acknowledging the ongoing technical investigation into the 'ghost' and the split shipment, "traffic can be instantly rerouted through multiple alternative paths through the network, dynamically and autonomously, without any loss of service or data integrity."

The secure line from Riyadh came through at 9:30 AM local time. Prince Omar's face appeared on screen, his expression carefully neutral but his eyes cold.

"Dr. Franco, Dr. Chen. I trust you understand why I'm calling."

"Your Highness," Ren began, but he raised a hand.

"The photographs have created... complications. The religious council is demanding we sever all ties with TTC. They view your relationship as incompatible with our values."

Terri started to speak, but Ren touched her arm gently—a gesture not lost on the Prince.

"However," Prince Omar continued, "I am not the religious council. I am interested in progress, in technology, in the future. But I need assurances."

"What kind of assurances?" Lynn asked, having joined the call.

"Complete discretion when you're in our territory. Separate accommodations, no public appearances together. And..." he paused, "information."

"Information?" Ren's voice hardened.

"About your competitors. About those who would use this technology for harm. We know Bora has approached several of our... less scrupulous neighbors. Help us stop him, and we'll weather this storm together."

After the call ended, Terri slumped in her chair. "We're being blackmailed because of who we love."

"No," Ren corrected, her jaw set. "We're being offered an alliance. One that might help us stop Bora." She met Terri's eyes. "But you're right. Our relationship is now a tactical consideration. We need to be prepared for that."

The push for redundancy wasn't just about efficiency; it was a direct, technological countermeasure against the demonstrated vulnerability, an attempt to make their network physically harder for the 'ghost' to isolate and interfere with single transfer streams. It was a defense built into the infrastructure itself.

The encrypted message came from an unexpected source— Admiral Cross of the Royal Navy.

"Dr. Franco, we need your help," his gruff voice came through the secure connection. "But understand, this conversation never happened."

"What's the situation, Admiral?"

"We've been tracking activity around abandoned oil platform Bravo-7 in the North Sea. Thermal imaging shows extensive activity in the underwater sections—areas below your teleportation threshold, we understand."

Ren exchanged glances with Terri. "How do you know about—"

"We know," Cross cut her off. "The point is, someone else knows too. They're using your technology's limitations to hide something. We're planning a joint operation with Norwegian and Danish forces, but we need to understand what we might find down there."

"You think it's Bora," Terri stated.

"We know it's Bora," Cross confirmed. "Intercepted communications mention 'quantum interference devices' and 'network disruption trials.' Whatever he's building down there, it's aimed at you."

"When's the operation?" Ren asked.

"Seventy-two hours. We're going in with divers and submersibles. Old-fashioned way, since your magical transportation can't help us underwater." There was no mockery in his tone, just military pragmatism.

"We'll provide whatever technical support we can," Ren promised.

"There's one more thing," Cross added. "The Saudis are funding him. Not officially, but through back channels. Prince Omar's opposition isn't as unified as he pretends."

"And energy buffer capacity across the entire network is up by fifty percent," Terri continued, showing indicators of increased energy storage within the orbital arrays, recharged by solar power and, in the case of the larger arrays, drawing supplementary power beamed wirelessly from dedicated, high-energy ground stations.

"This provides more resilience against unforeseen demands, allows for higher-energy transfers when necessary – like those required for Life MTU transfers or large-scale modular housing deliveries – and provides a crucial buffer if ground power infrastructure at an MTU site is compromised, allowing the satellite to sustain operations for a period using stored energy. It makes the ground network less vulnerable to physical attack or power disruption."

The expansion into the Arctic and Antarctic was particularly significant. These regions, long defined by their isolation, extreme conditions, and the formidable barrier of ice, were becoming critical players on the global stage, particularly in the context of climate change, resource exploration, and strategic geopolitics. Traditional logistics in these areas were incredibly difficult, expensive, hazardous, and environmentally impactful. Supply lines relied on specialized icebreaker ships capable of navigating frozen seas, often only for limited seasons, or highly limited air transport dependent on fleeting windows of favorable weather and dangerous ice runways. Teleportation changed that equation entirely, offering a clean, instantaneous alternative.

"Arctic coverage fundamentally changes operations in the high north," Terri explained, showing projected MTU sites appearing near remote research outposts, coastal settlements, mining operations, and proposed extraction sites for minerals and rare earth elements, resources becoming increasingly valuable globally. "Supplying these locations is no longer constrained by sea ice, landing strip availability, or darkness. Equipment, supplies, even personnel – once Life MTU is publicly operational and accepted – can be moved instantly, year-round, reliably, with minimal environmental disturbance from transit."

Terri found Ren in the observation deck at dawn, staring out at the North Atlantic's grey waters.

"You didn't come back to bed," Terri said softly.

"I've been thinking about what we've cost each other," Ren replied without turning. "Before us, you could have worked anywhere, been with someone who didn't make you a target."

"Stop." Terri moved beside her, not touching but close enough to feel her warmth. "I chose this. I chose you. With full knowledge of what it meant."

"But did you know it would mean being photographed? Being used as leverage against the company? Having your personal life weaponized?"

Terri was quiet for a moment. "My father once told me that loving someone in power means sharing their burden. I didn't understand then. I do now."

"I'm not in power, Terri. I'm in the crosshairs. And now you are too."

"Then we face it together." Terri finally took Ren's hand, their fingers interlacing. "But we need to be smarter. The polar base staff—we need to vet them more carefully. Someone on the inside leaked that photo."

Ren nodded. "Lynn's already running background checks. Three staff members had connections to Hartley Industries."

"Fire them?"

"No. We use them. Feed them false information, see where it goes." Ren's expression hardened. "If they want to use our relationship against us, we'll use their spy network against them."

The holographic display showed a remote research station in Greenland, surrounded by endless ice. A small MTU unit glowed yellow against the white landscape.

"This is Station Polaris," Bruce explained to the board. "Seventeen scientists studying ice core samples for climate research. Before our polar network, their supply drops came every six weeks, weather permitting. If someone needed medical evacuation, it could take days depending on conditions."

He swiped to a new image—the same station, but now researchers were unloading fresh supplies from the MTU. "Now they receive weekly deliveries regardless of weather. Critical medical supplies can arrive in minutes. They've expanded their research capabilities because they're no longer constrained by logistics."

Another swipe showed an indigenous community in northern Canada. "The Inuit village of Akulivik. Traditionally isolated for months during winter. Food prices were four times the national average due to transportation costs."

The image changed to show community members receiving

containers of fresh produce and medical supplies through a small MTU. "Now they have regular access to affordable fresh food, medicine, and educational materials. The economic impact has been transformative."

A final image appeared—a massive oil spill spreading across Arctic waters. "This simulation shows a potential disaster scenario. With our polar network, containment equipment could be teleported directly to the site within minutes of detection, potentially preventing catastrophic environmental damage."

The briefing room was crowded with an unusual mix—TTC executives and military officers from three nations. Admiral Cross led the presentation, with Commander Johannsen from the Norwegian Navy and Captain Lars Andersen from the Danish Defense adding details.

"Operation Deep Sweep commences at 0400 hours," Cross announced, indicating positions on a tactical map. "Three teams of combat divers will breach the underwater sections simultaneously while surface teams secure the platform's upper levels."

"What are we looking for exactly?" Johannsen asked.

Dr. Sharpa, who had been analyzing intercepted data, spoke up. "Based on the electromagnetic signatures we've detected, Bora's built devices that can generate localized quantum interference. They don't teleport anything—they're designed to disrupt teleportation fields."

"Weapons against our network," Terri clarified. "If deployed near our MTU sites, they could cause catastrophic failures."

"Or worse," Ren added grimly. "If activated during an active teleportation, they could cause molecular dispersion. The object being teleported would simply... cease to exist coherently."

The room fell silent as the implications sank in.

"That's why the timing matters," Cross continued. "Intelligence suggests Bora plans to demonstrate these devices within the week. A public failure of your network, something catastrophic enough to destroy public trust."

"Where?" Lynn demanded.

"We don't know yet. That's what we hope to learn from the

raid."

Captain Andersen looked skeptical. "You're asking us to risk our people's lives for corporate espionage?"

"No," Ren said firmly. "You're preventing a terrorist attack. If Bora succeeds, if he can destroy matter in transit, he's not just threatening TTC. He's creating a weapon that could be used against any teleportation transfer. Imagine if someone activated this during a humanitarian supply delivery, or worse—" she paused, the unspoken future threat of human teleportation hanging in the air.

"We're in," Johannsen said decisively. "But we need real-time technical support. Someone who understands what we're looking at down there."

"I'll do it," Terri volunteered. "I'll be on the command ship, walking your teams through whatever they find."

"No," Ren said immediately. "It's too dangerous—"

"It's necessary," Terri countered, her tone brooking no argument. "I know the technology better than anyone except you, and you're needed here to maintain network security during the operation."

Their eyes met, a silent battle of wills that everyone in the room pretended not to notice.

"She's right," Cross said diplomatically. "We need someone who can identify threats in real-time."

Ren's jaw clenched, but she nodded. "Fine. But she stays on the command ship. No closer."

Ren watched these examples with quiet satisfaction. This was why they had built TTC—not just for profit or technological achievement, but for tangible human impact. She felt Terri's presence beside her, a subtle warmth that reinforced the purpose behind their shared mission.

Lynn called an emergency meeting at 9 PM, just hours before the raid was set to begin.

"We found our leak," she announced, pulling up a personnel file. "Marcus Waterstone, one of our satellite communication technicians. He's been feeding information to Hartley Industries for six months."

The file showed a young man, mid-thirties, with security clearance for most of their facilities.

"But here's the interesting part," Lynn continued. "He doesn't know we know. And his last communication mentioned the raid."

"They know?" Bruce exclaimed. "We have to warn—"

"No," Ren said slowly, understanding dawning. "This is an opportunity. Lynn, what exactly did Webb transmit?"

"The timing, the location, and..." Lynn smiled grimly, "the fact that Terri would be on the command ship."

The room went cold. Terri straightened. "They're going to target me."

"Which means," Ren said, her voice deadly calm, "we can control exactly what they think they know. Lynn, I want you to let Webb transmit one more message. Tell him Terri will be on the Norwegian command vessel, specific coordinates."

"But I'll actually be on the Danish ship," Terri caught on quickly.

"With a security detail," Ren added. "And we'll have the Norwegian vessel ready for whatever Bora throws at it."

Katya looked concerned. "You're using Terri as bait?"

"I'm using their assumption about our relationship against them," Ren corrected. "They think attacking Terri will distract me, make me vulnerable. Instead, it'll expose their assets and reveal their capabilities."

"I don't like it," Dr. Sharpa said quietly.

"Neither do I," Ren admitted, her composure cracking slightly. "But they've made this personal. They've made our relationship a battlefield. So we fight on that battlefield with every advantage we can create."

The North Sea at 4 AM was a churning mass of black water and white foam. Three naval vessels held position around the abandoned oil platform Bravo-7, their lights extinguished except for the red glow of tactical displays.

Terri stood in the Danish command vessel's operation center, surrounded by monitors showing feeds from helmet cameras of the dive teams. Her hands trembled slightly—not from fear, but from the caffeine and adrenaline coursing through her system.

"Team Alpha in position," came the crackling voice of a Norwegian diver. "Beginning breach of underwater Section C."

On the monitor, Terri could see the eerie green-tinted view of the platform's submerged supports, encrusted with barnacles and seaweed. But there—a too-clean hatch, recently installed.

"That's not original construction," she noted. "Someone's added an airlock."

"Confirmed," Admiral Cross's voice came through from the British vessel. "Teams, expect pressurized compartments beyond those hatches."

Suddenly, an explosion rocked the Norwegian command ship, exactly where Webb had reported Terri would be. The vessel listed but remained operational—they'd been prepared.

"Torpedo impact, minimal damage," reported the Norwegian captain with satisfaction. "The countermeasures worked. We have a semi-submerged stealth ship signature, bearing 045."

"Danish frigate Absalon engaging," Captain Andersen ordered. "Fire control, solution ready."

Below the surface, the divers breached the airlock. The helmet cameras showed a surreal scene—a fully operational laboratory, somehow dry despite being twenty meters underwater.

"My God," one diver breathed. "It's huge."

The space extended into multiple chambers carved into the platform's underwater structure. Equipment lined the walls— servers, quantum field generators, and devices Terri didn't recognize.

"Those cylindrical units," she said urgently. "Don't touch them. They look like modified quantum interference generators. If activated, they could disrupt anything within a kilometer radius."

"Including our life support?" a diver asked nervously.

"Especially your life support if it has any electronic components. Your rebreathers, your heating systems—all of it would fail."

"Bloody hell," Cross muttered. "Teams, extreme caution. Treat everything as armed."

In another section, Team Beta found something worse— detailed plans of TTC facilities worldwide, with specific targets marked.

"They're planning simultaneous attacks," Terri realized, reading the documents visible on abandoned screens. "Sydney, Singapore, São Paulo—all our major hubs."

"When?" Ren's voice cut through from St. John's, where she was monitoring.

"The day of the polar network announcement," Terri replied, her blood running cold. "They want to turn our triumph into a disaster."

A new alarm sounded. "Semi-submerged stealth ship is flooding tubes," the Danish sonar operator announced. "Another torpedo, bearing directly for us."

"All ahead full," Andersen ordered. "Evasive maneuvers."

The Danish vessel lurched as it accelerated, the torpedo passing meters from their hull before Danish countermeasures destroyed it.

"We need those devices intact as evidence," Cross said urgently. "But we can't risk—"

"I can disarm them," Terri said suddenly. "Not physically, but I can talk your teams through it. The quantum cores have a specific shutdown sequence."

Over the next tense hour, Terri guided the dive teams through carefully disabling seventeen interference devices, each one capable of causing catastrophic failures in TTC's network.

"Platform secured," came the eventual report. "No personnel found, but extensive evidence recovered."

"And Bora?" Ren asked.

"Gone," Cross admitted. "But we have his weapons, his plans, and his semi-submerged stealth ship is leaking oil. The Danish Navy is tracking it."

Terri returned to St. John's exhausted but alive. Ren was waiting at the helipad, professional composure abandoned as Terri stepped off the aircraft.

"Don't ever volunteer for something like that again," Ren said, her voice rough with suppressed emotion.

"I won't if you won't," Terri replied, too tired for anything but honesty.

They stood apart, acutely aware of the ground crew watching, of the photographs that might be taken. The forced distance was almost painful.

"We have Webb in custody," Lynn reported, approaching with security. "He's talking. Heartley Industries paid him, but the money originated from accounts linked to Saudi opposition groups."

"The ones opposing Prince Omar's modernization efforts," Katya added. "They see TTC as a threat to oil revenues."

"So our enemies are multiplying," Terri observed wearily.

"But now we know who they are," Ren said, her strategic mind already working. "And we have their weapons. Dr. Sharpa?"

The older scientist stepped forward. "The interference devices are ingenious, actually. But knowing how they work means we can shield against them. I can have countermeasures ready within two weeks."

"Make it one," Ren said. "The polar announcement can't be delayed."

As the group dispersed, Terri and Ren walked toward the facility, maintaining careful distance.

"I was terrified," Ren admitted quietly, her voice barely audible over the wind. "When that torpedo hit the Norwegian ship, even knowing you weren't there, I couldn't focus, couldn't think."

"That's human, Ren. That's what love does."

"It's a liability. They knew it would affect me."

Terri stopped walking. "Is that what you think? That loving me makes you weak?"

"No," Ren said firmly, finally meeting her eyes. "It makes me vulnerable. There's a difference. Weakness is something to eliminate. Vulnerability... vulnerability just means I have something worth protecting."

The evidence from the raid was damning. In the secure conference room, Ren presented it to a carefully selected audience—Prince Omar via encrypted connection, Admiral Cross in person, and surprisingly, James Hartley himself, who had been "invited" by federal authorities.

"Your subsidiary funded terrorist operations," Ren stated flatly, showing the financial records. "Your employee, Marcus Waterstone, provided intelligence that aided attempted attacks on civilian maritime infrastructure."

Hartley's lawyer started to object, but Cross cut him off. "The evidence is overwhelming. Your choice is simple—full cooperation or prosecution under international terrorism statutes."

"This is ridiculous," Hartley blustered. "I had no knowledge—"

"Your signature is on the approval for Webb's placement," Lynn interrupted, producing the document. "You personally fast-tracked his security clearance."

Prince Omar spoke from the screen. "Mr. Hartley, you've created a diplomatic crisis. Saudi Arabia cannot be seen supporting terrorism. The rogue elements funding Bora will be dealt with, but you... you're a problem."

"What do you want?" Hartley asked, deflating.

"Complete withdrawal from any transport-related ventures," Ren said. "Full disclosure of all intelligence gathered on TTC, and public support for our polar expansion."

"That's corporate suicide!"

"That's justice," Cross corrected. "The alternative is actual prison."

As Hartley's lawyers huddled with him, Terri leaned toward Ren. "He'll fight back. This won't end him."

"No," Ren agreed. "But it defangs him. And more importantly, it sends a message—attacks on us, personal or professional, will have consequences."

The meeting continued for hours, but the outcome was predetermined. Hartley capitulated, signing agreements that effectively ended his ability to threaten TTC directly.

As they left the conference room, Prince Omar requested a private word with Ren and Terri.

"Your relationship has created challenges for me," he said bluntly. "But your technology is too valuable to lose over personal prejudices. I will manage the religious council, but you must be discreet in our territories."

"Agreed," Ren said.

"There's something else," Prince Omar continued. "Bora has approached Iran. They're interested in his interference technology. You've won this battle, but the war is escalating."

Dr. Volkov stood before a holographic display showing the polar satellite coverage, but her expression was grim.

"The interference devices change everything," she said. "If they can disrupt quantum fields, the polar stations are vulnerable. The aurora already creates natural interference—adding artificial disruption could create dead zones."

"Then we adapt," Ren said, studying the patterns. "Terri, what if we use the aurora itself as a shield?"

Terri's eyes lit up with understanding. "Reverse the polarity of our field generators. Instead of fighting the aurora's interference, we amplify it, create a quantum static field that drowns out artificial disruption."

"Brilliant," Volkov said, immediately grasping the concept. "The natural phenomenon becomes our defense. But the power requirements..."

"Would be enormous," Dr. Sharpa finished. "We'd need dedicated fusion reactors at each polar station."

"Then we build them," Ren decided. "Bruce, what's the cost?"

Bruce ran quick calculations. "Eight hundred million for full implementation. But Ren, that's our entire reserve fund."

"It's that or leave ourselves vulnerable," Katya pointed out. "The raid showed Bora's willing to use any weakness against us."

Lynn had been reviewing legal implications. "There's another issue. Fusion reactors in international waters require special permits. The Antarctic Treaty specifically prohibits nuclear installations."

"Fusion isn't fission," Terri argued. "It's clean energy."

"Try explaining that to bureaucrats who still think quantum teleportation is science fiction," Lynn replied dryly.

Ren made a decision. "We proceed with the installations but call them 'aurora research stations.' Technically true—we're researching how to use aurora phenomena for our network."

"That's a dangerous game," Volkov warned. "If discovered—"

"If we don't do this, Bora's next attack might succeed," Ren countered. "We're past playing safe."

Two nights later, after Terri's return, Ren found herself standing outside Terri's quarters, hesitating. Since the photograph leaked, they'd maintained careful distance, professional boundaries. But the near-miss during the raid had shaken something loose in her.

Terri opened the door before Ren could knock. "I heard you in the hallway. You pace when you're conflicted."

"May I come in?"

Once inside, the professional facades crumbled. Terri pulled Ren into an embrace, both women holding on as if anchoring each other against the storm of their lives.

"I can't lose you," Ren whispered against Terri's shoulder. "When that torpedo launched, when I thought—"

"You didn't lose me. You won't lose me."

"They're using us against each other. Our relationship is a weapon in their hands."

Terri pulled back, meeting Ren's eyes. "Then we make it a shield instead. We stop hiding, stop apologizing. We show the world that love doesn't make us weak—it makes us unstoppable."

"The conservative, old economy markets—"

"Will adapt or be left behind," Terri said firmly. "Ren, we're already revolutionizing global transport. Why not revolutionize corporate culture too?"

Ren kissed her then, pouring months of suppressed emotion into the contact. When they separated, both were breathless.

"After the polar announcement," Ren said. "We go public. Properly. No apologies, no explanations. Just truth."

"That's the Ren I fell in love with," Terri smiled. "The one who refuses to let anyone else define the possible."

They spent the night planning—not just their public revelation, but their counter-strategies against Bora, the polar network's defenses, and the future they were building together.

Terri's fingers intertwined with Ren's. "I've never told you about my family. My mother died when I was young. My father... he was brilliant but distant. Always working, always solving problems, never really seeing me."

"I'm sorry," Ren whispered, recognizing the parallels to her own behavior.

"I promised myself I'd never fall for someone like him," Terri continued, a sad smile playing on her lips. "Someone who would always put the work first. And then I met you."

Ren felt a stab of guilt. "Terri, I—"

"No," Terri interrupted gently. "That's not what I meant. You're like him in brilliance, in drive. But unlike him, you actually see me. Even when you're consumed by the work, you've never made me feel invisible."

The confession hung between them, raw and honest. Ren struggled to find words, so instead, she showed her understanding through touch—her hand reaching up to brush Terri's cheek, a gesture more intimate than any kiss.

Ren awoke gasping, the nightmare still vivid—the network collapsing, people trapped mid-teleport, her life's work becoming a monument to hubris and destruction.

"Hey, it's okay," Terri's voice came through the darkness, her arm tightening around Ren's naked waist. She had stayed the night, their newfound intimacy still fresh and tentative.

"I dreamt it all failed," Ren admitted, her voice uncharacteristically small. "That people died because of my arrogance."

Terri propped herself up on one elbow, her expression serious in the dim light. "That's not arrogance, Ren. That's responsibility. The fact that you worry about this shows why you're the right person to lead this revolution."

"Sometimes I feel like I'm balancing on the edge of a knife," Ren confessed. "One mistake and everything falls apart."

"You're not alone on that knife-edge," Terri said firmly. "I'm right there with you. We all are." She paused, then added softly, "But especially me. Always me."

Ren turned to face her, studying Terri's features as if memorizing them. "Why did you stay? All these years, through all the impossible challenges?"

"At first, it was the science," Terri answered honestly. "Then it was the mission. But for a long time now, it's been you, Ren. It's always been you."

The confession lingered between them, profound in its simplicity. Ren reached out, tracing the line of Terri's jaw with trembling fingers, allowing herself this moment of pure human connection amid the technological revolution they were building.

The call came at 3 AM. Ligia Volkov's face appeared on screen, her expression more severe than usual.

"We have a problem. The Svalbard monitoring station just detected something troubling."

"What kind of troubling?" Ren asked, instantly alert.

"Quantum resonance signatures consistent with Bora's interference devices, but stronger. Much stronger. Coming from underwater positions near three of our planned polar MTU sites."

Terri, who had joined the call, frowned. "He's already deployed? But we destroyed his stockpile."

"Those were prototypes," Volkov said grimly. "I think he's built something bigger. Something permanent. The signatures suggest installations the size of shipping containers."

"Semi-submerged stealth ship-deployed," Ren realized. "That's why he needed the funding. Not for the devices we found, but for something larger."

"If he activates those during our polar network launch..." Terri didn't need to finish.

"We need another raid?" Bruce asked, having joined the growing crisis call.

"No," Admiral Cross's voice came through—Volkov had already contacted him. "The positions are in international waters, under ice. It would take weeks to mount an operation."

"We don't have weeks," Ren said. "The polar announcement is in six days."

"Then we need a different solution," Terri said. "What if we don't destroy them—what if we use them?"

Everyone turned to stare at her.

"Explain," Ren demanded.

"Bora's devices create interference. But interference is just another form of energy. With the right modifications to our receivers, we could potentially convert that interference into usable power for our network."

"Turn his weapons into our batteries?" Sharpa sounded skeptical but intrigued.

"It's theoretically possible," Terri continued, her mind racing. "But we'd need to completely reconfigure our polar arrays. And we'd need someone on-site to make the modifications."

"In the Arctic. In six days. During polar winter," Volkov listed the challenges.

"I'll go," Terri volunteered.

"Absolutely not," Ren said immediately. "You were already targeted once—"

"Which is why I'm the perfect choice. They won't expect us to send the same target twice. And I'm the only one who understands the quantum mechanics well enough to make this work."

The argument continued, but everyone knew Terri was right. The chapter would end with preparations for a desperate race against time—Terri leading a technical team to the Arctic while Ren coordinated defenses against whatever Bora planned for the announcement.

12 THE WEIGHT OF SOULS

In the face of attacks designed to portray their network as unstable and unreliable, the most potent countermeasure, Ren believed, was not just to fix technical flaws or argue in the media, but to regain strategic control of their situation. They needed to plan their counter-offensive, to make decisions that could determine the very survival of TTC, not just as a company, but as a force for positive change, from a location where they knew they were safe. But where? The headquarters, despite its layers of security, felt compromised. The lingering mystery of the 'ghost,' its ability to potentially interact with their network at a fundamental level, raised terrifying questions. Could their communications be monitored? Were their physical movements tracked? Even the most shielded conference room felt potentially vulnerable to an adversary who could seemingly manipulate spacetime or inject fraudulent data into their highly encrypted network. Traditional security measures, designed for a world of physical entry and standard electronic eavesdropping, seemed inadequate against an enemy operating on a different plane, an enemy who understood their systems intimately.

The control room at TTC headquarters had transformed from a center of innovation into a war room. Multiple holographic displays showed attacks happening simultaneously: media headlines screaming about drug shipments, financial charts showing blocked credit lines, and a map highlighting the latest physical attacks on MTU facilities.

Bruce paced frantically, gesturing at a news report. "They're calling us 'The Teleport Cartel' now! Three major networks are running the story that we're the primary distributor for synthetic opioids in North America."

"Our legal countermeasures are being blocked at every turn," Lynn added, her voice hoarse from hours of video conferences with attorneys across five continents. "Every judge who's shown sympathy to our position has suddenly recused themselves citing 'conflicts of interest' that didn't exist last week."

Katya, normally the picture of composure, stared grimly at financial projections. "Six more banks have frozen our lines of credit. At this rate, we'll be facing liquidity issues within thirty days." She rubbed her temples. "The pattern suggests coordination at the highest levels of global finance."

Terri looked up from her terminal, face pale. "It's worse than that. We've detected three more intrusion attempts in the quantum stream in the last hour alone. They're getting more sophisticated, probing different points in the network simultaneously."

A junior technician burst into the room. "Dr. Terri! We've found something." He projected a complex waveform onto the main screen. "We detected this energy signature embedded in our satellite communications. It's... it's not just monitoring our transmissions. It's recording them. Everything. Even in our supposedly secure channels."

The room fell silent as the implications sank in.

"They're inside our communications network," Ren said, her voice unnervingly calm as she studied the signature.

The building's HVAC system suddenly groaned, followed by an acrid smell that made everyone's eyes water.

"Fire alarm!" someone shouted as smoke began pouring from the ventilation grates.

Bruce grabbed a fire extinguisher. "That's not just smoke—that's electrical fire. The whole ventilation system is compromised."

"Everyone out!" Lynn commanded, but Ren held up her hand.

"Wait." She checked her tablet. "The fire suppression system isn't activating. Security doors aren't responding. We're locked in."

Terri's fingers flew across her terminal. "This isn't an accident. Someone's taken control of our building systems. Temperature's rising—we have maybe ten minutes before this room becomes uninhabitable."

Through the reinforced windows, they could see smoke beginning to fill adjacent offices. Staff members were pounding on sealed emergency exits.

"Forty-seven people are trapped in various sections," Bruce reported, checking security feeds. "The stairwells are filling with smoke."

Katya looked at the sealed doors. "We need to get everyone out. Now."

Ren stood perfectly still for a moment, her mind racing through options. Then she turned to Terri. "How many Life MTU chambers do we have operational?"

The room went silent except for the growing roar of flames from the ventilation system.

"Three in the basement lab," Terri whispered. "But Ren, we've never—"

"We have no choice." Ren's voice cut through the smoke-filled air. "Initialize all three chambers. We're evacuating everyone through the Life network."

The descent to the basement lab was harrowing. Emergency lighting cast eerie shadows through the thickening smoke. Bruce led the way, using his security override to force open doors that the compromised system had locked.

"The smoke is lighter down here," Lynn observed, coughing despite the shirt she held over her face.

"Heat rises," Terri explained, her voice muffled. "But we don't have long before the fire spreads through the ventilation shafts."

They reached the Life MTU lab—a section of the building most employees didn't even know existed. Three cylindrical chambers stood like monoliths, each connected to massive power conduits and quantum processing arrays.

"I need to run diagnostics—" Terri began.

"No time," Ren interrupted. "Emergency protocols. We'll run basic bio-scans only."

"The risks—"

"Are less than burning alive." Ren turned to the others. "Terri, you'll operate the sending chambers. I'll go through first, initialize the receiving units at the backup facility."

"What backup facility?" Bruce demanded.

"Warehouse Seven. We installed Life MTUs there six months ago. Officially, it's additional cargo capacity." Ren stepped toward the first chamber. "Unofficially, it's our emergency evacuation site."

"You've been planning for this?" Katya asked, incredulous.

"I've been planning for many contingencies." Ren paused at the chamber door. "Including the possibility that someone might try to kill us all at once."

Through the security monitors, they could see staff members in other parts of the building struggling against locked doors, some already collapsed from smoke inhalation.

"We need consent protocols," Lynn said automatically. "Legal waivers, medical histories—"

"Lynn." Ren's voice was sharp. "Look at monitor seven."

On the screen, a young technician lay unconscious near a sealed exit, smoke pooling around her still form.

"She can't consent. None of the unconscious ones can. So we either break our own protocols to save them, or we let them die." Ren's jaw tightened. "I know which I choose."

Lynn nodded slowly. "Emergency medical exception. Life-threatening situation, implied consent for life-saving intervention. It'll hold up in court."

"Then let's move." Ren stepped into the chamber. "Bruce, start bringing people down. Conscious ones first—we'll need them to help with the others."

The chamber hummed to life around Ren, a deep resonance that seemed to vibrate through her bones. She'd overseen hundreds of tests, but being inside the chamber was different. The air itself seemed to thicken, pressing against her skin like water.

"Initiating scan," Terri's voice came through the intercom, professionally calm despite the circumstances. "Try to remain perfectly still."

Light erupted from every surface—not harsh, but penetrating, as if it could see through her, catalog every atom, every quantum state. Ren felt a tingling sensation, like static electricity dancing across her neural pathways.

"Scan complete. Initiating transfer in three... two... one..."

The world dissolved.

For an impossibly brief moment that felt like eternity, Ren existed as pure information—consciousness without form, awareness without substance. She could feel the data stream, her very essence encoded in quantum fluctuations, racing through the network she'd built.

Then, with a sensation like surfacing from deep water, reality reassembled around her.

She gasped, stumbling forward in the receiving chamber at Warehouse Seven. Her body felt electric, every nerve ending hypersensitive. The taste of copper lingered on her tongue, and her vision swam with afterimages of impossible colors.

But she was alive. Whole.

She immediately moved to the control panel, her fingers only slightly trembling as she initialized the other receiving chambers. Through the quantum-encrypted link, she could hear Terri's voice: "Ren's transfer successful. Biological readings nominal. Beginning evacuation sequence."

The first group came through minutes later—five staff members who'd been nearest the Life MTU lab. They materialized in flashes of contained light, each stumbling out with expressions of shock and wonder.

"Did we just—" one began.

"Yes," Ren cut him off. "And now you're going to help me save the others. We need medical teams ready for the unconscious ones."

Bruce came through next, and despite the dire situation, his face split into an amazed grin. "That was incredible! Like being lightning!"

Katya arrived third, immediately doubling over and vomiting into a hastily grabbed waste bin. "Oh God," she gasped between heaves. "The spinning... everything's spinning..."

"Vestibular disruption," Ren explained, supporting her. "Some people are more sensitive. It'll pass."

Lynn materialized with the controlled grace of someone refusing to show weakness, though her knuckles were white as she gripped the chamber's edge. "The legal implications—" she began, then stopped. "No. Later. How many more?"

"Thirty-eight," Ren replied, watching the status boards. "Including twelve unconscious."

The unconscious staff members were the hardest. Bruce and two security guards carefully carried them into the chambers, positioning them on specially designed transport platforms that would maintain their position during transfer.

"We've never transported unconscious subjects," Terri's voice crackled through the link, the first hint of fear breaking through her professional composure.

Ren watched the biometric readings of the first unconscious technician—the young woman from monitor seven. "We tested on sedated primates. Same principle."

"That's not—" Terri began, then stopped. Through the link, they could hear the roar of flames growing closer to the Life MTU lab.

"Do it," Ren commanded.

As the transfer initiated, Ren's mind flashed back to the early tests. The failures that haunted her dreams.

Subject 27—a laboratory rat that simply never rematerialized, its quantum signature scattered across the network like cosmic background radiation.

Subject 43—a rabbit that returned missing its left hind leg, the limb's data corrupted during transfer, leaving a perfectly healed stump as if the leg had never existed.

Subject 89—a chimpanzee that materialized physically intact but neurologically damaged, its higher functions erased, leaving only base instincts.

They'd solved each problem methodically, adding redundancies, improving error correction, refining the biological preservation protocols. But the weight of those failures, the knowledge of what could go wrong...

The young technician materialized, unconscious but breathing.

Medical scanners confirmed full biological integrity.

"Thank God," someone whispered.

They continued the evacuation, each unconscious form a testament to Ren's willingness to break her own ethical guidelines to save lives. With each successful transfer, the weight on her shoulders grew heavier—not from failure, but from success. The technology worked. Which meant the world would never be the same.

Bruce slammed his fist on the table. "So what do we do? We can't just stop operating!"

Before Ren could respond, her secure phone buzzed. Then Katya's. Then Lynn's. Then Bruce's.

They all looked at their screens simultaneously, faces draining of color.

"It's my daughter," Katya whispered. "Someone's sent photos of her at university. Walking to class. At the library. In her dorm room—" Her voice broke.

"My mother," Lynn said, her professional composure cracking. "Pictures from her care facility. Someone's been watching her."

Bruce's face had gone rigid with rage. "My brother's kids. At their school playground." He looked up, eyes blazing. "The message says 'Your move, Dr. Franco.'"

Ren's own phone showed images of Terri's parents at their retirement community in Mexico, unaware they were being photographed.

"He's threatening our families," Terri said, her voice hollow. "Bora's making it personal."

"We can't protect everyone," Bruce said, his security expertise turning the words bitter. "Not from someone with his resources. Not if they're willing to—"

"We need to meet. Plan. Somewhere absolutely secure," Ren interrupted. "Somewhere he can't possibly monitor or attack."

"Where?" Lynn demanded. "He's apparently watching our families across three continents!"

Ren stood slowly. "Killiniq Island. We'll use the Life MTUs to get there. No flight plans, no travel records, no way to track us."

"But he'll know we're gone," Katya protested. "He's watching everything."

"Let him watch empty offices," Ren replied coldly. "We'll leave decoys, false schedules, make it look like we're still here. By the time he realizes we're gone, we'll have our counter-strategy ready."

"The energy requirements for Life transfers are also significantly higher than for cargo," Ren added, citing technical data from Terri's display. "Maintaining the coherence of a complex biological system, with all its dynamic processes, its electrical signals, its chemical reactions, its consciousness… is power-intensive. Our expanded satellite network, especially with the recent Phase Three deployment and increased energy buffer capacity provided by the new polar arrays, is necessary to provide that power and processing capability for simultaneous transfers, or multiple transfers of a single person if an abort and retry is needed. We simply couldn't have done this reliably on a large scale even a few years ago."

The materialization at Killiniq Island was rougher than at Warehouse Seven. The receiving MTU, hastily assembled in sub-zero conditions, vibrated with barely controlled energy.

Bruce emerged first, immediately alert, hand instinctively reaching for a weapon that wasn't there. "Clear," he announced, though his breath caught as the Arctic cold hit his lungs like knives.

Lynn followed, maintaining her composure despite the way her legs shook. "The temperature differential is… significant," she managed through chattering teeth.

Katya materialized and immediately collapsed to her knees, dry-heaving. "I can't… the nausea is worse… everything's spinning faster…"

Ren appeared last, helping Terri support Katya. "It's the multiple transfers in rapid succession. The inner ear needs time to recalibrate."

As they helped Katya to a bench, a sound from outside made them all freeze—a deep, rumbling growl.

Through the habitat's reinforced window, they saw it: a massive polar bear, drawn by the unusual scents and energy signatures. It stood on its hind legs, nearly ten feet tall, testing the air.

"The barriers will hold," Terri said, though her voice was uncertain.

The bear circled the habitat twice, occasionally pressing its massive paws against the walls, leaving fog on the windows from its breath. After twenty minutes that felt like hours, it finally ambled away into the Arctic twilight.

"Welcome to Killiniq Island," Bruce muttered. "Population: fifteen humans and one very curious apex predator."

They had been meeting for two hours when Bruce's emergency beacon activated.

"Perimeter breach," he announced, checking his tablet. "Southwest sensor grid. Multiple heat signatures."

Through the window, they saw them—a pack of Arctic wolves, seven strong, circling the habitat with the patient intelligence of practiced hunters. Their pale forms were almost invisible against the snow except for their eyes, which caught and reflected the habitat's lights like yellow stars.

"They can smell us," Bruce explained. "Fresh scents in a place that's been uninhabited. We're curiosities. Potential prey."

"The barriers—" Lynn began.

"Will hold," Bruce assured her. "But we're essentially trapped until they lose interest."

Ren watched the lead wolf, a massive male with a scarred muzzle, as it tested the habitat's foundation, looking for weaknesses. "We're under siege by nature while under siege by Bora. There's poetry in that."

Her secure phone buzzed. A message from an unknown number: "Enjoying the Arctic, Dr. Franco? Your families are enjoying their evenings too. Your move."

Attached was a live feed—Terri's parents having dinner, unaware of the camera watching them.

"He knows we're not in St. John's," Katya said quietly.

"But not where we are," Ren replied. "He's fishing."

Another message arrived: "The Life MTU technology is too dangerous for private hands. Surrender it to international control, or watch everyone you care about disappear. You have 48 hours."

Outside, the wolves had settled into a patient wait, their breath creating small clouds in the freezing air. Inside, the team faced their own predators—human ones who understood exactly what buttons to push.

"We need to accelerate our plans," Ren said. "The humanitarian demonstration. We do it tomorrow."

"That's too soon," Lynn protested. "We need permits, medical staff, coordination with local authorities—"

"We need to change the narrative before Bora forces us into a corner we can't escape from." Ren turned to Terri. "Can you identify a suitable disaster scenario by morning?"

Terri nodded. "There's flooding in Bangladesh. Thousands trapped on rooftops. Traditional rescue is taking too long."

"Then that's our stage." Ren looked at each team member. "We save lives, publicly, undeniably. Let Bora try to spin that as evil."

The wolves howled outside, a sound that sent primitive shivers down their spines. But the real predators, they all knew, were the ones they couldn't see—the ones threatening their families, their company, their vision for humanity's future.

"We should establish rotation schedules," Bruce suggested. "Someone monitoring the situation here, someone watching our families through our security networks—"

A loud crack interrupted him. One of the wolves had tested the electric fence, yelping as it retreated.

"Even predators can be taught boundaries," Ren observed. "Bora's about to learn his."

Inside the habitat, the rest of the team coped with the stress in their own ways. Katya sat cross-legged on her bunk, surrounded by financial projections and risk assessments, more withdrawn than usual. Her normally impeccable appearance had given way to functionality—hair pulled back severely, minimal makeup, clothing chosen purely for warmth and comfort.

"The tribal banking network is our best option," she muttered to herself, making notes. "If we structure it as a series of independent entities with mutual cooperation agreements..." Her voice trailed off as she immersed herself in complex financial architecture, finding solace in numbers and systems.

Across the room, Bruce was doing push-ups, his face red with exertion. A bandage wrapped his right knee where he'd injured it during an overzealous workout the previous day.

"One hundred and forty-eight... one hundred and forty-nine..." he counted through gritted teeth.

Lynn looked up from her legal briefs. "Bruce, you're going to tear something. Again."

"Need to stay sharp," he panted. "Body and mind connected. Can't afford weakness."

"There's a difference between strength and self-destruction," Lynn pointed out. "You've been pushing yourself too hard since Rotterdam."

Bruce collapsed onto his back, breathing heavily. "We all cope differently, Counselor. You bury yourself in legal precedents. I push my physical limits."

Lynn sighed, returning to her work. "Fair point. But when this is over, you might consider therapy instead of ultra-marathons."

Two junior staff members, part of the technical support team, spoke quietly near the habitat's small kitchen area.

"I've never seen Dr. Franco like this," whispered Maya, a quantum engineer. "She actually asked for my opinion on the field stabilizer design yesterday."

Carlos nodded, stirring his coffee. "Things are changing. You can feel it. The pressure is either breaking us or... I don't know, transforming us somehow."

"Do you think it'll work? Going public with Life MTU?"

Carlos glanced toward the door where Ren and Terri had gone outside. "I hope so. But either way, nothing will be the same after this. For any of us."

The team gathered around the central table in the habitat, the raw beauty of the Arctic visible through the reinforced windows. Digital displays showed the global network, the pattern of attacks, and the web of connections they'd mapped to Bora and his allies.

"We need a concrete counter-offensive," Ren stated, her voice firm. "Reactive defense isn't enough anymore."

Terri brought up a complex schematic. "I've been developing what I call a 'ghost trap.' We create a deliberate vulnerability in a non-critical part of the network—something that looks like an oversight but is actually a carefully designed lure."

"Bait," Bruce said, nodding enthusiastically.

"Exactly," Terri continued. "When they attempt to exploit it, the system will trace the intrusion back to its source while simultaneously feeding them false data. We'll be able to identify their technical signatures and potentially their physical location."

"That's assuming they're careless enough to take the bait," Lynn cautioned. "These people have been meticulous so far."

"Which is why we need to make the opportunity irresistible," Terri replied. "A vulnerability in our core quantum encryption that would give them access to our transfer protocols."

Katya leaned forward. "Meanwhile, we need to secure our financial position. I propose we activate our contingency banking network through our tribal partners."

"The sovereign nation gambit," Lynn said with a hint of admiration. "Using tribal banking licenses to create a financial network outside federal jurisdiction."

"It's legally sound," Katya insisted. "The tribes have sovereign banking rights. By partnering with them, we create a financial infrastructure that the cartels and their banking allies can't touch."

Lynn nodded slowly. "It's aggressive, but defensible. I'm more concerned about your ghost trap, Terri. If we actively lure them in, even to catch them, we could be liable if anything goes wrong."

"And if we do nothing, we're finished anyway," Bruce countered, his voice rising. "I say we go further. Use what we know about Bora. Expose him. Use the Life MTU to put our people in position to gather evidence of his criminal activities."

"That's crossing a line," Lynn said sharply. "Using our technology for what amounts to corporate espionage—"

"It's self-defense!" Bruce insisted. "They've been attacking us from the shadows for months. They've tried to destroy everything we've built. They're hurting people with those drug shipments. Where's the line for them?"

"We don't win by becoming what we're fighting against," Lynn argued.

The tension in the room was palpable. Ren had been silent, listening to the competing perspectives. Now all eyes turned to her.

"Five years ago, I would have made this decision alone," Ren admitted to the group. "But I've learned—sometimes painfully— that my perspective has blind spots. Each of you sees angles I miss. So before we commit, I need to hear from everyone."

The admission seemed to shift something in the room. Katya, who had been reserved throughout much of the discussion, spoke up.

"We need to remember what we built TTC for," she said quietly. "Not just profit or technological achievement, but to solve real problems. To help people."

Bruce's expression softened. "That's actually my point. While we're under attack, people are suffering. The technology that could help them is being hamstrung."

Ren nodded, taking in all perspectives. "We need a multi-pronged approach. Terri's ghost trap gives us intelligence. Katya's financial network gives us stability. And we need to change the narrative."

"How?" Lynn asked.

"By showing the world what the Life MTU can really do," Ren said, her decision crystallizing. "Not as a weapon or a tool for espionage, but as what it was always meant to be—a way to help people in desperate need."

She stood, her voice gaining strength. "We begin tomorrow. The Life MTU goes public, but on our terms. We'll demonstrate it first with a humanitarian mission that no one can ignore or misrepresent. Moving disaster victims from dangerous conditions to safety within the same country."

"The media will go ballistic," Bruce warned. "Human teleportation—it's a paradigm shift beyond anything we've done before."

"Let them," Ren replied. "For once, the story won't be about us. It will be about the lives we save. And that's a narrative even Bora can't easily corrupt."

The strategy session continued deep into the Arctic night. Maps of Bangladesh covered every surface, showing flood zones, population densities, and potential Life MTU deployment sites.

"We'll need local government approval," Lynn insisted, making notes. "The Bangladesh authorities—"

"Are overwhelmed," Katya interrupted, pulling up news feeds. "They're begging for international assistance. Forty thousand people stranded, aid helicopters can only evacuate dozens at a time."

"We could save thousands in hours instead of weeks," Terri

calculated. "But we'd need at least six Life MTU pairs—three extraction points, three safe zones."

"The energy requirements alone—" Bruce began.

"Are manageable if we reroute power from the cargo network temporarily," Ren said. "This is what we built this for. Not profit. Not corporate growth. Saving lives."

Through the window, the wolf pack remained, patient shadows against the snow. One of the younger wolves played with something—a piece of equipment that had blown off during setup.

"They're adapting to our presence," Bruce observed. "Learning our patterns."

"Like Bora," Lynn said grimly. "Except the wolves are just hungry. Bora wants to destroy everything we've built."

Ren studied the flood maps. "What if we invited media to witness the Life MTU deployment? Full transparency?"

"Risky," Lynn warned. "If something goes wrong—"

"Everything's risky now," Ren countered. "But public success is our best defense against Bora's narrative."

A new message arrived on Ren's phone: "Your window is closing. 36 hours remain."

This time, the attached image showed Bruce's nephew at soccer practice, unaware of the telephoto lens capturing his every move.

Bruce's fist clenched. "When this is over, I'm going to—"

"Going to what?" Ren asked calmly. "Hunt him down? Use our technology for revenge? That's exactly what he wants—to make us into the monsters he's painting us as."

"So we just let him threaten kids?"

"We protect them by winning the right way," Ren replied. "By showing the world what TTC really represents. By making ourselves too valuable, too necessary to destroy."

Outside, the lead wolf suddenly stood, ears pricked. The pack responded instantly, disappearing into the darkness as quickly as they'd appeared. Something had spooked them—something the humans couldn't perceive.

"Polar bear returning?" Katya asked nervously.

Bruce checked the sensors. "No... nothing on thermal. They just... left."

The Arctic returned to its pristine silence, but the sense of being watched, hunted, remained.

"We should establish shifts," Terri suggested. "Two sleeping, three working. We can't all collapse from exhaustion."

"Agreed," Ren said. "But first, let's finalize the Bangladesh operation. Every life we save makes Bora's threats harder to justify to his allies."

They worked through the night, planning humanity's first mass teleportation rescue while Arctic predators circled in the darkness and human predators threatened their loved ones from afar. The Life MTU technology, born from a desire to unite humanity, had become both their greatest weapon and their greatest vulnerability.

Later that evening, Ren stood alone outside the habitat, the Arctic night surrounding her. The aurora danced overhead, ribbons of green and purple light against the vast darkness. Despite the insulated suit, the cold bit at her exposed face, a sharp reminder of the harsh reality beyond their temporary sanctuary.

The habitat door opened behind her, and Terri stepped out, carrying two steaming mugs.

"Thought you might need this," she said, offering one to Ren.

Ren accepted it gratefully, the warmth seeping through her gloves. "Thank you."

They stood in companionable silence for a moment, watching the sky's ethereal display.

"You haven't slept in three days," Terri said finally, her breath visible in the cold air. "Even you have limits, Ren."

Ren stared at the distant horizon. "I can't afford limits right now. Not when everything we've built is at risk."

"That's exactly when you need them most." Terri's hand found Ren's, their fingers intertwining. "You've always led with your mind. But right now, the team needs more than your brilliance—they need your humanity."

Ren turned to look at her, struck by the simple truth in her words. "I'm not sure I know how to give them that."

"You already are," Terri said softly. "Asking for everyone's input today—that wasn't the Ren I met years ago. You're evolving, adapting."

"Necessity," Ren murmured.

"Growth," Terri corrected. "And it matters. The team sees it. I see it."

Ren felt a vulnerability she rarely allowed herself. "I keep thinking about what we're about to do. Revealing the Life MTU... it changes everything, Terri. Not just for us, for humanity."

"That's been true since the day you conceived it."

"But now it's real. Once it's public, we can't control how it's used. Not entirely." Ren's voice dropped lower. "What if we're wrong? What if revealing Life MTU is exactly what they want? What if I'm leading us into their trap?"

The admission of uncertainty—so rare from Ren—hung in the frigid air. Then Terri stepped closer, her gaze steady and unwavering.

"Then we'll face it together. And adapt. Like we always have."

Ren felt something shift inside her, a tightness loosening. She had carried the weight of these decisions alone for so long, convinced that solitude was the price of leadership. But here, in this desolate, beautiful wilderness, with Terri beside her, she felt a different kind of strength forming—one born not of isolation, but of connection.

"I've been thinking about something Bruce said earlier," Ren said. "About using the Life MTU for surveillance. For gathering evidence against Bora."

"You seemed opposed to the idea," Terri observed.

"I was. I am." Ren frowned. "But not for the reasons Lynn cited. Not because of legal concerns."

"Then why?"

Ren turned to face Terri fully. "Because once we start using this technology that way—for covert operations, for purposes beyond its intended design—we begin a journey I'm not sure has an endpoint. Where does it stop? When does the justification of 'necessity' become something else entirely?"

Terri considered this. "That's why you want to start with humanitarian applications."

"It sets a precedent. It establishes the primary purpose in the public consciousness." Ren looked back at the aurora. "I've spent my life pursuing this technology because I believed it could liberate humanity from physical constraints. Not to create new forms of control."

Alone for a moment, Ren stared at her hands—hands that had created a technology that could save countless lives or, in the wrong hands, enable unprecedented oppression. The weight of that responsibility pressed down on her, making it hard to breathe.

The morning came with a blood-red sunrise that painted the Arctic landscape in shades of fire. The wolf tracks around the habitat told the story of their night-long vigil—patient circles, investigation points, places where they'd settled to watch.

Ren stood at the window, exhausted but determined. In six hours, they would begin the Bangladesh operation. In six hours, the world would learn about Life MTU technology. In six hours, everything would change.

"Can't sleep?" Terri asked, joining her.

"Calculating variables," Ren replied. "Success rates. Failure points. Public reaction scenarios."

"And?"

"Best case: we save thousands, change the narrative, force Bora to reconsider. Worst case: technical failure during live broadcast, confirming every fear about our technology."

"Most likely case?"

Ren turned from the window. "We succeed technically but Bora escalates. He's not the type to accept defeat gracefully."

Her phone buzzed. Another message: "24 hours. Your families are depending on your decision."

This time, no photo. Just GPS coordinates—the exact locations of twelve family members across the globe.

"He's showing us he can reach them all simultaneously," Terri observed.

"And we're about to show the world we can save thousands simultaneously," Ren replied. "Let's see which demonstration carries more weight."

The Arctic sun climbed higher, revealing the full desolation of their surroundings—and the fresh polar bear tracks that crossed the wolf trails, a reminder that in this harsh land, even predators had predators.

In a penthouse office overlooking Tokyo Bay, Bora studied the report on his secure tablet. His expression remained impassive, but a muscle twitched in his jaw.

"Unusual energy signatures detected in the Northeast Canadian Arctic," his aide explained. "The pattern matches what our source described as consistent with a Life MTU activation."

"So they've finally used it," Bora murmured. "Interesting timing."

"Should we investigate further?"

Bora's lips curved in a cold smile. "No need. Let them think they've found a sanctuary. Their desperate move tells us everything we need to know."

He closed the report and gazed out at the harbor lights. "Prepare The Ghost for the final phase. It's time we took control of what Dr. Franco has built."

13 DELIVERANCE IN THE SHADOWS

Terri answered carefully, "I've watched you build this from equations to reality, Ren. Your purpose has always been good."

"Purpose can corrupt," Ren muttered. "Destruction often begins with noble intentions."

"Remember when we first teleported living tissue? You said it's about connecting people, not moving things. We're connecting needs with resources. Countering enemies is secondary to saving lives."

Ren relaxed slightly. "When did you become philosophical?"

"Someone must be, when you're lost in quantum equations."

"I fear succeeding in ways that change us. Change me."

"Then we watch each other. Remember why we started."

Ren nodded. "Tomorrow, we deliver hope—with precision, care, humanity."

"That's why I follow you. Even as a strategic genius, you never forget the human element."

As Terri left, Ren faced the window, her reflection clearer against the darkness. The decision remained weighty, but felt lighter, shared.

"We mobilize aid to Pakistan and Iran," Ren stated, the decision firm, resonating with the purpose that had driven her for decades. "Food, medicine, essential equipment. We replace what was lost in Eastern Europe, and more. We double the amount of aid the cartels had destroyed or intended to replace with narcotics in their target regions, and we deliver it securely, directly, to those who need it, bypassing the broken systems and the corrupt hands."

This operation would be conducted in absolute secrecy. No media announcements, no fanfare, no coordination through standard international aid channels that might be monitored or influenced by the cartels or their allies in traditional logistics. Only the core executive team on Killiniq Island, a handful of the most trusted technical and logistics personnel back in St. John's (operating under strict security protocols and limited information), and carefully vetted partners on the ground in the receiving countries would know the full scope of what was happening. They couldn't risk another leak, another chance for the cartels to interfere, destroy the shipments upon arrival, or twist the narrative. The lessons were stark; discretion and security were paramount.

The door to the command center burst open. Bruce stood there, tablet in hand, face pale.

"We have a problem," he said. "Three of our suppliers just canceled. All within the last hour."

Ren straightened, exhaustion forgotten. "Which ones?"

"The pharmaceutical companies in India. Two in Brazil. They're citing 'regulatory concerns.'" Bruce's fingers flew across his tablet. "But the timing—"

"It's Bora," Terri finished. "He knows."

"How?" Ren demanded. "This operation was completely compartmentalized."

Bruce pulled up encrypted communications logs. "The suppliers all received identical messages from their respective governments, warning about 'unauthorized technology transfers.' The language is too similar to be coincidence."

"Can we source alternatives?" Katya asked, already running calculations.

"Not in time. Not for the antibiotics and vaccines." Bruce's usual energy had turned sharp with urgency. "Without those medical supplies, we're sending half an aid package. People will die."

Ren stood, pacing the small space. "Show me the supplier locations again."

Bruce projected a map. Three facilities, spread across two

continents. All with basic MTUs for standard commercial shipping, but nothing rated for life-critical medical supplies that required Life MTU protocols.

"We can't teleport directly to them," Terri said, following Ren's thought. "No Life MTUs at those sites."

"But we could establish temporary ones," Ren said slowly. "If we had the components."

"That would require sending technical teams," Terri countered. "Exposing our people, our methods—"

"Or," Ren interrupted, "I go myself."

The room erupted.

"Absolutely not," Terri said immediately. "You're the primary target. Leaving this facility—"

"Would be exactly what they don't expect," Ren finished. "They think I'm hiding, cowering. They're watching our facilities, our known personnel. But me, personally, walking into a pharmaceutical plant in Mumbai?"

"It's suicide," Bruce said flatly. "Even if you somehow avoid detection getting there, the moment you start installing Life MTU components, they'll know."

"Let them know," Ren said, her voice carrying an edge of defiance. "Let them see that we won't abandon those people. That their threats won't stop us from doing what's right."

Katya cleared her throat. "There's another problem. The Iranian military has mobilized around two of our planned delivery sites. Satellite imagery shows armored vehicles, aerial surveillance. They're not just investigating—they're preparing to intercept."

Lynn's secure line crackled to life. "My contact in Pakistan just went dark. His last message mentioned 'visitors' asking about unusual shipments."

The weight of the situation settled over them. Their humanitarian mission was unraveling before it had truly begun.

"We abort," Bruce said. "Regroup, try again when—"

"No." Ren's voice cut through the room. "We adapt. Terri, can you modify the routing to avoid the compromised sites?"

"I can try, but without ground coordination—"

"I'll handle ground coordination," Lynn interrupted. "I have a backup contact, but she'll need guarantees. And money. A lot of money."

"How much?" Katya asked.

"Fifty million. US dollars. Untraceable."

Bruce whistled low. "That's not a bribe, that's a ransom."

"It's the price of ensuring the aid reaches the people," Lynn said. "My contact has connections in both countries' intelligence services. She can guarantee safe passage, but only if we pay."

Ren turned to Katya. "Can we do it?"

"It'll drain our emergency reserves," Katya said, fingers flying across her tablet. "We'd be vulnerable if anything else goes wrong."

"Everything's already going wrong," Ren pointed out. "Do it."

"You're asking us to trust you with our lives," Bruce said bluntly. "While someone might be selling us out."

"Then we compartmentalize," Ren replied. "Everyone handles only their piece. No one sees the full picture except—"

"Except you," Terri finished. "Making you the ultimate target."

"I already am. At least this way, when they come for me, the rest of you can continue."

"That's not a plan, it's a suicide note," Bruce protested.

"It's necessity," Ren countered. "Unless you have a better idea?"

The silence that followed was answer enough.

Three hours later, Ren stood in the equipment bay, checking the portable Life MTU components strapped to her body beneath an oversized winter coat. Each component was worth millions, containing proprietary quantum processors that could establish a temporary Life MTU link.

"This is insane," Terri said, helping adjust the straps. "You're literally wearing our most advanced technology as a vest."

"It's the only way to transport them without detection," Ren replied. "Standard shipping is compromised, and we can't use the MTU network to send MTU components—the quantum signature would create a feedback loop."

"I'm coming with you," Terri said suddenly.

"No."

"You need someone watching your back. Someone who understands the technology if something goes wrong."

"I need you here, coordinating the transfers." Ren turned to face her. "This only works if you're managing the network. You're the only one I trust with that."

Terri's hand found Ren's. "Then at least let me set up a quantum-encrypted beacon. If something happens—"

"Nothing will happen."

"Ren." Terri's voice carried weight. "We both know that's not true. Bora has people everywhere. The cartels have reach we're only beginning to understand. You're walking into their territory."

"Then I'd better be quick." Ren squeezed Terri's hand, then pulled away. "Twelve hours. If I'm not back by then—"

"I'll come find you myself."

Despite everything, Ren smiled. "I know you will."

The next seventy-two hours were a whirlwind of precise, coordinated action. From their Arctic sanctuary, the executive team orchestrated a global response that would have been impossible from their compromised headquarters. Secure quantum channels hummed with encrypted communications as Ren's plan transformed from strategy to reality.

Katya immediately took charge of the financial aspects. This wasn't about making money; it was about spending it, strategically and on a massive scale, without attracting unwanted attention or being blocked by the financial pressures they were facing.

"We are purchasing aid directly, globally," she explained, setting up secure, rapidly deployable funding pipelines using a combination of TTC's vast, untracked reserves (built from Ren's early ventures and the highly profitable MDP chip sales) and complex financial maneuvers that bypassed traditional banking choke points.

"No calls for donations, no reliance on external aid budgets that can be traced or pressured by our enemies. TTC pays for everything, covering the cost of aid acquisition and teleportation. It's a massive investment, but a necessary one."

Katya worked intensely on her encrypted terminal in the Killiniq Island habitat. The faint light of the holographic displays reflected in her glasses. She initiated complex, multi-currency transactions, buying bulk quantities of goods from suppliers around the world – high-nutrient food packs from manufacturers in Southeast Asia, essential medicines and vaccines from pharmaceutical companies in

India and Brazil, emergency shelter kits from logistics hubs in South Africa. She bypassed traditional brokers and large-scale distributors, working directly with manufacturers and trusted, smaller logistics firms who could get the aid to TTC's MTU sites quickly and discreetly. She had to be vigilant, watching for any signs that suppliers were being pressured by the cartels or that transactions were being flagged by wary banks (despite her efforts to obscure their origin and destination). Her work involved layers of financial obfuscation, legitimate business transactions masking the true purpose and destination of the funds, a high-stakes game played out in the digital realm.

Mumbai, India. Sixteen hours earlier than Killiniq Island time.

Ren had never felt more exposed. The pharmaceutical facility's lobby was bright, modern, and filled with security cameras. The weight of the Life MTU components against her ribs was a constant reminder of what she carried—and what she risked.

"Dr. Chen," the receptionist said, using the alias Lynn had arranged. "Mr. Patel will see you now."

Patel's office overlooked the production floor. Through the windows, Ren could see the massive operation—and the basic MTU platform used for standard shipments, currently sitting idle.

"You're not Dr. Chen," Patel said quietly once the door closed. His weathered face showed no surprise. "You're her."

Ren tensed. "I don't know what—"

"Please." Patel held up a hand. "Your face has been on every news channel for weeks. The question is why Ren Franco is standing in my office wearing what appears to be twenty kilograms of hidden equipment."

"How do you—"

"Thermal imaging in the lobby. Standard security since the terrorist threats started." Patel moved to his desk, pulling out a bottle of whiskey and two glasses. "So. Will you tell me why you're really here, or shall I call security?"

Ren made a calculated decision. "Your government canceled our medical supply order. People in Pakistan and Iran will die without those supplies. I'm here to ensure that doesn't happen."

"By doing what exactly?"

"By upgrading your MTU to handle medical supplies directly.

Bypassing the distribution networks that have been compromised."

Patel poured the whiskey slowly. "You're asking me to violate direct government orders. To risk my company, my freedom, my family's safety."

"I'm asking you to save lives."

"At what cost?" Patel pushed a glass toward her. "Do you know what happened to the last facility that defied these new 'regulations'? Raided. Shut down. The owner imprisoned on terrorism charges."

"Then why haven't you called security already?"

Patel was quiet for a long moment. "My daughter. She's a doctor in Kashmir. Last month, her clinic ran out of antibiotics. Children died. Children who could have been saved if supplies hadn't been delayed by bureaucracy and corruption." He met Ren's eyes. "If you can guarantee these supplies reach the people who need them—truly guarantee it—then I'll give you one hour. No more."

"That's all I need."

As Ren began removing the Life MTU components, Patel moved to his computer. "I'm disabling security cameras in the MTU bay. Maintenance window. But if anyone checks—"

"They won't." Ren was already moving toward the door. "And Mr. Patel? Thank you."

"Don't thank me yet. We both might be in prison by nightfall."

Bruce, translating Katya's financial directives into tangible goods and logistical reality, became the orchestrator of global procurement and initial logistics for the operation. His encyclopedic knowledge of supply chains and his relentless drive, now channeled into a mission of profound importance, were invaluable.

"We need confirmed quantities, verified quality, and delivery to our origin MTU sites within tight, synchronized windows," he dictated during secure calls with his trusted logistics team back in St. John's. "Speed and discretion are paramount. Any anomaly, any delay, flag it immediately."

Bruce, energy still high despite the confined space of the habitat, coordinated on multiple screens, his voice firm and clear. He worked with suppliers, verifying manifests against purchase orders, scheduling pickup times, ensuring the aid packages met specific standards for humanitarian distribution – durability, nutritional value, clear labeling (though the labeling would need to be in local languages for the destination, adding another layer of operational complexity). He arranged for secure, unbranded electric trucks to pick up the aid directly from supplier warehouses and transport it to the nearest TTC origin MTUs, bypassing standard shipping routes entirely. His focus was on speed, volume, and absolute discretion.

"We need enough food packs for half a million people for a month, enough water purification tablets for the same, medical kits for fifty thousand, a hundred thousand emergency shelter units," he rattled off specifications, doubling the numbers from the destroyed aid. "Double what was lost," the phrase became a silent mantra for the procurement teams, driving them to secure unprecedented quantities under pressure, leveraging TTC's reputation and resources to get suppliers to prioritize their orders.

Terri's role was perhaps the most critical and the most technically challenging – ensuring the secure, undetectable movement of this massive volume of aid through the TTC network, directly countering the 'ghost' threat and potential interference from Bora's network. This operation would push the limits of their system's capacity and security protocols, sending thousands of simultaneous transfers across multiple continents.

Terri hunched over a complex network display, showing the flow of data and energy between global origin MTUs, the orbital satellites, and projected receiving sites in Pakistan and Iran. "We're routing transfers through newly deployed polar and inclined-orbit arrays," she explained to Ren via encrypted connection, highlighting specific pathways on the map that avoided major commercial routes potentially monitored by the cartels or their technical allies.

"Less traffic, potentially less exposure to whatever external monitoring capabilities our adversary possesses. We're masking the destination metadata within multiple layers of dynamic quantum encryption, making it look like standard, low-priority cargo transfers to generic receiving hubs if somehow intercepted mid-stream."

She detailed the technical challenges: managing thousands of simultaneous, high-priority transfers; ensuring consistent energy flow from the orbital network, particularly during peak transfer windows; coordinating receiving fields in potentially unstable or remote locations in Pakistan and Iran. Her team back in St. John's, working under strict lockdown and limited information (they knew they were facilitating a massive aid transfer to specific regions, but not the full political context or the specific adversary they were countering), were implementing enhanced, real-time quantum signature analysis on every single aid container during transit.

"Ma'am, we're detecting anomalies in transfer batch 447," a technician reported.

Terri's blood ran cold. "Show me."

On screen, the quantum signature flickered, splitting momentarily before reconverging. "Is it the ghost?"

"Unknown. But it's testing our defenses. Probing for weaknesses."

"Double the encryption layers. And prepare abort protocols for all subsequent transfers."

"We've refined the detection algorithms based on the split shipment data and the narcotics signatures," Terri said, though her face showed the strain, the lack of sleep etched around her eyes. "We can spot anomalies faster, identify potential interference signatures in real-time. But we still don't fully understand how they intervened. The risk of interference is present. We mitigate it with redundancy in routing, encryption, and constant vigilance. If an interference signature is detected mid-transfer, the protocol is an immediate abort and re-transfer via an alternative pathway, even if it causes a slight delay."

Lynn's task was perhaps the most delicate and politically sensitive: securing the necessary, albeit discreet, permissions and establishing reliable, secure receiving points in Pakistan and Iran – countries with complex geopolitical landscapes, wary of external interference, and potentially susceptible to the cartels' influence or existing criminal networks linked to the drug trade. Openly teleporting massive aid into these nations without explicit central government approval was impossible; seeking official, public approval risked tipping off their enemies.

Lynn, in a separate, private corner of the habitat, engaged in hushed, encrypted video calls. She wasn't contacting government ministries through official channels. She was working through back channels, leveraging contacts cultivated over years – trusted intermediaries within international aid organizations who understood the need for unconventional methods in desperate situations, local leaders bypassed by central authority, discreet individuals within the medical community, even informal contacts within regional security structures who prioritized aid delivery over bureaucratic protocol.

"We need to identify local partners on the ground," Lynn explained to the team. "NGOs with established, trustworthy networks, community leaders, respected local officials who can ensure the aid reaches the population directly, not local power brokers or criminal elements linked to the drug trade. People who understand the need for absolute discretion."

She explained the terms: TTC provides the aid, purchased outright, instantly and free of charge, delivered directly to their location. They handle distribution on the ground, ensuring it reaches those most in need, quietly and efficiently.

The operation unfolded over several days, a complex symphony orchestrated by the core team. In warehouses and logistics centers around the world, aid packages were loaded into TTC containers, often under the guise of standard commercial shipments to generic destinations.

The success of the first wave of deliveries lasted exactly forty-three minutes.

"Quantum signature detected," one of Terri's technicians announced. "It's... wait, this can't be right."

"What is it?" Terri demanded, looking over his shoulder.

"The signature. It's coming from inside our network. From one of our own Life MTUs."

On the screen, a single point pulsed red among the green lights of successful transfers. The location: St. John's. Their primary facility.

"Someone's transmitting our routing data," the technician said, his voice rising. "Real-time. Everything we're sending, every destination, every quantum signature—it's being copied and transmitted to an external receiver."

"Cut the connection," Terri ordered.

"I can't. It's hardcoded into the Life MTU's base protocols. Someone with administrator access—" The technician stopped, the implication clear.

Only five people had that level of access. The five executives currently in Killiniq Island.

Bruce's encrypted line crackled to life from his temporary station. "We've got bigger problems. Pakistani military just surrounded our delivery site in Quetta. They knew exactly when and where we'd be delivering."

"Same in Iran," Lynn reported. "My contacts are being arrested. Someone gave them names, locations, everything."

Terri felt the world tilting. "The leak is coming from inside. From one of us."

In the habitat's main room, the remaining team members looked at each other with new suspicion. Someone in this room, someone they trusted completely, was working for Bora.

"Nobody moves," Terri said quietly, her hand moving to the emergency lockdown controls. "Nobody communicates outside this room until we figure out who."

At origin MTU sites, containers were scanned, locked onto their quantum signatures, and queued for transfer, masked within the torrent of regular commercial traffic. In the main control room (operating under heightened security and with the knowledge that the executive team was monitoring remotely from an undisclosed location), Terri's trusted team managed the torrent of data and energy, prioritizing the aid shipments based on their internal codes, routing them through the new polar network, and applying the enhanced security monitoring protocols.

In the main control room during peak transfer hours, it was controlled chaos of light and information. Screens displayed the status of hundreds, then thousands, of simultaneous transfers, a glowing web of lines across the holographic globe. Lines of light pulsed between ground sites and orbital arrays, many arcing toward the high north before descending toward Asia. Energy levels on the satellites spiked and dipped as power was drawn for each transfer. Technicians monitored every parameter, their faces illuminated by the console glow, searching for any hint of the 'ghost's' signature, any deviation in the expected quantum flow.

"Transfer initiated, Manifest 448-A, 500 containers of food, Brazil to Pakistan, Routing Alpha-Polar 1-Gamma," a technician reported calmly, using the complex internal routing codes.

"Quantum signature integrity check... nominal," confirmed another, watching the waveforms. "No interference signature detected."

"Energy drawdown... within parameters. Satellite load balance... adjusted," a third stated, managing the power flow.

Terri, watching via a dedicated secure feed, felt the tension like a physical ache in her chest. The scale of the operation was immense, requiring perfect synchronization across continents and satellite arrays. The risk of interference, while mitigated by their new redundancy and monitoring, was never zero. Every successful transfer, every green light on the status board, felt like a small victory against the unseen enemy who had demonstrated the ability to strike at the heart of their system.

Thousands of miles away, in a small village in Pakistan devastated by recent flooding, twelve-year-old Amir sat beside his younger sister's makeshift bed. Fatima, only eight, had been fighting a worsening infection for days. The local clinic had run out of antibiotics three days ago.

"Water?" Fatima whispered, her cracked lips barely moving.

Amir held their last cup to her lips, his own thirst forgotten. "Drink, little one," he urged. Their parents had gone to the nearest town two days ago, seeking medicine. They should have returned yesterday.

The village elder, a man whose face had grown decades older in just weeks, placed a gentle hand on Amir's shoulder. "Save some," he advised quietly. "The relief trucks cannot get through the damaged roads. It may be days more."

Amir looked up, his young face set with determination beyond his years. "She cannot wait days."

The elder had no answer. They had been promised aid from international organizations, but promises couldn't navigate collapsed bridges or landslides.

A commotion outside drew their attention. Voices raised in confusion, then excitement. The elder stepped outside, Amir following despite his reluctance to leave Fatima.

In the village square, where nothing had been moments before, stood containers and pallets. People gathered around in disbelief as the village doctor, his hands shaking, opened a crate labeled in

English and Urdu: "ANTIBIOTICS – EMERGENCY MEDICAL SUPPLIES."

"How?" the elder whispered. "No trucks came. No helicopters."

The doctor didn't answer, already preparing an injection. Amir ran forward, hope surging through him for the first time in days.

"For my sister," he begged. "Please."

The doctor nodded, following Amir back to Fatima's bedside. As the life-saving medicine flowed into her veins, Amir finally allowed himself to cry.

The elder stood in the doorway, looking back toward the miraculous delivery. "Allah works in ways we cannot understand," he murmured. "Today, help came from the sky itself."

Lynn burst into the command center. "Iranian military has mobilized. They're surrounding our next three delivery sites."

"How much time?" Ren demanded from Mumbai, her voice crackling through the encrypted connection.

"Twenty minutes, maybe less."

"Can we redirect?"

"Not without losing the ground teams. They're already in position."

Ren made a decision that would haunt her. "Send it anyway. Maximum dispersal pattern. Make it rain aid across a five-kilometer radius. They can't stop what's already falling from the sky."

The reactions of the local aid workers and the people receiving help was simply disbelief, then overwhelming relief washing over faces hardened by hardship. They quickly began distributing the aid, organizing the supplies, their focus on the immediate, tangible reality of help delivered, bypassing the complex, corruptible systems they were used to. There were no cameras, no reporters from major networks, no speeches. The operation was a lifeline extended in the shadows, a powerful, quiet act of salvation.

The leaked video appeared on every major platform simultaneously.

Grainy thermal footage from Mumbai showed Ren installing Life MTU components. Another clip from Pakistan showed aid materializing in an empty field. A third from Iran captured local officials examining medical supplies with TTC's quantum signature still visible on the containers.

The headline was damning: "TTC ADMITS LIFE MTU EXISTS - SECRET TECHNOLOGY USED FOR UNAUTHORIZED INTERNATIONAL OPERATIONS"

But it was the commentary that truly hurt. News anchors questioning whether TTC had been transporting people illegally. Pundits suggesting the humanitarian aid was a cover for weapons smuggling. Government officials demanding immediate investigations.

"They've forced our hand," Katya said quietly, watching the coverage spread. "We have to respond."

"With what?" Bruce asked. "We admit to having Life MTU capability? That opens us to even more scrutiny."

"We deny it, we look like liars when the truth eventually comes out," Lynn countered.

Ren stood silent, watching the footage of aid being distributed to desperate families. Children receiving medicine. Families getting food. Despite the controversy, the mission had succeeded—partially.

"We don't deny or confirm," she said finally. "We redirect."

"How?"

"By showing them what really matters." Ren turned to Terri. "How many lives have we saved so far?"

"Based on the medical supplies alone? Thousands. Potentially tens of thousands if you count prevention of disease spread."

"Then that's our story. Not the technology. The lives." Ren looked at each team member. "Prepare a release. Focus on the humanitarian success. Let them question the method while we show them the results."

"And the Life MTU?" Katya asked.

"Remains unconfirmed. Let them speculate. Every moment they spend debating how we did it is a moment they're not stopping us from continuing."

"The volume delivered… it's unprecedented for a single, non-governmental operation," Katya reported back to the team on Killiniq Island after the main phase of the transfers was complete. She projected data showing the total weight and value of the aid.

"Enough food for over half a million people for a month. Medical supplies capable of treating hundreds of thousands. Over a hundred thousand emergency shelter units. More than double what was destroyed or targeted by the cartels in Europe. And all of it delivered in less than 72 hours."

TTC paid for every grain of rice, every tent pole, every pill, every liter of fuel for the ground distribution. It was a massive expenditure, drawing down significant reserves, but it was a strategic investment. An investment in their core mission, in the lives saved, and in building undeniable, ethical leverage.

Everyone was exhausted but felt a profound sense of accomplishment. They had faced the chaos the cartels had created and countered it with precise, instantaneous, large-scale aid. They had used their network, their technology, their resources, not for profit or power, but for pure, unadulterated good, bypassing the very systems their enemies controlled and exposing their own actions as destructive and self-serving by contrast.

"They wanted to show we bring chaos and enable crime," Bruce said, a tired smile on his face, looking at a report on the aid distribution logistics being handled efficiently on the ground by their local partners. "We showed we bring life and stability, even where traditional systems fail utterly."

The encrypted message arrived twelve hours into the operation.

"Ren Franco. You have something I want. I have something you need. Let's discuss terms. - B"

Attached was a video. Warehouse footage showing thousands of aid containers—the second wave of supplies meant for Iran and Pakistan. Armed men stood guard. The timestamp was current.

"He intercepted our shipments," Bruce said, his face pale. "How? Those were sent through conventional channels as backup—"

"He owns the shipping companies," Katya realized. "Or at least controls them. We've been playing in his sandbox the entire time."

Another message arrived.

"The price for releasing these supplies: 1) Cease all Life MTU development. 2) Transfer all quantum teleportation patents to a neutral third party. 3) $500 million in untraceable cryptocurrency. You have six hours."

"He's trying to cripple us," Lynn said. "Take our technology and our resources in one move."

"Counter-offer," Ren said suddenly. "Terri, can you track those warehouses?"

"Already on it. Three locations. All in territories with strong cartel presence."

"And all with basic MTUs nearby?"

Terri checked. "Within fifty kilometers, yes."

"Then we don't negotiate. We take them back." Ren turned to the team. "But not the supplies. That's what he expects. We take something more valuable."

"Which is?"

"His credibility. Bruce, how quickly can you mobilize ground teams in those regions?"

"Twelve hours, maybe less if I call in favors."

"Do it. But not to retrieve the supplies. To document everything. Every armed guard, every cartel symbol, every piece of evidence linking Bora to the theft of humanitarian aid."

"You want to expose him," Katya said, understanding.

"I want to destroy him. He made this personal when he stole medicine meant for dying children. Now we make it public."

The war between TTC and Bora's cartel had just escalated beyond corporate espionage. It was now a battle for public perception, moral authority, and the very soul of what quantum teleportation would mean for humanity.

"At least the first wave got through," Terri said, exhausted. "Before everything went sideways."

"Partially sideways," Ren corrected, finally back in the habitat after her harrowing Mumbai extraction. "We saved lives. That's what matters."

"And nearly lost you in the process."

The secrecy was paramount. The cartels still believed TTC was reeling from the drug scandal and the split shipment while battling a political firestorm and vulnerability. They did not know that TTC had just executed the largest, fastest humanitarian aid delivery in history, funded entirely by itself, targeting populations the cartels' actions had indirectly harmed. They did not know the scale of the counter-move being planned, a move that would leverage this very operation as proof of TTC's ethical commitment and capability, directly countering Bora's narrative of TTC being a tool of chaos.

This operation was not the final blow, but it was a critical step. It was TTC reclaiming its narrative, not yet in the court of public opinion, but in the quiet, undeniable reality of lives touched and suffering alleviated. It was leveraging their unique capability to demonstrate their purpose, building internal morale and external, discreet relationships with trusted partners on the ground. The aid delivered in the shadows was a promise of the power TTC held, a power Ren was now ready to use not just defensively, but offensively, revealing its full scope to the world and forcing the necessary conversation about its responsible use. The battle against the cartels was far from over, but TTC had just moved its pieces, silently and effectively, across the board, preparing for a move that would expose their enemy and redefine the rules of the game entirely.

After twenty straight hours of crisis management, Ren found herself alone with Terri in the small observation room. Outside, the Arctic dawn painted the ice in shades of rose and gold.

"You should have let me go with you," Terri said quietly.

"You were needed here."

"You could have died. Walking into that facility, exposed, vulnerable—"

"But I didn't." Ren turned from the window. "Because I knew you were here, managing everything, keeping the network secure."

"I almost lost you," Terri whispered. "When the feeds from Mumbai went dark, when we couldn't reach you for three hours—"

"Terri—"

"I need you to understand something." Terri moved closer. "This isn't just about the mission anymore. When I thought something had happened to you..."

The space between them disappeared. The kiss was desperate, filled with hours of fear and relief. When they finally pulled apart, both were breathing hard.

"We can't," Ren whispered. "The team—"

"Already knows. Has known for months." Terri's hand cupped Ren's face. "We're past hiding, Ren. From our enemies, from the world, from each other."

This time, when they came together, it was slower, deliberate. The exhaustion, the stress, the constant pressure—all of it fell away. In the soft Arctic light, they found each other, no longer CEO and security chief, but simply two people who had nearly lost everything.

Later, lying entwined on the small observation couch, Terri traced patterns on Ren's shoulder. "The Iranian government issued a statement."

"About the aid?"

"About us. Surveillance footage from one of the sites caught us on an encrypted call. They've identified me, connected us personally."

Ren stiffened. "The backlash—"

"Is already starting. But the aid workers on the ground are pushing back. Saying they don't care who loves whom as long as the medicine keeps coming."

"And Pakistan?"

"Similar. Some officials calling for the aid to be rejected on 'moral grounds.' Others pointing out that moral grounds don't cure tuberculosis."

Ren was quiet for a moment. "I won't hide who I am. Not anymore."

"Neither will I." Terri kissed her forehead. "Let them rage about our relationship while we save lives. History will remember which mattered more."

The vast, empty silence of the Arctic held their secret, a powerful counterpoint to the chaos raging in the outside world.

14 ORCHESTRAL MANEUVERS AND RECKONING

Ren and her executive team had orchestrated the massive, secret aid delivery to Pakistan and Iran. The success of that operation was a powerful affirmation of TTC's core mission, proving the network's resilience under pressure. Yet fundamental threats remained: the media campaign, the Secure Ports Act, financial pressures, and the 'ghost' in the machine—likely guided by Bora—lurking in shadows.

On Killiniq Island, accessed via Life MTU for absolute security, the conversation turned to their ultimate capability: the operational readiness of human teleportation technology.

After Lynn finished her sobering assessment of the ethical nightmare that could unfold with Life MTU, a heavy silence fell over the room. Ren stood by the window, her silhouette framed against the stark Arctic landscape beyond. The weight of the decision pressed down on all of them.

Bruce broke the silence, moving to stand beside Ren. He placed a hand on her shoulder, a gesture of solidarity that she hadn't realized she needed until that moment. The simple human contact grounded her, reminded her that despite the godlike technology they controlled, they remained fundamentally human, with all the frailty and strength that entailed.

"You've been carrying this alone for too long," Bruce said softly, his usual boundless energy tempered by understanding. "This decision was always going to come. Maybe not today, maybe not like this, but the world was always going to know eventually."

Ren nodded, grateful for his presence. "I know. I've just been hoping for more time. For the world to be more ready."

"The world is never ready for transformation," Terri said, joining them by the window. Her voice carried the quiet confidence of someone who had spent years wrestling with the impossible. "When we first succeeded with the cargo MTU, remember how terrified we were? How we spent those three days triple-checking every calculation before we even told the others?"

Ren smiled faintly at the memory. "You didn't sleep for 72 hours."

"Neither did you," Terri countered, her eyes crinkling at the corners. She turned serious again. "The difference between then and now isn't the technology—it's the scale of the human impact. But the core question remains the same: Do we trust humanity with this power?"

Katya, who had been unusually quiet, finally spoke up. "It's not about trust. It's about framework." Her financial mind was already calculating trajectories, mapping outcomes. "No technology is inherently good or evil. The internet connects billions, but also enables unprecedented surveillance. Nuclear power generates clean energy, but also creates weapons of mass destruction. The question isn't whether to reveal Life MTU—it's how to shape its implementation."

She stood and walked to the center of the room, her movements precise and deliberate. "Consider this: if we maintain secrecy and Bora or someone like her eventually develops similar technology, they set the rules. If we reveal it now, we define the ethical parameters." She locked eyes with Ren. "Economically speaking, first-mover advantage isn't just about market share—it's about establishing the standards everyone else must follow."

Lynn shook her head, pacing the small habitat with nervous energy. "Standards require enforcement. Who enforces global teleportation ethics? What judiciary has jurisdiction over quantum transport? We're creating an entirely new legal domain with no precedent, no framework, no oversight body."

Bruce interjected, "Then we create one! We establish an international oversight committee—independent experts, ethicists, and legal scholars. We fund it, but we don't control it."

"And who appoints this committee?" Lynn challenged. "Who decides who decides? This isn't just about logistics anymore—it's about fundamental human rights, national sovereignty, global power structures."

Ren turned from the window, watching her team wrestle with the implications. This was why she had gathered them—not just for their expertise, but for their diverse perspectives, their ability to see angles she might miss.

"What about a limited reveal?" Terri suggested. "A controlled demonstration with stringent parameters. We show what's possible without immediately deploying at scale."

Ren crossed the room to the small kitchenette, pouring herself a cup of tea. The familiar ritual gave her a moment to organize her thoughts. "A demonstration would only delay the inevitable questions. Once the world knows humans can be teleported, every government, every corporation, every individual will want access. The genie doesn't go halfway out of the bottle."

She returned to the group, cradling the warm mug between her palms. "I need each of you to be brutally honest. Not just about what could go wrong, but about what must go right. If we do this—when we do this—what's your greatest concern, and what's your greatest hope?"

The directness of the question silenced the room. Ren waited, giving them space to formulate their thoughts. These weren't just her colleagues; they were her friends, her chosen family. The people she trusted most in the world. Their physical presence around her—Bruce's steady hand on her shoulder earlier, Terri's knowing glance, Katya's unwavering gaze, Lynn's passionate gestures—all reminded her that she wasn't alone in this momentous decision.

Terri spoke first, her voice measured. "My greatest concern is technical failure leading to human harm. Despite all our safeguards, all our redundancies, we're still manipulating human consciousness at the quantum level. My greatest hope is that this technology becomes as routine and trusted as air travel, enabling human connection across distances that would otherwise separate us."

Bruce leaned forward, elbows on his knees. "My greatest concern is that we're too cautious, that we strangle this technology with restrictions before it can reach its potential. My greatest hope is that we use it to solve problems we currently consider unsolvable—instant disaster response, elimination of geographic inequality in healthcare access, the end of physical isolation."

Lynn stared at her hands for a long moment before responding. "My greatest concern is that we're opening new questions without sufficient legal infrastructure to handle the consequences. That governments, criminals, and criminal governments will use this technology to violate human rights in ways we haven't even imagined yet." She looked up, her expression softening slightly. "My greatest hope is that it forces humanity to develop truly global governance systems that transcend national interests and protect individual rights across borders."

Katya was the last to speak, her words carefully chosen. "My greatest concern is economic disruption without adequate transition planning. Entire industries will collapse overnight; jobs will disappear. My greatest hope is that by controlling the release of this technology, we can guide that transition, create new economic models, and distribute the benefits more equitably than previous technological revolutions."

Ren absorbed their words, feeling the tension in her shoulders ease slightly. These were the right people to be making this decision with. People who could see both the perils and the promise.

"Thank you," she said simply. She set her mug down and moved to the center of the room, where a small holographic projector displayed a rotating globe. With a gesture, she zoomed in on regions experiencing humanitarian crises—floods in Bangladesh, conflict zones in Eastern Europe, drought-stricken areas in Africa.

"What if we begin here?" she asked, her voice quiet but intense. "Not with commercial transport or government applications, but with humanitarian intervention where the need is most desperate and the potential for immediate, visible good is highest?"

Bruce's eyes lit up. "A humanitarian debut. It's perfect. Show the world the life-saving potential first, before anyone can frame it as a threat."

Lynn looked skeptical. "Even humanitarian deployment requires legal frameworks. Who decides which crises qualify? How do we verify refugee status? Where do we send them?"

"We partner with existing humanitarian organizations," Katya suggested, warming to the idea. "The Red Cross, Doctors Without Borders, UNHCR. They already have protocols for determining need, verifying identity, and coordinating international response. We provide the transport technology; they provide the humanitarian infrastructure."

Terri nodded slowly. "It's technically feasible. We could establish secure transport nodes at existing refugee processing centers, field hospitals, and disaster response headquarters. Limited deployment, maximum impact, controlled environment."

Ren felt a surge of hope. This was the path forward—not perfect, not without risk, but aligned with their core values. She reached out, placing her hand on the holographic globe, watching the light play through her fingers.

"This is how we begin," she said softly. "Not by announcing a technology, but by demonstrating its purpose. We show the world what it means to move human beings safely, ethically, and compassionately."

She looked around at her team, making eye contact with each of them. "But we couple this demonstration with our proposed ethical framework. We make it clear that this technology comes with responsibility, with rules that must be followed."

Lynn stepped forward, her legal mind already formulating the approach. "We present it as a package: the technology and its governance structure. One cannot exist without the other."

"Exactly," Ren agreed. "And we use the humanitarian deployment to establish precedent, to create real-world examples of how this can work when done right."

Bruce moved to Ren's side, his enthusiasm building. "We could start with a natural disaster response. Something unfolding right now, where conventional aid is struggling to reach victims."

"The flooding in Pakistan," Katya suggested. "Millions displaced, difficult terrain, limited access by conventional means."

Terri pulled up data on her tablet. "We already have cargo MTU nodes in the region from our previous aid operation. Adapting them for human transport would take approximately 72 hours."

Ren felt the plan crystallizing, the path forward becoming clearer. She placed her hand on Terri's shoulder, drawing strength from the physical connection to her oldest friend and colleague.

"Begin the preparations," she said, her voice firm with renewed purpose. "Secure the nodes, run the final safety protocols, establish contact with humanitarian partners on the ground."

She turned to Lynn. "Draft the ethical framework document— not just our internal guidelines, but a public declaration, something that can serve as the foundation for international agreements."

Lynn nodded, already mentally outlining the structure. "I'll have a preliminary draft within 24 hours."

"Katya, we need financial modeling for global humanitarian deployment. How do we fund this sustainably? How do we prevent economic shock?"

"On it," Katya confirmed, her mind already working through scenarios.

"Bruce, you'll coordinate with our media team. This isn't just an announcement; it's a narrative about human potential, about compassion at the speed of light."

Bruce grinned, squeezing Ren's arm. "Leave it to me. We'll make sure the world understands what this means—not just the how, but the why."

Ren took a deep breath, feeling the weight of the decision settle into a manageable burden, shared among them. "Three days. We prepare for three days, then we move."

As the team dispersed to begin their tasks, Terri lingered behind. She approached Ren, who had returned to the window, gazing out at the vast Arctic expanse.

"You know this changes everything," Terri said quietly. "Not just for the world, but for us. For you."

Ren nodded, not turning from the window. "I've always known this day would come. From the moment we realized it was theoretically possible to transport a living being."

Terri moved closer, standing shoulder to shoulder with her friend. "Are you ready for what comes next? The scrutiny, the responsibility, the impossible expectations?"

Ren finally turned, her expression a complex mixture of

determination and vulnerability. "No one could be ready for this. But I'm not alone." She reached out, taking Terri's hand in a rare gesture of physical affection. "We built this together. We'll face what comes together."

Terri squeezed her hand, a silent promise. "Always."

Two hours before the conference with Bora, Terri burst into the room, her face pale. "Ren, we have a problem."

She brought up a holographic display showing multiple TTC facilities worldwide. Red indicators pulsed at each location. "Security breaches at seventeen sites. Not digital—physical. Armed teams, moving simultaneously."

Bruce grabbed his tablet, pulling up security feeds. "They're not trying to steal anything. They're... planting something?"

"The non-functional MTUs," Lynn breathed, understanding dawning. "Bora's fake units. He's turning our own facilities into crime scenes."

Katya's fingers flew across her screen. "Financial markets are already reacting. Someone leaked that TTC facilities are being used for terrorist attacks. Our stock is in freefall."

Ren felt the trap closing. "He knew we were coming for him. This is his insurance policy."

"It gets worse," Terri said, her voice strained. "I'm detecting quantum interference at our Life MTU nodes. Not enough to prevent operation, but enough to cause... uncertainties in transfer."

"Define uncertainties," Ren demanded.

"Cellular degradation. Minor at first, but cumulative. Anyone using Life MTU repeatedly in the next 48 hours risks permanent damage."

"Wait," Bruce said suddenly. "How is Bora creating quantum interference? That's not possible unless—"

"Unless he has Life MTU technology," Terri finished, her face going pale. "My God, he's built his own based on one of our stolen prototypes."

"That's how he knows about them," Lynn realized. "He's not just interfering—he's been testing his own system."

Katya pulled up financial records. "Three months ago, several quantum computing components went missing from our Swiss facility. We assumed industrial espionage for the cargo MTUs, but if he's reverse-engineered—"

"He has a functioning Life MTU," Ren said quietly. "Probably poorly calibrated, definitely unstable, but functional enough to create interference patterns."

"And if he has one at his location..." Terri's fingers flew across her tablet. "Yes, I'm detecting it. The interference has a point of origin. His system is active, which means—"

"We can use it," Ren finished. "Turn his own weapon against him."

Bruce slammed his fist on the table. "He's forcing us to choose. Reveal Life MTU to save people from his false flag attacks, but risk killing them in transit."

"Or let his narrative stand," Lynn added grimly. "TTC as a terrorist network, using our facilities to stage attacks."

Ren stared at the displays, calculating. "How many hostages?"

"None yet," Bruce reported. "But the devices are armed. Timer shows two hours—exactly when our conference begins."

"He wants an audience," Katya realized. "He's going to detonate them during the call, frame us live on camera."

Ren closed her eyes, feeling the weight of the impossible choice. Save lives by using compromised Life MTUs, potentially killing innocents. Or let Bora's bombs explode, accepting the casualties and the narrative that TTC was responsible.

"There's a third option," she said quietly. "But it breaks every principle we've established."

The Rules for Life Transport appeared on the display:

These rules were intended to be a declaration to the world, a proposed international standard. But now, faced with Bora's trap, Ren was considering breaking one of them herself.

The countdown to the video conference with Bora had reached its final minutes. In the secure conference room in St. John's, tension hung in the air like an electrical charge. Ren stood at the center of the room, adjusting the collar of her simple black shirt, a contrast to the elaborate setting she knew Bora would choose to project power and confidence.

Bruce approached, carrying two cups of coffee. He handed one to Ren, their fingers brushing in the exchange. "Nervous?" he asked, his voice uncharacteristically subdued.

Ren took a sip, grateful for both the caffeine and the momentary distraction. "Not nervous. Focused." She met his gaze. "This ends today, one way or another."

Bruce nodded, understanding the weight of what they were about to do. "He won't go down easily. People like Bora, they don't know how to lose."

"That's their weakness," Ren replied. "They can't conceive of failure, so they don't prepare for it."

Lynn entered the room, tablet in hand, her posture rigid with tension. "Final confirmation from Interpol. All teams are in position, awaiting our signal."

Katya followed, her usual calm demeanor slightly strained. "Financial monitoring systems are active. The moment the arrests begin, we'll track any attempts to move or liquidate assets."

Terri's voice came through the room's communication system. "Connection protocols verified. Feed encryption secure. Backup channels standing by. We're ready, Ren."

Ren placed her coffee cup down and moved to the center of the conference table. She straightened her shoulders, centering herself. The others took their positions around her, a physical manifestation of their support.

Bruce stepped forward, adjusting Ren's microphone. His hand lingered on her shoulder, a gentle squeeze conveying more than words could. "Make him regret ever coming after us," he said softly.

Ren covered his hand with her own for a brief moment, drawing strength from the contact. "This isn't about revenge. It's about justice."

"Sometimes they're the same thing," Bruce replied with a grim smile, stepping back to his position.

Lynn moved to Ren's other side, her legal mind already anticipating the coming confrontation. "Remember, every word you say is evidence. Be precise."

Katya completed the circle, her analytical gaze steady. "We've mapped every possible response. You've got this, Ren."

Ren looked at each of them in turn, these brilliant minds who had chosen to follow her vision, to build something revolutionary, to stand against forces that would drag humanity backward rather than forward. Their presence around her—physical, tangible, real—anchored her in this moment of truth.

"Initiating connection in thirty seconds," Terri announced from the control room.

Ren took a deep breath, feeling the familiar calm of absolute focus settle over her. "Let's finish this."

The screens flickered to life, revealing Bora's composed face, the picture of confident authority. Behind him, a carefully staged setting projected wealth and power—subtle art pieces, elegant furnishings, the trappings of old-world influence.

"Ren-san," Bora greeted, his voice smooth as polished stone. "A video conference. How... practical. Have you reconsidered my offer from Switzerland? Are you ready to accept the inevitable and discuss terms?"

Ren met his gaze unflinchingly. "This isn't a negotiation, Bora-san. It's a final conversation. A statement."

Bora's smile widened. "Before we discuss statements, perhaps you should check your facilities. I believe you'll find some... unexpected additions."

On cue, alarms began blaring through TTC's network. Lynn's tablet lit up with urgent security alerts.

"Ah, there we are," Bora continued smoothly. "Seventeen of your facilities, each now hosting one of my special devices. Non-functional MTUs, as you've discovered, but packed with enough conventional explosives to level a city block. And the beauty is, they're your MTUs—at least, that's what the serial numbers will show."

"You're insane," Bruce snarled, stepping forward. "Those facilities have thousands of workers—"

"Who can be saved," Bora interrupted, "if Ren makes the right choice. You see, I know about your Life MTUs. I know they're compromised—my quantum interference ensures that. Use them to evacuate, and you'll save most of your people. Some will die from the cellular damage, of course. Perhaps ten percent? Twenty? But that's better than total casualties."

Ren kept her face expressionless, but inside, she felt something cold crystallizing. "What do you want?"

"Confession," Bora said simply. "Admit, on this call, that TTC has been running illegal human trafficking. Admit that you've been moving terrorists, criminals, anyone who pays. Destroy your own reputation to save your people."

"That's a lie," Lynn protested.

"Truth is negotiable," Bora replied. "Your choice, Ren-san. Confess and I'll disable the bombs. Refuse, and the world watches TTC facilities explode while you do nothing. Either way, your company dies today. The only question is how many die with it."

Ren looked at her team. Bruce's hand found hers, squeezing tight. She saw the horror in their eyes, but also trust. They would follow her decision, whatever it was.

"I need proof you can actually disable them," Ren said, her voice steady.

Bora's fingers moved across his console. One of the seventeen indicators on Lynn's screen turned green. "Building 7, Seoul. Disabled. The other sixteen await your decision."

"You have thirty seconds," Bora added, glancing at an antique watch. "After that, the timers become irreversible."

Ren felt time slow. Every principle they'd fought for, every ethical standard they'd established, weighed against thousands of lives. She thought of the workers in those facilities—people who'd trusted TTC, who'd believed in their vision.

"I'll do it," she said quietly. "But not just a statement. I'll come to you. In person. You disable the bombs, I surrender myself to your custody, publicly. A full confession, in person, more valuable than any video call."

Bora's eyes glittered with triumph. "You would trust me to honor that bargain?"

"I'll trust you to recognize the value of having me as your prisoner versus having me as a martyr. Disable the bombs, send me coordinates, and I'll come alone."

"Ren, no!" Bruce gripped her arm. "You can't—"

She turned to him, pressing her hand over his. "Take care of them," she whispered. Then, louder, to Bora: "Do we have a deal?"

Bora considered for a moment, then smiled. "You have one hour. The coordinates are being sent now. Come alone, or the bombs activate immediately."

The screen went dark.

"You're not going," Bruce said immediately. "We'll find another way—"

"There is no other way," Ren cut him off. She turned to Terri. "Can you lock onto Bora's Life MTU signature? Use his own system as the receiving point?"

Terri's face went pale. "Ren, transporting through his compromised system, with the quantum interference—the cellular damage would be—"

"Survivable?"

"Barely. And that's assuming his MTU doesn't fail during transport. If it does—"

"I'll be scattered across quantum space," Ren finished. "But if it works, he won't expect me to arrive instantly. He thinks I'm coming by conventional means."

"You're betting your life on his arrogance," Bruce said.

"No," Ren corrected. "I'm betting it on Terri's ability to stabilize even a poorly built system long enough for one transport."

Terri's face went pale. "Ren, the cellular damage from a single compromised transport could be—"

"Survivable?"

"Yes, but—"

"Then do it." Ren turned to the others. "While I keep Bora occupied, you execute the original plan. The journalists release their stories. Interpol moves on all targets simultaneously."

"Including Bora's location," Lynn realized. "You're going to be there when they raid it."

Ren nodded. "He expects me to arrive by conventional means. That gives us an hour to prepare. Terri, can you also create temporal stasis fields around each bomb using cargo MTUs?"

Terri's eyes widened with understanding. "Create pocket dimensions where the explosions happen disconnected from our reality. It's theoretically possible, but the timing—"

"Will have to be perfect," Ren agreed. She looked at each of them. "This is our only shot. We save our people, expose the cartels, and end this. Today."

Fifty-five minutes later, Ren stood in the modified Life MTU chamber. The quantum interference made the usual smooth hum of the machinery sound discordant, wrong. She could feel the instability in the field, like standing too close to a live wire.

Bruce stood at the chamber entrance, his face etched with worry. "There has to be another way."

Ren stepped close to him, placing her hand on his chest. "There isn't. You know there isn't."

"The cellular damage—"

"Is a price I'm willing to pay." She looked into his eyes. "Promise me something. When this is over, when Life MTU goes public, make sure it's used the way we intended. For good. For humanity."

Bruce pulled her into a fierce embrace. "You're going to be there to make sure of that yourself."

She held him tight for a moment, then stepped back. "Initiating transport."

The last thing she saw was Bruce's face before the world dissolved into quantum probability.

The rematerialization was agony. Every cell in her body screamed as it reformed, the quantum interference causing microscopic damage throughout her system. Ren collapsed to her knees in Bora's elegant office, gasping, blood trickling from her nose.

Bora stood from his desk, satisfaction evident on his face. "The great Ren Franco, brought to her knees. How poetic."

Ren forced herself to stand, though every movement sent fire through her nerves. "The bombs. Disable them."

"All in good time. First, your confession. The camera is ready."

But instead of moving to the camera, Ren smiled. "You made one mistake, Bora-san."

"Oh?"

"You assumed I came here to surrender."

The door behind Bora burst open. But instead of officers initially, Ren had timed it perfectly—she'd arrived moments before the raid, giving her just enough time.

Bora's shock lasted only a second before transforming into rage. "Impossible. The quantum interference—"

"Affects repeated use," Ren said, her voice strained. She could feel the damage in her cells, a burning sensation that would likely never fully heal. "A single transport, accepting the consequences, still works."

"You sacrificed yourself for theater?" Bora snarled.

"I sacrificed myself for justice," Ren corrected. "You see, your bombs were real, but your leverage wasn't. While you gloated, my team isolated each device in temporal stasis fields—cargo MTUs creating pocket dimensions where your explosions happened in spaces disconnected from our reality. Your terror ended before it began."

Bora lunged at her with surprising speed, a concealed blade flashing from his sleeve. Ren, weakened from the damaged transport, couldn't dodge entirely. The blade caught her shoulder, sending her spinning into the wall.

Bruce's voice crackled through her earpiece. "Ren! We're reading your vitals—"

"I'm fine," she gasped, though blood was already soaking through her shirt.

Bora advanced, blade ready. "You think you've won? You have no idea what you've started. The old world doesn't die quietly, Ren-san. For every head you cut off—"

"Two more grow back?" Ren pushed herself up, meeting his eyes. "That's the problem with hydras, Bora. They're myths. And myths die when exposed to light."

The officers finally entered, weapons drawn. "Federal police! Hands where we can see them!"

As they reached for him, Bora pressed something on his ring—a deadman switch.

"If I fall, everything releases. Every dirty secret, every government official we own, every TTC employee who ever took a bribe. Mutual destruction, Ren-san."

Ren smiled coldly, her hand pressed to her bleeding shoulder. "Release it. We already have. Every document you possess, we've preemptively published with context. Your blackmail is now evidence. Your leverage is now testimony."

As the officers restrained him, Bora's composed mask finally shattered completely. "You don't understand what you've done. The chaos you'll cause—"

"Change isn't chaos," Ren said quietly, sagging against the wall as medics rushed to her. "It's evolution. And you're extinct."

"Ren-san?" Bora smiled even as they cuffed him. "Check your Shanghai facility's accounts. Your CFO there has been very cooperative with us. The authorities will find some interesting transactions."

Through her earpiece, Ren heard Katya's voice from St. John's: "Checking now... Oh no. He's right. Zhang has been—"

"Handle it," Ren said wearily. Even in defeat, Bora had drawn blood.

Three hours later, Ren lay in a medical facility, the cellular damage from the compromised Life MTU transport being assessed. The doctors had stopped the bleeding from Bora's attack, but the internal damage was another matter.

"Fifteen percent cellular degradation," Terri reported, her voice thick with emotion. "Ren, this is permanent. Your life expectancy—"

"Has been reduced by approximately five years," Ren finished. "I knew the risks."

Bruce hadn't left her bedside, his hand constantly finding reasons to touch her—adjusting her blanket, checking her bandages, holding her hand. "You didn't have to do this. We could have found another way."

"Could we?" Ren asked. "How many would have died while we searched for it?"

Lynn entered with a tablet showing news feeds. "The arrests are holding. Forty-seven individuals across nineteen countries. Not all arrests proceeding smoothly," Lynn reported, reading updates. "Three suspects in Singapore escaped before teams arrived. Two in Hamburg destroyed evidence. The Monaco target had diplomatic immunity."

"But we got the principals," Katya confirmed. "Forty-seven of sixty planned arrests. It's enough. The journalists' stories are dominating every major outlet. But Ren, the cost—"

"Was mine to pay," Ren interrupted. She struggled to sit up, Bruce immediately supporting her. "We've all sacrificed for this. Terri, years of your life in research. Katya, your family's reputation when you sided with us over traditional finance. Lynn, the threats against you for challenging legal precedents. Bruce..." she touched his face gently, "your freedom, constantly watching over all of us."

"That's not a sacrifice," Bruce said roughly. "That's a choice. My choice."

Katya stood by the window, watching the sun set over St. John's harbor. "Bora was right about one thing. We've killed the old world today. What we birth tomorrow—that's our real test."

Ren nodded slowly, feeling the weight of her damaged cells, the shortened future she'd accepted. "Then we'd better make it count. Every day we've bought with this victory, every life saved through what we've built—it has to matter."

She looked at each of them, these people who'd become more than colleagues, more than friends. They were the family she'd chosen, the ones she'd literally sacrificed years of her life to protect.

"Tomorrow, we announce Life MTU," she said, her voice gaining strength. "Not as conquerors, but as servants. Not as gods, but as humans who've found a better way. The old world dies today, but only so something better can be born."

Bruce squeezed her hand, and she squeezed back, drawing strength from the simple human contact. Outside, the world was changing, transforming at the speed of light. But here, in this room, surrounded by the people she loved, Ren found peace in knowing the sacrifice had been worth it.

The future would be shorter for her, but infinitely brighter for humanity.

"Now," she said, "we build the future."

The narrator's voice from the independent news collective overlaid the scene, providing context for the journalists' networks broadcasting simultaneously across the world.

"This unprecedented global law enforcement action, coordinated through Interpol and based on extensive independent investigative journalism and intelligence shared through international channels, targets key individuals believed to be orchestrating a vast criminal enterprise from within the traditional transportation sector... Evidence includes systematic drug trafficking leveraging new technologies, economic sabotage against competitors, the deliberate destruction of humanitarian aid, and disturbing links to long-standing human trafficking operations... The suspects were apprehended simultaneously in multiple secure locations worldwide, utilizing intelligence gathered during a final video conference that was monitored as part of the ongoing investigation..."

The authorities arrested swiftly, precisely, and globally. Executive staff at numerous large and mid-size ship and aircraft manufacturers and related logistics firms faced intense scrutiny, with law enforcement arresting many key figures based on overwhelming evidence the journalists presented and corroborated. The unprecedented scale of the operation testified to the power of combining cutting-edge technical capabilities, dedicated journalistic integrity, and international law enforcement cooperation working outside compromised channels.

15 THE SERPENT'S OFFER

Ren reviewed the aftermath reports in her office. The cartel arrests had reversed public opinion overnight, the Secure Ports Act was dead, and thirty percent of transportation companies had agreed to preliminary discussions. Then the invitation arrived—a consortium meeting in the Swiss Alps, deliberately opaque in origin.

"It's obviously a trap," Lynn warned from her position by the window, her lawyer's instincts on high alert.

"Perhaps," Ren conceded, studying the elegant invitation with its embossed letterhead. "But if we're going to understand what we're still facing, I need to meet with them."

"At least let me come with you," Lynn said.

Ren shook her head. "I need you here, preparing our legal position for the regulatory hearings. All of you have critical roles right now." She turned to face the team. "Besides, a larger delegation would signal fear."

"And going alone signals what? Recklessness?" Katya challenged.

"Confidence," Ren replied. "And respect. I'll take a small security team, of course, but this needs to be a conversation between principals."

"Wait," Terri interrupted, pulling up her tablet. "Before you go, take this." She handed Ren a small device, no larger than a button. "Emergency beacon. One-time quantum burst using satellite reflection. If they're jamming communications, this will punch through for about three seconds. Also—" she tapped Ren's collar, affixing a nearly invisible recording device, "—continuous local recording with burst transmission if activated. The recording stays on the device even if transmission fails."

"Always prepared," Ren said with appreciation.

"I don't like it," Lynn said flatly.

"Noted," Ren replied with a small smile. "But I'm still going."

Two weeks later, the helicopter crested a ridge of snow-capped peaks, revealing a secluded valley nestled in the heart of the Swiss Alps. Ren gazed down at the estate—a sprawling complex of traditional Alpine architecture blended with modern elements of glass and steel. A frozen lake glittered beside it like a mirror.

"Approaching the landing zone now, ma'am," the pilot announced. "Security sweep shows no obvious threats, but there's significant signal jamming in effect."

"To be expected," Ren replied. She turned to the head of her security detail, a former German intelligence officer named Dov. "Remember, I need you to be invisible but accessible."

Dov nodded, his weathered face impassive. "We'll maintain the perimeter. Any sign of trouble, we extract immediately. The nearest police station is forty minutes away in good weather—this location was chosen for its isolation."

The helicopter touched down on a pad at the edge of the property. A tall man in a tailored overcoat stood waiting, flanked by two security personnel whose professional stance betrayed military training.

"Dr. Franco," the man greeted as Ren stepped onto the snow-covered ground. "Welcome to Adler Estate. I'm Heinrich, the property manager. Your security team may use the guesthouse as their base of operations. The principals await you in the main building."

Ren nodded to Dov, who directed his team toward the indicated guesthouse while maintaining a professional distance. As they walked, Dov spoke quietly into his comm. "Overwatch positions confirmed. Three snipers on the high ground, at least a dozen security personnel patrolling. This is more than a business meeting."

The main building was a masterpiece of old-world craftsmanship and wealth. Centuries-old timber beams supported vaulted ceilings. Antique furniture and modern art created an atmosphere of timeless luxury. The scent of wood smoke from massive stone fireplaces permeated the air.

Heinrich led Ren to a set of ornate double doors. "The conference room, ma'am. They're waiting."

Ren paused, taking a moment to center herself. Then she pushed open the doors.

The room was dominated by a massive old growth wooden table, around which sat about a dozen people. Most wore expressions ranging from cautious neutrality to barely concealed hostility. Ren recognized several faces from industry publications— executives from shipping conglomerates, airline corporations, and logistics firms. Their body language spoke of defensive posturing, wounded pride.

"Dr. Franco," said a silver-haired woman at the near end of the table. "I'm Victoria Henryson, former COO of Oceanic Maritime Alliance. Thank you for agreeing to meet under these unusual circumstances."

Ren took the empty seat at the opposite end of the table. "Thank you for the invitation, Ms. Henryson. I am a steadfast believer in dialogue, especially during times of transition."

A man with a thick German accent scoffed. "Transition? Is that what you call the destruction of entire industries? The overnight obsolescence of trillions of euros in infrastructure?"

"Klaus," Victoria cautioned, "we agreed to maintain civility."

"Civility?" Klaus retorted. "My company lost sixty-eight percent of its value in three weeks. Thirty thousand employees face unemployment. All because of her technology."

Ren met the man's gaze steadily. "I understand your anger, Mr. Schumacher. The disruption TTC has caused isn't something I take lightly. That's precisely why I'm here—to discuss how we might mitigate the impact on workers and find new roles for existing expertise."

"Pretty words," said another executive, a thin man with sharp features. "But your actions tell a different story. You exposed our colleagues to public humiliation, criminal charges—"

"Your colleagues," Ren interrupted calmly, "according to the evidence, were running narcotics through our network, sabotaging humanitarian aid, and trafficking human beings. Are those activities you wish to defend, Mr...?"

"Yoshida. Banri Yoshida, Nippon Forwarders." The man's jaw tightened. "And no, of course not. If those allegations prove true, they deserve prosecution to the fullest extent of the law. But you've painted our entire industry with the same brush."

"That was never my intention," Ren said. "TTC has always recognized that traditional transportation infrastructure will remain essential for many applications. Last-kilometer delivery, specialized cargo, redundancy systems—there are numerous areas where our technologies complement rather than replace."

Victoria leaned forward. "That's why we requested this meeting, Dr. Franco. We're facing an existential crisis, yes, but we're also realists. Your technology isn't going away. The question is whether there's a path forward that doesn't end with millions unemployed and centuries of logistics expertise simply... discarded."

Ren felt a flicker of hope. This was exactly the conversation she'd wanted to have. "I believe there is. TTC doesn't want to destroy industries; we want to transform global logistics. That transformation can and should include the expertise, infrastructure, and workforce of existing transportation networks, adapted to new roles."

For the next hour, Ren outlined her vision: a managed transition where traditional carriers could partner with TTC to develop hybrid systems. Shipping companies could maintain specialized routes while integrating MTU technology for certain cargo types. Airlines could repurpose passenger fleets for experiences rather than mere transportation. Logistics firms could leverage their expertise to optimize the growing network of MTU hubs.

Some executives listened with cautious interest, while others remained skeptical, occasionally interjecting with pointed questions about timelines, financial models, and regulatory frameworks. But over time, the atmosphere gradually shifted from outright hostility to guarded consideration.

"These are interesting concepts," Victoria finally said. "But they require tremendous capital investment at a time when our valuations are in free fall. The transition period would be brutal."

"TTC is prepared to establish a transition fund," Ren replied. "Financial support for retraining programs, infrastructure conversion, and even early retirement packages for workers in positions that truly cannot be adapted."

Klaus looked suspicious. "At what cost? What do you want in return?"

"Cooperation," Ren said simply. "An end to the coordinated opposition. Support for reasonable regulatory frameworks instead of punitive legislation. And your expertise in helping us build a global system that serves everyone, not just the privileged few."

A murmur ran through the group. Some exchanged glances, others made notes. Victoria was about to speak when the double doors opened.

It was as though the temperature in the room had plummeted to zero when Bora entered.

Ren's shock must have shown on her face, because Bora smiled—a cold, predatory expression.

"Forgive my tardiness," he said, his voice smooth as silk. "Travel arrangements were complicated, given certain... legal misunderstandings."

Victoria's expression turned to shock. "You're supposed to be in custody. There are warrants—"

"International arrest warrants, yes," Bora acknowledged with a slight smile. "Issued after my bail was revoked three days ago. A clerical error, they called it—bail never should have been granted for charges of this magnitude. Yet here I am, in a country with no extradition treaties for my particular combination of citizenships. Swiss law is wonderfully complex when one knows how to navigate it."

"The authorities—" Klaus started.

"Will arrive eventually," Bora interrupted. "But Switzerland requires probable cause for immediate arrest, and I've committed no crimes on Swiss soil. By the time they sort through the paperwork, I'll be gone. International law moves slowly, Mr. Schumacher. Money moves much faster."

The dynamic in the room had instantly transformed. The

cautious openness that had been building evaporated, replaced by a tense awareness of the power struggle now made explicit.

"The cartels have been dismantled," Ren stated, her voice calm and steady, meeting his gaze. "Their criminal activities have been exposed. Their political influence severely weakened."

Bora smiled, a cold, humorless expression. "Criminals are... interchangeable, Ren-san. They are symptoms, not the disease. They are tools. And tools can be replaced. The disease is the disruption of order. The disease is control slipping from those who understand how to wield it effectively. Your technology... it is a powerful tool. Too powerful to be left in the hands of... idealists."

He leaned forward, his intensity filling the room despite his quiet tone. "My clients, as you called them, were... useful partners. They understood power. They understood leverage. They provided the means to pressure you—financially, politically, through media—to expose your system's vulnerabilities, to turn public opinion against you. A necessary, if... unseemly... alliance."

Ren's expression remained unchanged. "Unseemly? They destroyed humanitarian aid meant for earthquake victims. They trafficked human beings. They used our network to attempt to transport narcotics. Those aren't 'unseemly' actions, Bora. They're monstrous."

"Collateral damage," Bora replied with a dismissive gesture. "Regrettable, perhaps, but inconsequential in the larger strategic context."

Victoria cleared her throat. "I think we've strayed from the purpose of this meeting—"

"On the contrary," Bora interrupted smoothly. "We've arrived precisely at its purpose." He turned to the other executives. "Ladies and gentlemen, I believe we should continue this discussion privately. Dr. Franco and I have specific matters to address."

The executives exchanged uncertain glances. Klaus started to protest, but Bora's security team—who had been standing invisibly along the walls—stepped forward slightly. The message was clear.

"This is highly irregular," Victoria said, but she was already gathering her papers. One by one, the executives filed out, some looking relieved, others concerned. Yoshida paused at the door, meeting Ren's eyes briefly before hurrying out.

When they were alone, Bora's demeanor shifted. The pretense of civility dropped away, replaced by naked ambition.

"Now we can speak plainly," he said. "The remnants of the consortium, under my leadership, recognize the inevitable. Teleportation is the future. But it must be controlled. Regulated, not by chaotic governments influenced by quaint notions of democracy or human rights, but by those with the vision to manage global flow efficiently and profitably."

He fixed his gaze on Ren. "I want control of TTC's core technology. But I'm willing to negotiate. You see, I've learned something interesting about your Life MTU technology. The authentication protocols, the UN oversight—all quite impressive. But my cyber intelligence teams have been busy. We obtained partial schematics through... let's call it aggressive data acquisition. Not enough to replicate, but enough to understand."

Bora produced a tablet, showing technical diagrams that made Ren's blood run cold. They were incomplete Life MTU designs—fragmentary but accurate.

"How?" Ren kept her voice steady.

"Your partner companies aren't all as secure as TTC," Bora replied. "Component manufacturers, software contractors—every partnership is a potential vulnerability. We couldn't get everything, of course. The quantum encryption keys, the bio-authentication protocols—those remain beyond our reach. For now."

"Those designs are useless without the complete system," Ren said.

"True," Bora acknowledged. "Which is why I'm offering you a trade. You provide limited access—say, a hundred Life MTU units for my private network—and I'll ensure this technology doesn't fall into less responsible hands."

"You mean terrorist organizations," Ren said flatly.

"Such harsh words. I prefer 'non-state actors with aggressive negotiation tactics.'" Bora's smile was predatory. "Imagine what they could do with even partial Life MTU technology. The chaos they could cause trying to reverse-engineer it. All because you refused to compromise."

"You're threatening to release dangerous, incomplete technology unless I give you controlled access to the real thing."

"I'm offering a partnership," Bora corrected. "You maintain your humanitarian network. I operate a parallel system for premium clients. We both profit, and the technology remains contained."

"The answer is no."

Bora's expression hardened. "Then you force my hand." He touched his earpiece. "Begin Phase Two."

A new image appeared on his tablet—a live feed showing a TTC facility in Mumbai. "Your secondary hub in India. Forty-three employees currently on shift. The lighting towers around your facility—so vulnerable, so overlooked. My people embedded devices in six of them three months ago. Originally intended for... let's call it infrastructure disruption during our political campaign. But now? They'll serve a more immediate purpose. The blast radius won't destroy your MTUs directly, but the power surge when they detonate? Your entire grid will overload. Millions in damages, operations crippled for weeks."

"You're lying," Ren said. "Our security—"

"Checks the MTU facilities obsessively, yes. But the municipal lighting towers? Those are city property, maintained by lowest-bid contractors. We simply outbid them." He smiled coldly. "In approximately ten minutes, if you refuse my offer, they detonate."

"This is terrorism," Ren said quietly.

"This is negotiation," Bora countered. "You have eight minutes to decide."

Ren stood slowly. "You've made a critical error, Bora."

"Have I?"

"You've confessed to terrorism, attempted mass murder, and extortion." She tapped her collar, where the recording device gleamed. "All recorded. This will be transmitted the moment I leave this building."

Bora's amusement didn't waver. "A recording made under duress won't hold up in court. Besides, you still have to leave this building." He gestured, and Heinrich entered with a contingent of security personnel—at least twenty armed men.

"Dr. Franco," Heinrich said, his tone now openly hostile. "Bora's holdings have increased substantially since your arrival. He now controls forty percent of this estate through his companies.

The consortium knew I had investors, but not the extent of his involvement. You're trespassing on what is partially his property. Please surrender your devices and remain seated."

Victoria stood abruptly. "Forty percent? The disclosure documents showed fifteen—"

"Recent acquisitions," Bora said smoothly. "Completed this morning, in fact."

Ren activated the emergency beacon. Nothing. She triggered it again—a brief chirp, less than a second of connection before the jamming crushed it. Again. Again. Her fingers worked frantically, adjusting the frequency microscopically each time.

"Technical difficulties?" Bora asked, amused.

On the fifteenth attempt, something aligned—atmospheric conditions, a gap in the jamming rotation, pure luck—and the signal punched through. One second. Two. Three full seconds of beautiful, clear transmission before the device burned out, its circuits fried from the overload.

She pressed the recording device, praying its burst transmission would find the same window. A green light—partial success at least.

"Done," she said, hoping it was true. "Mumbai has been warned."

Bora's amusement faltered slightly. "You're bluffing. Three seconds isn't enough—"

His phone buzzed. His expression darkened as he read. "The lighting towers... how did they—"

"We got lucky," Ren said simply.

Bora's expression finally showed anger. "Heinrich, secure her—"

The lights suddenly cut out. Emergency lighting cast red shadows across the room.

"Ma'am, we have entry!" Dov's voice burst through the darkness. The doors exploded inward as her security team breached, flash-bang grenades disorienting Bora's guards.

"Move! Move!" Dov grabbed Ren's arm, pulling her toward the exit. Gunfire erupted behind them—Bora's security responding to the extraction.

They ran through the darkened hallways, gunfire echoing behind them. Dov's man Marcus cried out, spinning as a bullet caught his shoulder. Another operator, Silva, grunted as return fire grazed her ribs.

"Two down! Keep moving!" Dov barked, half-carrying Marcus while Silva pressed against her wound, still providing cover fire.

Terri's voice crackled through their partially restored comms: "Mumbai—still working on it! Wait—a maintenance worker just called in. He noticed strange devices on the lighting towers. They're checking now!"

"Swiss authorities inbound," another voice reported. "Twenty-one minutes out, helicopters launching despite weather."

More gunfire. Rodriguez screamed as a round punched through his thigh. The extraction was becoming a bloodbath.

"How many casualties?" Ren demanded as they reached the vehicles.

"Two critical, six wounded," Dov reported grimly, his own arm bleeding from a graze. "We hurt them worse, but this wasn't clean. Get in! We're going overland."

They burst out into the snow, where one of Bora's own security vehicles sat idling—Dov's team had already secured it during the chaos. They piled in, tires spinning on ice as they accelerated toward the main gate.

"Gate's locked down!" the driver shouted.

"Ram it!" Dov ordered.

The reinforced vehicle smashed through the ornate metal gates, alarms wailing behind them. In the side mirror, Ren saw muzzle flashes from the estate—Bora's security firing at their retreat, though not pursuing into the storm.

As they sped down the mountain road through increasingly heavy snow, Ren glimpsed helicopter lights rising from the estate—Bora making his own escape before authorities arrived.

"He'll claim diplomatic immunity or have another legal excuse ready," Dov said grimly.

"It doesn't matter," Ren replied. "We have his confession. The world will know what he really is."

Ninety minutes later, Ren stood in Zurich's police headquarters, providing testimony to Swiss authorities and Interpol agents. The rapid response team had arrived at the estate exactly twenty-one minutes after her emergency signal, finding evidence of the firefight but no sign of Bora—he'd fled minutes before in a private helicopter, flying below radar toward the Italian border. His recorded confession was already making headlines worldwide.

"How did you find the devices so quickly?" the Interpol agent asked.

Ren's phone buzzed with a message from Terri: "Pure accident. Maintenance worker named Rajesh noticed unusual wiring on a lighting tower during his rounds. He'd been complaining about it for weeks, thinking it was unauthorized cable theft. When your warning came through—garbled but enough—he connected the dots. We found six devices total, all on municipal infrastructure, not our facilities. Bomb squad says they were sophisticated, definitely would have caused the power surge Bora described."

"We were lucky," Ren told the agent. "An observant employee and good timing."

"Lucky," the agent agreed. "But Bora won't count on luck failing twice. He'll escalate."

"The recording is admissible for intelligence purposes," the Interpol agent explained. "For prosecution, we'll need corroborating evidence, but the Mumbai devices are a start. We've frozen his known assets, though he certainly has resources we don't know about."

Ren's phone buzzed. Bruce's face appeared on the secure connection. "Ren, we have a situation. Seventeen transportation companies just announced they're pulling out of negotiations. They're citing 'security concerns' after the Switzerland incident."

"Bora's parting gift," Ren muttered. "He knew this would happen. Turn potential allies against us through fear."

"There's more," Katya added, joining the call. "Several of our component suppliers are reporting attempted buyouts through shell companies. Someone's trying to strangle our supply chain."

"And I'm tracking suspicious network activity around our Life MTU facilities," Terri reported. "Probing attacks looking for vulnerabilities in our authentication systems. Very sophisticated."

Ren closed her eyes, feeling the weight of the coming storm. "He's not done. This was just his opening move."

Lynn appeared on screen. "Ren, I've been thinking. We should use the recording, release everything. Turn public opinion completely against him."

"The legal implications—" Katya started.

"Don't matter if we're all dead," Lynn interrupted. "He's shown he'll use terrorism. We need to destroy his credibility completely."

"No," Ren said firmly. "We release the facts about the Mumbai threat and his connection to it. But we don't become him. We don't use fear as our primary weapon." She looked at each of her team members. "We do this our way. Strengthen security, yes. Prepare for his attacks, absolutely. But we don't abandon our principles."

"Then what do you propose?" Bruce asked.

Ren straightened, decision crystallizing. "We accelerate the Life MTU rollout. Every humanitarian organization, every hospital, every refugee camp that's been waiting—we fast-track them all. We make the technology so essential, so woven into saving lives, that any attack on it becomes an attack on humanity itself."

"That's risky," Katya warned. "We'd be stretching our resources thin. And if Bora has partial designs, he might try to interfere."

"It's the only way," Ren replied. "Bora thinks he can control this technology through fear and force. We'll prove him wrong by making it indispensable for good. Every life saved, every emergency responded to faster, every family reunited—that's our answer to his vision of control."

She looked out the window at the Zurich skyline, knowing that somewhere out there, Bora was planning his next move.

"He thinks this is a chess match," Ren said quietly. "Capture the king and win. But he's wrong. This is Go. We surround him with so much good that his darkness has nowhere left to spread."

"Ma'am," Dov interrupted, entering the room. "Swiss intelligence just shared something. They found documents at the estate—Bora had detailed files on all of you. Your families, your habits, your vulnerabilities. Surveillance going back months, maybe longer."

The team fell silent on the call, the implication clear. This was now personal for all of them.

"Double security for everyone," Ren ordered. "Relocate family members if necessary. He's declared war not just on TTC, but on us personally."

"Ren," Lynn said softly. "Are you prepared for what this means? He won't stop. Not until one of you is destroyed."

Ren met her gaze through the screen. "Then we'd better make sure we're the ones left standing. But we do it without becoming monsters ourselves. That's the only victory worth achieving."

As she ended the call, her phone buzzed with a single message from an unknown number: "The game has only just begun. —B"

Ren deleted the message and turned to Dov. "Get me on the next flight to Mumbai. If he wants to target our facilities, I need to be there. Leadership from the front."

"Ma'am, that's exactly what he'd expect—"

"Good," Ren interrupted. "Let him expect it. But we'll be ready this time. And we'll show him that fear is his weapon, not ours."

The ride to the airport was tense, Dov's team maintaining a defensive formation around their vehicle. Ren used the time to coordinate with her team, setting in motion a series of defensive measures and acceleration plans.

"Bruce, I need you to work with our partner companies," she instructed over the secure line. "Anyone still willing to work with us gets priority access to our technology. Show them that standing with us is the profitable choice."

"Already on it," Bruce confirmed. "I've got meetings scheduled with twelve CEOs tomorrow. They're scared, but they're also smart enough to see the opportunity."

"Katya, work with legal teams in every country where we operate. I want restraining orders, injunctions, whatever legal protections we can get against Bora and his associates."

"Working on it," Katya replied. "But he's slippery. Multiple citizenships, diplomatic connections—he's hard to pin down legally."

"Terri, I need our systems hardened. Whatever vulnerabilities he might have found through those contractors, I want them closed."

"Already patching," Terri said, her fingers flying across her keyboard even as she spoke. "I'm also implementing a new authentication protocol that will detect any unauthorized Life MTU units. If he tries to build his own with those partial designs, we'll know immediately."

"Lynn, prepare a media strategy. Not aggressive, but firm. We tell our story, our vision, and we let people choose between his world and ours."

"I'll have a press release ready within the hour," Lynn promised. "Focusing on the Mumbai attack attempt and his terrorist tactics."

As the lights of Zurich faded behind them, Ren reflected on the battle ahead. Bora represented everything she had feared when developing the MTU technology—the concentration of power, the commodification of human movement, the use of revolutionary technology to reinforce rather than break down barriers.

But she also knew that his vision, for all its darkness, had appeal to those who benefited from the current system. The promise of maintaining power, of profiting from control—it was seductive to those who had never experienced powerlessness.

"Ma'am," Dov said quietly, "I've been thinking about what Bora said. About people choosing security over freedom."

"And?" Ren prompted.

"He's not entirely wrong," Dov admitted. "Fear is a powerful motivator. But he's missing something crucial."

"What's that?"

"Hope," Dov said simply. "People will choose hope over fear every time, if given a real choice. That's what TTC represents— hope for a better world, not just a more controlled one."

Ren smiled slightly. "Then we'd better make sure we keep giving them reasons to hope."

Her phone buzzed with a message from Victoria Henryson: "Not all of us agree with Bora. Some of us want to find a middle path. Can we talk?"

Ren typed back: "Yes. But on my terms, in a location of my choosing."

The response was immediate: "Agreed. The old order is dying, Dr. Franco. The question is what rises in its place. I'd rather it be something we build together than something imposed by men like Bora."

As the airport lights came into view, Ren felt a glimmer of possibility. Bora might have his allies, his resources, his ruthless vision. But she had something more powerful—people who believed in a better future and were willing to fight for it.

The war for the soul of instant global transportation had begun. And Ren was determined that when it ended, the world would be more connected, more equitable, and more free than ever before.

"Dov," she said as they pulled up to the airport, "contact our security teams at all facilities. Tell them we're moving to high alert. And reach out to local law enforcement in each city—we're going to need allies."

"Already done, ma'am," Dov replied. "We're as ready as we can be."

Ren nodded, stepping out of the vehicle into the cold Swiss night. The stars above were brilliant, countless points of light in the darkness. Somewhere among them were the satellites that made TTC's network possible—the physical infrastructure of a dream made real.

Bora could threaten, he could scheme, he could try to corrupt or destroy what they had built. But he couldn't change the fundamental truth that had driven Ren from the beginning: the future belonged to those who dared to build it, not those who sought only to control it.

The battle ahead would be difficult, dangerous, and deeply personal. But as Ren boarded the plane to Mumbai, she felt not fear, but determination. They had come too far, achieved too much, to let one man's vision of control override the promise of liberation.

The game, as Bora had said, had only just begun. But Ren was ready to play it on her terms, with her rules, and for stakes that went far beyond profit or power. She was playing for the future itself, and she intended to win.

16 SCARS AND STARS

The physiotherapy center in St. John's overlooked the harbor, its windows fogged with October cold. Ren gripped the parallel bars, her knuckles white with effort as she forced her left leg forward. Six months since the explosion at the Barcelona facility—six months since she'd pulled three technicians from the wreckage of Bora's sabotaged cargo MTU.

"That's enough for today," Dr. Jones said, moving to support her.

"One more lap," Ren said, her voice strained but determined. The burns along her left side had healed, but the nerve damage from the quantum field exposure when the sabotaged unit detonated—that was permanent. Seventy percent function in her left leg, maybe eighty-five percent in her left arm on good days.

"You have the UN address in four hours," Terri reminded her from the doorway, worry etched across her face. "You need to conserve—"

"I need to walk onto that stage without assistance." Ren started another lap, each step deliberate and painful. "They can't see weakness. Not today."

Dr. Jones exchanged glances with Terri. "The media is already running stories about the forty-three casualties from the sabotaged units. They're calling you reckless, saying you rushed the technology—"

"Let them." Ren reached the end of the bars, breathing hard. "Every revolution has its casualties. The question is whether we let fear stop us from moving forward."

Marcus Cardosi entered the rehabilitation center, his face grim. At twenty-eight, Bora's son carried himself with a weight beyond his years. "My father has agreed to testify."

Ren turned carefully, favoring her right leg. "In exchange for?"

"Reduced sentence. Minimum security facility. He's claiming the explosions were never meant to harm anyone—just to demonstrate the technology's vulnerability."

"Forty-three people would disagree," Terri said coldly.

"I know." Marcus's jaw tightened. "Which is why I'm testifying against him. Whatever he was before, whatever he meant to TTC's founding—he became a terrorist the moment he rigged those units."

Ren studied him. Marcus had been instrumental in identifying the sabotaged units, working twenty-hour days to prevent more casualties. His loyalty to the truth over his father had cost him everything—family, inheritance, his place in Boston society.

"After the trial, what will you do?" she asked.

"Disappear, probably. Change my name. Try to build something that isn't tainted by what he did." He paused. "I wanted to thank you, though. For not holding his sins against me."

"We're all more than our worst mistakes," Ren said quietly. "Or our parents' worst mistakes."

Marcus nodded and left. Ren turned back to the bars, starting another lap despite the pain.

"The Barcelona victims' families will be at the UN," Terri said. "Including the Yamato family. Their daughter—"

"Yuki. Seven years old. Lost her right eye and hearing in one ear." Ren's grip tightened on the bars. "I know every name, Terri. Every injury. They're the reason I have to get this right."

She completed the lap, then finally accepted the forearm crutch Dr. Chen offered—sleek carbon fiber that could pass for a walking stick if she carried it with enough confidence.

"You can't hide the limp entirely," Dr. Chen said. "But if you pace yourself, control your breathing—"

"I've been hiding pain my whole life," Ren said. "What's a little more?"

The United Nations General Assembly hall was filled to capacity. World leaders, diplomats, and reporters from every major nation watched as Ren took the podium. She approached with measured steps, the carbon fiber cane barely visible against her dark suit. She could feel the weight of thousands of eyes—some sympathetic, many hostile. In the gallery, she spotted the victims' families, including Mrs. Yamato holding her daughter Yuki, whose prosthetic eye gleamed under the lights.

"Distinguished delegates," she began, her voice steady despite the burning in her leg. "Three years ago—"

"You stand before us wounded by your own creation!" The Russian ambassador rose, his voice cutting through the hall. "How dare you advocate for expansion when you yourself bear the scars of this technology's dangers?"

Ren shifted her weight slightly, refusing to show the spike of pain. "Ambassador Volkov, I bear these scars because I chose to enter a compromised facility to save lives. The danger came not from the technology, but from those who would weaponize it."

"Semantics!" The Chinese representative stood. "Forty-three casualties, Ms. Franco. Children maimed. Families destroyed. Your safeguards failed."

"Yes," Ren said simply. The admission rippled through the hall. "They failed because we underestimated human malice. Because we believed that the promise of instant global transport would unite us rather than divide us. We were naive."

She clicked her remote, and images filled the screens—not the triumphant saves, but the casualties. Every face. Every injury.

"Yuki Yamato, age seven. Lost an eye when a sabotaged unit exploded in Kyoto." The child's image lingered. "David Chen, age thirty-four. Third-degree burns over sixty percent of his body pulling coworkers from the Bangkok incident. Maria Santos, age twenty-two. Paralyzed from the waist down in São Paulo."

The hall was silent.

"I could stand here and quote statistics about the two million lives saved through medical transport and refugee evacuation. But that would dishonor these forty-three people who paid the price for our failure to anticipate the worst of human nature."

The U.S. Secretary of State stood slowly. "Ms. Franco, what exactly are you proposing?"

"The International Teleportation Accord." The document appeared on screens. "Every Life MTU installation to be monitored by international inspectors. Mandatory quantum signatures that make units impossible to modify without detection. A global fund for victims of transport-related incidents, funded by TTC and participating nations."

"And if nations refuse?" the Russian ambassador asked.

Ren's hand tightened on her cane. "Then TTC will cease operations in those nations. No cargo, no humanitarian aid, no medical transport. Nothing."

"You would punish innocent citizens for their governments' decisions?"

"I would prevent future casualties by ensuring only responsible nations have access to this technology." She looked directly at the victims' families. "I cannot undo what happened. I cannot give Yuki her eye back or restore David's skin or make Maria walk again. But I can ensure it never happens again."

"Even if it costs you everything?" The Chinese representative's tone had shifted from accusatory to curious.

Ren lifted her cane slightly, acknowledging her own injuries. "It already has. The question is whether we learn from that cost or let it be meaningless."

A small voice rose from the gallery. Yuki Yamato, her young face serious above her eye patch: "My mama says you saved the other kids. The ones who would've died."

The breach of protocol should have brought security, but no one moved.

Ren turned to face the child directly. "Not enough of them."

"But some," Yuki said. "Some is better than none."

The simple truth from the wounded child broke something in the room. The Russian ambassador sat down slowly. The Chinese representative began studying the Accord on his tablet.

"We'll need amendments," the U.S. Secretary said finally. "Oversight provisions. Accountability measures."

"Then let's begin," Ren replied, knowing she'd need to stand for hours of negotiation despite her screaming leg. "We have work to do."

The Hague International Detention Center was a monument to modern justice—clean, humane, and utterly inescapable. Ren moved through the security checkpoints slowly, her limp more pronounced after eight hours of standing at the UN.

Bora sat in the visitor's room, no barriers needed given the armed guards. He'd lost weight, his designer physique reduced to something harder, leaner. His eyes tracked her cane as she approached.

"The great Ren Franco, humbled at last," he said softly. "Though not as humbled as you should be."

Ren lowered herself carefully into the chair, suppressing a wince. "Forty-three people, Bora. Including children."

"Forty-three casualties to prevent thousands more." He leaned forward. "Every day that technology spreads without proper control—"

"Without your control, you mean."

"Yes!" The word cracked like a whip. "My control. Because I understood the dangers. You were so intoxicated by the possibilities that you ignored the threats."

"I trusted people to use it responsibly."

"And I knew they wouldn't." Bora's hands clenched. "Terrorists, criminals, rogue states—they were all coming for it. My demonstrations were meant to force regulations before—"

"Your demonstrations killed a seven-year-old girl's eye." Ren's voice was ice. "Paralyzed a young woman. Gave third-degree burns to a father of three."

"To prevent worse!"

"No." Ren pulled out her tablet, showing him footage from the Barcelona facility. "This is you, Bora. Setting the quantum destabilizer. You could have set it for minimal yield—property damage only. But you maximized the radius. You wanted casualties."

Bora's face went pale. "How did you—"

291

"Marcus gave us access to your personal servers. He chose truth over blood." She put the tablet away. "You weren't trying to save anyone. You were trying to maintain your empire."

"My empire?" Bora laughed bitterly. "I'm in prison. My son testifies against me. My fortune is being distributed to victims. What empire?"

"The one you built on controlling global logistics. The one that teleportation threatened." Ren stood with difficulty. "You became a terrorist not from principle, but from greed dressed as concern."

"You don't understand," Bora said desperately. "The world needed gradual change. Controlled introduction. Not your radical democratization—"

"The world needed hope," Ren interrupted. "It still does. And despite what you did, despite these scars, we're going to provide it."

She turned to leave.

"Ren." His voice broke slightly. "Tell Marcus... tell him I understand his choice."

She paused at the door. "Tell him yourself. He'll be testifying tomorrow. Look him in the eyes when he describes finding the bodies in Barcelona. When he explains how his father became a killer."

She left him there, smaller somehow in his prison grays, the weight of his choices finally crushing the man who once stood as a titan of industry.

The Newfoundland safe house perched on granite cliffs, autumn storms battering its windows with salt spray. Ren sat in the whirlpool bath, jets pounding against her damaged muscles, when Terri entered with a tea tray.

"The Accord passed," Terri said quietly, setting the tray aside. "Unanimous, after China and Russia added their amendments."

"What did we lose?"

"Military applications remain banned. They wanted an exception for defense—"

"No." Ren's response was immediate. "No military use. Ever."

"That's what I told them." Terri knelt beside the tub, studying Ren's scars—the puckered burns along her ribs, the surgical incisions from removing quantum shrapnel. "How bad is it today?"

"Six out of ten." Ren never lied to Terri about the pain. "Maybe seven."

Terri reached for the medical kit, pulling out the topical analgesic. "Let me help."

Ren shifted forward, allowing Terri access to her back. The cream was cold at first, then warming, Terri's hands gentle but thorough as they worked it into damaged tissue.

"I watched you today," Terri said softly. "Eight hours on that leg. Most people would have collapsed after two."

"Most people didn't put forty-three others in harm's way."

"Stop." Terri's hands stilled. "Bora did that. Not you."

"I gave him the means."

"You gave the world the means to transcend distance. He chose to corrupt it." Terri resumed her ministrations, moving to Ren's shoulders. "The families don't blame you. Yuki's mother told me she's grateful—you saved twelve other children that day."

"It should have been all of them."

"You're not omnipotent, Ren. You're just human. Brilliant, determined, stubborn as hell, but human."

Ren turned in the tub to face her, water sloshing. "Is that enough? Being human?"

"It's everything." Terri cupped her face gently. "Your humanity—your refusal to become like Bora, to use power without conscience—that's what saved us."

They kissed, soft at first, then deeper as months of stress and fear dissolved into need. Terri pulled back, searching Ren's eyes.

"Can you—with your injuries—"

"Everything works," Ren said with a slight smile. "Just... differently. Slower. More carefully."

"I can do slow and careful." Terri helped her from the tub, wrapping her in warm towels, supporting her weight without making her feel weak.

They moved to the bedroom, taking time with buttons and zippers, pausing when Ren's leg cramped, working around limitations with patience and creativity. Terri mapped every scar with her lips, treating each mark not as damage but as evidence of survival, of courage.

"You're still beautiful," she whispered against Ren's hip, where the worst burns had been.

"Liar," Ren said, but she was smiling, threading her fingers through Terri's hair.

"Never about this. Never about you."

They made love slowly, accommodating Ren's limited mobility, finding positions that didn't stress her injuries. What they lost in athleticism they gained in intimacy, in the vulnerability of asking for what they needed, in the trust of showing weakness and finding strength in return.

Afterward, they lay intertwined, Ren's head on Terri's chest, listening to her heartbeat.

"Marry me," Ren said suddenly.

Terri's hand stilled in her hair. "What brought this on?"

"Watching Yuki today. Seeing her mother's fierce love despite everything. Thinking about Marcus choosing principle over his father." Ren lifted her head. "I don't want to wait for some perfect future that may never come. I want to commit to you now, scars and all."

"Yes," Terri said immediately, then laughed. "God, yes. Though I should probably be the one proposing—you can barely kneel."

"I'll sit while you kneel," Ren suggested, and they both laughed, the sound mixing with the storm outside.

"There's something else," Ren said after a moment. "The lunar project."

Terri tensed slightly. "What about it?"

"The first official Space MTU is complete. The receiving station is already on the moon, delivered by conventional rocket last month. We're ready for cargo trials."

"Ren, after everything that's happened—"

"Because of everything that's happened." Ren shifted to look at her. "We can't let fear stop progress. But this time, we do it right. Full international oversight from day one. Complete transparency. And we start with cargo only—no Life MTU applications until we have years of safety data."

"The moon," Terri said wonderingly. "We're really going to do it."

"We're going to try. Together." Ren kissed her again. "Partners in everything."

"In everything," Terri agreed, pulling her close despite the storm, despite the scars, despite all the challenges ahead.

Six months later, the Vancouver Space Center hummed with controlled tension. The first lunar cargo trial—a simple shipment of water and supplies to the automated moon base—was scheduled for T-minus ten minutes.

Ren stood at the observation window, her weight distributed carefully between her cane and the railing. The physiotherapy had helped; she could manage four hours without significant pain now, though she'd never run again. The burn scars still pulled when she moved too quickly, and cold weather made her bones ache in ways that reminded her of every moment in that Barcelona facility.

"Quantum field alignment at optimal levels," reported Dr. Sarah Kim from her station. She'd returned to work after three months of recovery, her own burns hidden beneath long sleeves.

"Receiving pad on Luna Base confirms ready status," added James Wright, one of the technicians Ren had pulled from Barcelona. His hands shook slightly—nerve damage from quantum exposure—but his voice was steady.

Terri stood beside Ren, their wedding rings catching the light. They'd married quietly two months ago, just family and the surviving members of the original TTC team. No media, no fanfare, just promises made between two people who'd already proven their commitment through fire.

"International observers confirm all protocols met," someone announced. Representatives from twelve nations watched from the gallery, including the Chinese and Russian delegates who'd fought hardest for oversight provisions.

"T-minus five minutes."

Marcus Cardosi entered the observation deck—not as a TTC employee, but as a reporter for the Independent Science Journal. He'd rebuilt himself as a technology journalist, using his engineering background to explain complex developments to the public. His coverage of the trial would be syndicated worldwide.

"Ms. Franco," he said formally, his recorder visible. "Any

statement before the trial?"

Ren considered. "Only this: We're taking the next step. Not rashly, not without consideration of consequences, but with determination to expand human possibility while protecting human life."

"Critics say it's too soon after the Barcelona incidents."

"Critics said powered flight was impossible. That splitting the atom was madness. That connecting the world through the internet would destroy society." She shifted her weight, suppressing a grimace. "Progress requires risk, but calculated risk with extensive safeguards."

"T-minus one minute."

The room fell silent. Even the observers leaned forward. This was history—not the dramatic unveiling of three years ago, but something more measured, more careful, more aware of the price of innovation.

"Thirty seconds."

Ren found Terri's hand, squeezing it. Through the window, they could see the MTU—redesigned with triple redundancies, quantum signatures that would detect any tampering, and automatic shutdowns if any anomaly was detected.

"Ten... nine... eight..."

She thought of Yuki Yamato, who'd sent a drawing of the moon with a note: "Make it safe this time."

"Three... two... one... Transport initiated."

The flash was brilliant but contained, the quantum field stable and controlled. Energy readings stayed within predicted parameters. No alarms. No emergencies.

Five seconds of silence.

Then, from 384,400 kilometers away: "Luna Base confirms successful receipt of cargo. All materials intact and accounted for."

The room erupted in applause—not the wild celebration of the first human teleportation, but something more subdued, more aware of what such achievements cost.

"It worked," Marcus said quietly, and Ren heard the echo of his father in his voice—not the Bora who'd become a terrorist, but the one who'd once dreamed of changing the world through technology.

"The first step worked," Ren corrected. "We have years of testing before we even consider Life MTU applications for space. We learned that lesson."

Through the window, the moon was rising, visible in the afternoon sky. Somewhere up there, in the Sea of Tranquility, sat crates of water and food that had traveled impossibly far in impossibly little time.

"What's next?" a reporter called out.

Ren looked at Terri, who smiled and answered for them both: "We take it one careful step at a time. We test, we verify, we protect, and slowly, carefully, we expand what's possible."

As the press conference continued, as data streamed in confirming the complete success of the trial, Ren stood at the window, her reflection overlaid with the rising moon. She saw her scars, her cane, the slight list to her stance. She also saw determination, wisdom earned through pain, and the knowledge that progress wasn't about speed—it was about direction.

Somewhere in a maximum-security prison, Bora watched the news coverage alone in his cell. His son's byline on the article made him close his eyes, though whether in shame or pride, even he couldn't say. The revolution he'd tried to stop through violence had evolved beyond his influence, tempered by tragedy but not halted by it.

The age of lunar transport had begun—not with reckless abandon, but with careful steps taken by those who bore the scars of harder lessons. And in that caution, that wisdom, that refusal to let either fear or ambition override conscience, lay the true revolution: humanity learning to wield transformative power with the responsibility it demanded.

The moon hung in the sky, no longer untouched for nearly a century, but approached now with the respect it deserved.

ABOUT THE AUTHOR

Daniel J. Formoso is a business consultant who spends his days grappling with real-world engineering and construction issues. When he isn't contemplating the future of global transit, he lives with his family in Alaska, United States.

He loves the cold.